SEARING PLEASURE

"Damn you!" He slammed the door shut behind him. "God
damn you!"

Jenny's head jerked up. The sketches on her lap scattered.
Her face went ashen as she confronted the terrible fury in
Christian's bitterly icy eyes. Fury that she had invaded his
most private sanctuary. "I know how you feel—" she began.

Christian's long stride carried him to Jenny's side in an
instant. "You can't begin to know how I feel," he murmured
harshly. "But perhaps I will show you." He wanted to shake
her. Instead he found himself forcing her on tiptoe, raising her
face to his.

Her mouth was slightly parted, her lips wet. Christian's
mouth covered hers punishingly.

The kiss went on. And on. Desire stirred in him. He raised
his head and captured her eyes with his own.

Then his hands were in her hair, his fingers threaded in the
dark sable strands, keeping her immobile. . . .

And there was no escaping his passion. . . .

MIDNIGHT PRINCESS

Jo Goodman

ZEBRA BOOKS
KENSINGTON PUBLISHING CORP.

This book is dedicated to l g j

Chapter 1

It was torment, not treatment. How else could one describe the agony of the screams? They echoed hollowly in the room and sent a wave of nausea through Christian Marshall. For a brief moment he closed his eyes. The luxury was short-lived. When he realized what he was doing he opened them and forced himself to watch. He glanced surreptitiously to his left and saw that his companion had not noticed the lapse. Christian's stomach tightened, curled. He could taste bile at the back of his throat. His hands were thrust into the pockets of his woolen jacket and they trembled with equal parts of rage and fear.

A drink. That's what he needed. A tumbler of whiskey, two—no, three—fingers deep. Another scream, as raw and tortured as any that came before it, gradually became a choking sound. There was a struggle and Christian understood immediately that the intensity of the battle was lessening. The attendants would realize it too. They would be able to ease their bruising grip on the slender shoulders of their patient as soon as she became unconscious. A minute or so, perhaps as many as three, would pass before they lifted her out of the tub of cold spring water. Most likely she would vomit again when they

5

revived her. If they revived her this time. Her lack of strength against the orderlies had probably saved her the pain of a dislocated collarbone or a broken forearm.

One drink wouldn't be enough when he got home tonight. He would have to sit with the bottle.

Dr. Perry Glenn had struck a pose that Christian associated with sea captains rather than physicians. His legs were slightly splayed, his hands clasped behind his back, and he rocked forward on the balls of his feet. His demeanor was relaxed, his expression one of profound satisfaction. It was Glenn's expression that was responsible for Christian's fear. The doctor was not unaffected by what was taking place in the treatment room at Jennings Memorial. He was genuinely pleased with it.

The doctor nudged Christian lightly with his elbow and lifted his chin to indicate the scene in front of him. "I wonder how well you understand what you're seeing," he said. "I've observed that you've stopped making notes."

It was true. Christian had put his pencil and leather-bound notepad in his breast pocket when he had been escorted into the treatment room. What he had witnessed since had made him forget that he had a role to play. When he spoke he was careful to keep the dry, caustic tenor of his thoughts out of his voice. "Notes seem superfluous when I've committed everything I've seen to memory." Memories that I'll have to drink away tonight, he added silently. Christian was relieved when the doctor accepted his words at face value.

"A convenient talent for any reporter." The doctor's hands loosened from behind his back. His right hand found his chin in an absent gesture and he stroked the wiry steel-gray threads of his beard with his thumb and forefinger. He smoothed his drooping mustache and large side-whiskers, then went back to rubbing his chin. He stopped the motion long enough to indicate to the orderlies that they should let their patient surface. "The efficacy of terror as a form of treatment is not disputed by the professionals in this hospital any longer," Dr.

Glenn said as his patient was laid on her side on the stone floor.

One of the attendants pressed the young woman's head forward so that her chin lay against her upper chest. The other aide slapped her back rhythmically. Christian's expression was inscrutable, his aquamarine eyes shuttered as he waited for a response from the patient. He could not give himself away by allowing his innermost thoughts to be read. "I can see that you're a proponent of terror in the treatment of the insane. I believe, however, there are any number of physicians in this country—indeed, in this city—who would disagree with its effectiveness."

Dr. Glenn nodded. "I can't dispute that. It's the primary reason Dr. Morgan thought you should observe the treatment firsthand. You'll see for yourself that far from being inhumane, this method of treatment is the kindest thing one can do for poor creatures like this girl."

Pompous ass, Christian thought, controlling a grimace. The patient's slight whimper held Christian's attention. It was a pathetic, mewling sound more suited to an injured alley cat than a young woman. The loose shift that she wore was merely a wet second skin now and offered no protection against the cold. As she came out of her induced unconscious state Christian released the shallow breath he had been holding. He felt the tension in his neck and back ease. "Tell me about her," he said evenly.

The doctor considered Christian's thinly veiled demand for a moment before answering. He could admit to himself that he was not entirely comfortable with this interview or Christian Marshall. He stroked his beard and Dundreary whiskers again as a way of gaining time and taking measure of the man at his side.

Dr. Glenn knew who Christian Marshall was. Even if he hadn't known, Dr. Morgan, the hospital administrator, had been quick to address the salient points, ticking them off on his fingers and having to use both hands to complete the list. Artist and architect. Second of four sons and the only one to survive

7

the war—albeit with serious injury. Decorated for valor. Publisher and sole owner of *The New York Chronicle* since the death of his father six months earlier. Reputed to be a hard drinker. Ladies' man. Horse-fancier. High on every important hostess's guest list. And oddly enough, reclusive in his own fashion.

Dr. Glenn would have liked to deny the request for an interview and tour, but apparently one didn't say no to Christian Marshall. The doctor imagined the supervising board wrestling with the request, then capitulating because it was Christian Marshall himself and not merely his paper doing the asking. No one had mentioned "gambler" when discussing Christian Marshall's character, yet that description was very much on Perry Glenn's mind. It was the bored insolence in the pale aquamarine eyes that concerned the doctor. He couldn't shake the feeling that this man was playing cards very close to his chest. There was an air of implacability about the hard angles and taut planes of Christian's face, a steely bitterness that went right to the man's core and that no smile ever quite cut through.

Christian Marshall was smooth-shaven. Perhaps a touch of rebellion against the dictates of current fashion, the doctor thought as he continued to stroke his own whiskers. Or perhaps the man knew the strength of his character could be seen in the rigid thrust of his jaw and the hard line of his mouth, and saw no reason to hide behind a mustache stiffened with beeswax and pomade.

The granitelike cast of Christian's face might have altered slightly if he had been privy to the doctor's thoughts. At the very least he would have been dryly amused by Perry Glenn's speculations. Christian's clean-shaven face had nothing to do with his sense of his own character and everything to do with a thick head of hair the color of an old penny. Strands of copper highlighted his crown, temples, and brows, but on the few occasions he had been forced to go without shaving, his beard had always come in with the fiery brilliance of red autumn

8

leaves. "It's rather, er, colorful, don't you think?" his mother had once commented delicately. His brothers and father had shown far less tact while making the same point. Christian got rid of the beard and sideburns that same evening.

Dr. Glenn's brows drew together as he made a sweeping assessment of his companion, taking in the breadth of his shoulders, the ease with which the man wore the invisible trappings of power, and the incongruous infirmity which made Christian Marshall favor his right leg while walking or standing. The wound had made the man a hero, elevating him to a stature above other mortals. The limp served as a reminder that no man deserved such a lofty position, in his own heart or anyone else's. Dr. Glenn didn't think that Christian had asked for any of it.

The doctor cleared his throat. "There's not a great deal we know about her," he said at last. "She's a Jane Doe. I make her age to be early twenties, though that's only a guess. She could easily be younger. She carried no identification when she was found wandering Paradise Square, lost and incoherent." He paused and let Christian have some time to put that information into perspective. One didn't have to be a native of New York City to know about Paradise Square.

It was a deliberate irony that Paradise Square was actually a triangle of open land at the center of the most dangerous quarter of Manhattan—the Five Points. Armed policemen only entered the Five Points in pairs, and New Yorkers who cared as much for their reputation as their life avoided the district even in the bright light of day. Tenements and decrepit clapboarded houses lined the filthy, narrow streets of the area. Lodging houses could be found in cellars below the street. They were breeding places for rats and vermin, and in the case of the prostitutes who often rented the rooms, they were a breeding ground for disease and bastard children. The Five Points was also a seedy fortress for one of the most powerful gangs operating in the city. The Dead Rabbits were the authority in the Five Points, rulers of a criminal empire whose

9

loyal subjects were prostitutes, murderers, hoodlums, and thieves.

"Our Jane Doe has been here a little more than a month," Dr. Glenn continued. "About six weeks I think. I was away when she was brought in, but I've worked with her steadily since my return. There's virtually no admissions information, but no one seems to have missed her. We've had no inquiries, and none were really expected. It's hard to imagine that anyone in the Five Points will come forward to identify or claim her."

"She was brought here first?" asked Christian.

"Yes, as far as I know. It's hard to believe they would put themselves out for anyone, but two members of the Dead Rabbits escorted her here.

One of Christian's brows kicked up in frank amazement. "The Dead Rabbits? Here?"

"Oh, you're wondering why she wasn't taken to one of the city asylums."

"It occurred to me. I wasn't aware that Jennings Memorial even treated the insane. And this woman is indigent as well."

"I'm disappointed in you, Mr. Marshall. Jennings Memorial has a mandate from its Board of Directors to treat a percentage of charity cases every year. I thought you had come to Jennings with something of an open mind. I can see, however, that you're guilty of the same preconceived notions the general public embraces about this hospital—that we're only here to serve the rich." Dr. Glenn cut short his observation just as he was warming to the subject. His patient was coughing violently and a series of convulsive shudders wracked her body. He pointed to the freshly made cot which sat in one corner of the room. "She's had quite enough for today," he said. "Put her to bed. It will be a few hours before I'll know how well her mind has responded to the treatment."

It required only one of the attendants to lift Jane Doe and carry her to the cot. The other pulled back the thin sheet and snapped open the coarse wool blanket which had been folded at the foot of the cot. Both of the hospital attendants were large men, heavily built and bull-necked. Their size was unremarkable given the job they were required to do. Christian imagined they were called on frequently to initiate the plunge-bath treatment with patients much less delicate than their current charge. What struck Christian most profoundly was the odd tenderness each of the attendants showed for their patient after very nearly causing her death. One of the men carefully pushed aside the strands of dark hair clinging to Jane Doe's cheek and forehead. The other covered her with the sheet and blanket, tucking them around the shivering contours of her body. Almost in unison they stepped away from the bed and looked at Dr. Glenn for direction. There was a dull, lethargic look common to both men, and Christian was moved to wonder if they were capable of making any decisions on their own or if they could only follow orders. If the latter were true, and Christian suspected it was, then Dr. Perry Glenn had found the ideal men to carry out his treatment.

"Ronald. William. She requires restraining." Dr. Glenn's voice softened and the singsong cadence of his voice was perfect for gentling animals and thick-witted men. "We've been over this before. You know she can't be free to move around. She may hurt herself."

Christian saw hesitation on the part of both men, but it was momentary. If Christian had not counted himself a keen observer he might have been convinced he had imagined their small attempt at mutiny. As they moved to obey the doctor, Christian allowed his eyes to stray about the room. He could not help but wonder how Dr. Glenn thought Jane Doe could harm herself. Other than the wooden cot and the tub of spring water, the treatment room was barren. Located as it was in the basement of the hospital, it was an airless, windowless room that had more to recommend it as a medieval dungeon. Two lanterns on either side of the oak and iron door provided the room's light. They would be removed—as would the tub— when the patient was left alone, plunging Jane Doe into certain darkness. There had been one small concession to creating a more pleasant environment: The damp stone walls had been whitewashed. Now their crevices and niches were a garden for mosses and lichens. No one would ever mistake the effect for classic green-veined marble.

Dr. Glenn had been quick to point out that the room was only intended to house the patient during the treatment process. That knowledge did nothing to ease Christian's mind. He wouldn't have been surprised if there were thumbscrews, shackles, and racks stored in the adjoining rooms.

Christian watched the attendants secure Jane Doe to the cot's frame with wide, padded leather belts attached to her wrists. He was only slightly relieved to see they weren't using iron manacles. "What is it you expect her to do unrestrained?" he asked.

"Left to her own devices," the doctor answered, "she could easily hurt herself by beating her head against the wall or break her hands by punching them. Undoubtedly you think us cruel, yet consider the alternative. The first time she was treated here she was not restrained afterward. The tips of her fingers were raw and full of splinters from her attempts to claw open the door. Those splinters had to be removed, Mr. Marshall, wedged as they were beneath her fingernails and embedded in her skin. Aaah, I see you have some feeling for her pain," he said when Christian betrayed his thoughts with a slight grimace. "Believe me, we were not immune to it either. Jane, however, gave no indication that she felt anything—even when the lacerations in her fingertips and palms became infected. Perhaps this is the best measure of the state of her mind. She simply does not respond in the manner we have all come to accept as normal. Still, we can't ignore our own sensibilities. Therefore it is necessary to restrain her. You can see for yourself that she has calmed now. It won't be long before she is sleeping peacefully. The effectiveness of the treatment is best judged upon her waking."

Christian stepped to one side as the attendants dragged the

tub out of the room. He managed to casually bump one of them so water sloshed out of the tub. Some of it splashed on the back of his hand. It had all the warmth of freshly melted ice. He glanced quickly at Jane Doe again. She was breathing shallowly, her eyes closed. Her ash-white skin was pulled taut over the fine bones of her face. In contrast, her lips had taken on a bluish hue and her heavy lashes couldn't hide the jaundiced cast of the shadows just beneath her eyes. Where her arms were not covered by the blanket the flesh was pale and pimply with cold. "Shouldn't someone change her shift?" Christian asked. "Dry her hair?"

"It's all part of the treatment. The bracing cold helps her make contact with reality."

Make contact with pneumonia, Christian thought. He was careful to keep his comment to himself, and withdrew his notepad and pencil. "How often does she have these treatments?"

"Once a week is recommended until there's been noticeable improvement. This is her fifth—no—sixth plunge bath."

Christian made a note of it. "How many other patients are receiving this course of treatment?"

"Four. As I told you before we came down here, this method is not prescribed for all lunatics. You know from the tour that lunatics account for a very small fraction of our patient population. I wouldn't recommend this treatment for patients suffering from, let us say, melancholia, certain phobias, idiocy, or torpid madness. Does that give you an idea of the select nature of the treatment?"

Christian nodded briefly. He limped toward the door to take advantage of the light from the single lantern the attendants left behind. "Tell me again about the use of terror. I think I'm in a better position to understand it now that I've seen its application." It was easy for Christian to imagine that Dr. Glenn was mentally congratulating himself. He thinks he's brought me over to his side, Christian considered cynically. He thinks I'm impressed with his professional credentials and his

13

self-righteous assurances that he knows what he's doing. Ignoring the dampness of the wall, Christian leaned his shoulder against it, striking a relaxed, interested pose that he had found effective for inviting conversation. He was a little startled that he remembered how to do it. It had been a long time since he'd cared enough to bother.

Dr. Glenn moved to the circle of lantern light. His stocky shadow fell against the wall. He maintained a comfortable distance so he didn't have to strain his neck looking up at Christian. Without realizing he had fallen into the old habit, the doctor tugged lightly on his beard as he spoke.

"The use of terror as a treatment method had its origin in the old asylums of France and England centuries ago. It was thought at the time that lunatics, particularly the violent ones, were men and women who had, at the deepest point of madness, become no different than wild beasts." He chuckled lightly as he considered the folly of thought of his professional forebears. "We know now that this isn't true—at least not to the extent it was once thought to be. The treatment then was meant to break the lunatics' spirit—tame them, as it were. Food deprivation and methods better suited to breaking wild horses were often used."

"Pardon me," Christian said, a dry edge to his voice, "but I don't see much difference in those methods and the way in which that young woman was just treated."

"But there is," the doctor assured him. "The cold-water plunge is meant to induce the most powerful, primitive fear known to humankind—the fear of death. It's respected medical theory that fear is a passion which diminishes excitement. I believe Dr. Cullen said that a century ago."

"I'm not familiar with that name," Christian said as he made a few notes. Without looking at the bed he began making sketches of Jane Doe. His pencil worked quickly, but not so fast that Dr. Glenn would suspect what he was doing. The simple line drawings came from memory.

"Dr. Cullen was a teacher of Benjamin Rush. You know who

14

he was, don't you?"

"A signer of the Declaration, if I'm not mistaken."

"That and more. He was a doctor, scholar, and pioneer in the care and treatment of persons suffering from insane and disordered minds. Like many men of his time he advocated the therapeutic use of terror. He recommended the use of a tranquilizing chair—his own invention, by the way—which keeps the patient in a fixed, upright position for hours at a time. It reduces the heart rate because it limits muscular action and motor activity. He found the mad jacket, as it was called then, an unreliable and unnecessarily cruel device. Far from being an advocate of torture, Dr. Rush was a leader in the move toward rational humanitarianism. He understood that terror is a powerful agent on the body and the conduit is the mind."

"Rush must have died some forty years ago," Christian pointed out. "It's logical to assume that some of his methods would be dated by now. I know there are physicians who would ridicule Rush's practices."

"But who's to say they're right and he was wrong?" Dr. Glenn asked rhetorically. "The work I'm doing with my patients—work I am documenting, I might add—will speak to my fellow physicians and finally to the general public about the value of terror as a treatment. I propose that lunatics can be frightened *into* their wits, so to speak."

Christian flipped the page of his notepad and began sketching another scene, the one he had witnessed upon entering the room. Poor, mad Jane Doe struggled without any hope of being released in the solid arms of the two attendants. Her dark brown eyes seemed impossibly wide in the smallness of her face. They were glassy with fear, yet strangely lusterless. For an infinitesimal span of time her eyes held Christian's and he knew her helplessness, resignation, and despair in the part of his soul he thought had been long since immune to another's distress. He captured that look now on paper, and the power of it caused his stomach to lurch uneasily. He thought about the bottle of whiskey he had promised himself. It helped. "What about the other methods of terror? I believe the plunge bath is not the only one in use."

"Oh, no. Of course not. We use it here because it's the simplest method of invoking the fear of death by drowning. It's also the safest. The patient can be easily scooped out of the tub, and therefore we virtually eliminate the possibility of actual drowning. Some places still use the well cure."

"What's that?"

"The patient is chained to the bottom of an empty well. Water is slowly poured in to instill the fear."

"The well cure," Christian murmured to himself. "No pun intended, I'm sure."

"Hmmm? What was that?"

Christian caught himself before he repeated his caustic thought more loudly. "Nothing. I'm sorry. You were saying . . ."

Dr. Glenn took his stethoscope out of his coat pocket and slipped it around his neck. "There is the so-called bath of surprise," he said as he walked over to his patient. He checked her pulse and heartbeat, then resumed his explanation. "That consists of a trapdoor which can be opened under an unsuspecting patient. It drops him into a pool of cool water, frequently deep enough to force him to save himself by swimming or treading water. You can imagine that such a method meets with its share of fatalities." Dr. Glenn moved back to the pool of yellow lantern light, took up the pose of sea captain once more, and rocked slightly on the balls of his feet. "There have been many ingenious devices invented. There is a particularly powerful water pump which is manned by four men. The patient is chained to the wall and a highly pressurized stream of water is focused on the lunatic's spine."

"My God," Christian said softly, wondering at the mind that had thought of such a terror-inspiring and painful mode of treatment. It was difficult to credit who were the real madmen.

Dr. Glenn echoed Christian's sentiments. "I'm happy to say

16

it's not a widely used device today, though I daresay in some backwoods country hospital you might find one. Terror, not pain, is the preferred therapy. The gyrator is employed here from time to time. Again, its use is practiced judiciously. The gyrator was never intended as a cure-all."

"What is it?"

"I could let you see it," Dr. Glenn said, taking a step toward the door.

"No . . . no, that's all right." Dear Jesus, I don't want to see it. "Just explain how it works. A general description will do for my article."

The doctor shrugged. "It's a relatively simple device. It consists of a rotating board on which the patient is strapped, his head farthest from the center. The board spins at a high rate of speed, causing blood to rush to the patient's head. Its effect is opposite of the tranquilizing chair. I feel compelled to emphasize that none of the treatments I've described are employed indiscriminately. The gyrator, for instance, is used with patients who are sluggish, inactive, or unresponsive. What we call torpid madness. To use it on our Jane Doe here would be practicing the worst kind of medicine. Jane is in an almost constant state of excitement. I realize you didn't have the benefit of seeing her prior to treatment so you must trust my word. She is invariably agitated and restless. When not restrained she paces the hall on the lunatic ward. She has screamed so often and with such fervor that her speaking voice is now a bleak and biting whisper. We despair of it healing."

"What's to become of her?"

"As to that, I can't say. We're hopeful the treatment will work, of course. We have our share of successes, you know. In that case our plan would be to release her to family or friends once she can identify herself."

"And if she's unable to do that?"

"Then we would try to arrange for some type of employment."

Christian's steady gaze fell on the pathetic young woman

17

again. He couldn't imagine who could be induced to hire her after they learned her history. Most likely she would end up on the streets, wandering the Five Points again and making her living on her back. "And if the treatment doesn't work?" Or if it kills her? he wondered silently. "What then?"

"As I mentioned before, we're able to keep a small percentage of charity patients, though in time I believe she would be removed to one of the city's public asylums to make room for someone who can be helped here."

"I see," Christian murmured. He began to ask another question, but stopped himself as the sound of urgent, heavy footsteps echoed in the passageway beyond the treatment room door.

One of the attendants who had assisted in Jane Doe's plunge bath flung open the door. His expression was harried, his breathing labored, as he sought out the doctor. "It's Mr. Drummond, Dr. Glenn," he said, tripping over his words in an effort to get them out quickly. "He's havin' himself a fit. Cornered two of the guards in the ward and he's holdin' them off with a broken chair leg. The other patients are cryin' or screamin'. Everyone wants to know about the princess." His chin jerked briefly in the direction of the cot to indicate Jane Doe. "I told 'em she was fine but—"

Dr. Glenn laid his hand on the attendant's forearm. "They can't be reasoned with when they're agitated, William. Take the lantern and wait for me in the hallway, I'll be with you in a moment." He turned to Christian. "I'm sorry, Mr. Marshall, but you can appreciate that these sorts of incidents are never timed to anyone's convenience. I'll have to go with William. You're welcome to wait in my office if you have more questions for me, or show yourself out if you're done. I'm afraid you can't stay here."

For all the doctor's air of calm Christian could see that he was anxious to be gone, and just as anxious that Christian wouldn't press him for permission to accompany him back to the lunatic ward. Christian tucked away his notebook and

18

pencil and stepped into the hallway. "Don't let me keep you, Doctor. I'll certainly find my own way out." He held out his hand to Dr. Glenn, who grasped it and shook it firmly. The attendant moved around them and took a small iron ring of keys from his pocket. He sifted through them, found what he wanted, and shut and locked the door to the treatment room. As an extra precaution he threw the bolt. The door was designed not to let the unauthorized in or the patient out. From the corner of his eye Christian watched the orderly pocket the keys again. The pressure of his grip on the doctor's hand increased slightly as Christian's fingers itched to hold those keys. "I appreciate the time you've taken with me, Dr. Glenn. It's been most interesting." He smiled blandly, almost daring the doctor to try to read his thoughts.

Dr. Glenn hesitated momentarily and glanced at his pocket watch. "You're welcome. If you'll excuse me, William will see you to the first floor lobby. Keep the lantern, William. I can find my way without it." He turned and hurried down the dark and narrow hallway.

William started to follow almost immediately, but Christian held him back by taking out his pencil and surreptitiously dropping it. "Just a minute, Bill, I lost something." He made a pretense of looking for it while William showered the area with light. When Christian heard the door at the end of the hall close and Dr. Glenn's steps recede in the stairwell, he found the pencil under his shoe. "Here it is," he said sheepishly. "Don't know how I managed that."

The attendant impatiently shifted his weight from one foot to the other and swung the lantern so light chased shadow in an arc along the damp corridor. "If you don't mind, Mr. Marshall, we really have t'go. The doctor'll be needin' me."

This was going to require a delicate touch, Christian thought. At another time William's determination to attend to his duties would have been admirable. Now it put them at cross-purposes. Christian slipped the pencil behind his ear, where it was immediately lost in his thick, copper struck hair.

19

"I'm ready," he said, stepping to William's side. As they began to walk down the hallway Christian deliberately exaggerated his limp and subtly manipulated the attendant to follow suit. "It's the dampness," he apologized, taking a moment to stretch his leg. "Can't think how the princess survives it," he added offhandedly.

Bill was visibly disconcerted. "The princess?"

"Hm-mm. Jane Doe. That's what you called her, isn't it?"

"Did I?" He frowned and his steps slowed as his thoughts clouded. "I didn't mean to. Habit, I suppose. Dr. Glenn won't like it. Wonder if he noticed."

Christian ignored the attendant's questions and pressed his own. "The other patients call her princess also?"

"What?" Bill asked distractedly. Before Christian could repeat himself Bill began answering the question. "Oh, sorry . . . yeah, they do. Only it's more of a title than a name, if you take my meaning . . . you know, when people think she's out of earshot they use it. Ain't never heard no one call her princess to her face. Old Alice Vanderstell give her the title. That one's as loony as they come, but she has her moments. Started callin' our Jane the princess right off. Everyone picked up on it 'cause it suited her. We're not supposed to do it, though. Doc Glenn says it's bound to confuse Jane."

Christian couldn't see that it would confuse her any more than being called Jane if her name were actually Mary. He withheld comment. "Alice Vanderstell," he said consideringly. "Any relation to Gordon Vanderstell? His mother perhaps?"

"His aunt," corrected the orderly. "A regular harpy she is too. It's no wonder he tucked her away here."

Christian was aware that Jennings Memorial counted a number of wealthy, influential people among its patients, but Alice Vanderstell's presence on the lunatic ward took him slightly aback. Which madwoman had she been? The one who rocked an imaginary babe in her arms? The one who stared sightlessly out of her window?

Christian tried to recall what he knew about her, and berated

20

himself for rarely taking any notice of what was printed in *The Chronicle*'s society pages. Or any of its pages for that matter. Deciding he could kick himself later, preferably while working on that bottle he had promised himself, Christian focused his mind back to the task at hand.

Though he had never met Alice Vanderstell personally, Christian knew she had had at least a nodding acquaintance with his late parents. The Vanderstell name was synonymous with old money. Very old money. It was rumored that when Manhattan was sold for a few strings of beads, the Vanderstells were there monitoring the transaction. There probably wasn't a grain of truth to the story, but it underscored the depth of the roots the Vanderstell family had laid down in the city. There was power and prestige in the name and, Christian believed, more than a few skeletons in the closet as well.

"His aunt?" Christian questioned softly. "I thought she died more than a year ago."

The attendant cleared his throat, realizing he had said more than he should have. "This way, Mr. Marshall." He opened the door to the stairwell. "I really must be goin'."

"Don't let me stop you," Christian said, waving William up ahead. He saw that he had delayed the orderly enough to make him even more anxious to return to Dr. Glenn's side. "I can find my own way out."

William hesitated again, glancing up the narrow stairwell. Gas jets dimly lighted the passageway at the entrance to each floor. The wing for lunatics occupied half of the fourth and highest floor of the hospital. He offered Christian the lantern.

"No." He held out his hand, palm up. "I don't need it. You go on."

The orderly's dull eyes dropped to Christian's game leg.

"I know what you're thinking, but the stairs are no problem," Christian told him. In a slow movement that was almost against his will Christian found his hand dropping to his left thigh and massaging the spot where the Confederate lead ball had struck flesh and bone. "Gettysburg."

An embarrassed flush stole over William's square-cut features. "G'day, Mr. Marshall." He turned quickly and hurried up the stairs.

Christian followed at a pace that had nothing to do with his old wound. Something that felt very much like excitement fired his heart, and he ceased to notice the nagging ache in his leg. If he had stopped to think about it, he would have been much struck by this occurrence. Now he didn't give it a thought. He could only think of the risk he was planning to take. Nothing else mattered. Above him he heard William pause on the stairs. Christian looked up to see the attendant peering over the railing. Christian gave him a cursory salute to indicate everything was fine. The door on the fourth floor opened and closed. William was gone.

Christian's limp was hardly noticeable as he retraced his steps to the treatment room. With his right hand he followed the contours of the wall, counting four recesses which marked doors to other rooms. He stopped at the fifth and knelt in front of the treatment room. From the moment he had seen the keys William used to lock it he knew his task would be a simple one. A determined child could pick it with the right tool. In this case the only tool required was a pencil. Christian inserted it into the wide keyhole, manipulated it with a deft touch, and consequently broke the pencil.

"Dammit." He felt in the dark for the part that had not fallen in the lockpiece and pocketed it. Under his breath he cursed the man who had encouraged him to come to Jennings Memorial. Christian took out his notepad and slipped a flat metal file from beneath the book's leather spine. It took thirty seconds to release the lockpiece.

Christian pulled himself upright, threw back the bolt, and entered the room, shutting the door behind him. It was useless to expect that his eyes would adjust to the total darkness of the room, so he didn't waste time waiting for it to happen. He regretted not having the lantern, but he couldn't take the chance that someone would happen by and see light from under the door. Exercising caution, Christian crossed the room, stopping when his knees touched the cot. He sat down on the very edge and placed his head where he expected Jane Doe's shoulder to be.

It wasn't there. Neither was her neck, her head, or her arm. Christian ran his hands all across the cot, and was forced to admit that she was gone. "What the hell?" he whispered. "Where did you go, Jane? You couldn't have left the room." A small whimper at the far corner alerted him to her presence. Afraid that he would frighten her more than he already had, Christian stayed where he was. "Jane?" he questioned softly. "I'm a friend, Jane. I'm not going to hurt you. I only want to talk."

Another shivery whimper was all the response Christian received.

"You're very resourceful, Jane. Someday I hope to learn how you escaped those straps." He paused, reaching toward the head of the cot where the leather straps had been. They were still there. Further investigation proved they hadn't been cut or unbuckled. He ran his index finger around the inside of one of the straps. It felt wet. He drew back his finger, sniffed, and touched the tip of his tongue to it. It was blood. The flesh on her wrists would be twisted and raw from her efforts to free herself. He heard her teeth chatter and decided to ease what suffering he could. "You're welcome to my jacket. It'll ward off the chill. Shall I bring it to you?" He waited a moment for a reply. When none came he tried another tack. He stood up and took the jacket off, holding it out at the end of his fingertips. "Would you like to come for it yourself? I'm holding it out to you. Just follow the sound of . . ." Christian didn't finish. He never heard her move. One moment the navy blue jacket was dangling at the end of his hand, in the next it was gone. He cocked his head to one side and heard her scurry back to her corner. Had she crawled along the floor on all fours? The thought was repugnant. "Does that help at all? Are you warmer?"

23

"Hmm."

Christian hoped that meant yes. "My name is Christian Marshall. I'd like to call you by your name. Will you tell me what it is?"

Nothing.

"Then shall I call you Jane like everyone else?"

Nothing.

"I'm going to sit down again," he said, doing just that. He sat heavily so the cot groaned a little beneath his weight. It was important to him that she not feel threatened. "I know you don't have any reason to trust me, but I'm asking you to do it anyway. Are you listening to me, Jane?"

"Hmm."

Her teeth had stopped clicking, but her reply was little more than a moan. Not for the first time Christian questioned the rightness of what he was doing. "There's someone here at the hospital who believes in you. He's a friend of mine." Or he was, Christian amended silently, before he talked me into this bit of blatant idiocy. "You've met Scott, haven't you? Dr. Turner?"

Nothing.

"I can't see you, Jane," Christian explained patiently. "If you're shaking your head one way or the other I've no way of knowing. Do you remember meeting Dr. Turner? It would have been shortly after you were brought here. Before the treatments started."

There was a short gasp as Jane Doe caught back a sob. Then, "Hmm-mm."

"Good." Progress at last. "Dr. Turner thinks you may not belong here but it's not in his power to get you out. I might be able to help if you'll let me. It won't be accomplished easily, Jane, and certainly not without your assistance. Today is simply the introduction. Will you remember me later? Know my voice?"

"Taak meh." A sob followed the unintelligible words. "Doan leef meh."

Christian's stomach coiled as the sounds of the tortured

voice washed over him. So much effort had gone into the few words she spoke that Christian could not bring himself to ask her to repeat them. He said them again in his mind, then mouthed them, and finally whispered them until he had a sense of their meaning. When he realized what she was asking his insides curled tighter. "I can't take you today. I have to leave you. I didn't come in a carriage. I rode Liberty. She'd take both of us but I don't think you can ride—not in your condition. And it can't be more than twenty degrees outside. You'd freeze to death before we made a city block. I live too far north of here, on Fifth, between Thirty-eighth and Thirty-ninth." Christian knew he was rambling in what amounted to a poor attempt to justify his inability to take any action at this time. It definitely wasn't in the plans he and Scott had outlined. "It won't work. I'll have to come back. It will be a few days. No longer." Inadequately he added, "I promise."

"Doan leef meh," she said again, choking on a shallow sob. "Plee doan."

It was immediately apparent to Christian that Jane Doe could no longer hold back her tears. He left the bed and moved to her side as she began sobbing in earnest. He was careful not to touch her as he hunkered down. "I'm here. I'm not going to hurt you," he repeated gently. "I want to help. Dr. Turner wants to help. But I can't do anything today, and Scott can never be implicated. Do you understand? You must never mention his name or anything that I've told you. Jane, are you listening? Please, you must understand. I can't stay any longer. I have to leave now."

He gave a small start as her crying stopped abruptly and her fingers curled around his wrist in a surprisingly strong grip. She seemed to know the exact placement of his arm. "Do you have cat's eyes, Jane Doe?" he asked softly, trying to extricate his hand. She was not giving any quarter. He remembered the things Dr. Glenn had told him about this patient. Was Glenn right and Scott wrong after all? "Is that it?" he asked again in a tone suited to a fractious child. "Cat's eyes? I don't remember

25

them that way. They're very pretty, though. Deeply brown, I think. Touches of cinnamon and dark chocolate." Christian gave up trying to remove her fingers. With the intention of leading her back to the cot, Christian started to rise. Her choices were clear. She could be led or dragged or she could let go and stay where she was. He was only slightly relieved when she allowed herself to be led docilely. When they reached the cot she still had a bloodless grip on his wrist. There was no question in Christian's mind but that he could pull away if he wanted. A quick downward snap would set him free. He also thought it would agitate Jane, and Scott Turner had cautioned him against that. He was still trying to decide what to do when she lifted his wrist and laid his hand against her left breast.

"Taak meh." She stepped closer to Christian and moved sinuously against him so that her breast rubbed the heart of his palm.

Confusion was uppermost in Christian's mind. He was only peripherally aware of the breast that filled his hand or the damp, clinging shift that covered it. Had he misunderstood her request all along or was she bartering herself to gain her release? Did she want him to take her on the cot or take her out in the cold? Was she simply a demented syphilitic whore who'd caught Scott Turner's eyes one day? Christian had difficulty believing that. He decided to believe that she was bartering herself in order to get him to change his mind. "This isn't what you want," he said firmly. God knows, he thought, it wasn't what *he* wanted. He'd count himself as debased as one of the Five Points pimps if he were attracted in any physical way to Jane or her offer.

"I have to go before I'm discovered here. Someone's bound to come and check on you soon. If I'm found I won't be able to come back." Was she listening to him? Christian didn't think so. She continued to press her body against his. The jacket he gave her slipped from her shoulders and he felt it touch his arm on its way to the floor. How could she withstand the cold? Dr. Glenn warned him she didn't feel things the way a normal person would. Of course she was close enough to him that she was practically basking in his body heat, he decided wryly. Incredibly, he felt his body respond to the small hand that began to slide back and forth across his groin. Too dumbfounded to be angry, Christian simply stood there and waited for Jane to realize that he wasn't going to make a single willing overture. "Are you used to getting what you want?" he asked dryly. "Is that why Alice Vanderstell calls you the princess?"

The words were barely out of Christian's mouth when he felt a sharp, excruciating pain in his groin. Belatedly he understood that Jane had delivered the humiliating and incapacitating blow with her knee. It had never occurred to him that he was being set up like a mark in a Bowery saloon. She was sly and cunning and probably everything else that Dr. Glenn said she was. He began to think with more conviction that Scott Turner had made the mistake.

Christian's legs trembled and he instinctively doubled at the waist to prevent further injury and ease the existing pain. He regretted not being able to hold back the small, surprised grunt that gave sound to Jane's blow. It helped her target his face in the pitch-black room. The double-fisted punch she landed on his cheek and temple knocked Christian sideways and back and onto the bed. He rolled toward the wall in an attempt to get out of her way, but her thin arms seemed to rotate like windmills, pummeling and flailing him until inevitably she got lucky. Jane's fists found the same spot on Christian's left leg that the lead ball at Gettysburg had.

A different kind of darkness encroached on Christian's vision. It was murky and thick and unrelentingly powerful. Christian was unconscious almost before he had finished screaming.

Marshall House was one of a number of brownstone mansions built at the mid-century mark when New York money was moving uptown. At that time Fifth Avenue north of Twenty-third Street was still unpaved and resembled nothing so much as a quaint country cowpath. It was largely unpopulated, and many New Yorkers predicted the northern migration would fail. They were wrong. Fifth Avenue, from Washington Square to Madison Square, established itself as the center of society and fashion and the brownstone mansions bore the mark of money.

Marshall House, like its neighboring residences, was both grandiose and solid-looking. It reflected the wealth and the conservatism of the original owners. Men who'd made millions by taking risks to build their empires chose conformity when it came to building their homes. There was a fine line between originality and a vulgar display of wealth.

Commissioned by Christian's father, Marshall House favored conformity. The entrances were made imposing by the Corinthian columns and pilasters which flanked them. The mansard roof, the high, arched windows, and the heavy stone ornamentation weighted the house with formality and respectability. Inside, the mansion was no less stately. The rooms on the first floor included a spacious banquet hall which was not to be confused with the dining room, a solarium, a study, an exceptionally well-appointed library, three parlors, and a gallery which displayed tapestries and sculpture.

Before the war Marshall House had played a significant role in the social life of the Fifth Avenue elite. Now, with only Christian remaining the seldom-used rooms of Marshall House seemed to echo silence.

Scott Turner splashed a crystal tumbler with whiskey and held it out to his patient. The searing look Christian gave him made him pull back and add a generous two fingers of liquor before he handed it over. He arched one wheat-colored brow critically. "You're certain you want this?"

"Stop playing doctor and be my friend. Or leave." He leaned forward in his red leather armchair to accept the tumbler and pushed the ottoman away with his feet. The plaid shawl which

28

covered his lap and legs slipped to the floor. He kicked it aside. "Damn right I want it. I'm not an invalid." Christian knocked back the drink in one long swallow. He winced slightly when it hit the pit of his empty stomach.

Scott shrugged. He could sense that Christian was spoiling for a fight. Scott Turner counted himself among a half dozen or so people who wouldn't back down from the opportunitiy to flatten Christian Marshall. Not that Scott was certain he could do it, but there were times he'd be grateful for the chance. The game leg didn't make Christian untouchable as far as Scott was concerned. It tended to make things a little fairer. Scott stood a full head shorter than his best friend and carried only three-quarters of the weight. He had regular, even features that his wife assured him were quite handsome—even if they didn't turn female heads the way Christian's profile was prone to do. "Doctor or friend, my advice is still the same. Drink in moderation or don't drink at all. This isn't doing you any good."

"What would you know?" he asked sulkily, holding the tumbler up to the firelight and examining it idly.

"Now you sound like Amy," Scott said, remarking on Christian's tone. "May I remind you that my daughter is five?"

Lowering the tumbler, Christian rolled it back and forth between his hands. His eyes dropped away from the hearth. "Jesus, what a day."

"And night. It's long gone eight, you know."

That surprised Christian, but it didn't show on his face. His features were a study of stillness. "Is it? What time was it when Mrs. Brandywine sent for you?"

"About six. Just after Dr. Morgan and an attendant from Jennings brought you home and took their leave. I've already commended your housekeeper for not mentioning me to Morgan. He'd have been apoplectic if he'd known I'd be called in."

"Thinks you found your medical degree in the *Herald*'s classified ads, does he?"

Scott grinned and ran his fingers through his hair, pushing back the golden fringe that tended to fall on his forehead. The rueful smile lifted his lips and lighted the striking blueness of his eyes. "Something like that. Morgan's Harvard. The University of Pennsylvania's Medical School doesn't carry much weight with him. He's very old guard. Innovation and change frighten him." He chuckled briefly. "I scare the hell out of him."

"Then he approves of the things I saw today?"

"Don't ever doubt it," Scott said seriously. "Perry Glenn is precisely what Morgan likes in a physician. Ancient techniques only slightly modified to fit a few modern sensibilities. Morgan's been running Jennings Memorial under those guidelines for too many years. The people who put money into that hospital don't begin to understand what it is they're getting in return. In the case of the lunatic wing it's often out of sight, out of mind." He stoppered the whiskey decanter and took a seat opposite Christian, stretching his legs in front of him. "You know, Christian, if you'd let me give you a powder for the pain, you wouldn't be sitting there as stiff as a three-day corpse."

"You'll turn my head with your delightful bedside manner," he said dryly. "Next you'll be suggesting an operation." He held up his hand to stop Scott's obvious reply. "I don't want to hear about it and I don't want a powder. The whiskey will do just as well, thank you very much."

"Stubborn fool. Alcohol's no good as a painkiller. That's a myth."

Christian's lip curled. "Then it's a damn good myth," he said sourly. "No wonder you scare the hell out of Morgan. Your medical education is full of holes."

Experience had taught Scott when to make a strategic retreat. "So tell me what happened at the hospital. You've been dozing off and on in that chair for the better part of two hours. No concussion that I can see, but Mrs. Brandywine should have kept you in bed where Morgan and William put you."

30

"Don't blame her. Your luck wouldn't have run any better."

"Don't I know it."

"So," Christian sighed, coming to his feet and heading toward the sideboard. Ignoring Scott's cross look, he poured himself another drink and carried it and the decanter back to his chair. "You want to know what happened. I assume Mrs. Brandywine gave you some version of the truth."

"She told me what Dr. Morgan told her. That after William MacCauley called Dr. Glenn away from the treatment room you went back inside instead of leaving the building. Your bleeding heart got the better of your common sense and you released Jane Doe. She returned your favor by knocking you out, stealing your clothes, strapping you to the bed, locking you in, and added insult to injury by taking flight with Liberty. Is that the gist of it?"

"Close enough," Christian grimaced. "I didn't release her, though. She had wiggled out of those straps by the time I returned to the room."

"Yes, but she couldn't have gotten out if you hadn't gone in. The bolt was meant to secure her just as it secured you after she was gone."

"In my case the bolt was completely unnecessary. She had me trussed so tightly to that cot my fingers went numb."

"You deserved it," Scott said bluntly. "Now she's out wandering the streets in weather that would freeze a witch's—"

"How was I supposed to know she'd do a damn fool thing like that?" Christian interrupted impatiently. "This was your idea, Scott. You're the one who said there was nothing wrong with her mind. I hope you'll understand that my experience with her has led me to a slightly different conclusion."

Scott threw up his hands. "Don't you see? If she's sane, then she'd be even more desperate to get away from the hospital? You offered her hope and snatched it away in virtually the same breath."

"If?" Christian demanded, latching onto the one word he heard above all the others. "What do you mean *if?* When you

31

approached me with this scheme you never once used the word if. 'I'll stake my reputation, Chris,' you said. 'Everything I've been taught tells me something's wrong at Jennings and not with Jane Doe,' you said. 'Help me, I swear she's being kept there against her will.' Does that sum it up?'' Christian asked angrily.

"Don't you forget anything?" Scott's handsome features contorted slightly as Christian belted back another drink. He fought the urge to take the decanter, knowing full well that Christian would only switch to something else. "I really haven't changed my opinion either," he said. "It's just that I never anticipated something like this. I had no idea that you'd be allowed to observe the treatment."

"It surprised me too. I think he wanted to impress, add another slant to the story he thought I was writing." Christian raised his glass in salute. "The Marshall name. *The Chronicle*'s power."

Scott ignored that. He knew better than to think Christian cared about either one any longer. "You were only supposed to take this opportunity to see which patient she was. The idea was for her to have some recognition of your presence."

"Well, we all got more than we bargained for. I didn't know I was going to see your Jane in that treatment room. I just assumed I had missed her on the ward. Hell, Scott, you could have warned me."

"I thought I did."

"Then you could have made a better job of it. Glenn almost killed her with his idiotic plunge bath. And the man believes in what he's doing! How can you keep on working there?"

"How can I not? Who battles for reform if I don't?"

"Saint Scott." Christian sipped from his glass. "Sorry. I didn't mean that."

"Yes, you did."

"All right, perhaps I did. You can't deny that you've been battling to save my wretched soul these past six months."

"I've been battling *alone* these last six months," Scott

corrected. "I used to have your father's help." He watched Christian's hands tighten around his drink at the mention of his father. "So," he said lightly, "you realized all along that this business with Jane Doe was just another skirmish in the war to make you take account of the real world."

"From the beginning."

"I see."

Christian savored the biting flavor of hard liquor on his palate. "And now that you've failed?"

"I wasn't aware that I had."

"Jane Doe's gone, Scott. Vanished. Probably frozen stiff by now." Christian's words were rounded at the edges as the whiskey began to slur his speech. He never claimed the same tolerance for alcohol that trapped an unwary drunk. "Not a damn thing we can do about it. Shame about Liberty, though. Best mare in my stables. Hoped she'd find her own way back, but suppose that's unlikely now. Past eight, you say? No, she's good as gone now. Jane's good as dead. And I good as killed her. That about sums up my day. Why don't you tell me about yours? Susan well? Amy?"

Scott had had enough. "What's this, Chris? A real display of self-pity? You usually play the callous bastard so well. Choose one or the other but stop vacillating. I damn well know you felt something today. You couldn't have toured the lunatic ward, seen the treatment room, and not been touched, not if you went to the hospital sober. And I know you did," he added for good measure. "Mrs. Brandywine told me."

Seemingly unmoved, Christian finished his drink. "I'll fire the old biddy."

"Even you aren't that stupid."

"No," he said consideringly. "Probably not."

"Open that decanter again and I'm leaving," Scott warned as Christian's fingers fiddled with the stopper. "You can drink yourself to death, but not in front of me." He held out his hand and waited for Christian to give over the tumbler and decanter. When he had them he set them on the floor by his chair. "And

33

anyway, this was never all about you. It's about Jane Doe as well. What are we going to do about her?"

Christian blinked, shaking his head to clear it. "Do about her? You're as mad as she is, Scott."

Scott leaned forward in his chair to press his point. "Listen to me, Christian. The hospital has every available person on staff out looking for her. Interesting, don't you think, given the fact that Jane's supposed to be a virtual nobody? I can tell you, they've had other patients leave without permission and they don't trouble themselves like this. Just as interesting, the police haven't been notified. No one is circulating any flyers with her picture."

Christian's fogged brain began to clear a bit. "How do you know there's a search?"

"Susan sent word here that the hospital's been trying to reach me. They want me involved because I know what she looks like."

"What are you going to do?"

"I *am* involved. *We're* involved. Did you make any sketches of her?"

"Several. They're in my jacket. Jane has that, remember?"

"Can you make more? One would serve. Something for the morning edition of *The Chronicle*?"

"Don't you think we're too late?"

"For the presses or for Jane?"

Christian glanced at the clock on the mantelpiece. "Probably both."

"Dammit, Christian. Stop throwing up blocks."

The hesitation was palpable. "All right," he said finally. "My sketchpad's on my desk." Christian pointed to the oak rolltop by the study's bowed window. "There are pens in the top right-hand drawer."

Scott wasn't even offended by Christian's assumption that he would get the things. "That's flagrant manipulation. You get them. I'll guard the whiskey."

"Damn you, Scott," Christian said matter-of-factly. "There

are times when I wonder why I don't lay you low."

"I've wondered the same thing." He realized how that could be misinterpreted and rushed to explain himself. "Why I don't lay you low, I mean."

"As if you could."

"I could."

Mrs. Brandywine chose that moment to enter the study. She'd had a hint of the conversation as she approached and it didn't ease the deep frown lines between her brows. Christian had created enough confusion and concern these past few hours to last a lifetime. And now Dr. Turner was egging him on. Neither one of them had the least sense. She took a deep, steadying breath. "Pardon me, Mr. Marshall," she said, smoothing her starched apron over her generously rounded hips. "Joe Means just came to the back door. He says he needs you in the sta—"

"It will have to wait," Christian said, pushing himself to his feet. The effects of his drinking, rather than his limp, marred Christian's walk to the desk. "I'm busy now."

"He said it was urgent," she pressed. "It's—"

"Maybe it's Liberty," Scott pointed out. "Joe would want you to know she's back."

Mrs. Brandywine rolled her eyes in exasperation. "Of course it's Liberty. Joe said she's just returned and—"

Christian spun away from the desk. "Was there a rider, Mrs. B.? Did Joe mention anything about a rider?"

"If someone would just let me finish." Her dimpled chin jutted forward militantly. "Yes, there's a rider. Joe's got him—"

In spite of his drinking, in spite of his limp, Christian sprinted out of the study ahead of Scott. Mrs. Brandywine threw up her hands in despair of ever learning what was going on.

Neither man gave a thought to a coat as they ran out into the cold. Scott passed his friend on the stony path to the stable. Christian gritted his teeth and managed a loping stride that

35

served to get him to the stable within a few seconds of Scott. Joe Means, Christian's trainer and stablemaster, met them at the entrance. Joe was a small man whose diminutive stature belied a seasoned wiry strength. He sported a stiff, outrageously large handlebar mustache that Christian swore could balance two of Harry Hill's dance-house showgirls.

"Where is she?" Scott demanded.

Joe's thick brows creased to form a single line above his nearly colorless eyes. He hadn't thought the doctor's first concern would be for the mare. "Liberty's being taken care of in her stall but—"

"Not the horse, Joe," Christian interrupted breathlessly. "The girl. Mrs. B. said there was a rider."

Confused, Joe's hands dug into his pockets. "This way. There was a rider, all right. A young man as near as I can tell." Joe took them to the tack room where he and one of the grooms had carried Liberty's rider. He threw open the door. Sleeping or unconscious, Liberty's rider was curled in a fetal position in one corner of the room. "In here."

Christian never doubted the young man was Jane Doe. His first glimpse of her explained why the mistake had been made. To combat the cold she had used his shirt as a turban. It completely covered her dark hair and one of the sleeves fell over the lower part of her face like a muffler. She couldn't begin to fill out the clothes she had stolen. The shoulder seams of his woolen jacket hung halfway to her elbows. The reddened tips of her fingers were all that were visible at the cuffs. His trousers were rolled twice at the ankles. She still wore his socks but not his shoes. He wondered how long ago she had lost them.

Scott fell on his knees beside her. He raised each of her pale eyelids in turn and checked her fingers. His pronouncement was grim. "Frostbite. Joe, send one of the grooms to Mrs. Brandywine. Have him tell her to draw a warm bath. Not hot, just warm. Then come back here with some blankets. We've got to get her up to the house."

"Shouldn't we rub snow on her hands?" Joe asked.

"Do what Dr. Turner wants, Joe," Christian said tightly, emphasizing Scott's title. After Joe was gone Christian joined Scott on the tack room floor. "What can I do?"

"You can build a litter."

"I'll carry her," he objected.

"Dammit, Christian! I'm not suggesting you can't." But he had been. They both knew it.

"I'll *carry* her," he said again. "I can't explain it. I need to do this." His voice softened as his fingers fluttered against the arch of Jane's exposed cheek. "It's as if I owe her something."

Chapter 2

Christian paced the hallway outside the guest room where Jane Doe had been taken. After following Scott's instructions and depositing Jane in the warm bath drawn by Mrs. Brandywine, Christian had been summarily dismissed. His protests had fallen on deaf ears. Now Christian was nursing whiskey from a silver flask he usually kept in his bedside table while Scott nursed their patient.

Mrs. Brandywine stepped out of the room and clicked her tongue in disapproval when she saw Christian touching the flask to his lips. She knew the futility of actually saying anything so she didn't. Her clicking tongue was eloquent in its own right.

With an air of defiance more suited to a ten-year-old than someone three times that age, Christian tipped back the flask and swallowed deeply. He wiped his mouth with the back of his hand. His cool blue-green eyes, as clear and pointed as shards of crystal when he wasn't drinking, were clouded and slightly unfocused. He pocketed the flask and laid a hand on Mrs. Brandywine's shoulder as she attempted to brush past him. "Where are you going?"

"Towels," she said tersely.

"Does Scott need any help?"

"He needs fresh, clean towels and nightclothes for your

39

guest." She managed to control a disparaging sniff. "May I go, sir?"

"*Sir?*" Both of Christian's brows flew upward. "You must be *extremely* put out with me."

"How clever you are," she said dryly. "Perhaps too clever for your own good."

"A lecture, Mrs. B.? And I thought you had given up on me." He tried to coax a smile from her with his own boyish grin.

Mrs. Brandywine's expression remained dour. The lines at the outer corner of her eyes deepened as she stared up at Christian. The earnest, slanted smile was reminiscent of the boy she had helped raise, but the eyes belonged to a man she did not know. "I light a candle for you every day," she said softly.

Christian's smile vanished. He felt as if he had been given a vicious blow to his midsection. "I don't need your prayers."

"May I go, Mr. Marshall? Dr. Turner will be wondering what's become of me."

Christian released her. "Go. Get the hell out of here." Even in his fogged state of consciousness he saw Mrs. Brandywine's blink of hurt surprise. "Jesus, Mrs. B., I'm sorry. I didn't mean . . ." He stopped because she was walking away. Christian leaned against the wall and shut his eyes briefly, rubbing them tiredly with his thumb and forefinger. Dear God, he thought, when was the last time he had done something right?

Some minutes later Scott's call for help from the guest room roused Christian from his self-pitying trance. He crossed the hallway in two uneven strides and twisted the door handle. "What's wrong?" he demanded. "What's happened to Jane?"

Scott didn't even glance in Christian's direction. He was kneeling over the tub, one arm braced around his patient's shoulders to keep her upright. "Nothing's happened to her. I was calling for Mrs. Brandywine. Where are the blasted towels?"

"She's getting them." He shifted his weight uneasily, not

40

certain if he should stay or go. "Is there anything I can do?"

"Get over here and hold her up. She keeps slipping and I need to examine her feet again."

Christian exchanged places with Scott, sliding his arm around Jane's naked shoulders. Her head rested heavily in the crook of his elbow. Her closed lids were pale, nearly translucent, making the silky fringe of her lashes seem jet black in comparison. His eyes shifted uncomfortably as he tried to avoid looking past Jane's shoulders. The water did not quite reach the level of her breasts, and it did nothing to hide the length of legs or the slim angles of her waist and hips. The mere fact that he had to control an urge to look at her more closely made Christian feel uneasy if not precisely perverted.

Scott lifted Jane's left foot out of the water and examined her toes. He depressed the tip of her toes gently and firmly, then the sole of her foot and the heel. "It embarrasses you, doesn't it?" he asked, glancing at his friend.

Christian could have pretended he didn't know what Scott was talking about. He didn't bother. "A little. I'm not sure I even understand it. It's not as if I've never seen a naked woman before."

"Now there's an understatement." Scott chuckled. "This house used to see more naked women than Madame Restell's."

"They were models. And they were nude, not naked."

"There's a difference?" Scott asked skeptically.

"Most times," Christian said, forcing a straight face. "They also didn't parade in and out of here unclothed, and my mother was a frequent visitor to my studio. Neither she nor my father would appreciate you comparing this house to that abortionist's bordello."

"Would you want to paint her?"

"Who? Madame Restell?"

Scott rolled his eyes. "No. I mean Jane."

Christian didn't take the bait. "I don't paint anymore."

"You sketched her. You told me you did and you were willing to make another—from memory, I might add."

41

"That was different."

"Oh?"

"Leave it, Scott. Why are we even having this conversation? Shouldn't you be concentrating on your patient?"

Scott's eyes met Christian's for a long moment. "I have two patients," he said quietly. His eyes dropped away and he gently lowered Jane's foot into the water. "She has second-degree frostbite on her fingers and toes." He lifted her right foot and touched each of her toes in turn. "As near as I can tell the deep tissues aren't damaged," he explained. "See, the surface of her skin is still hard but the underlying tissue is soft. I can depress it. If this were deep, unthawed frostbite, then her flesh would feel more than hard. It would feel solid and I wouldn't be able to depress it."

"But her skin is so red."

"That's due in part to the rewarming." He pointed to the small blisters on the tips of Jane's toes. "These may be a good sign. If the frostbite were worse it's likely she wouldn't have any blisters, or at least not this early. We'll know more in twelve or so hours. If more appear, then it means her tissues are more badly damaged than I think they are now. There will be additional swelling and some burning and tingling as the surface area thaws."

"Will she lose her toes?"

"It's too early to tell, but I don't think so. Her fingers are in better condition, though her wrists are abraded from the restraints." Scott scooted to the middle of the tub, reached in the water, and raised Jane's hands for inspection. The blisters were less pronounced. "It looks like sunburn, doesn't it?"

"I suppose," Christian said doubtfully. "Shouldn't you be trying to warm her from the inside out?" With his free hand he reached for the flask in the breast pocket of his jacket. "I've got something here that—"

"You give her even a whiff of that stuff and I'll break your fingers," Scott said bluntly.

"But—"

"I'm serious. Alcohol is the last thing she needs. The warmth it provides is only temporary, and in the main it's false. It eventually results in an increased loss of heat."

"Is that what passes for medical knowledge where you come from?" scoffed Christian. "I begin to see why you're so often at odds with Morgan and Glenn."

Scott shrugged. "I saved your leg, didn't I?"

Christian replaced the flask. "My leg. My life. And now you want my soul."

"No comment." Scott sat back on his heels. "Where the hell is Mrs. B.? I just sent her for towels."

"Should I get her?"

"No, stay where you are." Scott got to his feet and stretched his legs. He walked over to the fireplace and removed the kettle the housekeeper had set in the hearth. "I need to add some hot water. Can you move her legs a little to the side and make sure they stay there? I don't want to burn her."

As Scott was adjusting the temperature of the tub water Mrs. Brandywine reentered the room. "Mr. Marshall, you shouldn't be in here," she said, setting her armload of towels on the seat of the rocker. She kicked at the braided hearth rug with the toe of her shoe, straightening out its curling edge. "You're a man and that poor child hasn't a stitch on."

Christian and Scott exchanged humor-filled glances. "Your ability to state the obvious takes my breath away," said Christian. "You could make the same observation about Scott."

"He's a doctor," Mrs. Brandywine said. "He has a purpose, you don't. It isn't decent that you're here."

"I don't think Jane cares who's holding her. In fact I'd say she's probably grateful just to have someone keeping her above the waterline for a change."

The housekeeper snorted delicately and addressed the doctor. "I'm sorry about the delay. There was a bit of trouble at the front door. A Dr. Glenn came by asking to see you. Apparently Mrs. Turner mentioned you might be here."

Scott frowned. "Glenn must have tricked Susan into saying it. She wouldn't have offered that information."

"I told him you'd been gone for hours. I don't think he believed me."

"It's all right. I'm certain you did fine."

Christian voiced his doubts. "She doesn't lie very well, do you, Mrs. B.? Some people have a knack for it, and then there's Mrs. Brandywine," he explained to Scott. "She thinks it's a sin."

"It *is* a sin," she said firmly. "But in this instance I can live with it. I can tell you, I had half a mind to let him see *you*, Mr. Marshall."

"He asked?"

"Of course he did. Wanted to see for himself how you were getting on. I could have told him you were nearly three sheets to the wind, but I held my tongue."

"There's a wonder," he said wryly. "What did you tell him?"

"I said you were sleeping comfortably and had left strict orders not to be disturbed."

"That never stopped you before."

The housekeeper's chin jutted forward. "But Dr. Glenn didn't know that."

Scott held up his hands. "Enough. I could use more assistance and less conversation. Mrs. B., will you steam the towels? I need them warm and moist. Chris, pull back the covers on the bed, then help me get Jane out of the tub. I'll hold her." He set down the kettle and traded places with Christian. Scott gently brushed back Jane's dark hair at the temples and examined her ears. "This could be a problem," he said to himself.

"What's that?" asked Christian, pausing in turning back the covers.

"Her ears. They're blistered too. That shirt she had wrapped around her head wasn't enough protection, not with her wet hair."

44

Christian swept back the sheets and blankets, smoothed the bottom sheet with his hands to warm them, and returned to Scott's side. "Let's get her into bed. How are you coming with those towels, Mrs. B.?"

"Just fine. You take care of your, er, end," she said, blushing to the roots of her ash-blond hair as Christian eased Jane's legs out of the tub.

"Have a care with her feet," Scott cautioned. "That's it. Easy. Where's that nightgown, Mrs. B.? We need to put her in it."

"Here it is," she said, plucking it off the back of the rocker. "None of the maids had one to spare and mine wouldn't suit, so I took one of Mr. Marshall's nightshirts." She glanced guiltily at Christian. "You don't mind?"

"I'm going to pretend you didn't ask me that," he said. "That way I won't be insulted." He softened his words with a faint smile. "The towels, Mrs. B." When she was out of earshot he looked at the nightshirt and then at Scott, a question in his eyes. "Have you ever tried to *dress* a woman?" he whispered.

"How hard can it be?" Scott asked.

Christian knew evasion when he heard it. "Should I ring for one of the maids to assist Mrs. B.?"

Scott took the nightshift out of Christian's hands. "We'll both do this. Lift her head. That's it. Now slip this over her shoulders. Raise her arm. No, the other one first. Be careful of her hand. Gently . . . gently. Good. Now the other. Pull the hem down over her breasts. There, we've got it now. I'll roll back this cuff, you do the other."

Christian was glad for Scott's chatter and the opportunity to keep busy. Perhaps no one would notice that his hands were trembling. Christian wanted to tell himself he needed a drink, but he knew it wasn't true. He hadn't descended so far into any bottle that he shook when he went without.

It was Jane Doe that made his fingers shake. The woman was unconscious. She was ill, probably mad as well. Her skin, where it wasn't red and blistered, was as pale as salt. There

45

were deep shadows beneath her eyes. Her hair was tangled and matted. He felt sick to his stomach that he noticed things about her.

Like her legs. The splendid line of her legs caught more than his artist's eye. He felt the tug of a man-to-woman attraction. He despised himself for that. And how was he supposed to ignore her breasts? They were beautiful, pink-tipped and ivory-smooth. Strictly speaking they were a bit too large for the narrowness of her waist and ribcage, but they held a fullness that made him want to cup their underside, lift them, and . . . He was disgusting, he thought. He disgusted himself. His thoughts were disgusting. If Scott or Mrs. B. suspected what he was thinking, they would be disgusted with him.

"Did you say something?" Scott asked.

Christian blinked. Scott was looking at him strangely. Oh, God, Christian wondered despairingly, had he spoken any of his thoughts aloud? "What?"

"Did you say something?" Scott repeated. He took one of the warm, moist towels that Mrs. Brandywine held out to him and gingerly wrapped it around Jane's head, covering her ears with the wet heat. "I thought you were talking to me."

"No," he said quickly. "No, I didn't say anything."

Scott frowned slightly, gave Christian a hard look, then shrugged. "How about wrapping her feet? Don't rub them and don't break the blisters. We'll leave the towels on five minutes, then replace them. Mrs. B.?"

"Yes, sir?"

"Is there a warming pan somewhere in this house?"

"Certainly. I'll get it right away." She dropped the towels in Christian's lap. Ignoring his pained look, the housekeeper bustled out of the room.

"What's going to happen to her?" Christian asked after they had pulled the covers over Jane and retreated to the far side of the room. "Why doesn't she come around?"

Scott began steaming more towels using the kettle in the hearth. "She's had a shock," he said simply. "Don't forget all that's been done to her these last six weeks. Her mind is resting now, restoring itself."

"How do you know that?"

"I don't, not with any certainty. There's no hard, scientific evidence to support that belief, but I suspect it's true." He paused and added quietly, "I have to hope to God it's true."

Christian glanced over his shoulder at Jane, then looked at his friend accusingly. "You don't really know any more than Dr. Glenn, do you? This is all just a gamble. Your game may be a little more humane than the good doctor's, but it's still a game, isn't it? You're both using Jane as your personal blue-chip stake. You both think you know what treatment's best for her and the truth is, neither of you knows a damn thing!"

Scott's face flushed with anger but he took a calming breath. "I damn well know that one doesn't need to repeatedly attempt to drown a person to cure a disordered mind. And don't put words in my mouth. I'm not saying that Jane's a lunatic. Or at least she wasn't when she was brought to Jennings. Violent? Yes. Disoriented? Certainly. She was hysterical, confused, delusional and possessed of a scream that could send chills up your spine. It remains my best professional opinion that everything I observed initially was related to some drug she was given."

"What drug does all that?" Christian asked skeptically.

"A very common one," he said, his eyes narrowing sharply on Christian, then the outline of the flask in his pocket. "Alcohol. Ever heard of delirium tremens?"

Christian's applause was light and cynical. "Nicely done, Scott. You can be satisfied that your warning has been heard if not heeded. However, I don't believe for a moment that alcohol had anything to do with Jane's problem. So what drug was it?"

"Cocaine. Opium. Rat poison. Foxglove. Datura. There are a host of possibilities. The actual dose would make a difference. Something relatively harmless at a low dosage could account for most of Jane's symptoms in larger amounts. Or the drug may have been introduced into her system over time. It could

47

have an accumulative effect. Hell, Christian, it may have been something I've never heard of. I've no way of knowing with one-hundred-percent accuracy. I'd have to do tests, and for those I'd need a sample. You can appreciate the fact that Jane wasn't admitted with any."

"How do you know the effects of the drug aren't permanent?"

"I don't."

"How do you know Glenn's treatments haven't damaged her mind?"

"I don't."

"How do you know it's not the pox?"

That question, at least, Scott was prepared to answer with more certainty. "Generally syphilis takes years to generate insanity. Anyway . . ."

"Yes?"

"She's a virgin."

Christian almost dropped the towels Scott had been piling in his arms. "What?" He shook his head. "You must be mistaken. Once we were alone in her cell she was all over me. Trust me, she knew what she was doing. Jane's used to trading herself for favors."

"Desperation."

Christian snorted.

"I did a thorough examination shortly after she was admitted," Scott said, pressing his position. "It's routine. I had to rule out pregnancy and venereal disease." He paused a beat, then said offhandedly, "Is it so hard to believe that she could be a virgin?"

"Sure it is. Who ever heard of a virgin her age from the Five Points? They pimp children in that quarter."

Scott tapped the side of his head and smiled, indicating that Christian was finally beginning to grasp the right idea. "Makes one suspicious, doesn't it?" he asked. "Could even lead one to believe that Jane may not be from the Five Points at all."

Christian followed Scott back to the bed. They began the

48

process of exchanging the towels. "It's not enough, Scott."

"Not by itself," he agreed. "But I told you how she came to be at Jennings."

"Dr. Glenn told me the same story."

"Didn't you find it unlikely that two of the Dead Rabbits gang brought her to the hospital? And why Jennings? It's not even close."

"Perhaps the asylums turned her away."

"You're grasping, but go ahead. It makes my case stronger. I checked other hospitals. There were beds that night. More to the point, no one could recall anyone fitting Jane's description being brought in for admission. That's because the Dead Rabbits didn't even try. They took her straight to Jennings."

"Why?"

"For the same reason they do anything—money. They were paid."

"By whom?"

"Now there you have me." He gathered up the used towels while Christian covered Jane again.

"To what purpose?"

"I would imagine it was to get her out of the way."

Christian bent over Jane and rearranged her pillow so that her head and neck were no longer resting at such an awkward angle. Satisfied that she was more comfortable, he turned away from the bed and sighed, thoroughly out of patience with Scott's thin explanations. "This is all about that book you read a while back, isn't it? The one about that woman in Illinois. What was her name?"

"Mrs. Packard."

"Hmmm. Mrs. Packard. She was committed by her husband and—"

"You don't have to tell me the story. I *read* it, remember? She was committed to the state insane asylum in Jacksonville, Illinois, while perfectly sane. Her husband, a minister if you recall, managed the thing quite easily. She spent three years there, Christian. *Three years.* Is it really so difficult to believe that the same thing could happen here, under our very noses?"

"Frankly? Yes, it is. It sounds as melodramatic as one of those penny dreadfuls Harris Press is always trying to foist on the public." Christian's lip curled derisively. "This must be one of the oldest contrivances in literature."

"We're not writing a novel, damn it. This is real." He shook his head, running his fingers through his hair. "What's the matter with you, Christian? I thought you used to tilt at windmills, champion unpopular causes. What the hell happened?" Scott caught himself, took a deep breath, and let it out slowly. "I'm sorry. That wasn't called for. I know what happened almost as well as you do. Damn, but you try my patience. I never expected that you'd require so much in the way of convincing, certainly not after you saw firsthand what Jane was going through."

Christian removed the towel from Jane's head and indicated that Scott should examine her ears again. "Would it be all right if I comb out her hair?" he asked.

"You amaze me," Scott said, shaking his head in disbelief. "You're arguing with me every step of the way, yet you care enough to want to untangle that rat's nest?"

"My arguments have nothing to do with whether or not I care." Christian rifled the contents of a chest of drawers and came up with a boar's-hair brush. He tested the bristles against the palm of his hand, concerned that they would be soft enough for Jane. It wasn't what he wanted but it would do. He held it up and looked at Scott inquiringly.

"Go ahead. Just don't touch her ears with it."

Christian sat down cautiously at the head of the bed and eased Jane's mass of matted hair from beneath her head. He fanned out her hair on the pillow, tugging on it gently with his fingers, separating the strands as best he could before he used a brush on them. Her hair was the color of dark semi-sweet chocolate, a deep, rich brown that could almost be mistaken for ebony in the dim lamplight.

"I was appalled by what I saw today," he said after a

moment. "Nothing you told me going into this prepared me for what I experienced in the treatment room. I can't even be sorry that Jane tricked me into helping her escape. That was our plan after all, and she merely took matters into her own hands. I don't believe for a second that anyone deserves the kind of torture that was being used on Jane. What I'm having difficulty understanding is your conviction that Jane is quite sane and that she was brought to Jennings Memorial against her will. There's not enough proof to support that view."

"There is one more piece of evidence," Scott said, "but I hesitated to bring it up. No doubt you'll think it's as farfetched and fanciful as everything else I've told you."

Christian smoothed back Jane's hair at the temples and continued brushing with light, rhythmic strokes. Her hair was like chocolate lace against the stark white pillow sham. "Let me make up my own mind," he said. "Alcohol hasn't dulled all my faculties for judgment. At the moment I'm feeling disgustingly sober."

Mrs. Brandywine picked that moment to return with the warming pan. Scott took it from her and directed her to have some broth and tea prepared in the event Jane woke. She hurried off again, but not before she had taken in the sight of her employer enrapt in his ministrations to Jane. As she retraced her steps back to the kitchen happy tears smarted her eyes. She made no attempt to wipe them away. They felt too good.

Scott wrapped the warming pan in a towel to protect Jane's skin and slid it under the covers. She moved slightly but did not wake. Scott gathered the cool, damp towels and took them back to the hearth. He stoked the fire under the kettle and started the process of warming them again. "You've heard Jane called the princess, haven't you?"

Christian nodded. "You've used it once or twice before, though I really didn't think much about it. It caught my attention today when one of the attendants called her that."

"Did you ask about it?"

51

"You know me too well." He grinned. "Yes, I asked William. He said that Alice Vanderstell gave Jane that title. That took me by surprise. I thought Old Alice was dead."

"Her family probably wishes it were so. She's been at Jennings quite a while, and there's really no hope that she'll ever be allowed to return home."

"You're not going to tell me she's there against her will as well, are you?"

"I'm sure she's there against her will," Scott replied. "If she had a choice in the matter she would choose to be in her own home. However, she can't take care of herself there and her family finds her a social embarrassment. She's disrupted parties they've given and invited complete strangers into the home. She still enjoys an occasional cigar." Scott gave a short half-laugh. "That wouldn't be a problem except that she's started a number of fires as a result of her habit. Her unpredictable behavior and forgetfulness make her something of a danger to herself and others."

"I'm not certain where this is leading."

"Alice has moments of complete lucidity," Scott explained. "But it seems they are all tied in, one way or the other, with her past. She recalls events of years ago with startling clarity and accuracy."

"That's not so unusual, is it?"

"No, not really. But it's important."

"How so?"

"Because she called Jane Doe the princess after only seeing her one time."

"So? Jane reminded her of someone she knew from her past."

Scott shook his head impatiently. A lock of hair fell forward and he brushed it back with the heel of his hand. "It wasn't like that. It was more definitive. I was there when it happened, and Alice seemed so certain. Don't you see? What if Jane *is* someone from Alice's past . . . someone she actually knew?"

"Farfetched and fanciful. You were right on both counts."

Christian put down the brush on the bedside table and eased off the bed. He sat down in the rocker and massaged his leg absently. "It's difficult to credit that Jane and Alice Vanderstell ever walked in the same social circles."

"Why? The Marshalls and the Vanderstells could have easily shared a rung on the social ladder. And look at you now. Who would believe it?"

Christian's jaw sagged a little and his eyes widened at Scott's plain speaking. "You're not pulling any punches, are you?"

"I can't afford to. This is important to me."

"Well, to give your theory a bit of credit, my parents knew the Vanderstells. That family always was a touch too high in the instep for my tastes, though it seems I missed something by never making Alice's acquaintance. She really smokes cigars, eh?"

"Yes, she really does."

"Imagine that." He slipped the flask out of his breast pocket and unscrewed the cap with his thumb. He ignored Scott's dark look. "You know what's even harder to believe?" he asked, raising the flask to his lips.

"What's that?" Scott asked, discouragement rife in his voice.

"That Jane over there could ever come by a nickname like the princess. I can't think of anyone less suited to a title like that."

"I'm not so sure you should judge Jane on the way you've seen her thus far. When she's feeling more the thing, I think she'll be rather pretty."

Christian almost came out of his chair. Pretty, he thought in amazement. What an insipid description! Her delicate, elegant bone structure was worthy of second notice. When Jane was well she would easily transcend being merely pretty. She would be striking.

"I was thinking of her demeanor," Christian said, "not the way she looks."

"I'd think it would be rather hard to affect the manner of a princess when one is being brutalized," Scott said dryly.

"I suppose so." Christian capped his flask and put it away.

Scott made a short, mocking bow. "How kind you are to concede that one small point."

"Listen, Scott, I'm not saying I won't help. I'm in this up to my neck so far and I'm not complaining about that, am I? I simply think your theories are without adequate foundation. That doesn't mean I'm going to abandon you or Jane. I have no intention of kicking her out. Tell me what you want me to do and I'll do it. Just don't ask me to involve the paper in any way again. I want as little to do with *The Chronicle* as possible, and that includes pretending I write stories for it."

"Am I missing something here? For God's sake, Christian, you own the damn paper. You're the publisher!"

"A set of circumstances that I would remedy if I could legally do so. My brothers cared about *The Chronicle*. I never did. I don't know why you expect their deaths should make a difference in the position I take with the paper. I do what I have to do for it."

Scott dropped the subject. "Help me with the towels again. This should be the last time we have to change them." He carried them over to the bed. "I had considered taking Jane to my home, but if you're serious about letting her stay, then this room should be prepared. I think she'll be safer here. As long as I can see her frequently, your staff can provide better care than Susan can by herself. She has plenty enough to do with Amy being underfoot most of the day."

"You should hire someone to help. More than just the cook you have now."

Scott laughed. "I'm a doctor, not the beneficiary of more inherited wealth than I know what to do with." He lifted Jane's right hand, unwrapped the towel, and examined it closely. "This is much better. She's making good progress. Once she's conscious she'll have to exercise her fingers. Just some mild movements, nothing strenuous. Under no circumstances is she to be allowed to walk. She could do serious damage to her

54

feet at this point."

"Does that mean we'll have to strap her down?"

"God," he said feelingly, "I hope not. That wasn't what I was thinking when I said the room had to be prepared."

"What did you mean?"

"Basically that we remove sharp objects and reduce the number of corners in the room. Get rid of that chest for instance. The mirror too. The figurines on the mantel should be taken out. I would prefer she didn't have anything to throw. It would be a good idea to wrap the brass posts of this bed with blankets. Does the door to this guest room lock from the outside?"

Christian had been listening to the list of changes with growing amazement. "Yes, it locks. But I'm damned if I'm keeping her prisoner! She can go anytime she wants."

"Didn't you hear what I said less than a minute ago? She can't be allowed to walk. And even when she's ready to walk, she may not be ready to leave our care. I have to satisfy myself that she's well enough physically and mentally to do that. It was never part of my plan to release her from Jennings and permit her to make her own way. Nothing's that simple."

Christian bit off his reply as Jane stirred. "I'll ring for some help. It appears we may not have much longer."

"There's no great hurry. She'll be as weak as a newborn kitten for a few days."

"Don't you believe it. I have personal experience with her recuperative powers that says differently. Moreover"—he grimaced—"she fights dirty." Christian went to the fringed bellpull and gave it two yanks. "That should bring Mrs. B. on a run," he said with a devilish smile.

Scott had to laugh. "You're cruel to her."

"Me?" Christian held up his hands innocently. "That woman stays awake nights thinking of some new way to get under my skin and you call me cruel? Surely you jest."

"Then you take shameless advantage of her. I wonder why she puts up with you."

Christian turned away and stared at the fire for a long moment. An ember popped, fizzled, then died. "We're the only family each of us has," he said finally. When he turned back to Scott he managed a rueful smile. "I didn't mean to get maudlin. Next thing you know I'll be turning to drink. Come on, help me with this chest."

Scott didn't know what to make of Christian's lightning-quick mood changes or his black humor, and he was too weary to dwell on it now. He couldn't help wonder if he had done the right thing by involving Christian in his own personal crusade. He had thought Christian needed a direction, some purpose, but what the hell did he know about anything? His wife had warned him Christian might not fall in easily with his plans. Susan had also pointed out that Christian Marshall, unlike Jane Doe, might not be worth saving. There were moments when Scott found himself considering the possibility that Susan was right.

They finished moving the chest into the hallway just as Mrs. Brandywine topped the stairs. She didn't appreciate their efforts, not when it meant that her floors were scratched because of their clumsiness. "I'll have Sam and Eddy take it from here," she said haughtily. "Is this why you rang for me?"

"In part," Christian said. "Scott wants a few things done to the room to accommodate his patient." He cast a sidelong glance at his friend to underscore the fact that he was not taking responsibility if Mrs. Brandywine threw a fit.

The housekeeper was immediately all smiles. "What can I do for you, Dr. Turner?"

Scott outlined the changes that needed to be made, expecting Mrs. Brandywine to formulate some objections at any time. When she listened carefully, nodded occasionally, and said that everything would be done to his satisfaction, he realized that this was her subtle way of needling Christian. Odd, he thought, but they both seemed to enjoy it. "Do you have that broth ready, Mrs. B.?" Scott asked.

"It's warming on the stove. I can have it brought up

56

whenever you want it."

"I'll come down with you and get it myself. Christian can stay with our patient for awhile. You can do that, can't you, Chris?"

Christian knew that Scott had some ulterior motive for accompanying Mrs. Brandywine, but he didn't bother pointing it out. Let them have their fun, he thought, magnanimous enough to be amused. If it gave them so much pleasure to discuss his welfare, who was he to stand in their way? Their meddling was generally harmless. "You go on. I'm sure I can manage." He waved them off with an impatient gesture and returned to the bedroom. "Mark my words, Jane Doe," he said, shutting the door behind him, "they'll be back here with broth for you and a small feast for me." He tapped the flask in his pocket. "They're both of the opinion I've had too much to drink this evening." He shrugged and pushed away from the door. Taking the rocker, he slid it toward the bed and sat down, propping his feet on the side rails. "They're right, of course, but then neither of them saw what I saw today. You're quite a woman, Miss Jane Doe. Not many people could have survived what you did."

Christian was staring at the polished tips of his shoes as he spoke, so he didn't see Jane's lashes flutter or notice that the cadence of her breathing had changed. "The question remains, how well did you survive it?" His brief smile was self-mocking. "I know something about getting on in the world. We could compare notes, you and I. Over a few drinks, I think. How would that suit? I prefer whis—"

He broke off in midsentence, taken completely off guard by Jane's sudden movement. She scrambled to the far side of the bed, hugging a pillow protectively about her middle, and stared at him accusingly. Though she opened her mouth and made some attempt at speech, the sounds were guttural, pained, and unintelligible.

Christian's feet dropped to the floor and he leaned forward in the rocker, but didn't make a move toward her. "Please

57

don't try to talk," he said. "You don't do it very well and it can't be good for your throat."

Her pale lips came together tightly. It was a mutinous line and Christian didn't mistake it for anything less.

"Since you're a guest in my house," he went on softly, "you may take it as an affront that I'm here in your bedroom, invading your privacy. It's for your own good, you know. And we won't be here alone for long. Dr. Turner will come back soon and so will Mrs. Brandywine. She's my housekeeper and a constant thorn in my side, but we deal well together so she lets me think I still employ her." He drew his brows together and he lifted the left one fractionally, hoping he looked properly bemused and perhaps a little skeptical. "Was that a smile I just saw hovering about a pair of blue lips? That won't do. Not at all. Scott will berate me for taxing your energies, and Mrs. B. will think I'm trying to cajole my way into your good graces and possibly into your bed." He held up his hands, palms out. "Nothing could be further from the truth." Christian saw her shoulders slump slightly as she relaxed her posture and her guard.

"Your hands and feet are wrapped in those towels for a reason." He watched her look down at her hands and register mild astonishment that they were covered. "It's for your protection. You have frostbite. Your skin is blistered, and if you're not careful you'll break the blisters. I imagine your fingers and toes are tingling now, but that's to be expected. It would be better if you would lie down again."

Jane's beautiful, soft doe eyes widened. She dropped the pillow and shook out her hands trying to get the towels off.

"No! Don't, Jane! You'll hurt yourself!"

She stopped what she was doing and recoiled as Christian came out of his chair. Her back was pressed flat against the brass headrails.

Christian held himself in check. Jane looked prepared to shimmy between the rails to get away from him if that was what was required. "I've frightened you, haven't I? I'm making such a mess of things." He swore softly under his breath, berating himself, and gave her a sheepish glance. Easy, he warned himself, don't overplay your hand. If she thinks you're too helpless in this situation, she won't trust you to assist her. "Could I just sit here on the edge of the bed? I'd remove those towels for you and you could twiddle your thumbs. Scott said that would be good for you."

Jane continued to stare at him, confusion and wariness darkening her eyes. She finally gave him a hasty nod.

Christian sat down slowly and drew one bent knee onto the bed, twisting slightly toward her as he did so. "If you're worried about what happened earlier today, perhaps I can ease your mind. I don't hold it against you. All things considered, I thought you were rather intrepid. Funny, I never thought that was a quality I'd find to admire in a woman, but there you have it. You're intrepid. Hold out your hands and we'll take another measure of your bravery."

She hesitated. Her eyes darted over him.

"Please? I really do want to help you."

Two large tears formed in her eyes, and before she could blink them back they slipped over her lower lids and dripped silently down her pale cheeks. Embarrassed, she turned her head away, tucking her chin against her shoulder, and held out her hands in a gesture that was at once defiant and helpless.

"Good girl," Christian said gently. He slid more fully onto the bed in order to reach her. With infinite tenderness he removed the damp towels from Jane's hands and moved his own fingers in the manner he wanted Jane to exercise hers. "Just like that," he told her when he caught her attention. "Not too quickly. Just enough to aid your circulation." He tossed the towels carelessly on the floor and took Jane's wrists, circling them with his thumb and forefinger. They seemed incredibly fragile to him. He turned her hands one way, then the other, checking them for broken blisters. "You're going to be all right, you know," he said, hoping it was so. "You're quite lucky. Liberty brought you here in time. She took you right to the stables where Joe found you." He released her wrists and watched her withdraw her hands and cross them modestly against her chest. To Christian it seemed an odd thing to do. It hadn't been so many hours ago that she had pressed her body intimately to his. She was full of interesting, intriguing contradictions. He wondered if she was even aware of them.

"That nightshirt is perfectly respectable," he said, not quite able to mask his grin. "It seems of late that I'm sharing a great deal of my wardrobe with you. Aaah, you blush, as well you should." He wagged a finger at her and smiled more openly to take away the sting of his words. "You took terrible advantage of me earlier. I, on the other hand, gave you over to the tender ministrations of my housekeeper." Christian had no regrets over the lie when he saw relief clear her clouded eyes. "May I remove the towels from your feet?" he asked, edging the tangle of sheets and blankets over her knees. Christian thought his question and his movements were casual, but his guest took almost immediate exception. She skittered away from him, drawing her knees up to her chest. As a result she lost the protection of the blankets, but she removed herself from Christian's easy reach.

"Would you like to take the towels off yourself?" he asked calmly. "The way you're sitting now is putting too much pressure on your feet. Dr. Turner is going to skin me alive if you hurt yourself. Why don't you stretch out your legs?" Christian could tell that she wanted to. There were clear signs of pain in the tight set of her mouth and the pale waxiness of her complexion. He glanced over his shoulder at the clock on the mantelpiece. Where the hell were Scott and Mrs. B.? He considered ringing for them, but he was afraid to leave the bed. Given Jane's fragile state of mind, he thought it was too likely that she would take the opportunity to get out of bed herself. She did not seem to fully comprehend there was any danger to herself other than the danger she attributed to his own presence. Christian couldn't help wondering what it was she expected him to do.

"I'd appreciate some reassurances on your part, Jane," he said.

Her brows drew together and she stared at him, puzzled. Her beautifully molded lower lip trembled slightly. She caught it between her teeth and held it still.

"I'd like to think that you aren't going to hurt yourself more than you already have this evening. It was a dangerous stunt that you pulled earlier. I'm not certain you grasp what could have happened to you. You were half frozen when Liberty delivered you here. You were unconscious. Another hour or so out in the cold and you very well may have been brought here dead. My only motive in bringing you inside was to see that you survived. Now, if you prefer to survive as a cripple that's entirely up to you. But let me give you a small idea of what you can expect that to look like." Hoping that he had her complete attention, Christian sidled to the edge of the bed and stood up. Without exaggerating his limp he walked to the fireplace, then he turned to face her.

Jane's blistered hands flew to her face. She smothered the strangled gasp that rose in her throat, but could not suppress the look of vivid horror in her eyes.

Christian was embarrassed by her reaction, and embarrassment quickly turned to anger. The taut planes of his cheeks flushed red and his already cool eyes iced over. He knew his limp made him ungainly, but it damn well didn't unman him. After Gettysburg that was one of the first things he had proved to himself, as well as to a succession of painted ladies at Mrs. Quilley's House of Blue Hearts. There was no reason that he could see for her complete revulsion to his infirmity. Gritting his teeth, he nearly growled at her. "It's not pretty, is it?" When she only continued to stare he advanced on the bed again, unaware that his approach was menacing or that his aquamarine eyes were colder than anything his guest had experienced during her escape from the hospital. "The same thing can happen to you," he said tightly. "Why do you think—"

61

Christian didn't have the opportunity to finish his sentence. He swallowed his thoughts and his words as Jane scrambled off the far side of the bed. She wavered on her feet for a few seconds, barely able to remain upright. The towels on her feet nearly unbalanced her, and before Christian could offer advice to the contrary, she shook out her legs and kicked the towels away.

"What the hell are you doing?" he exploded, throwing up his hands. "Didn't you hear anything I said? Are you out of your mind?" Belatedly Christian realized what he had just asked her. He knew he could be an insensitive bastard, but he believed he had finally crossed some invisible line that marked the difference between callousness and cruelty. Frustrated, he ran his fingers through his hair and raised his eyes upward. "What in God's name am I doing here anyway?" he muttered impatiently. He caught a glimpse of Jane as her eyes darted about the room and settled momentarily on the door. There was no doubt in Christian's mind that she had every intention of trying to escape. He quickly moved to the foot of the bed so that he could block her way when she came around it. "I'm not sure what just happened here, but I'd be a lot happier if you'd get back in that bed. I'd prefer not to have to put you there, but I'll do it if I have to." Unconsciously his hand dropped to his thigh and he massaged his wound. "And I can. You were lucky earlier, but I don't think you'll be so lucky again."

Jane's dark eyes dropped to Christian's leg and the horrified look appeared again.

With sudden insight Christian understood what was wrong. She thought *she* had caused his limp. The very idea was laughable because it was so absurd. "I don't think you understand," he began, rounding the corner of the bed. "You didn't—"

Once more Christian was forced to stop in midsentence. As soon as he came around the bed Jane threw herself onto the mattress, rolled to the other side, and dropped to the floor. Before Christian could reach her she was hobbling toward the door.

Christian had seconds to decide his best course of action. Every step she took was doing her more harm than good, and she didn't seem to comprehend the effects of her own recklessness. Christian's choices were clear. Two years ago, two months ago, even two days ago, he might have let her experience the consequences of her own folly, but that wasn't what he wanted to see happen now. Something had been altered in his thinking. He couldn't dwell on it because he was hardly even aware of the change, but it was there and he acted on it.

Christian flung out his left arm and managed to grab a handful of his nightshirt as Jane skittered past him. He yanked hard and caused her to lose her footing. She cried out as the soles of her feet slid painfully against the polished hardwood floors. Christian tightened his grip on the nightshirt and used it to lift her. His free arm slipped neatly beneath the back of her knees. She was so light that she bounced in the cradle of his arms as he let go of the nightshirt and supported her back. He had to lift her high to his chest to keep her from wiggling out of his hold. Her arms flailed at him, but he noticed that she did not hit him with her fists. She pounded him with her forearms and the unblistered heel of her hands.

Unlike the first time she had fought with him, Christian commanded the position of strength, and her blows were ineffectual even if they were not particularly pleasant.

He drew in a sharp breath as Jane managed to chop him on the side of the neck. "Easy, darlin'," he said, turning on his heel. "There's no cause for all this commotion. I'm going to put you down on the bed." He groaned as she landed another nicely aimed blow. "God! Where do you get that reserve of strength?" He dropped her on the bed. "I could have used a few more like you in my company during the war. No, you don't," he warned her as she started to roll toward the other side of the bed. Christian reached out, grabbed her by the nightshirt's collar, and hauled her back. He winced as he heard the material give way around the buttonholes.

Jane's hair flew around her face as she was turned onto her back and her wrists were captured just above the marks left by the restraints. She glared defiantly at Christian while she tossed her head like some young filly, trying to throw back her mane. Unaware of the split neckline that exposed her breasts nearly to their pink-tipped nipples, she continued to fight with her knees and legs, hoping to force him to release her.

The fact that she could still struggle at all amazed Christian as much as it worried him. Surely this was further proof that Jane Doe was no ordinary woman. For all her delicacy she was a fierce opponent and her strength was something to be reckoned with. Scott needed to see this, he thought. Perhaps it would change his opinion about Jane's state of mind.

Christian tightened his grip on Jane's wrists and forced them against the mattress on either side of her head. She kicked out at him, and the nightshirt rucked up about her thighs. So much for her earlier attempts at modesty, Christian thought distractedly. He narrowly avoided being laid low by her knee again as he moved to straddle her hips. His brows rose a notch and his half-grin was part exasperation, part relief. "I told you you wouldn't be so lucky again. Oh, stop looking at me as if you expect me to rape you. What do you take me for? I'm not an animal, and you're hardly likely to consume me with lust. I wasn't willing before when you offered yourself, and I'm definitely not willing now." He gave her wrists a shake. "Can't you get it through your head that I'm doing my level best to help you?" Christian had studiously avoided dropping his eyes to the gaping neckline of her nightshirt, but when she expressed her frustration in a frantic little wiggle he couldn't help himself. The merest glance showed him that she had managed to bare one breast. He released her wrists and sat up straighter, careful not to rest his weight on her but on the backs of his calves instead. "Cover yourself, please," he said lightly.

Mortification brought a sheen of tears to her wide doe eyes

64

and a rose blush to her cheeks. Rather than simply try to right her nightshirt, Jane twisted beneath Christian in an attempt to turn on her stomach. Though it wasn't her purpose she managed to unseat her captor.

Christian fell to one side. "You little hellcat," he gritted, grabbing her wrists again and throwing his good leg over both of hers. He was only vaguely aware of the intimacy of their positions and the snug fit of her hip against his groin. "You could be a hell of a bit more cooperative. You owe me *something*, dammit!" He trapped her with his hard, wintry stare and spared a brief glance for her neckline. "Now, let me do it."

From the doorway Mrs. Brandywine screamed and dropped the tray of food she carried. The tangle of sheets and blankets and arms and legs was damning enough, but the housekeeper would have given Christian the benefit of the doubt if she hadn't heard his words. The fact that his mouth hovered mere fractions of an inch above Jane's and that one arm rested directly beneath her bare breasts only helped seal Christian's fate.

Christian glanced over his shoulder at his housekeeper, disgust rife in the set of his mouth. "Mrs. Brandywine," he said calmly, "would you please—"

But Mrs. Brandywine wasn't listening to her employer. In that moment nothing could have swayed her from the belief that Christian had finally arrived at the only place a steady diet of drink could lead him. She screamed again, this time for Dr. Turner. "Help! Mr. Marshall's gone mad! He's going to hurt her!"

"Oh, Jesus," Christian swore, shaking his head and raising his eyes heavenward. "Mrs. B., can't you see that—"

Scott skittered to a halt in the doorway directly behind the housekeeper. His jaw fell slack, then dropped open at the sight that greeted him. "What the hell?"

"Oh, for God's sake," Christian said wearily. He turned his attention from the door to Jane, intending to ask for her help in explaining the situation. Her eyes were closed, her breathing shallow through lightly parted lips. She had passed out. "Wonderful," he muttered, releasing her and flopping onto his back. He cradled the back of his head in his palms and stared down the length of his aquiline nose at his friend and his housekeeper. "Just bloody wonderful."

Chapter 3

Christian stared out the window of his study, his expression brooding. He didn't take any particular notice of the sporadic traffic on Fifth Avenue. The occasional passing coach didn't interest him. The after-theater supper crowd had finished parading the avenue in their elegant coaches and evening finery and retired to their own homes. He didn't see Liam O'Shea walking his beat or hear his club tap rhythmically against the spiked iron fence that bordered the Marshall property. Moonshine fell brightly on the lawn of new snow and glittering flakes rivaled the stars in the night sky. It was the kind of clear evening that made the street lamps superfluous. Somewhere nearby a stray dog howled mournfully, and when he was done another took up the unhappy call.

Inside the deep pockets of his quilted smoking jacket Christian's hands curled into tight fists. His mouth was dry, his throat parched, and his fingers itched to pour a shot of whiskey. He resisted the temptation and reached for the cup of tea Mrs. Brandywine had brewed for him almost an hour ago. It was stone cold, left a bitter aftertaste in his mouth, and suited his mood perfectly. He finished the cup quickly and moved away from the window. Drained of energy and most emotion, he found it easy to mask his surprise when he turned and found Scott watching him from the doorway.

"Have you been there long?" he asked without interest.

"Long enough," Scott said easily, unperturbed by Christian's black mood. He leaned his shoulder against the doorjamb and crossed his arms against his chest. "You should be in bed."

"In a little while." Christian walked to the fireplace and picked up the poker. He stirred the ashes idly. "How is she?"

"All tucked in and sleeping peacefully."

Christian nodded. "Good. And Mrs. B.?"

"She's recovered from her earlier shock as well. More than a little embarrassed by the conclusions she drew when she saw you and Jane together on the bed. Have a heart, Chris, let her off the hook. A few words from you and she wouldn't feel as if she committed some sort of crime. The poor woman's beating herself up for not trusting you."

There was a pause. The poker scraped loudly in the grate. "I'll speak to her in the morning," he said finally. "She doesn't deserve to be let off too easily. I've never done anything to give her the impression that I force myself on women."

"Haven't you?" Scott asked softly.

Christian's grip on the poker tightened. "What the hell is that supposed to mean?"

"Look at yourself, Christian." The line between Scott's brows deepened as he thoroughly surveyed his friend. "Look at what you've become. Do you think Mrs. Brandywine really knows what you're capable of anymore? It's not quite the same for me. Our acquaintance . . . our friendship . . . only goes back a few years, but Mrs. B.'s known you all your life. She sees the things you do in a different light. The change in you is much more dramatic to her than it is to me."

"We all change," he said tersely.

Scott decided nothing more could come of the confrontation. Christian had his defenses firmly in place. If he were to push too hard Christian would be reaching for a bottle. It could still happen, and probably would, the moment Scott left the house. "Go easy on her," said Scott. "That's all I'm suggesting. She's feeling her own censure. She doesn't need yours in addition."

Christian replaced the poker and turned away from the fireplace. "I'm not some damn ogre," he said.

Scott grinned. "You give a hellish good impression then." His smile faded and his thoughts became introspective. "God, listen to me. D'you hear how much I'm swearing?" He shot Christian a sideways glance. "That's your influence, m'friend. Susan always knows when I've spent more than thirty minutes in your company."

"She has you on a short leash."

"She has me precisely where I want to be," Scott corrected. "There's a difference."

"If you say so." He shrugged. "Tell me, what are your instructions for Jane?"

"Mrs. B. has them all." When he saw that wasn't going to satisfy Christian, he explained further. "We've arranged a night watch among your female staff. Someone is to be with Jane at all times, though I suspect this first night at least will be uneventful. I've given her a mild dose of laudanum and she should sleep till late morning. I'll stop by in the afternoon to examine her. If she requires me at any time before then, I can be reached at my home or the hospital. Naturally no one at the hospital must know that I'm being summoned here."

"Her hands and feet?"

"I'll know better tomorrow. I don't want to say more than that now. You did the right thing, Christian, so stop blaming yourself. She needed to be restrained."

"I should have rung for you as soon as she woke."

"Perhaps," Scott said. "But there's no certainty that I would have arrived in time to prevent her from getting out of bed."

Christian hardly noted Scott's objection. "She really thought she hurt me," he said. His voice was softly puzzled as if he were no longer aware of Scott's presence. Unconsciously his hand dropped to his thigh. "She thought this was her doing and she was *sorry* for it."

"That surprises you?"

"What?" Christian's train of thought was broken. "Oh, yes. Yes, it does. I didn't think she would feel things that way."

"You listened to too much of Glenn's balderdash this afternoon. I thought you had more sense. Apparently not." Scott pushed away from the door and walked into the study. He lifted his coat and top hat from the chair where he had flung them earlier. "She feels hot and cold, pleasure and pain, just the way we do," he said impatiently. "Why shouldn't she feel other emotions as well? She's as capable of feeling guilt as you are."

"But she didn't do anything," he protested.

"Dammit! Neither did you!" Scott watched a dull wash of color touch Christian's face. Good. He had been understood then. They both knew he hadn't been talking about what had happened above stairs. Christian's imagined wrongs went back years and guilt had been his parasitic, soul-sucking companion since the beginning. "Good night, Christian," Scott said lowly. "Perhaps I'll see you tomorrow when I visit Jane."

"Perhaps." He didn't bother seeing Scott to the door. Christian had poured a tumbler of whiskey before his friend reached the front gate. He carried the tumbler and decanter to his favorite chair in front of the fire and propped his feet on the ottoman. With no thought to the consequences Christian Marshall proceeded to quietly drink himself to sleep.

"Where is he today?" Scott asked Mrs. Brandywine as he shrugged out of his coat. He gave it to her along with his muffler and hat and picked up his black leather bag. Taking in the housekeeper's long-suffering expression, which was earned in this instance and not feigned, Scott's eyes darted to the double oak doors of Christian's study. "Not still in there, I hope. My God, it's been almost two weeks."

70

Mrs. Brandywine paused in hanging the doctor's coat and hat on the brass rack in the entrance hall. "Two today," she said, lowering her voice. "Remember, you've not been here since Monday. Christmas is less than a week away and I'm thinking he's purposely set about missing it. It's his first one without any family at all, you know. Last year at this time he still had his father."

"He has us." Scott sighed heavily. "This is ridiculous and I don't have the patience for it anymore." He started down the hallway, his shoes clicking lightly on the parquet floor, but stopped when he felt Mrs. Brandywine's urgent tug on his jacket sleeve. He glanced at her over his shoulder, saw the panic in her eyes, and turned to give her his full attention. "What is it, Mrs. B.? Are you afraid I'm going to hurt him?"

She shook her head. "I'm afraid you'll hurt each other," she corrected. "He's been looking for a fight and you'd make a fine target. None of my house staff will go near the doors, but Joe Means braved entry the other day. He made a simple inquiry about ordering feed for the horses, and Mr. Marshall nearly separated Joe's head from his shoulders with his sharp tongue."

"Does he never come out of there?"

"Several times during the day." She blushed deeply. "As much as he's drinking he has to . . . well, you can see that . . ."

Scott took pity on her. "I understand about nature's call. How is he getting the alcohol? Surely he must have emptied his sideboard twice over by now. No one here is supplying it, are they?"

The housekeeper was clearly affronted by the suggestion. "He's threatened to fire each and every one of us," she said with quiet dignity, "but that's the drink talking and we don't pay it no mind. Anyone giving him a drop of the stuff is to be let go without a reference, and those are *my* instructions. But Mr. Marshall was always a clever one, and when he wants something he has his own ways of getting it. He stood out on the front stoop not two days ago, barefoot and shirtless, and called to a

71

ragpicker out on the avenue. Offered the man a handsome sum to deliver a case to the house. There was no intercepting it." She shuddered. "I can't imagine what the neighbors are thinking. The avenue's not seen the likes of this decadence since Mrs. Stevens began giving musicales on the Sabbath."

With some difficulty Scott bit back a smile. "Perhaps no one noticed Mr. Marshall," he said solicitously, then brought the subject around to what was important. "Is he eating anything?"

"Mrs. Morrissey fixes regular meals and he takes them in there. The dishes come back empty."

"Then for all you know he could be feeding them to the ragpicker through the study window."

She nodded firmly. "Precisely. To the ragpicker, Mrs. Astor's pet horse, or Liam O'Shea on his beat."

"What do you think he's doing?"

"I think he's feeding every dog in the neighborhood and drinking himself to death."

Scott sighed again and made a sweeping gesture through his hair with his fingers. "All right, Mrs. B., we're going to have to help Christian in spite of himself. Why don't you choose three or four men among the employees who won't be intimidated by Christian's threats or his size? Have them meet me in the kitchen. We'll plan our strategy after I've examined our other patient." He changed his black case from one hand to the other and retraced his steps to the stairs. "How is she doing?"

Mrs. Brandywine smiled for the first time since she opened the door to Scott. "That one's going to be just fine. Her voice still isn't what it should be so she doesn't say much. Hears just about everything, though, and pays attention to it. She's anxious to be out of bed."

"We'll see," he said, carefully noncommittal.

"If it's a question about what to do with her when she's well, then I may have an answer."

"Oh?" Scott was glad to hear the housekeeper had given the problem some thought. With Christian being at his most unapproachable, Scott didn't know what to do with his patient.

"She can work right here. I'm permitted to hire staff and I choose to hire her."

Scott had some doubts and they showed. "I don't know, Mrs. B. I don't think Christian would necessarily approve. The last time I spoke with him he still believed she was deranged."

"Then it would serve him right for not inquiring these last fourteen days," she said firmly. "That young woman has more sense than he does." She rolled her eyes as she realized how little that accolade meant at the moment. "She has as much sense as *I* do. I'm not afraid to have her here. Neither is anyone else on my staff. No one's breathed a word to any of those doctors who came around here, and no one has any intent of doing so."

Dr. Turner smiled gently. "That was the least of my worries. I knew I could depend on you to keep her safe. The search was called off as of Monday. The hospital believes she died of exposure the same night she escaped. Dr. Glenn even identified a body the police discovered in the Five Points as her."

"This all happened Monday?"

"Hmm-mm. There was a small item tucked in *The Chronicle*'s obituaries about finding a frozen body in a drift in Paradise Square. It mentioned the woman was identified as an escaped lunatic patient from Jennings."

"How could they make a mistake like that? People knew she was wearing Mr. Marshall's clothes when she left. This other woman couldn't have been dressed the same way."

"She, er, wasn't dressed at all. She'd been, um, ill-used before she was left to die. The body wasn't in good condition for identification, but I think Dr. Glenn really believes it was his Jane Doe. I thought you might have read the article."

"No, I missed it. What a world it's become. Saw that heiress's obituary in yesterday's paper, though. Poor thing. Her sick for so long and all." She shook her head slowly in a gesture of empathetic sadness. "How she must have suffered.

The Van Dykes had more money than God, excuse the expression, and little good it did them. That family's had its own share of tragedy, what with Mr. Van Dyke dying in that train accident like he did. Then him not even cold in the grave and his wife taking up with—" She ground to a halt when Scott held up his hand.

"Some other time, Mrs. B.," he promised. "Let me look in on our patient first. You go see about those strong bodies we'll be needing."

Realizing she had gotten carried away, Mrs. Brandywine flushed. Dr. Turner was not the same rapt audience she had had yesterday. His patient, however, had had the good manners to listen to *The Chronicle*'s account of the death of Caroline J. Van Dyke, and had even been moved to ask a few questions. There was a certain sensitivity about the girl that warmed the housekeeper's heart. Mrs. Brandywine had ended up reading the account to her charge twice, then relating gossip about the Van Dykes to which only the hired help were privy.

"I'll see to the matter at once," she said.

"Very good." Scott climbed the stairs with a light step. Visiting this patient was a pleasant task in any circumstances. When he compared it to the upcoming confrontation with Christian Marshall, it was like having an interview at heaven's door. Below stairs, however, the devil was waiting to have his due.

Mrs. Brandywine picked up the breakfast tray that had been prepared for Christian. There was a short stack of pancakes slathered with butter and maple syrup, two soft-cooked eggs, three bacon strips, orange slices, and a pot of weak tea. "You take this up to Mr. Marshall," she said, turning to the newest member of the household staff.

Jenny Holland looked at the contents of the tray and raised dark doe eyes to the housekeeper, her expression doubtful. Dr. Turner had only given her his cautious assent to get out of bed and begin light duties two days ago—the same two days ago that he had forced her new employer from his sanctuary in the study and into the master bedroom. Jenny hadn't laid eyes on Christian Marshall since the eventful moment when he had wrestled her back into bed and she had passed out beneath him. She wasn't sure she was ready to see him now.

Even though her room was in another wing of the house Jenny had heard the commotion Christian had caused. She could only guess at the meaning of some of the words that had been exchanged. The battle had been heated and loudly contended. If colorful expressions and baldly phrased threats had been weapons, then Mr. Marshall would have won easily. From the accounts Jenny had heard since, it seemed he had almost won anyway. It had taken two grooms, the gardener, the cook's helper, and Dr. Turner to remove Christian from the study. Later that day Jenny had heard the tale of Mrs. Brandywine breaking bottles and giving a stiff piece of her mind to the hapless ragpicker who came to the back door.

The only people to have cared for Mr. Marshall since he had been taken to his room were Mrs. Brandywine and Dr. Turner. Jenny didn't know why she had suddenly been singled out. "I thought you were pleased with my work," she said huskily. Dr. Turner had warned her that she might never recover the full range that had been her voice. She hardly recognized herself when she spoke. "I thought you were pleased to have me here."

The housekeeper laughed. "Lord, Jenny, of course I am. I didn't mean it as a punishment. You've got such a calmness about you that I thought Mr. Marshall might take to it. He's made it clear he doesn't want anything to do with me."

"But that's not right," Jenny protested, seeing the hurt in the older woman's eyes. "You're only helping him."

"Oh, pooh. I don't take much mind of it, not really. He needs to lash out at someone, and I've made myself a fair target. There's no reason for him to feel the same about you."

Jenny worried the soft inner side of her lip. She could have said that she knew different. Though the staff at Marshall House had been exceedingly kind to her, welcoming her into their fold, even protecting her, it was really no secret that Christian Marshall's seclusion and long drinking bout were in some way related to her presence in the house. There was a general consensus among the employees that she had inadvertently tipped the delicate balance Christian had struck between timely drinking and drinking all the time. The upcoming holiday had only given him another excuse.

"All right," she said. "I'll take it up to him." It was still early. There was a very good chance he wouldn't be awake yet.

"There's a good girl." The housekeeper dropped the key to Christian's room in Jenny's apron pocket, and thought to herself how fine her young protégée was beginning to look. The plain black wool dress and crisp white linen apron, rather than diminishing her color, served to expose the becoming peach blush that caressed Jenny's cheeks. Her dark hair shone from a recent washing and was arranged in a soft chignon at the back of her head. There were small silky curls on her forehead and she had drawn the hair back to display her ears. The stylishness of Jenny's coiffure had surprised Mrs. Brandywine when she first saw it. It was more suited to a lady rather than a lady's maid, which is what Jenny said had been her training. Further questions on the matter had sealed Jenny's lips, and Mrs. B. had known enough to withdraw rather than upset the girl.

Dr. Turner had warned her to proceed cautiously with Jenny. The glow in her complexion, the eagerness to be out of bed, and the desire to make herself useful were all fine as far as they went. There remained, he'd told her, a number of questions unanswered and a certain aura of mental fragility that belied Jenny's physical strength.

Mrs. Brandywine had made a little shooing gesture with her hands. "Go on with you. It'll be fine. You'll see."

Unconvinced but game, Jenny headed for the master bedroom. She balanced the tray on one hip while she fumbled for the key. Following Mrs. Brandywine's instructions, she locked the door upon entering the room and slipped the key back in her pocket. None of it sat well with her. In some ways this was worse than what was done to her at the hospital, she thought uneasily. The man snoring softly in the middle of the wide tester bed was a prisoner in his own home.

Jenny set the tray on the bedside table and stepped back, surveying the room. It was too dark and gloomy for her tastes. The wallpaper was beige, but an unappealing shade that looked as if it was supposed to be cream and hadn't been washed in an age. The flocking was a swirling rust pattern of embellished curls that made Jenny think of a garden in need of weeding. The woodwork, the tester bed, the chiffonier, and the minor pieces of furniture were all dark walnut. The counterpane was hunter green, as was the canopy. Tassels the color of goldenrod fringed both the canopy and the drapes. The fireplace was a corner affair which might have been charming if it had had a sitting area nearby. No attempt had been made to make it the focal point of the room. It was purely functional and, at the moment, not doing even that very well. The kindest thing Jenny could think to say about the room was that it had considerable potential. The other words that sprang to mind were oppressive, cheerless, and dreary.

Something would have to be done. Clearly Mrs. Brandywine's influence had never been felt in this room. Jenny knew the housekeeper had been given free rein elsewhere in the house. This bedchamber reflected Christian Marshall's mood, Jenny thought, and oh, what a black mood it was!

The first thing Jenny did was to add coals to the fire and stoke it until she had a blaze that was capable of warming the room. Her next task should have been equally easy, but some things, she decided philosophically, were not meant to be.

The curtain rings had attracted some condensation from the frosted window and had actually rusted to the drapery rod. It appeared that natural light hadn't seen the inside of the master bedroom in weeks, if not months. Dust motes clung to the outer folds of the drapes, and when Jenny flicked at them with her fingers a dry cloud choked her. She grimaced, trying to decide what to do. Mrs. B. had obviously been wary of making changes. Jenny wondered if she should be as circumspect.

Then she remembered how Christian Marshall's entry into her life had changed everything. She did not owe him undue caution. She owed him her best judgment, and at the moment he deserved better than waking up in a room that was so melancholy.

Jenny picked up the ladderback chair that sat at the small writing desk and moved it to the window. She unhooked the tie-back sashes that were hanging uselessly on either side of the window frame and snapped the dust out of them. More was required here than simply parting the drapes at the middle and securing them with the sashes. She wanted to pull back the drapes at the top. For want of anything better to do with the sashes, Jenny slipped them around her neck as she climbed onto the chair.

The drapery rings were not difficult to move once she could reach them properly, but she was disappointed with the effect once the drapes were parted. Even if the sun deigned to make an appearance on this wintry day, it was still too early for it to have much force. She leaned toward the window and rubbed at the frosted panes with the heel of her hand, hoping to let in what light was available. When she tried to lean back to survey her work she felt a tug at the nape of her neck. Belatedly she realized her chignon had been caught by one of the open drapery rings.

Jenny's efforts to unhook it were unsatisfactory. She didn't want to ruin the hairstyle she had taken such pains with only hours earlier. She stamped her foot in frustration and the chair teetered a little. One of the sashes around her neck had slipped beneath her collar. Not only did it itch uncomfortably, it made her want to sneeze. She reached for it, intending to draw it off.

If Jenny hadn't been concentrating on her work she might have noticed the cessation of her employer's light snoring. Christian Marshall had turned on his side moments earlier, opened bleary eyes, and was immediately confronted with a vision that almost stopped his heart.

In the gray light that filtered into the room he saw the shadowy outline of a woman in the process of using his drapery rod to hang herself! Given her intent, there was no doubt in Christian's mind as to her identity. As far as he knew there was only one woman in his household who might have reason to contemplate suicide. The chair teetered and he sucked in his breath. She lifted the rope around her neck.

That's when Christian made his move.

Throwing the covers back, he leaped out of bed. His legs, weak from inactivity, nearly gave way. In spite of that he stumbled toward Jenny and flung out his arms to catch her when the chair fell. She screamed when his hands clamped around her waist, but because her voice was still so fragile, the sound she made was pathetically weak. The chair tipped over, set in motion more by Christian's lunging than anything Jenny did, and thudded to the floor. The chair was immediately followed by Christian and Jenny, and since Jenny tried to save herself by grabbing the drapery rod, they were in turn followed by the heavy velvet drapes, the rod, and a light sprinkling of plaster dust when the valance supports pulled away from the wall.

Christian twisted, taking the brunt of the fall, and brought Jenny down on top of him. They both narrowly missed the chair. The drapery rod caught Jenny across the shoulders, but it wasn't a painful blow. She ducked her head instinctively, burying against the crook of Christian's shoulder. The rod slipped to one side and the drapes cocooned them.

Christian raised his head, groaned, and lowered it to the floor again. His eyes were closed. Jenny thought he'd passed out but when she started to move away, his large hands tightened on her waist. In one fluid motion he turned them both until she was lying beneath him. The drapes were tangled between them. She had been here before, she thought giddily as she stared up into cool aquamarine eyes. They were piercing in their slow perusal of her face.

"It *is* you," Christian said finally. She looked far healthier than the last time he had seen her. Her complexion was agreeably flushed and her wide brown eyes with their splinters of cinnamon color were bright. Her beautifully modeled lips were slightly parted, moist, and pink. The body that pressed against him was familiar as well, uncomfortably so. His hands could nearly span her waist and her breasts, in spite of the ridiculously severe gown she was wearing, still felt full against his chest. "What in the hell do you think you were doing?" he demanded roughly.

With great dignity Jenny replied, "Don't swear at me, please." When this request merely had the effect of making Christian's eyes narrow to hard slits, Jenny's small chin shot out with a measure of defiance. "What does it look like I was doing?"

"I asked you."

Jenny shrugged. The movement was awkward because he was so heavy on her. "I knew you might not like me opening the drapes but really, don't you think you're making too much of it? I only wanted to bring some light into the room. The drapery rings were rusted to the—"

Christian's hands left her waist and grasped her shoulders. He gave her a little shake. "Do you take me for a fool?"

Bewildered, Jenny blinked widely. "I assure you, I don't," she said throatily.

Christian frowned, his mouth pursing to one side as he continued to regard her skeptically. "You weren't trying to kill yourself?" he asked slowly.

"Kill myself?!" She looked past his shoulder to the window and saw the holes where the flimsy valance hooks had been. "Hang myself, you mean?"

He nodded.

Jenny couldn't hold back a smile. A bubble of laughter caught in her throat, but it didn't stay there long. It tripped lightly along her tongue and tickled her lips.

Her husky laughter teased Christian's senses and he didn't thank her for it. "I'm not sure I understand your amusement. Your intent was quite obvious."

"Obviously it wasn't," she countered. "Would you please let me up?"

Christian considered her request a moment, then eased himself off her. He sat up and rubbed his wounded thigh. His nightshirt had climbed above his knees and when he glanced at Jenny, he caught her staring at his naked legs. She blushed deeply and quickly averted her eyes.

Jenny used the toppled chair for support and got to her feet, smoothing her dress and making the same attempt with her hopelessly creased apron. She righted the chair and moved it back to the desk, putting some distance between herself and Christian. "I was only trying to open the drapes," she explained. "My hair got caught in one of the drapery rings and I was trying to free it."

"What about the rope around your—" He stopped as she lifted the drapery sashes from around her neck. "I see."

"I hope so." She wondered if he had hurt his thigh. She knew about the wound at Gettysburg from members of the household staff. There were as many versions of the story as there were people to tell it.

Unaware of Jenny's interest, Christian stopped massaging his leg and looked up at the window as she had done moments earlier. "I suppose the rod wouldn't have held your weight anyway," he said grudgingly. "If you wanted to hang yourself there would be better locations."

"There certainly would be." She added quickly, "Not that I've been looking for any."

Christian grunted softly and cleared away the draperies which were covering his broad shoulders like an emperor's cloak. "What's wrong with your voice?" he asked bluntly. The hint of huskiness was unnerving because there was something very attractive about it.

"Dr. Turner says it may stay this way forever. Would you

81

rather I didn't speak?"

"Scott, eh? Don't pay attention to anything that charlatan says," he growled lowly. "Bastard thinks I'm a drunk."

Jenny refrained from responding. She watched Christian draw up his legs and settle his elbows on his knees. He cupped his head in his hands, supporting it, then gently moved his head from side to side to clear the muzziness. Jenny observed that the area around his eyes was drawn and haggard. His skin was sallow and it contrasted horribly with the unkempt growth of his fiery beard. He had lost some weight. His cheeks were sunken so that the bones of his face stood out in hard relief, and his lean fingers seemed almost skeletal.

"Not a pretty picture, is it?" he asked, glancing at her face and divining her thoughts. "I haven't had a bender like that since . . . hell, I don't think I've ever been on a bender like that." When she remained quiet he demanded a response. "Say something, dammit! I don't care if you sound like your throat is filled with gravel."

"Please don't swear at me," she said calmly. Inwardly she was seething. Gravel! He was rude, obnoxious, disgusting, and boorish. It was not out of gratitude that Jenny remained serene on the surface, but out of her need to remain at Marshall House. She couldn't very well bite the hand that was feeding her. Not yet, anyway.

Christian's tone was scathing. "My, what a self-righteous little prig you are. Have you met Scott's wife Susan? A matched set of bookends, that's what you'd be."

"How kind of you to say so," she said sincerely. "I shall look forward to making her acquaintance."

Christian snorted. "Don't just stand there. Help me up. The damn—er, the *darn*—floor is tilting."

"I shouldn't wonder." She circled the desk and went to his side, holding out her hand for him to take.

He shook his head. "If I pull on your hand you'll be sitting on the floor again."

Jenny realized the truth of that. She hunkered down beside him and put one arm about his shoulders and a hand beneath his elbow. With a little cooperation on his part, she managed to get Christian to his feet. She escorted him back to the bed, letting him lean on her, and plumped his pillows before he collapsed like a felled tree onto the feather tick. Belatedly she understood how much his errant rescue of her had taxed his strength. Jenny rearranged the covers, pulling the dark counterpane up to Christian's chin. His eyes were closed now and he groaned softly a few times, but he didn't object to her fussing.

Jenny stepped back from the bed and caught sight of the breakfast tray out of the corner of her eye. She couldn't imagine that he would want anything to eat, but good manners, as well as her new position in his home, compelled her to ask.

"God, no," he muttered, turning on his side away from the tray. "Take it out of here. The smell alone is enough to make me—"

"I understand," she interrupted. She picked up the tray. "I'll come back later with something more agreeable. I can clean up then also."

She was gone, the door locked behind her, before Christian realized he had never asked her what business she'd had in his room in the first place. He'd find that out later, he thought muzzily. Christian thumped on his pillows until they were just right for hugging. He kept one under his head and clutched the other to his chest. In minutes he was asleep again.

Jenny eased herself quietly into Christian's bedchamber two hours later. This time the breakfast tray carried a light repast: one soft-cooked egg, a slice of dry toast, and a pot of weak tea. There was also a slender pewter bud vase with a white winter rose. Several of the housemaids were skeptical that this added touch would do anything to soften Christian Marshall's mood, but Jenny was insistent and Mrs. Brandywine had agreed. Jenny put the tray down and gathered the fallen draperies. Following the housekeeper's directions she tossed them into the hallway to be picked up later, then locked the door.

"I'll take that key," said Christian.

Jenny ignored him, dropped it in her pocket, and turned to face him. Her smile was a trifle too bright to be completely sincere. "Good, you're awake. I was hoping you would be. I didn't think you'd want a cold breakfast."

Christian sat up in bed, tucked a pillow behind the small of his back, and rubbed his beard. "I don't want breakfast. I want that key."

Her smile faltered. "We'll see."

"We damn well will *not* see. Give it to me."

"Oh, very well." She reached in her pocket and pulled out the key to her own room. "Here it is. You impressed me as someone with a stubborn streak. I thought you might bully me for it." Jenny walked over to the bed and placed the key in Christian's open palm. His hand closed over it quickly as if he suspected she might snatch it back.

"Thank you," he said with sarcastic sweetness. He slid the key behind his back and under his pillow. When Jenny lifted the tray to set it on his lap he shook his head and grimaced. "I told you I don't want any breakfast."

"All right." She set the tray down again.

"That's better." Christian leaned toward the bedside table and opened the top drawer. He put his hand in and felt around blindly, withdrawing only when he realized someone had anticipated his actions. "Where's the bottle I kept there?"

"I couldn't say, Mr. Marshall."

"I couldn't say, Mr. Marshall," he said, mimicking her stiffly correct reply. He watched her turn her back on him and head toward the dressing and bathing area adjoining his bedroom. "Where do you think you're going?"

"To the next room," she explained patiently. "I'm going to

pour some water so you can wash, clean your teeth, and shave."

"Where's Mrs. B.? Is something wrong with her? Is that why you're here?"

"Mrs. B. is fine. A little out of patience with you, it's true, but I suspect the feeling is mutual. I'm here because she sent me." Jenny disappeared into the other room.

"What if I don't want to wash and shave?" he asked sourly. "Don't you ever ask anything first?" When there was no reply Christian continued his tirade. "What the hell did that old harridan do with my bottle? It was here yesterday. Scott put her up to it. I know he did. She wouldn't have had the nerve otherwise. That's why she sent you up here to beard the lion. She doesn't trust herself not to give me what I want." His smile was confident and a trifle smug. "I know precisely how to get around her." He glanced at the tray, grimaced, then picked up the piece of dry toast and began eating it. It wasn't so bad. His dulled taste buds and churning stomach would have revolted against anything less bland.

"Can't you do something about all the light in here?" he demanded. "If I wanted to make my room in the solarium I damn well would have done so. And what was Mrs. B. thinking of anyway, letting you in here? You might do anything. Strip me naked. Tie me to the bed. It's not as if you haven't done those things before." The pain behind Christian's eyes was tremendous. He couldn't remember a hangover equal to this one. Chewing hurt. "Has everyone in this house gone balmy? Are you infectious by any chance? Should we have the house quarantined before it spreads to the rest of the city?" Still no response from the other room. "Dammit!" he yelled. "Can't I even offend you?!" He thought his head would explode. "You don't ask! You don't answer! What else don't you do?"

Jenny stepped back into the room carrying a porcelain washbowl and pitcher in one arm and a small salver and water glass in the other. "I don't swear to make a point. Would you

85

move the breakfast tray a little to the back so I can set these things down?'' When Christian grudgingly complied Jenny went on. "I don't purposely set out to hurt another person's feelings and I don't yell. Not because I don't want to. I can't. If I had tried to make myself heard from the other room I wouldn't have a voice now.'' She sat down on the edge of the bed and handed him the water glass. "You can rinse your mouth out with this. And don't look so hopeful. It's water, not gin."

"Are you related to Mrs. B.?" he asked suspiciously.

She smiled and picked up the salver. There was a baking soda paste on it for Christian to clean his teeth. "No, I'm not, but thank you for the compliment."

"It wasn't meant as a—"

"I know. Here, you can clean your teeth."

Christian wrinkled his nose, but he swiped at the paste with his finger and brushed it on his teeth. He took a sip of water, sloshed it around and looked for a place to spit. Jenny helped him out by pulling a juice glass from her pocket and holding it up to his mouth.

"Better?" she asked, placing the spit glass and salver aside and removing the water glass from Christian's hands. She noticed they trembled slightly.

"Better than what?"

Jenny didn't have an answer for that. She poured some water into the basin and wet a cloth. "Do you want to wash yourself or shall I do it for you?"

Christian began to believe he had been out of his mind when he took this viper into his home. "I'll do it." He took the cloth and rinsed his face. She held out a bar of soap for him and he took that as well. "I'll need hot water if I'm going to shave."

"Of course." Jenny rose from the bed and found a small kettle in the dressing room. She set it over the fire to heat. "Shall I pour you some tea?" she asked.

Christian's face was buried in the cloth. He was on the edge of feeling human again and not certain he liked it. "No tea," he muttered.

She shrugged. "As you wish."

"This is a dream, isn't it? An alcoholic hallucination. Scott warned me it might happen and here it is."

"I don't know what you mean."

"You. I mean you." He tossed the cloth and soap into the basin and leaned back against the headboard. "My God, this all seems real."

Jenny had more than a little empathy for the disorientation Christian was feeling. "I'm afraid this is real," she said gently. "I'm very real."

"You *would* say that." He slanted her a skeptical look. "You're looking better than the last time I saw you."

She couldn't resist the opening he gave her. "And you're looking worse."

"I'm flattered you noticed enough to make a comparison now." Color tinged her cheeks and she looked away. Good, Christian thought, that would teach her not to play games with him. "How long have you been out of bed?"

"Off and on for two days."

"Scott agreed to that, I take it?"

She nodded. "I was ready a day or so before that, but he wouldn't hear of it."

"He's a tyrant."

"When he has to be."

Christian noticed how quickly she defended Scott. It grated on his nerves. When he was better he was going to strangle the friend he thought he had. "So, Jane, why were you chosen to play nursemaid? I thought it was Mrs. B.'s idea or Scott's, but perhaps it was your own?"

"My name is Jenny," she corrected. The water in the kettle had begun a rolling boil so she removed it.

"What?"

"My name is Jenny Holland." She poured the hot water into

87

the basin, tested it, and added a measure of cooler water from the pitcher.

"Jenny. As in Jennifer?"

She put the kettle on the apron of the fireplace. "No. Just Jenny." She went into the adjoining room and returned moments later with Christian's shaving things. "It was your housekeeper's idea that I take over the role of nursemaid. Your word," she reminded him, "not ours."

Christian's coolly colored eyes regarded her thoughtfully. She sat on the edge of the bed, added a little water to his shaving mug, and began making lather with his brush as if she had done this for him a hundred times. It was a trifle disconcerting. Christian still wasn't entirely convinced that he wasn't hallucinating. "Scott was right, wasn't he? You're not a lunatic."

"Perhaps I'm not the best person to judge that. It's rather like asking a drunk if he has a drinking problem. He says, 'No, not as long I'm drinking.'"

"My God! You have incredible nerve!" He snatched the shaving mug from her hands and began brushing lather on his face. "Get a mirror from the other room for me. There's one right on top of the small linen cupboard." When she returned with it he pointed at her to sit down again and hold the mirror up for him. "Where's my razor?"

"Shouldn't you soften your beard first? That's why I boiled the water."

Though it pained him to admit it, she was right. "Get me a towel," he snapped.

She turned away quickly so he wouldn't see her smile. A lunatic, indeed. Everything she heard—and saw—about Christian Marshall convinced her he was a much better candidate for commitment than she ever had been. She got the towel, let him wipe away the lather he had smeared on his face, then took it and dipped it in the hot water. After wringing it out she returned it to him. He placed it around the lower part of his face and pressed it against his beard.

"For what it's worth, I don't think I'm demented," she told him when he couldn't interrupt. "I already thanked Dr. Turner for his part in helping me. I want to thank you also. You made it possible for me to escape that hell. And that's all I really want to say about it. If that doesn't satisfy you, I'll leave, but you should know that Dr. Turner says I don't have to talk about anything until I want to . . . if I ever want to."

Beneath the steaming towel, Christian smirked. It showed in his eyes. "How convenient."

"It might appear that way to you," she conceded. It was not a matter of convenience to her, however, Jenny would have liked to confide in someone, but experience had taught her there was no one she could trust. Christian Marshall, Dr. Turner, even Mrs. Brandywine would be no different. They would think her deranged and the real madness would start again. Silence and time were the only means of combating the problems facing her. "You'll find out soon enough, so you may as well hear it from me. Mrs. Brandywine's hired me."

Christian tore off the towel. "Hired you! That's absurd! I forbid it!"

A measure of Jenny's bravado deserted her. She had always known this could happen but she hadn't wanted to consider it. What was she going to do if he made her leave his home? "Why?"

"Because . . . because you're not well enough to be working."

"That's true to some extent. My duties are very light, but that will change as time goes on."

Christian picked up the shaving mug again and lathered his softened beard. When he was done he set the cup and brush aside and held out his hand for his razor. "Hold up the mirror. A little higher. That's good." He scraped through his beard carefully, cleaning the razor by wiping it against the edge of the basin. "I think Mrs. B. may have overstepped herself," he said.

"You were a guest. Scott's patient, really. I can't imagine what she was thinking. Or Scott for that matter. He shouldn't have gone along with it."

"It was my idea."

"Oh?"

"I've worked in service before. I was a lady's maid, hairdresser, and companion."

"Well, I sure as hell figured out you weren't from the Five Points. But a lady's maid?" He had to lower the razor because he was in danger of cutting himself. Laughter rumbled in his chest. He sucked in his breath as the pain in his head sharpened unbearably.

Jenny was immediately aware of Christian's distress. His eyes closed briefly and his complexion lost even its sallow coloring. Her attention dropped to his right hand. Gently she took the razor out of his trembling fingers. "I'll do this for you."

"I can do it," he snarled, embarrassed.

"Of course you can," she said. "But let me."

He looked at her suspiciously. "I thought you were a lady's maid. Who was the lady? A bearded curiosity in one of Barnum's sideshows?"

Jenny's mouth twisted to one side, showing him what she thought of his sarcasm. "I used to do this for my father. Tip your head back a little." When he hesitated she sighed. "Are you afraid I'll have a fit of madness and slit your throat?"

It was her questioning of his bravery that hooked Christian. Prudence be damned, he thought. He tilted his head so the crown of his copper-streaked hair rested against the headboard and exposed his throat to her. He didn't realize that his Adam's apple bobbed as he swallowed hard.

Jenny's tongue peeped out at the corner of her mouth as she concentrated on her task. Angled as it was, he had a relatively easy face to shave. The jaw was strong and, unlike her father, there was only one chin and no dimple. "I would have thought

90

a man in your position would have a valet."

"I did," he answered without moving his lips. "He left. Ow!"

"Sorry," she said guiltily. "You jerked."

"Hhhmmph."

Jenny drew her own conclusions about why Christian's valet was no longer in residence. It was a little astonishing that anyone remained in his employ. Though the staff was loyal, Mrs. Brandywine in particular, no one ever said Christian Marshall was an easy man to work for.

So many things were still hazy about the day he broke into the treatment room and offered his help that Jenny could almost believe she had imagined it. What left an indelible impression, however—what she would have maintained even under torture—was that Christian Marshall had been kind to her. His voice had soothed her as she cowered like a wild animal in one corner of the cell. He had offered his coat as comfort against the cold. He had talked to her as if she could understand him, not as if she were demented or deranged. Christian had spoken *to* her, not *at* her; something no one, not even Dr. Turner, had done since she had been taken to Jennings.

In some ineffable way he had returned to her a measure of dignity. It was a gift without price.

"There," she said, a hint of pride in her tone, "all done." She wiped a bit of lather from the corner of his jaw near his ear. "One nick, and it's already stopped bleeding. Would you like to see?"

He shook his head—gently, because it was still pounding. "No, I'll take your word for it." He wasn't ready to confront his face in the mirror again. A quick glance earlier was enough. Christian felt as aged as the whiskey he had been drinking.

Jenny began cleaning up, removing all the shaving articles and the basin and pitcher to the other room. "Tea?" she asked when she was done. She placed her palm against the pot. "It's

91

still warm."

"And weak as water, no doubt."

"Just about. Mrs. Morrisey was under strict orders to keep everything mild."

"I detect Mrs. B.'s fine hand."

Jenny nodded. "Dr. Turner left some headache powders with her. Would you like me to get you one?"

"No."

Jenny looked around the room. There was nothing else she could do for him. "I'll go then. I promise I'll do something about the drapes later."

"The light's not so bad."

Her dark brows rose a little at Christian's grudging admission. He had certainly made a fuss over it earlier. She turned to go but had only taken a few steps when he called to her.

"Who was the woman you used to work for?"

She looked at him and saw his eyes were still closed. He seemed so weary that speaking must have been an effort for him. Her fingers fidgeted with a crease in her apron. "I don't think you would know—"

"Jenny. Her name."

"Vanderstell. Alice Vanderstell." There was no reaction from him, nothing to indicate whether he believed her or even if he was surprised. She couldn't imagine that he knew Alice, but the Vanderstell name would be known to him. When he made no reply she assumed he was done with her. She reached for the door.

"Aren't you forgetting something?" he asked, regarding her through narrowly slitted eyes and a dark sweep of lashes. He opened his palm and showed her the key she had given him earlier. "You'll need this to get out. And I don't know if I can trust you to give it back."

A sly smile touched Jenny's pink lips. She reached in her pocket and dangled the key to his room between her thumb and forefinger. "You shouldn't have trusted me to give it to you in the first place." Before he decided to get out of bed and come after her, Jenny inserted the key into the lock and twisted the brass handle.

Christian regarded the key in his possession with complete astonishment. "But you said—"

"I lied." It was her parting shot.

Chapter 4

Stephen Bennington lowered the paper he was reading as his father entered the dining room. He looked over the top edge, saw the grim set of his father's mouth, and wished he had never peeked in the first place. In Stephen's opinion breakfast was meant to set the mood for the day. Therefore one should make it pleasant. His sigh was inaudible as he snapped the paper briskly, folded it in quarters, and laid it beside his plate.

"The biscuits are especially good this morning," he said as his father helped himself to the food set out on the sideboard.

The senior Bennington's acknowledgment was something between a snort and a grunt. He spooned scrambled eggs onto his plate, speared a few strips of hot bacon, and took two biscuits. When he approached the table his chair was held out for him by the maid who had fluttered in with a fresh pot of coffee. She poured a cup for William and added a good measure to Stephen's, then removed herself from the room quickly, pulling the double doors closed behind her.

With an angry flourish William Bennington opened his linen napkin. He smoothed it across his lap and shot his son a sour look. "Where were you last night?" The question was not so much an inquiry as it was a demand. It was the senior Bennington's way to never ask a question when he could demand an answer.

Stephen was too familiar with his father's manner to take offense or even be much bothered by it. He returned his father's glower with a slight smile. "I informed you days ago that I had plans for last evening," he said coolly.

Though father and son were possessed of decidedly different temperaments, there could be no doubt, even among the most casual of observers, that these two men were related. When they stared at one another from opposite ends of the table as they were doing now, the physical similarities were striking. The Benningtons shared sharp angular features that were by turns aristocratic and predatory. The strong jaws were softened only marginally by large side whiskers. William had a meticulously groomed beard and mustache while Stephen sported a mustache alone. Both men had thick heads of pale ash-blond hair, though William's hairline showed signs of receding and some strands of hair were now gray rather than ash. On their feet William and Stephen stood shoulder to shoulder, lithe, handsomely featured men with a natural grace that invariably captured a woman's eye.

William's manner of dress was a shade more conservative than his son's. He preferred formal cuts and somber tones which he believed lent him dignity and forcefulness. Stephen was more likely to wear the colorful clothes of his generation: check trousers, short, loose sports coat, and a jaunty bowler. William was often seen coming or going from his office at the bank. Stephen was more likely to be spied taking part in a daring coach race down the center of Broadway.

A score of years separated father and son. At twenty-five Stephen still lapsed into moments of profound immaturity and petulance. At forty-five William did not always shoulder responsibility well. Somewhat to his regret William realized that in the case of his only offspring the apple had not fallen far from the tree.

William's cobalt-blue eyes snapped at his son. "I would have thought you had sense enough to change your plans. I don't think you truly understand what we're up against. Things are not going to stay the same no matter that we might wish it otherwise. Caroline's death has changed everything."

"I don't see that my presence at the bank mattered one way or the other."

William jabbed at his eggs with his fork. "Then it's high time you began to see! You were Caroline's fiancé, for God's sake. Don't you think the board found your absence conspicuous? After all, this was the first meeting since her death."

"Didn't you tell them I was too grief-stricken to attend?" Stephen asked. He lifted his coffee cup and sipped slowly, watching his father over the gold leaf rim. "The meeting was ceremonial, wasn't it? Hanging Caroline's portrait or some such? Their reasoning escapes me entirely. It's not as if she had anything to do with the bank. Her great-grandfather founded the blasted institution. What Caroline knew about finance was strictly confined to accounts payable. She died owing A. T. Stewart's thousands of dollars, and that was only one of the places she set up credit after her return from Europe. Left to her own devices she would have owed city merchants more than a half million dollars by spring. If that's what the members of the board want to pay tribute to, then let them. I don't have to sanction it with my presence."

"My," William said, raising both eyebrows, "this is something new. Principles, perhaps?"

Stephen mirrored his father's skeptical expression exactly. "I think you know the answer to that," he said.

"Then it's sour grapes." William picked up a biscuit, sliced it, and smeared it with sweet cream butter. "That money should have been yours."

"Ours," Stephen corrected, lowering his cup and leveling a significant, knowing look at his father. Stephen pushed away from the table and stood, slipping the paper under his arm. He went to his father and touched him lightly on the shoulder. "Don't worry so. Caroline Van Dyke was not the only heiress in the country, or in New York for that matter. I'll find someone to take her place."

97

"The sooner the better, Stephen. There are rumblings at the bank about changes being proposed. I would not like to find myself on the outside looking in. I don't believe you would relish that position either. Money would give us control, secure my place as president. The terms of the Van Dyke will would be less significant to us. Keep that in mind."

Stephen offered a small smile. "I will, Father. I'm meeting a young woman this morning for a ride in Central Park."

"The same woman whose bed you warmed last night?"

"Hardly." He paused at the door. "Last evening was strictly pleasure. This morning is business. You taught me how important it is to keep the two separate."

William watched his son go and hoped Stephen knew what he was doing. His son did not seem to understand there were a number of significant loose ends. William raised his pocket watch and glanced at the time. The line of his mouth tightened and a muscle worked in his cheek. He was due to meet with one loose end in less than thirty minutes. Applying himself to his breakfast as if it were the last meal of a condemned man, William Bennington finished eating just as his visitor was admitted to the entrance hall.

He looked up when Reilly, the house butler of some twenty years, opened the dining room doors with an officious air. "Yes?" he asked. "What is it, Reilly?" As if he didn't know.

"Dr. Morgan is here to see you," he said without inflection.

Had William been less concerned about the interview he might have noticed the hint of insolence in the butler's dark eyes and the challenge in the jut of his chin. "Very well. Show him to the library. I'll see him there."

Christian Marshall's coolly colored eyes fastened on the door as soon as he heard the handle being twisted. His face reflected disappointment, which was quickly masked as Scott walked into the room. "Oh, it's you."

"You were expecting someone else?" he asked. He dropped

98

his bag on the floor and locked the door. His brief, knowing smile had vanished by the time he faced Christian again. "Miss Holland, maybe?"

"Not likely," Christian denied. "She's made my life a pure misery. Why would I want to see her?"

"I'm sure I don't know." Scott looked around the room. Mrs. Brandywine had warned him there had been some changes, but he was still a little taken aback by what he saw. He could hardly believe Christian had permitted so many alterations. He whistled softly, at once amused and bemused.

"You think it's funny?" Christian practically snarled, sitting up in bed. He tossed his copy of *The New York Ledger* on the nearby table. The magazine slid across the polished surface and skidded to a halt at the edge. "If I have to be incarcerated in my own room, then I may as well find some pleasure in the surroundings."

"I was here not two days ago," Scott pointed out. "Everything's different. How did she accomplish so much in so little time?" The draperies, canopy, and counterpane had all been replaced. The heavy hunter-green velvet had been exchanged for lighter fabrics in ivory tones. The walls seemed brighter now and the fireplace drew one's attention with its collection of pipes and colorful tins of tobacco. A divan and an antique rocker had been placed on the large, braided rug in front of the hearth, forming a surprisingly inviting sitting area. The dark walnut woodwork contrasted suitably with the room instead of being part of the dark and somber whole.

"Who?"

"Miss Holland, of course. How did she do it?"

Christian drew his knees up to his chest and wrapped his arms about them. "Except for tearing down the old, perfectly suitable drapes, damaging my wall, and polishing my floor with her backside, Jenny didn't have a damn thing to do with it. Mrs. B. made the suggestions and I agreed to them. There was a small army of people in here doing the work, cleaning and polishing and hanging and whatnot, and Jenny wasn't one of them. Thank God," he added with what he believed was complete sincerity. "There were generals in the Union army who weren't as whip-handed as she is."

"Which is why it took us four years to lay down Ol' Dixie," Scott said dryly.

Christian's mouth curled to one side and he snorted a shade derisively.

Scott walked over to the fireplace and examined the pipes and tins. "I didn't know you smoked a pipe."

"I don't. They were Braden's."

That surprised Scott. He wasn't aware that Christian kept many personal reminders of his family in places where they could be admired. Scott had been all through Marshall House and he had never seen this collection. "He was the eldest, wasn't he?" Casually he picked up a meerschaum pipe and studied it. The craftsmanship was detailed and exquisite. From the teeth marks on the end Scott imagined it was a favorite.

"Yes." And the first to die, he almost added. He struggled with bitter thoughts, and banished them for now. "Mrs. B. found them in the attic. I didn't even know they were there. Mother probably had them put away after Braden was killed."

Scott replaced the pipe. "Bull Run, wasn't it?"

Christian nodded. "The first battle."

Turning away from the mantel, Scott approached the bed. The last thing he wanted was for Christian to begin dwelling on the past. He put his leather bag on the table and opened it up, withdrawing his stethoscope. "How are you feeling?"

"Rather like an idiot."

"Not precisely what I meant." He chuckled. "But it'll do." He made Christian lean forward and listened to his breathing, then checked his heart and took a pulse. "You've been dry . . . what? Four days?"

"It's been five and you know it."

"I thought you probably had been counting."

"Not because I want a drink," Christian snapped. "Because I want out of this room."

100

"Temper . . . temper."

"Temper be *damned!*" He slapped Scott's hand away from his wrist. "My pulse is fine. My heart is fine. My lungs are fine. But my muscles are atrophying and my brain is turning to oatmeal. I don't need a drink. I need to get out of here!"

"And do what?" Scott asked pleasantly.

For a moment Christian was bewildered. "What do you mean?"

"Precisely what I said." Scott put the stethoscope away, shut the bag, and went to the rocker. He turned it so it faced the bed and sat down. "What is it you intend to do?"

"There's business at *The Chronicle* which requires my attention."

"But you hate going there. You've said so often enough."

"So? There are responsibilities I can't entirely avoid. Not if I don't want to bury the paper."

"I thought that was exactly what you wanted. Isn't that what you told me not so long ago?"

Christian's lean fingers raked his hair impatiently. "What I said was that I didn't want to be the publisher. I also said I had as little to do with its running as possible. But I never said I wanted to bury the paper. Too many people depend on it for their livelihood as well as for fish wrapping."

Scott chuckled. "Susan says *The Herald* is better for fish. Particularly the personal columns."

"Listen, Scott. I never meant to imply that I wanted the paper to go under. I just don't have an interest emulating Greeley at *The Tribune* or Bennet at *The Herald* or even Raymond over at *The Times. The Chronicle* carried the stamp of my father and my brothers. It still does. There are people managing it now who make certain that happens. I couldn't do that. When it came to editorializing I rarely shared *The Chronicle*'s view. That hasn't changed. The staffers suffer my presence in the building twice a week because it's necessary to get certain things done. I sign papers they put in front of me, ask a few questions, question a few answers, and generally encourage their efforts. They give the paper its prestige, not me. I'm merely the only surviving son of the founder." He drew in a calming breath and let it out slowly. "Now that that's settled, why not let me get on with what I need to do?"

Scott hesitated. He envisioned Christian drinking himself under another table if his only motive for leaving was the paper. It was clear from Christian's tone that what he felt for *The Chronicle* was best described as an obligation, a sense of duty to the memory of those who had cared. Part of what Christian did for the paper—and what he neglected, perhaps purposely, to mention—was to make it visible in certain fashionable circles. Christian lent his formidable presence and power to *The Chronicle*. He made people think of the paper, gave it a high profile, and did not object if society thought his opinions and the paper's were one and the same. He subscribed to a stall at Wallack's Theater and a box at the Academy of Music, each for the season. Christian could be seen there, as well as at the elite social gatherings, the races out on Harlem Lane, and at the New York Yachting Club. He promoted *The Chronicle*, suppressing his own views and pretending an interest he did not feel. The facade was taking a steady toll. Scott was very much afraid that if Christian did not bury *The Chronicle*, the paper would bury him.

"We'll see," he said finally. "Why not wait until after the holidays? Christmas is the day after tomorrow. Let the paper rest until the New Year."

Christian threw up his hands. "Who in the hell appointed you my guardian? Don't you think this is absurd?" He threw his legs over the side of the bed and began pacing the floor. "I should have you brought up on charges, that's what I should do."

"If only it weren't so embarrassing," Scott said knowingly.

Christian shot his friend a wry look. "My thoughts exactly. I'd be the laughingstock of the avenue. Probably of the entire city." He paused a beat. "I have social obligations, Scott. There must be twenty or more invitations downstairs waiting to be answered."

"There were twenty-eight," Scott said. "And they're all taken care of. You sent your regrets."

"You dared!"

"I did. Miss Holland has a fine writing hand. She's been taking care of all your correspondence. You could do a lot worse than to keep her on as your secretary."

"I don't believe I'm hearing this! You're completely taking over my life! And my own employees are helping you! God, spare me from humanitarians!"

Unperturbed by Christian's helpless anger, Scott went on. "Susan and I would like you to share Christmas dinner with us."

"What?" he asked sarcastically, raising his brows. "You didn't send my regrets to yourself as well?"

"We didn't send round an invitation. I didn't think one was necessary since we'll be eating here."

That brought Christian up short. "No," he said firmly. "Absolutely not. I forbid it. I will not have you *and* Susan up here. My dining room is downstairs. We'll eat there."

"Very well," Scott said amiably. "We'll see you on Christmas Day. Say seven? I assume my daughter's included as well."

"Why do I feel as if I've been completely outmaneuvered?"

Scott laughed. "Because you have been."

Christian stopped pacing and sat on the edge of the bed. He leaned forward, clasping his hands and pressing his thumbs together. His nightshirt caught around his knees. "I don't know what to do to convince you that I'm not about to drink myself senseless if you let me get out of this room. You can't keep me here forever, Scott. I think I've showed admirable patience and considerable tolerance for your high-handed methods thus far. That's about to end. If you're going to permit me downstairs on Christmas Day, then you can damn well give me the key now."

"Promise me you'll stay away from Printing House Square.

103

Forget about the paper and social obligations. Do something you *want* to do."

Christian's eyes narrowed on his friend's nose, imagining what it would look like if it were knocked slightly askew. "Don't tempt me."

Scott could almost feel the pressure of Christian's fist. He rubbed the bridge of his nose with his forefinger and smiled sheepishly. "What about painting? You could open up the studio and—"

"You're about to get thrown out of here. I don't need the door to do it either. The window will serve my purpose just as well."

"I see."

"I hope you do."

"What about the paper?"

Christian swore softly. "All right," he said, exasperated. "I'll pretend the paper doesn't exist. It's obviously managed this long without me. It can manage a while longer."

Scott nodded, pulled the key to Christian's room out of his vest pocket, and tossed it to him. "You can check it if you wish."

"I will. I've been tricked once already."

"I know. Miss Holland told me what she had done."

Christian was at the door, inserting the key before he answered. "You approved, of course."

"Of course."

The door opened and Christian poked his head into the hallway. It was almost as good as being outside. After a moment he withdrew. "You're leaving?" he asked when he saw Scott had moved to the table and was picking up his bag.

"I've worn out my welcome for today and I'm satisfied with what I've seen and most of what I've heard."

Christian opened the door a little wider so Scott could pass.

"If you need me . . . just to listen . . . don't hesitate to send for me." He ducked his fair head slightly, avoiding Christian's probing eyes. "I couldn't just do nothing, Chris. Watching

104

you . . . what you were doing to yourself . . . I couldn't."

"You don't have to apologize for being the man you are," Christian said. "I may even thank you one day."

"I'll look forward to it."

"You asked to see me, sir?" Jenny's feet rooted to the floor as she crossed the threshold into Christian's room. So this was how he was getting some of his own back, she thought when she saw him sitting in a copper tub in front of the fireplace. He was not going to let her off lightly for the trick she had played him the other day. Jenny had not seen him since then and she believed that she was seeing too much of him now.

His naked shoulders and chest were tawny in the firelight. Droplets of water glistened on his arms and his muscles bunched as he groped for the towel that lay on the floor. His aquamarine eyes studied Jenny's face.

For a moment she thought he was going to stand and dry himself. She tensed, closing her eyes tightly, and stayed that way until she heard him laugh. Risking a peek, she saw that he had only used the towel to dry his hair. The streaks of copper were visible now. In the mere seconds she had stood in the doorway she had noticed too many things to pretend nonchalance. Jenny swallowed hard, made a small quarter turn, and let her eyes rest elsewhere. She reached blindly for the door handle and grasped it like a lifeline when she found it. "I'll return when you're finished," she said. "You only have to ring once. I'll know it's me you want."

"I want you now," he countered, watching her carefully. She was wary and it showed. The hint of peaches in her cheeks deepened a little, and unconsciously she tugged at her lower lip with her teeth. She wore the same severe dress she had worn the last time he saw her, the same type of dress all female employees wore, yet Christian couldn't remember ever thinking the dresses were particularly becoming to their wearers. The effect was otherwise on Jenny Holland. The

105

delicate structure of her face was highlighted. The line of her neck seemed longer, slimmer. For all her uncertainty her carriage was regal. She held her shoulders stiffly; her spine might well have been steel. Christian's eyes dropped away from the high curve of her breasts to the papers she carried under one arm. His temperature was becoming warmer than the water. "Is that the correspondence I asked for?"

"Yes."

"Well?" he drawled, raising one eyebrow.

"Well what, sir?"

"Put them on the desk. I can't very well review the stuff while it's a parasitic growth on your hip."

Avoiding his gaze, Jenny quickly crossed the room to the window, dropped Christian's letters on the writing desk, and made certain she stayed beyond his arm's length. "You're not very kind, Mr. Marshall," she said when she reached the door again.

"Oh?"

"This . . ." She made a gesture with her hand to indicate the room, the tub, and Christian's presence in the tub. "I lied to you about the keys for your own good. I can't help but think that you're revenging yourself now. This could have waited until you were more appropriately prepared to receive me." She bowed her head slightly. "I'm going now."

Christian sat up straighter in the tub and held up his hand. "No, wait," he said, dropping the towel around his shoulders when she stopped her retreat and looked at him. "You may as well hear it from me as from any of my staff. Dr. Turner is kind. Mrs. Brandywine is kind. I am not kind. And yes, I suppose part of my purpose in asking for you now was to make you a little uncomfortable. You may call it revenge if you wish. It seems small enough repayment for what you did to me."

"What I did? But—"

"What you did," he repeated, his features implacable, giving no quarter. "You were my guest here, now my employee. Neither of those positions give you any right to mother or coddle me as if I were an infant. I do not need you to determine what is for my own good. I may not be a kind man, but I am a man. You'd do well to remember that the next time you find yourself under me."

The back of Jenny's hand covered her mouth and smothered the gasp that rose in her throat. Color vanished from her cheeks. Her dark eyes were wide and wounded. "You're like the others," she whispered. "No different at all . . . I thought . . ."

"What?" Christian leaned forward. A frown puckered his brow. "What did you say? I couldn't hear—"

Jenny's hand dropped away and she shook her head, denying that she had said anything.

Christian did not press the issue. He'd heard more than he'd admitted but until her denial, had thought he must have been mistaken. "You may remain in my employ, but it would be prudent of you not to take on tasks which are none of your concern." He pointed to the stack of letters. "Contrary to what you may think, Dr. Turner is not the one who pays your wages." He pointed to the drapes, the sitting area, and the freshly washed walls. "In spite of what I said to Scott, I don't believe for a moment that Mrs. B. was entirely responsible for this. I permitted the changes because I wanted the company of the people who did the work. In other circumstances I would have told everyone to go to hell. Am I making myself clear?"

She nodded.

"What?"

"Yes, Mr. Marshall," she said dutifully. "You've made yourself clear."

"Then one more thing," he added. His tone was too honeyed to be sincerely felt. Anger was very near the surface. "Stay out of my way, Jenny. I'd prefer not to know you're here. Convey my wishes to Mrs. Brandywine. She'll give you appropriate duties."

"Yes, sir," she said softly. "May I go?"

"With my blessing." When she was gone Christian drew the

towel off his neck and sank lower into the tub. He stared at the fire in the grate, frowning. He reviewed his conversation with her, wondering if he had inadvertently sent her packing. Not that she had anything to take, he realized, or anywhere to go. Still, his purpose had been to get her out of his immediate sight, not send her on her way. Out of sight, out of mind. It would be enough.

That night Jenny's sleep was troubled. Except for the intensity of her fear and confusion it was not a new experience for her. She had known sleepless nights before she went to Jennings, had known them throughout her stay in the hospital, and had come to expect that she would always suffer them, even in Marshall House. When she had confided as much to Dr. Turner, he had assured her distressing nights would eventually become less frequent. Time, he'd told her. She required time, and peace of mind would follow.

Jenny was not so certain. Outside, the sky opened up and icy shards of rain pelted her window. Wind swirled violently, rising and falling, battering the house and pressing its cold cheek to each pane of glass. The snow that had brightened New York was driven away and sidewalks and streets were frosted with a thin layer of ice. Just beyond Jenny's room the spindle-fingered tips of an oak tree scratched at her window. The ends of the branches were covered with diamond chips of ice and in combination with the wind became the equal of any glass-cutter's tool.

Jenny buried her head beneath a pillow to shut out the drumming and the pinging and the scratching. Blotting out Christian Marshall's image was not so easily accomplished. When she closed her eyes he was there, at the back of her lids, staring at her with his own cool eyes and giving her a faint smile that was both derisive and cruel. When she opened her weary eyes and focused on the opposite wall she saw his image projected there as well. His profile was hard, his mouth grim, and a muscle worked in his cheek as he ground his teeth together.

He wanted her gone, Jenny thought despairingly. Somehow she had offended him. He regretted everything he had done for her, she was sure of it. She told herself she shouldn't have badgered him. And she wished she hadn't begged Mrs. B. to approach Christian about the alterations to his room. Better he should have rotted in his dreary bedchamber. She should have followed her instincts and kept well clear of Christian Marshall. His callous comments notwithstanding, the last thing Jenny thought she needed was yet another man dictating to her. That he should purposely set out to embarrass her still raised hackles at the nape of her neck. His biting reminder that he was a man was unnecessary and unseemly. She had been deliberately provocative with him only once, and Jenny believed anything she did in order to leave Jennings Memorial had been justified. She had no wish to find herself beneath Christian Marshall ever again!

Jenny tossed and turned, hardly knowing if she was asleep or awake. Dreams and reality became indistinguishable, and all she felt was a gnawing pain in her middle that tightened her stomach to the point of nausea. She curled fetally in her bed and prayed for sleep to ease her tormented thoughts. But then the nightmares came. She heard someone screaming and thought it might be her. But that didn't make sense because she knew better than anyone that she couldn't scream anymore. She shuddered so violently that she thought her bones would crack.

The room was cold. Bitter, biting cold. Jenny reached for blankets only to find there were none. The floor was wet and her nightshift was damp. Her fingers and toes were stiff from the cold and they hurt unbearably. She curled more tightly, seeking warmth from somewhere inside herself, and sucked on her fingers. At her back the stone wall was uncomfortably rough, but she was afraid to get back in bed. They would tie her down if she did that and she would go mad if they tied her again.

There were footsteps in the hallway. Three pairs of feet. She recognized William MacCauley's heavy tread, Ronald White's shuffle, and Dr. Glenn's almost military stride. They were coming for her. She frowned, trying to concentrate, and felt a wave of nausea threaten to turn her insides out. What she had been thinking couldn't be right. She wasn't in the hospital anymore. But why was she so cold and why were the attendants here? And Dr. Glenn! He was ordering a treatment. She heard him. They were going to bring the tub and fill it with water and they would try to drown her again. Tears slipped beneath her closed eyes as she shivered and tried to make herself invisible against the whitewashed wall. Perhaps no one would see her and she would escape while they were looking for her.

It didn't work. The tub was brought in and although she struggled, William and Ronald held her down. They weren't gentle now. Their grips were like iron. They were only gentle when someone was observing or they wanted something from her. Sometimes they'd give her an extra blanket or another serving of soup or even loosen her straps, but she'd have to let them touch her then. Most often she let them do whatever they wanted. It was that or freeze or starve or strangle. They rarely did anything but run their hands over her body. It was almost as if they were afraid of her. She was mad, of course, and Jenny thought that probably accounted for their peculiar reaction to her. William always wanted to cup her breasts. He would stand behind her and rub himself against her while he held her breasts in his hands. He never removed her shift. Sometimes he slipped his hands beneath the gaping neckline; other times he simply touched her through the material. Ronald liked looking at her. His pleasure came mostly from watching. He made certain William wasn't caught by looking out for doctors at the door, and in exchange he saw everything. When that wasn't enough he would press her hand against his groin and hold it there for a long time while he watched her with dull, flat eyes. Then he would begin to move her hand and the look in his

110

eyes would change.

"I'll do it for you now," she whispered huskily because her throat wouldn't let her do anything else. "You can touch me, too. I'll let you. Just don't put me in the . . ." She clutched his shoulders as she was lowered toward the icy water. "Don't. Please don't." Jenny changed her tactic. She vowed to hold him so tightly that she would pull him with her. That would put an end to Dr. Glenn's treatment and her nightmare. Everyone would laugh when she and Ronald fell in the tub together.

"Mr. Marshall! Mr. Marshall! Come quick!" Mrs. Brandywine pounded on Christian's door. "Wake up, Mr. Marshall! We need you!" The housekeeper glanced at Mary Margaret, the young scullery maid, and pointed her in the direction of Jenny's room again. "See if you can't pick the lock with one of your pins." She gave the door a sharp kick with the toe of her slipper and didn't even feel the pain. "Oooh! Won't that man ever wake?"

"Maybe I should pick this lock instead," Mary Margaret offered helpfully. She plucked a pin from her bright red hair and started to kneel, wrinkling her pert nose in concentration.

"What the hell is going on?" Christian demanded as he opened the door. He frowned at Mary Margaret, who was so shocked by his sudden appearance that she almost stuck him with her pin. Christian steadied her as she started to fall and set her on her feet. He raked his fingers through his hair and turned his attention to his housekeeper. "Mrs. Brandywine? What's this all about? It must be two o'clock."

The housekeeper tightened the belt of her robe. She knew precisely what time it was and that was hardly an issue. "Can't you hear it?"

"Hear what? All I hear is you and the blasted howling wind." She tapped her foot impatiently. "From Jenny's room."

Christian listened, but heard nothing alarming. Jenny's room was in the opposite wing, separated from his room by the

111

wide main staircase. "Is she ill?" he asked.

"I think she's hurt. Mary Margaret heard a window break and woke me. We've narrowed it to Jenny's room. There's a rush of air from under her door but she won't come to it when we knock. We can't get in because it's locked and she gave you the extra key. Remember?" Christian shrugged into his quilted robe and found Jenny's key in his bedside table. "Let's go."

Mary Margaret and Mrs. Brandywine ran to keep up with Christian's long slightly uneven stride. He fairly leaped down the six steps that led to the main staircase's landing, ran across it, then took the six steps that led up to the south wing in two quick jumps. Outside Jenny's room he stopped. Christian could feel the draft from under the door on his bare feet. "Jenny!" he called. "Can you hear me, Jenny?"

"Use the key," Mrs. Brandywine urged breathlessly.

Christian did so. A horrible, pained scream filled the frigid air as Christian thrust open the door. "Oh, my God," he said quietly as he felt the full impact of what he was seeing. Behind him the scullery maid and housekeeper stood on tiptoe to see over his shoulders.

Jenny was crouched in the corner of the room nearest the window. Firelight made a gold and orange glitter of the shards of glass and ice chips in her hair. A tree branch had broken through the window and the wind was carrying stinging pellets of rain to all parts of the room. Even in her corner Jenny wasn't safe. Her shift was soaked and her hair was plastered to her head. Her feet were cut and to stop her own screaming she had one hand pressed to her mouth, sucking on her fingers like an injured child. Her eyes were open, but Christian thought it was doubtful she saw anyone. He'd seen men in the army who slept with their eyes open, who relived some hell while in a deep trance that confounded their comrades. Jenny looked as terrified as any of the men who crawled away from the bloody, open fields at Shiloh.

"Mother of . . ." Mary Margaret crossed herself three times in quick succession. "She's balmy! Just like I said to Carrie.

112

We shouldn't have—"

"Be quiet," Mrs. B. snapped. "She's frightened and chilled to the bone. Anyone can see that!"

Careless of the glass scattered on the floor Christian went straight to Jenny's side. He hunkered down and gave orders with staccato precision to Mrs. Brandywine and the maid. "Heat water for a bath right away and add it to my tub. It hasn't been emptied yet. I'll take her to my room where there's already a fire going." The housekeeper nodded once and hurried out of the room. "Mary Margaret, get me a blanket, then start cleaning up this glass. When it's cleared, wake up George and tell him to board up the window. And get something warmer on. You'll catch your death in here."

The maid stripped the bed and tore off a blanket that wasn't too damp. Her hands shook with cold as she gave it to Christian. She couldn't understand why Jenny hadn't left the room or at least moved away from the window. Mary Margaret held to her original conclusion that Dr. Turner's patient was not in her right mind.

Christian thanked her briskly. "Go on," he said when she hesitated. "Get a coat or borrow another robe and go find a broom. I can handle things from here."

"Beggin' your pardon, Mr. Marshall, but should you be alone with her? She could do something crazy. She might hurt you."

"Go!" Christian growled.

Mary Margaret nearly tripped over her own feet in her efforts to be gone from the room quickly. Her nightgown flapped about her legs and her hair lost most of its anchoring pins.

Christian drew the blanket about Jenny's shoulders and lifted her. She seemed completely unaware of his presence. She remained as tightly curled against him as she had been in the corner. Her body was rigid with cold and she shuddered so deeply that Christian felt his own body shaking in response. A faint trail of blood marked Christian's passage back to his own

113

room. He kicked open the door, carried Jenny to the rocker, and sat down with her in his lap. The blanket fell away, but Christian thought the fire would be enough. He looked over his shoulder for Mrs. Brandywine.

"What's keeping her?" he muttered. "How long can it take to boil water?" His eyes dropped to Jenny. She was every bit as pathetic looking as he remembered from the hospital. "Poor Jenny Holland," he said softly. "You've had quite a time of it, haven't you? Jumped from the frying pan right into the fire. I'll bet you didn't count on any of this when you left Jennings. Probably thought you'd escaped everything for good. You couldn't have known this house harbored its own lunatic, namely me." His fleeting smile was self-mocking. "I suppose you've forgotten all about staying out of my sight." Christian began to pick bits of glass from her hair. Tiny rivulets of melting ice ran over her forehead and across her cheeks. It took a second and third look before he realized that the source of some of the water was Jenny's tears.

"I could use a drink just about now," he said, flicking chips of glass into the fireplace. They snapped and popped and turned tongues of yellow flame to shades of green and blue. He glanced at the door again. "Damn! Where are you, Mrs. B.?"

Tiny shards of glass dug more deeply into Christian's feet as he continued rocking. He wiped Jenny's pale face with the cuff of his nightshirt and watched her eyes close slowly. It helped a little. He didn't have to look at the terror that was in her sightless and unblinking stare.

"Thank God you're here," he said feelingly when Mrs. Brandywine appeared on the threshold. She carried two large kettles of hot water.

"Will it be enough, do you think?" she asked, setting them down beside the tub.

"It will have to be." Christian stood and looked in the tub. There wasn't a lot of water in it. He thought the kettles would be sufficient to heat it up. "She's nearly frozen through. I'm worried about her hands and feet. Scott said they would be

114

susceptible to frostbite for the rest of her life. You add the water and test it. I'll put her in the tub when the water's ready."

Mrs. Brandywine drained one kettle and most of the second before she declared it ready. Christian changed his grip on Jenny to make it easier for him to put her in the tub. "This will warm you up," he told her. "Just like the first night you were here."

But Jenny was still caught in her nightmare. "I'll do it for you now," she whispered huskily because her throat wouldn't let her do anything else. "You can touch me too. I'll let you. Just don't put me in the . . ." She clutched his shoulders as she was lowered toward the tub of water. "Don't. Please don't."

Her words brought Christian up short. He heard Mrs. Brandywine's gasp and looked at his housekeeper helplessly. "I don't know what she's talking about."

"Like before," Jenny insisted, pressing her face into Christian's shoulder. "You can do whatever you want." Her hands left his upper arms and her fingers curled around the lapels of his robe. She tried to get closer to him.

The shift in Jenny's weight threw Christian off balance. He faltered, caught himself, then felt his bad leg give way. He swore out of sheer frustration, realizing he was going to drop her and probably follow her in as well. There was no time to maneuver a graceful descent. Jenny plunged into the water, never releasing the bloodless grip on Christian's lapels, and pulled him in top of her.

Mrs. Brandywine jumped away as water showered the sitting area. Flames spit and sizzled in the fireplace. Puddles darkened the braided rug. The hems of her nightgown and robe were immediately soaked. Eyes wide, her brows nearly lifted to her hairline, the housekeeper stifled a hoarse cry by pressing her fist to her mouth as the battle between Jenny and Christian began in earnest.

Jenny fell into the tub on her back, and for a brief moment her head went beneath the water. Just as she surfaced,

Christian's heavy weight bore her under again. He tried to get out quickly, but it was difficult to get purchase on the sides of the tub. No human body, he thought, was meant to be folded at so many uncomfortable angles. He pushed at the sides of the tub again, attempting to raise himself, only to discover that Jenny had yet to release his robe.

As soon as Christian grabbed Jenny's wrists his weight was no longer supported by the rim of the tub. Jenny's scream was choked off as she slid beneath the water a third time. Her panic was complete. She kicked, squirmed, and pushed and her terror-filled eyes opened under water. Above her she saw the distorted shadow of the man who was trying to drown her.

Jenny's fingers finally loosened their grip on Christian's robe. Before he could raise himself she landed two hard blows on his chest and neck and scored his cheek with her nails.

Christian's exit from the tub was as awkward as his fall had been. He sat heavily on the floor, out of breath and soaked to the skin. Dipping one hand in the water, he caught Jenny by the collar of her nightshift and roughly jerked her upright. "Stay where you are, Mrs. B.," he said with fatigue as the housekeeper advanced in his direction to help. "This she-cat will pull you in as well. You can't imagine how strong she—owwww!" Christian withdrew his hand sharply as Jenny's teeth sank into the fleshy ball of his fist. "Mad little bitch," he gritted, raising himself up to a kneeling position. "I've a good mind to bite you back."

Shaking as if with ague, Jenny merely regarded him blankly.

"Oh, Jesus," he swore softly, pushing aside several thick strands of hair that were plastered to her cheek and neck. "What a piece of work you are." He glanced over his shoulder at the housekeeper. "Mrs. B., get one of my nightshirts out. We have to put her in something dry. There are some towels in the dressing room. Get those as well." Christian slipped his hands under Jenny's arms and dragged her out of the tub. He pulled her against him, and she stayed there without protest, fitting the contours of his body as if she belonged there. She

116

was stiff and cold and reminded Christian of a fledgling chick. As for himself, he thought he was behaving in the best tradition of a mother hen. The soggy sleeves of his robe even resembled wings as he wrapped his arms around her. His legs were splayed and Jenny's trembling body slipped comfortably between the cradle of his thighs. He had the absurd notion that he was patiently waiting for his egg to hatch.

Christian rubbed her back, trying to keep her warm while he waited for Mrs. Brandywine to bring the towels. "I suppose the bath wasn't such a good idea," he said to himself. "Let me see your hands and feet."

There was no response from Jenny, and Christian really hadn't expected one. He lifted each of her hands in turn, examined them, then pressed them together between his own warmer ones. Nudging aside the hem of her nightshirt where it covered her feet, Christian saw the tiny cuts had stopped bleeding. He supposed the slivers of glass embedded there would have to wait for removal until she could understand what was being done to her. He could imagine touching her with a pair of tweezers and having her react as if he were stabbing her with a knife. There was no telling what manner of torture had passed for treatment at Jennings.

Christian laid his thigh very gently over her feet to keep them warm. His chin rested against the crown of her head and his mouth was set in a grim line as he stared at the fire. "What's to become of you, Jenny Holland?" he questioned softly. He released her hands and one of his arms stole around her, slipping just under her breasts to keep her warm as well as upright. He nearly came out of his own skin when he felt her place his hand over her left breast.

"There," she said dully. "That's what you wanted."

Her voice was so low that Christian had to dip his head to hear her. When he did he felt the press of her mouth just below his ear. She didn't bite him but she might just as well have. Christian reacted the same way, pulling back sharply and cursing her under his breath. What in God's name did she

117

think she was doing? "Mrs. B.! Hurry, will you? I can't be held responsible for what I do to this woman if you—"

"I'm here," she said breathlessly, skittering to a halt in front of Christian. "There were towels all over the floor in there and no fresh—"

"No explanations, please. Just give me one for her hair. You can start stripping off her shift."

"Oh, but—"

"I'm not in the mood to listen to your tittering objections. Will you just, for once, do as I say?" He reached up and caught the corner of one of the towels that the housekeeper held. He yanked it out of her hand and began patting down Jenny's hair. "I'm not going to ravish her. Though I'm not so certain I can vouch for her intentions toward me."

Mrs. Brandywine snorted. "If you would show a moment's patience you would know that I wasn't going to say anything of the kind. I merely wanted to point out it would be easier to remove her shift if you would put her on the bed."

"Oh." He raised sheepish eyes to Mrs. B. and held her glowering stare long enough to let her know he had been suitably chastised.

The housekeeper reflected that some things hadn't changed in the thirty years since Christian's birth. He had been manipulating her with his penitent expressions from the cradle onward. "Go on with you," she said. "I know when my leg's being pulled. Put her on the bed."

Christian finished drying Jenny's hair before he moved. Flinging the towel over his shoulder, he got to his feet, carefully supporting Jenny as he did so. Christian grasped her by the upper arms and hauled her to her feet. She was still curled so tightly that her feet actually left the floor. "She's not making this easy," he muttered as he swung her into his arms. It was more the ungainliness of her position than her actual weight that made everything awkward for Christian.

"Should I get help?" Mrs. B. asked anxiously. "One of the men—"

118

"I'm fine," he said, cutting her off.

Mrs. Brandywine held her breath as Christian slipped a little in a pool of water. He caught himself, paused, then continued more carefully. Mrs. B. threw down a towel on the wet floor and began mopping up water with the toe of her slipper.

"Leave it for later," Christian said. "I need your help here." He dropped Jenny on the bed, and used the towel that was hanging over his shoulder to briskly rub her down. "Did you find one of my nightshifts?"

Mrs. B. held it out to him. "Take it. I'll get her out of this wet thing."

Jenny moved restlessly, moaning softly, as she felt the hem of her shift being moved up her calves, over her knees, then sliding along her thighs. William had promised he wouldn't make her get undressed. She didn't want him to see her. Touching was bad enough, but if she let him see her she would never feel clean. "No," she protested. Tears gathered beneath her lids. "Nooo." Her hand moved from side to side. "Please, no."

Christian sensed what was going to happen before Mrs. Brandywine. He tried to move the housekeeper out of the way but his timing was off by a single beat. Jenny's knees came up and rammed into Mrs. Brandywine's bosom as the housekeeper bent over her. Mrs. B. was thrown off balance, first by Jenny, then by Christian as he pushed her out of Jenny's reach. She stumbled away from the bed and sucked in her breath, trying to fill her lungs with air.

"Don't, Christian!" she gasped when she saw him take Jenny's wrists in a rigid, painful grip. "She didn't know what she was—"

Christian was only marginally aware that Mrs. B. was speaking to him. It was one thing for Jenny to bite, kick, and scratch at him, but when she turned her hellish madness on Mrs. Brandywine Christian saw red. He jerked her upright, caught her by the shoulders and shook her roughly. "Don't you ever, *ever* hit her again—"

"Christian," Mrs. B. pleaded, tugging at the soggy sleeve of his quilted robe. "She can't even hear—"

Neither could Christian. Jenny had become a wild thing in his arms again, fighting him with a strength that was suited to a man half again her size. "Oh, no you don't," he snarled as she began to flail at him. "Not this time." He slammed her back on the bed, and this time when he straddled her it was not at the hips. He slid over her chest and pinned her upper arms to the mattress with his knees. Jenny's hands and fingers went numb almost immediately. They fell uselessly above her head. The attempts she made to unseat him were unsuccessful. Her legs, with nothing but air to push against, gradually stopped kicking. There was a drop of blood on her lip where she had bitten it. Her eyes darted frantically but saw nothing. Finally they closed.

"Mr. Marshall," Mrs. B. said gently after several highly charged minutes had passed. "She's long done struggling with you."

Christian let out a long, calming breath and nodded slowly. He eased himself off Jenny and turned to Mrs. Brandywine. "Are you all right?"

"Yes," she assured him swiftly.

His eyes made a careful study of the older woman as he satisfied himself that she was speaking the truth. "I was afraid she had hurt you."

She dismissed that idea. "Winded a little. I'm fine."

"I'll take it from here," Christian told her. "There's no sense in you even trying to help." His head gave a slight jerk backward toward the bed, indicating Jenny. "She's completely unpredictable."

There was a whimper from the bed, and Mrs. Brandywine looked around Christian's shoulder as he spun on his heel. Jenny was sitting up now, her knees pressed to her chest and her spine as stiff and straight against the dark headboard. She was looking at them, at the room, and finally herself with helpless confusion.

"It happened again, didn't it?" she asked huskily, talking more to herself than to her rapt audience. Her fingers plucked at the wet sleeves of her nightshift and she blinked rapidly, stemming the tears that threatened to flow. "Perhaps they were right after all. I may well be mad . . . I can't even . . ."

Both Christian and Mrs. B. leaned forward, straining to hear what Jenny was saying. Her voice trailed off into nothingness and they were no longer privy to her thoughts. Suddenly it was as if there was no strength left in Jenny. Her body went limp, unfolded, and she fell on her side away from them. The only evidence they had to suggest she was crying was the intermittent shuddering of her shoulders. She had jammed one corner of a pillow against her mouth to smother her sobs.

"Poor thing," Mrs. B. said sympathetically. "Let me go to her, Christian."

He nodded and stepped back. "See if you can't get her to change her wet gown. I'll clean up." Christian closed his ears to the soothing, cooing noises Mrs. B. showered on Jenny. He dragged the half-empty tub into the dressing room, changed his own wet clothes, and mopped the floor with the towels that Jenny didn't need. "She may as well sleep there tonight," he said, stretching out on the divan when he was done pulling glass splinters from his feet. "There's not another room prepared or one warm enough for her."

"Where will *you* sleep?" Mrs. B. asked. She was sitting on the bed now with Jenny's head in her lap. Her fingers gently stroked Jenny's hair and cheek. Jenny's eyes were closed, her lips slightly parted, her breathing even.

"Right here," he said, patting the cushion.

Mrs. B. looked skeptically at Christian's bare feet, which were hanging over the edge of the divan. "You won't be comfortable. I'll take her to my room."

"How? She's finally sound asleep, and I'm not going to carry her to the other wing. My feet still feel like pincushions."

"Then I'll sleep here with her and you can spend the night in my room."

121

"Mrs. B.," he sighed. "I won't let you be alone with her. There's no telling what she may do, and you simply haven't the strength to deal with her. Take yourself off to bed now. You're falling asleep where you sit."

There was truth in that that Mrs. B. couldn't deny. Still, she couldn't leave without voicing her objections. "It's not proper, Mr. Marshall," she began.

Christian cut her off before she could warm to her subject. "There, you've made your token protest. That's all I'm going to allow you. What the rest of the staff doesn't know won't hurt them. Off to bed, Mrs. Brandywine."

It was futile to go on and she didn't have the energy. "Very well. But let me get you some blankets first." She eased Jenny's head off her lap and back onto a pillow.

"To bed," Christian said, pointing toward the door.

"At least let me stoke the—"

"Bed."

"Tyrant."

"Busybody."

Mrs. Brandywine turned the handle on the door. Her tender smile disappeared as she yawned hugely. "Good night, Mr. Marshall."

"Good night, Mrs. Brandywine."

Chapter 5

Christian couldn't sleep. He had been exhausted when Mrs. Brandywine left and now that he was alone—almost alone—he was bone weary and restless. Somehow it did not seem a contradiction. The divan was hopelessly inadequate for his needs, but Christian knew better than to think that was the reason for his wakefulness. *She* was to blame. He couldn't sleep for watching her.

Turning away from her didn't help. Jenny's pure profile confronted him no matter where he looked, no matter if his eyes were open or closed. He decided it made more sense to look at her than not. Christian sat up and threw his legs over the side of the divan. Resting his elbows on his knees, he cradled his head in his hands and studied Jenny's face.

It had been a long time since he had looked at a woman's face with an artist's eye to line and form. The first thing Christian found himself considering was the reason Jenny Holland had awakened his interest. There was no single feature that engaged his attention, yet the whole of her face, especially now while she slept, was a work of striking loveliness.

Her expression was serene and untroubled. The traces of tears had been wiped away. There were no lingering lines of tension at the corners of her mouth, her eyes, or her brow. Had Christian not seen her earlier, he couldn't have guessed that she had ever known terror. The shadows that lay in the faint hollows beneath her cheeks and below her eyes were caused by the firelight, not apprehension.

Through thoughtful, narrowed eyes, Christian studied the line of a jaw that was strong without being masculine. The bones of her face were too finely drawn to lay any claim to manliness, yet there was undeniable strength that Christian associated with his own sex not hers. Jenny's dark eyebrows curved in a natural arch that owed nothing to plucking and primping. Her thick lashes framed expressive eyes when she was awake and fringed delicate, blue-veined lids when she was asleep. Her pared nose was not so much as a centimeter off center, but her mouth was a shade too wide, the bottom lip too full for Jenny to be acknowledged by society as a conventional beauty. Jenny's mouth gave her an earthy sensuousness that was clearly lacking in the pure, perfect lines of her other features.

Again and again, Christian found his eyes drawn to the full curve of her mouth. When her lips parted on a sigh and she unconsciously wet them with the tip of her tongue, Christian sucked in his breath. It was not strictly carnal arousal that he felt. Though he did not deny that was part of his reaction, what struck him with all the force of a physical blow was his desire to paint her, to capture on canvas the face whose features were a contradiction of purity and voluptuousness.

Christian stood, agitated. He did not know what to do with his hands. There were no pockets in his nightshirt to jam them in. His robe was still wet. His fingers folded and unfolded fists clenched and unclenched. He lighted a lamp on the table by the rocker, then paced the room restlessly, stopping periodically to poke at the fire or add more coals.

The contradiction he saw in Jenny's face existed in her character as well, Christian thought sourly. He didn't appreciate Scott handing him this particular feminine puzzle. According to his friend, Jenny was a virgin. Christian had seen enough to know she was innocent. He had observed her almost

124

painful shyness when she had come upon him in his bath, and she'd seemed genuinely distressed when his language was salted with a number of curses. Christian did not think her embarrassment had been faked. She gave every indication that she found his manner insulting.

But how did that fit with the fact that she had used her body with the shamelessness of a whore?

He couldn't think of a satisfactory answer. He particularly could not accept that Jenny Holland was mad, that two disparate personalities existed within her. The notion seemed as absurd as believing in demons and devils and possession. There was something he was overlooking, he decided, some vital missing piece. If he could discover it, the mystery of Jenny Holland would be solved.

All the time Christian had been contemplating Jenny he had studiously avoided looking at his writing desk. Now he approached it, unable to hold himself back. Quietly sliding open the desk's only drawer, he withdrew a single sheet of paper and one charcoal stub.

The pool of light from the lamp erased the shadows on her cheeks. Christian's eyes traced the contours of her face and found his starting point in the strand of hair that outlined the gentle curve of her ear. His grip on the charcoal stub loosened and he made a sweeping line, hardly touching the bit to the paper. He made the same motion several times before the charcoal touched down and produced the exact arc, angle, and curve he wanted.

Christian worked quickly, against time, against his fear that the vision in his mind's eye would dissolve. He caught the smooth planes and hollows that defined her cheeks and forehead, the exact arch of her brows. He used the side of his little finger to smudge the charcoal and suggest the color of her dark brown hair. He found the sharp edge of the charcoal and created each lash individually.

His picture was beginning to take form when the image he held began a subtle metamorphosis. On the bed Jenny

125

continued to sleep; the serenity of her repose was unchanged, yet Christian's perception had dramatically altered. He was not even aware it was happening. The full line that was her mouth became a gaping hole in her face, and a silent scream seemed to erupt from the paper. The bones of her cheeks were accentuated so that the hollows below were deeper. The effect was a certain emaciation that bordered on the skeletal. She looked starved, half-dead, and still she was screaming. He redrew her eyes and opened them this time. They were opaque, without light. They held nothing but death.

By slow degrees Christian began to see what was happening, and when his vision cleared he threw down the charcoal as if it were a hot ember in his hand. His chair scraped harshly against the floor as he pushed away from the desk. He grabbed the drawing, crumpling the haunted death mask that was Jenny's face in his fist. He went to the fireplace and pitched the paper to the flames. It vanished in a brief flash of heat and light. Limping slightly, he returned to the divan and sat down, cradling his head in his hands. His shoulders heaved once as a shudder, too powerful to be contained, ripped through him and hot tears scalded his eyes.

It was the grating sound of the chair being pushed against the floor that woke Jenny. Her sleep-filled vision cleared in time to see Christian throw something into the fireplace. Watching him through the feathered fan of her lashes, she bit the soft inner side of her lip to keep from making any sound. The despair she saw in Christian Marshall—despair over what, she did not know—touched a chord in her heart and made her want to cry as well.

Christian drew in a deep breath. What he needed, he decided, was a drink. He didn't remember that Mrs. Brandywine had removed all his liquor until he opened each drawer in the bedside table and found them all empty. He considered whether he wanted a drink badly enough to go out for it. The answer was no. He decided to put on a pair of trousers and go to the kitchen for a cup of warm milk. Just the

126

thought of drinking warm milk was mind numbing. He'd probably fall asleep at the table.

Jenny understood exactly what Christian was looking for when he went through the drawers, and assumed when he padded into his dressing room that he was preparing to go out for a drink. She decided to stop him in the only way she could think of.

Christian had gotten one leg into his pants when he heard Jenny's whimper. He cursed softly. He wasn't up to another battle with her, he thought as he hobbled into the bedroom, trying to finish dressing as he went. He tucked in his nightshirt and snapped his suspenders in place just as he reached the bed.

"What is it you want from me?" he asked plaintively. "I'm damn—darn—certain I'm not crawling into that bed with you."

Jenny moaned softly and clutched her pillow. She ground her teeth together, tautening the muscles in her face. Her fingers opened and closed spasmodically. Christian responded by sitting on the edge of the bed.

"Oh, hell," he whispered as he lifted her head and placed it on his lap. "Mrs. B. would be better suited to this." He stroked her hair, threading his fingers through it gently. "She likes cats and children. I can't abide either. And there's a bit of both of those in you, Jenny Holland." Christian grimaced as she snuggled against him and made it more difficult for him to ease out from under her. At least he didn't have to wrestle her again.

Christian leaned back against the headboard and tried to find a comfortable position for himself. His bare feet were cold. He adjusted the blankets that covered Jenny so they covered his feet too. He pushed a pillow behind his back for extra support. Every time he moved he did so with caution, so as not to wake Jenny or frighten her.

It took some ten minutes of adjusting this way and that before Christian was satisfied that he could nap without disturbing her. He'd get out of the bed before she woke in the morning and she'd never know they'd shared the same blankets. Christian suppressed a yawn and felt his lids growing heavier. He'd forgotten to turn back the lamp, he realized. Too late now. It would have to burn itself out because he wasn't moving. Jenny Holland was a better soporific than a cup of warm milk.

Jenny waited until she was certain Christian was sleeping before she gingerly moved away from him. There was plenty of room in his wide bed for both of them. She scooted to the far side and hoped that Christian, given time, would stretch out more comfortably. She slipped one arm under her pillow, elevating her head slightly, and was deeply asleep in minutes.

It was the heat and hardness against her buttocks that woke her. She knew she had slept a few hours at least. The lamp had burned itself out and the misty gray light of dawn filtered through the drawn curtains. Outside, the storm had stopped and there was a heavy silence beyond the windows that Jenny associated with falling snow.

There was a brief, panicked moment when she thought she wasn't awake at all, but trapped in another nightmare with William MacCauley. The truth of her situation, when it came to her, was much more difficult to know how to handle. This was Christian Marshall who held her now, and if William's grip about her waist had been strong, this man's grasp was unbreakable. His arm curled completely around her middle so that she was actually lying on the hand he had slipped under the curve of her waist.

Jenny held herself very still, afraid to make any movement that might encourage him. Was he sleeping? He had to be. Against the nape of her neck she could feel the even cadence of his breathing. It was soft and warm and it tickled. His mouth must be very close to her skin, she thought. Somehow she resisted the urge to touch the back of her neck with her hand or lower her head out of his way.

When one of Christian's legs nudged Jenny's she almost came out of her skin. His knee was seeking to part her thighs, and it was the first time she realized just how far her nightshirt had ridden up her legs. She heard him moan softly, something between a sigh and a yawn, then he adjusted his position so that he was cuddling her even closer. Jenny held her breath until she felt him relax, then released the air in her lungs slowly and began to ease away. She bit her lower lip when she realized his fingers were tangled in her hair. What was she supposed to do now? Jenny couldn't help but think of times William McCauley had come to her in just this manner. If Christian touched her breasts she knew she would gag.

But Christian did not touch her breasts. What he did was lower his head so that his cheek rested against the silkiness of her sable brown hair and whisper a name. "Maggie."

Jenny was surprised by a surge of outraged feminine sensibility. She elbowed Christian sharply in the ribs.

"Owww!" he grunted, blinking. His vision was bleary. "What the hell did you do that for? You used to like it when—"

"I *never* liked it," she gritted, pushing at his arm. Unable to budge him, she pummeled his shins with her heels instead. "Now let me go!"

Christian shook her. "Dammit! Stop—"

"And kindly stop swearing!"

That admonishment brought Christian to his senses as nothing else could have done. He released her immediately and rolled away. "You're not Maggie," he accused, sitting up in bed.

Jenny sat up as well, wrapping herself in a blanket. Her dark brown eyes were equally accusing. "I certainly am not!"

Christian closed his eyes a moment, pressing his thumb and forefinger to his lids. "I don't believe this," he murmured. "What are you doing in my bed?" Then he remembered the events of last night and swore again under his breath. He glanced at the clock on the mantel. It was after seven. So much for his intention to return to the divan. How did he keep getting himself into these situations? "Never mind," he said with weariness. "Stay where you are. I'm getting out."

Jenny immediately felt a stab of pity for him. This was, after all, his bed, and she was the intruder. How could she blame him for thinking she was some Maggie person when she had thought he was William McCauley? She gathered the blanket about her shoulders like a shawl. "No, you stay. I hardly know what I'm doing here myself."

"You don't remember?"

Jenny turned away from him and put her legs over the side of the bed, modestly covering her bare legs with the hem of the nightshirt. "Bits and pieces. That's the way it usually is." She could have told him she recalled some things more clearly than others, such as the moment when she awoke and found him sobbing in the cradle of his hands.

"This has happened to you before?"

"Sleepwalking? Many times." Jenny lifted her chin and cast a defiant look over her shoulder. "Do you think that makes me insane, Mr. Marshall?"

"I have no idea, but if you set one foot on the floor right now I'm bound to tell you that the scales will be tipped on the side of insanity."

Whatever was that supposed to mean, she wondered, sliding off the edge of the bed. Both of her feet touched down on the floor and she stood. The sensation was alarming and she gasped. It was as if she were walking on pins and needles. The sharp pricks of pain brought tears to her eyes and she fell back on the bed. "How could you know?" she demanded, raising one foot so she could see the sole. "What have you done to me?"

"Done to you?" he repeated, feeling his temperature rise at her unfounded assumption. "You have incredible gall. There are dozens of glass crystals embedded in your feet. And no, I didn't put them there. Apparently you walked all over the glass that shattered in your room before we found you."

Jenny knew she was looking at him stupidly, blinking at him hugely as if he were the one who had lost his mind. "Glass?

What glass? What are you talking about?"

Christian frowned. "You really don't remember, do you?"

"I told you, bits and pieces." She looked away, trying to put the events right in her own mind. "I was having a nightmare and I remember being very cold and wet and . . . frightened."

"An understatement. You were frozen, dripping, and terrorized. It was one hell of a nightmare. What were you dreaming?"

Jenny shook her head. It had been, as he said, one hell of a nightmare, but she was not going to share it with him. "I'd like to go back to my own room now," she said lowly.

"Haven't you heard anything I've said? There are splinters of glass in your feet. That's why it hurts to walk. The storm shattered a window in your room."

"I remember the storm. I couldn't sleep."

"Yes, well, you had a restless evening even after Mrs. B. and I brought you in here." Christian refused to say any more. She could make what she liked of the fact that he had been in bed with her—was still in bed with her. "Lie back down and get a little more sleep. You can't do anything until Dr. Turner takes care of your feet." Christian swung his legs out of bed. "I'll ring for Mrs. B. and have her send someone for Scott."

"No! My feet don't require Dr. Turner's skills. I'll take care of them myself. Do you have a pair of tweezers?"

"You're not serious."

"I am. Please, Mr. Marshall. I'm sick to death of troubling people." When he merely rolled his eyes, Jenny sniffed. "Very well. I'll find them myself. I seem to remember a pair in the dressing room." Jenny slid to the opposite side of the bed, not even aware that Christian made a grab for her. Gripping the footboard of the bed, she tiptoed around the edge of the bed. Confident of her own cleverness and self-reliance, she shot a smug smile at Christian. The smile he returned was a sneer that brought Jenny up short. She wavered on the balls of her feet between the bed and the rocking chair. Her arms flung out, seeking purchase on the furniture and balance for herself.

131

"I despise martyrs," he bit out, watching her weave. "Now put yourself back in that bed or I swear I'll throw you there!"

Jenny was too startled to move in any direction. What had she done to deserve his anger? Her fingers gripped the back of the rocker and she tried to steady herself. She winced slightly as the soles of her feet touched the floor. "I will not be bullied by you, Mr. Marshall," she said with what she thought was great dignity. "You may be my employer, but—"

"That does it," he growled, cutting her off. "You've just reminded me that I don't need your permission. You *work* for me."

Jenny had time enough to turn but no opportunity to run. "Let me go!" she said in her harsh whisper as Christian's arm snaked about her waist. His grip was so powerfully hard that she was winded for a moment. Her next protest died in her throat.

Christian picked Jenny up easily. Although she flailed at him, he managed to dodge her blows. "I've had just enough of your self-styled martyrdom, Jenny Holland!" He pitched her on the bed. "Now stay there! I'll get the tweezers and take the splinters out myself. You can't imagine how pleasurable I'll find that task." He stalked off into the dressing room, the set of his shoulders and his doubled-up fists daring her to move while his back was turned.

Jenny was sitting at the head of the bed when Christian came back. Her arms were crossed in front of her and her mouth was set mutinously. She glared at him.

"Your show of defiance is duly noted," he said, sitting down. He brusquely motioned her to move back a little and put her feet on his lap again. He lifted her left ankle and pressed his thumb into the ball of her foot. Shards of glass glittered. He took aim at one with the point of his tweezers.

"You probably torture small animals as well."

Christian frowned. "What's that again?"

"What you said last night . . . about disliking cats and children. I see that it's true. A great bully like you would . . ."

Jenny bit back her words and knew even as she did so that it was too late. She could practically hear Christian's thoughts as his scowl deepened.

"You were awake," he said accusingly. He dropped the tweezers and grabbed Jenny by the back of her knees, dragging her toward him. She kicked, but he subdued her quickly. Her calves lay across his lap and the back of her thighs pressed his. Jenny's nightshirt had ridden up almost even with her hips and neither of them noticed. Christian leaned over her, holding her wrists still with a grip that made no allowance for her fragile bones. "Damn you! You were awake!"

Jenny shivered at the rigid anger she saw on his face. She closed her eyes, blocking out the sight of his taut jaw and the tiny white lines of fierce, hot fury that were forming around his mouth and between his brows.

"Look at me!" he gritted out between clenched teeth.

Her attempts to get away failed. Jenny's back arched and she tried to dig into the mattress with her heels. The placement of Christian's thighs prevented her from getting purchase. The tender skin of her wrists was pinched and twisted as Jenny struggled to free herself. Christian's hands were more powerful and far less giving than the leather restraints she was used to. Only when she acknowledged the futility of escaping his hold did Jenny open her eyes. Her gaze fastened on a point beyond his shoulder.

"At me! Not at the wall! Look at me!"

Jenny's eyes darted wildly before they settled on Christian's face. Even now she could not look directly at his pale blue-green eyes. Her focus was the muscle working rhythmically in Christian's lean cheek.

"How long were you awake?" he demanded. When she didn't answer quickly enough to suit Christian, he gave her a little shake to punctuate his question. "How long?"

"Please let me up," she said, unaware of the tears that glistened in her eyes.

But Christian was very aware of them. "Don't you dare start

133

crying," he fairly growled. "Now, answer me. How long were you awake?"

Jenny couldn't get a single word past her thickening throat. She swallowed hard and shrugged. Her eyes pleaded with him for understanding.

"I swear to God I'm going to beat you unless you tell me what I want to know," Christian snarled.

His threat effectively dissolved the lump in her throat. She caught a sob when he shook her roughly and made her head snap forward. "I-I woke up when you s-sat down on the bed. You p-put my head on your l-lap and j-just held m-me."

"Stop that infernal stammering! I'm not swayed by tears! Credit me to know a lie when I hear one, especially when it's told as pitifully as you tell it."

"I c-can't help it." Jenny did not know if she was apologizing for crying or lying. She couldn't seem to control either.

Christian lowered his head just enough so that he caught her gaze. Once he had it, he held it with the cold, mesmerizing charm of a cobra. "You were awake when I came over to the bed, weren't you? You played the outraged innocent this morning, but last night you let me crawl under the covers with you. You laid your head in my lap and let me stroke your hair. Why, Jenny? Why did you do it? What game are you playing with me . . . with all of us?"

"No game," she said quickly. "I swear there's no game."

"Tell me more."

"I-I woke up and s-saw you . . ."

"Yes? Saw me what? Dammit, Jenny! What was I doing?"

"Y-you were cr-crying and I f-felt s-sorry for . . ." It was the wrong thing to say. If he hadn't been pressing her for answers, Jenny knew she would have been able to invent something more palatable than the harsh truth.

"I don't want your pity," he grated, his cool eyes boring into hers. "More than that, I don't need your pity." His grip on her wrists tightened fractionally. "What else did you see?"

Jenny's fingers were numb from the pressure Christian

134

applied to her wrists. She bucked, trying to escape him again. Her neck arched, exposing the vulnerable white curve of her throat as she dug the crown of her head into the mattress. Her head jerked in small, agitated movements and her eyes dropped away from his.

Christian rearranged his position. He lay alongside Jenny and threw one of his legs over both of hers. His hands maintained the hold on her wrists, but he pressed more of his weight against her, pinning her with his chest and hips. It became clear in a matter of seconds that her strength was insufficient to move him.

Jenny's fingers itched to get hold of Christian's suspenders. Nothing would have given her greater pleasure than to draw them back as far as New Jersey and let go. She'd sling shot him to Albany . . . to Canada . . . to—

Christian interrupted Jenny's musings as he repeated his demand. His eyes slid from the pulse beating at the base of her throat and fastened on the tremulous pink curve of her mouth. "What else did you see?"

Bewildered, she frowned. "I don't know what you're talking about. What else was I supposed to see?"

He didn't know if he could believe her. Had she really not witnessed his attempt to sketch her? "Look at me and tell me that."

Raising her eyes, Jenny found herself trapped by his gaze once more. "Tell you what? I can't tell you what I don't know and I don't know what I was supposed to see." She felt tears congealing in her throat again and cursed herself for them. Christian Marshall wasn't the only person who wanted privacy for his tears. "I-I s-said I saw you cr-crying and that's all I s-saw."

"All right," he said after a long moment, "I'll accept that— for now." If she hadn't seen him drawing, then she had no explanation for what moved him to tears. That suited Christian perfectly. As far as he was concerned, Jenny Holland knew too much about him already. "So, you saw me crying and the compassionate side of your nature came to the front. You faked the little scene that got me into bed." Perhaps she had faked the nightmare as well. She could be capable of anything. The thought fueled his anger.

"It w-wasn't like that," she denied. She hated the sneer she heard in his voice and his continued suspiciousness. "You're making it sound . . . I don't know, as if I w-wanted something from you."

"Didn't you?"

"No!"

"Didn't you want me in bed with you?" His head bent lower so that his mouth hovered above hers. "Isn't that why you laid your head on my lap?" he demanded. "Isn't it? You have the most perfect mouth. I couldn't help thinking . . . Did you want me then? Hmmm? Jenny Holland? Did you want me?"

"No," she whispered, horrified by the image he was forcing her to see. She couldn't look away from him. Her body burned where he touched her. "No, I didn't . . . I don't want—"

Christian's head dipped quickly, without warning, and his lips ground against hers. Surprise was on his side, and Jenny's startled gasp gave him an unexpected opening to the sweetly warm recesses of her mouth. The pressure of his lips increased so the kiss held more in the way of contempt than passion. His mouth slanted across hers, bruising her with the force of his anger. His tongue speared her, ravaging her mouth, raping her senses.

Jenny twisted beneath him as panic began to overwhelm her. The weight of his body on hers was like being held underwater. He was sucking the air from her lungs and she was drowning. There was no screaming this time. Christian's mouth swallowed the sounds she made, and even to her own ears her protests sounded like the throaty erratic murmurs of desire.

Jenny managed to turn so that her hip pressed sharply into Christian's groin. He groaned, but not from pain. She felt him swell and harden as he rubbed himself against her. Jenny knew she was going to be sick.

Jenny clamped her mouth shut the moment Christian's head lifted a fraction. She knew he intended to renew his assault, but she was not going to make it easy for him. Her teeth ground together so that when his mouth touched hers again she gave him no opening. She felt his tongue darting, probing, as he tried to gain entry. Jenny jerked her head aside and Christian's mouth grazed her cheek.

"No," he said lowly, his breath hot on her skin. "That isn't what I want. Give me your mouth, Jenny."

She shook her head and tried to wriggle her wrists free of his bruising grip.

Christian's lips nuzzled the curve of her jaw just below her ear. "Your mouth," he said again. "Open it for me."

Agitated, Jenny made a tight sound of refusal.

"What's this?" he asked, anger edging his voice when she didn't cooperate. "Have you forgotten what I told you before?"

This time Jenny refused to answer or even look at him. She continued to stare in the direction of the fireplace and wished she could cover her legs. She hated the feel of him against her bare skin. His trousers were no barrier at all. They only served to remind her that she was the one exposed and vulnerable. Male strength and predatory power were all on Christian's side. Frustrated, she pushed at him again, arching and jerking. Her breasts ached from the crushing pressure of his weight.

Christian's own breathing was harsh. He watched Jenny's nostrils flare slightly as she sucked in air through her nose. Stubborn, mad bitch, he thought. She wouldn't even open her mouth to breathe. Her heart was thumping against his chest like a racehorse's and still she was holding her own. It had the effect of angering him further. He was damned if she was going to best him or use him or pity him. He'd warned her to stay out of his way, and here was the proof of how well she obeyed his wishes.

Changing tactics, Christian released her wrists and dug his fingers into the thick, sable richness of Jenny's hair. His forearms still rested heavily on her upper arms, making it difficult for her to attack with her fists. As near as he could tell, her fingers were still so numb she could not even make a fist yet. "Why is it that you never answer my questions, Jenny?" He waited, knowing she wouldn't talk to him but giving her the opportunity nonetheless. Inexorably his fingers tightened and the pressure on either side of Jenny's head increased. He turned her face toward him. "No? Still not speaking, hmmm? Well then, I'll say what needs to be said. I warned you against interfering in my life, but it seems that you've taken my warning as a challenge. You as good as invited me into this bed last night. I thought I'd made myself clear regarding what you could expect if you found yourself in this position again . . . beneath me. Do you still feel sorry for me? Do you still want to comfort me?"

Jenny blinked up at him then. Her eyes were wide, still, and wary. She felt her stomach heave, and she couldn't even warn him that if he kissed her again she was going to be sick. The threat in his eyes, in his voice was enough to keep her insides roiling.

"You can, you know," he went on softly, menacingly. "You can comfort me in a way I can appreciate. It's been a long time since I've been with a woman." His head dipped again and he touched the corner of her mouth with his lips. "Hmmm? Does the little virgin from the Five Points want to show Christian Marshall what she *doesn't* know?"

To maintain her silence, Jenny bit the underside of her lip until she tasted blood. Christian Marshall was a monster!

"Perhaps she isn't a virgin any longer," he said thoughtfully, moving his mouth along the edge of hers, tracing the full line of her lower lip with his tongue. He felt her shiver. "Is that it, Jenny?" He laughed softly, without humor. "It's more likely that Scott made some sort of mistake, isn't it? I've heard that whores from the Five Points have all sorts of ways of making a man think he's the first. I should have suspected that you could fool a doctor too. Of course, you're not from the

138

Five Points, are you? Or is it just that working for Alice Vanderstell gave you airs?"

He kissed the tip of her chin, and when her neck arched as she tried to avoid his touch, Christian's mouth slid along the smooth, taut flesh of her throat. "Who are you, Jenny Holland? Virgin? Whore? Nursemaid?" Each question was punctuated by a tiny nibble on the sensitive cord of her neck. After he had pressed a kiss to the hollow of her throat, Christian raised his head. "Still want to comfort me?" he asked again. His hips moved against the cradle of her thighs, forcing her to feel the pressure and heat of his wanting.

Goaded beyond reason, Jenny's hoarse cry rent the air. "Bastard! Let me up, you great, hulking son of a whore!"

It was Christian's turn to be startled into silence. These words from the priggish little maid who prettily begged him not to swear in front of her?

"Dammit! Let go of me! If you want comfort, go find it in a bottle! That's where you usually go, isn't it? That's what you wanted last night! I saw you searching for your whiskey, so don't deny it!" Her eyes accused him, dared him to call her a liar now. "And when you couldn't find it, you started to dress to go out and get some! There!" she said triumphantly. "That's what else I saw you do last night! You were going to get drunk and I thought I could stop you. Well, I did, but I wish I hadn't. I wish you would go drown yourself in the stuff. You're pathetic, Mr. Marshall, and I can't think of a single reason you shouldn't drink yourself to death."

Christian's knuckles turned white as he squeezed his fingers around thick masses of Jenny's hair. "Whatever you are," he gritted, "you don't know me at all. I suggest you remember that the next time you try to interpret my actions." Christian could hardly believe he was able to keep such a tight leash on his temper. He had never struck a woman before, but he was tempted to lay Jenny Holland out cold. "I was going downstairs for warm milk, not whiskey," he told her.

Jenny laughed incredulously. "Your lies are even pathetic."

Something snapped in Christian. He'd been bent on frightening her before, teaching her that her interference was unnecessary and unwelcome. She may have thought he had lost control of his actions, but he knew differently. He had known precisely what he was doing. That was true even now, except that one thing had changed. Now he wanted to hurt her. "Sweet bitch," he said. "You'll pay for that."

Jenny's raw scream was silenced by Christian's mouth. He released her hair and caught her by the shoulders. Though she renewed her struggles, her energy was sorely tapped and her blows fell against him harmlessly. His hands moved downward until they found the V collar of her nightshirt. Then Christian raised himself up and yanked hard. The material gave way as easily as if he had been using scissors.

Throwing up her arms, Jenny tried to cover herself. But Christian held her wrists together in one of his hands and brought them above her head.

His eyes dropped to her chest. With her hands trapped above her head Jenny's breasts were thrust forward and offered up to him. They were as beautifully formed as he remembered and he was not embarrassed looking at her now. She was awake and she knew what he was doing. He had not forgotten those times when she had placed his hand on her breast and begged him to touch her. "Why aren't you saying anything now?" he asked. His fingers whispered a trail between her full, taut breasts, paused, then slid lower across the midline of her abdomen. Her skin was warm beneath his fingertips. "Usually you beg me to touch you."

Jenny turned her head to one side and closed her eyes. "This is rape," she said, her husky voice barely audible.

"Not if I make you want me," he said. "Shall I, Jenny Holland? Shall I make you want me?" As he spoke, Christian's palm cupped the curve of her hip. He ran his hand back and forth, raising the hem of her nightshirt a little more with each pass. "I can do it, you know." He lowered his head long enough to trail his tongue along Jenny's collarbone. When he reached the base of her throat he felt as well as heard her bitter invective.

"Bastard."

"I'm not bragging," he said, lifting his head. His voice and his eyes were equally cool. His fingers slipped under the nightshirt and traced the line of her hipbone. "Women appreciate men who can give them pleasure. I've been told I'm quite good."

"A whore will say anything if she's paid enough." Jenny's entire body went rigid as Christian's hand slid between her thighs. "Oh, God! No!" She pressed her legs together to stop his probing, stroking fingers and merely succeeded in trapping his hand.

Christian laughed softly and countered by insinuating his knee between her legs, forcing her thighs apart. "That's better," he said softly, coaxingly. "It won't do any good to hold yourself so stiffly. Feel that? I can make you wet with wanting me." She writhed, trying to move away from his intimate caress. His touch was light, exploring, though Jenny sensed he knew precisely what to do to make her respond. "Much better when you move, even when you're only moving to get away. After a while that will stop and you'll only be moving to get closer."

Watching her closely, Christian saw her quick, indrawn breath as he continued to stroke her. His eyes were once more drawn to her breasts. The coral tips were a few shades darker than the flush that heated her skin. He wanted to touch her, but both of his hands were occupied bending her to his will. Christian used his mouth instead. His tongue flicked back and forth across her nipple, raising the tip to a perfect little bud. She was moaning by the time he treated her to the hot suck of his mouth. Oh, Jesus, he thought, she tasted fine.

Between her thighs, the heel of his hand pressed her mound and cupped her fully. Her hips jerked in response, her thighs parted under the pressure, and Christian's fingers stroked more deeply. God, she was hot and tight. She'd close around him like a velvet fist. Soon, he thought, soon she'd do anything for him. Anything at all.

Tears gathered behind Jenny's eyelids and her insides continued to turn over. Christian's finger slipped inside her. "Please, don't," she rasped in her ruined voice as Christian's mouth began its slow, hot trail to her other breast. "Don't." Her head moved restlessly from side to side in negation of what was being forced upon her. His teeth tugged at the hard nub of her nipple while his tongue made it wet. "Let me up. I'm going to be sick. I swear it, I'm going to be . . ." She choked on the bile that rose in her throat. Gagging, she tried to wrench free of Christian.

Stunned, Christian released her instantly. At first he thought he had fallen for some new trick and was prepared to make her suffer for it. It only took seconds for him to realize Jenny wasn't playing him false. He watched her bound out of bed, covering her mouth with her hand, and careless of her feet, oblivious to the pain, she ran into his dressing room. Moments later he heard the sounds of her being sick.

Christian closed his eyes briefly and pressed the tips of his fingers to his temples. Slowly, still dazed by the enormity of what he had been doing to Jenny, Christian rose from the bed, tucked his loose shirt into his trousers, and followed her into the dressing room. She was sitting on the floor, her head bent over the chamber pot. "I'll get you a glass of water," he said wearily, raking back his hair with his fingers.

Jenny would have liked to tell him that she didn't want anything from him, but as soon as she opened her mouth she retched again.

Christian poured fresh water from the porcelain pitcher on the washstand into a glass. He set it aside while he looked for a cloth. Behind him, the continuing noises of Jenny being sick made his own gut churn. He swallowed hard and closed his ears to the sounds of her distress. Wetting the cloth, he knelt beside her and waited. "Here," he said, when he thought she had emptied her stomach. "Take this."

142

Jenny nodded weakly and took the cloth without looking at Christian. When she was done with the cloth she folded it neatly, concentrating on the task because it gave her something to do with her hands. Christian eventually took it from her and substituted the glass of water. Jenny rinsed out her mouth, spat, and drank a little to cool the burning in her throat.

Christian held out his hand to help her to her feet. Jenny recoiled, clutching the gaping collar of her shift. Christian stood up and rifled the drawers of the chest until he found another of his nightshirts. "Put this on," he said. "I'll wait in the other room. Call me when you're done and I'll carry you back to bed." He sensed her objection before she had time to speak it aloud. "I'm ringing for Mrs. B. right now. I think you'll feel safer once she's with you. I'd like you back in bed by the time she gets here."

Jenny was tucked in bed only minutes before Mrs. Brandywine answered Christian's summons. Jenny's face was still flushed unnaturally, but she managed a shaky, relieved smile when the housekeeper swept into the room.

"Jenny's been sick," Christian told the housekeeper. His tone was matter of fact, without inflection. "I'm going for Scott myself. Her feet need attending as well. Just let me get some fresh clothes and I'll be out of your way."

Mrs. B. acknowledged Christian's words with a brief nod as she bent over Jenny. "Poor dear," she clucked, touching Jenny's forehead with the back of her hand. "You feel a trifle hot. Can't say that I'm surprised after your ordeal last night. You were fair to froze when Mr. Marshall plucked you out of your room." The housekeeper spoke over her shoulder to Christian. "Before you leave, would you ask Mrs. Morrisey to brew some tea?" Her eyes made a quick study of her employer. "You look as if you could do with a cup too. Your face is as pale as ash. Are you certain you should be going after Dr. Turner yourself?"

"I'm certain."

"Then have a care. There's three inches of new snow out there and Joe tells me there's a good quarter inch of ice beneath it. Bundle up." Mrs. Brandywine frowned when Christian merely nodded and disappeared into the dressing room to get his things. "He's surely sick," she murmured to herself. "He's usually quick to take exception to mother-hen remarks." Her attention returned to Jenny, and her frown deepened as she observed the young woman avoiding her gaze.

Mrs. Brandywine sought Jenny's hand and squeezed it gently. "We'll have you feeling more the thing in no time," she promised, forcing a smile. "Mrs. B. cares for all her chicks."

Chapter 6

Scott Turner laid the medical journal he was reading to one side and looked up expectantly as his wife entered their bedchamber. "Has she finally exhausted herself?" he asked.

The look Susan slid her husband was frankly disbelieving. "Amy's asleep because Christian exhausted her, not because she did it to herself. I thought we were going to have to leave her at Marshall House this evening. That would have set Chris back on his heels for spoiling her the way he did. What was he thinking giving her that kitten?"

"I was as surprised as you were," he said, quickly defending himself. Then he defended Christian. "He did say he would keep it for her if you didn't want it here."

"As if Amy would have let me do that. And Christian knew it. That was really too bad of him, Scott." There was more bemusement in her voice than sting, however.

Scott chuckled and patted the space beside him in bed. "Over here, wife. I'll play the lady's maid."

There was a distinct gleam in Scott's eye that made Susan's heart skip a beat. Her smile coy, she ignored his outstretched hands and sat at the vanity. Beyond her reflection in the mirror Susan caught her husband's exaggerated expression of hurt. She pushed out her lower lip in a beautifully sulky pout that told him precisely what she thought of his tactics to make her feel guilty. "All in all it was a lovely day, wasn't it?" she sighed, plucking pins from her auburn hair.

"Lovely," he replied absently as the heavy coil of Susan's thick hair fell away from the crown of her head. Her slender fingers deftly undid the braid, and in a matter of moments her shiny hair lay like a silky shawl across her back and shoulders. In Scott's opinion Susan's hair was her finest feature. Not that he wasn't full of admiration for the almond-shaped eyes and winged brows that gave her a vaguely mysterious air. That secretive aura would have driven him mad if it weren't for the fact that Susan's green eyes were so frank and honest. She wasn't capable of real deception. Prevarication inevitably brought a flush of color to her cheeks and made the spray of light freckles on her nose darken.

Scott's eyes dropped to the choker of pearls that Susan was fingering lightly. He didn't blame her for admiring them. They were beautifully matched and accented the slender stem of her neck perfectly. Christian had outdone himself this holiday, Scott thought. "Some day I'll buy you earrings to go with that necklace," he said.

Susan's fingers fell away from the choker instantly. She picked up a brush, drew her hair over her shoulder, and began untangling the curling tips. The eyes she raised to Scott were anxious. "You know I don't care about things like that," she said. "Should I give the pearls back to Christian? I will, if you want me to. I wouldn't have kept them in the first place if you hadn't thought it would be all right. I can't even think where I could wear them. People would talk if they knew how I came by the choker."

"Christian wanted you to have them," Scott said. "We both know why. He doesn't know any other way to say thank you."

"But he's not thanking me, he's thanking you."

"Yes, but I don't have the neck for pearls."

Pretending to be unamused, Susan gave Scott a sassy glimpse of the tip of her tongue. "Still, it was extravagant of him."

146

"They were his mother's."

"Then it was extravagant *and* sentimental," she said firmly.

"One day they'll be Amy's. That was Christian's real intent, to repay me by providing for her. It would have been churlish not to accept, and until Amy's old enough to appreciate them, I don't know why you shouldn't have the enjoyment of his gesture."

Susan was doubtful but definitely wavering in her conviction. The pearls *were* astonishingly lovely and she knew Christian's gesture had been meant well. She felt compelled to make one last protest. "These should go to his wife."

That raised Scott's brows. "Do you really see Christian marrying? I always thought he seemed quite content with his bachelor existence. No obligations or responsibilities to a single other person. He has his choice of female partners from debutantes to fallen women, and if you'll pardon my frankness, he makes use of them with a fair amount of frequency. I can't imagine that he'll ever settle down."

"Are you really so obtuse?" Susan shook her head and gave her hair a half-dozen crackling strokes with the stiff-bristled brush. "I think he's terribly lonely," she disagreed. "Oh, he enjoys pointing out that you dance to my tune, but he knows that isn't so. And even if it were, I think there are times when Christian himself would like to waltz, so to speak. Now, don't look at me so," she said to Scott's reflection. "I didn't say that he wanted me for a partner."

Scott snorted. "He'd better not."

"Christian likes to goad me," she continued, "and I don't doubt that it's done with a certain amount of affection. By all accounts, his parents had a very happy marriage. It makes sense to me that someday he'll want the same thing for himself." She set down the brush and swiveled in her seat, facing Scott. "I can't help but believe that he's envious of what you and I share. If I didn't think that were true I couldn't tolerate his needling."

"He needles you because you rise so beautifully to the bait."

147

"I rise to the bait because it gives Christian one of his few pleasures," she corrected primly. "It's the least I can do for a man who gives me pearls."

Scott laughed. "If only he knew how easily you see through him. He'd hate it."

Susan rose from her chair and approached the bed. "Help me with the buttons, darling, will you?" Above her, the snowy white canopy billowed slightly as she sat down and gave Scott her back. "Christian was particularly attentive to Amy this evening. I could hardly credit my eyes when he got down on his hands and knees and helped her chase down the kitten."

"Hmm-mm." Scott leaned forward and kissed the back of Susan's bowed neck just above the gold clasp of her choker. His fingers fiddled with the cloth buttons of her gown. "He did seem to enjoy himself tonight, didn't he? I was afraid, after yesterday, that he wouldn't. He was more than a little upset by Jenny's accident." In truth, upset did not begin to describe the state of Christian's mind when he had sought out Scott, yet all Scott could discover was that Jenny had had a nightmare and that somehow she had hurt herself. Scott followed Christian back to Marshall House, took care of Jenny's feet, and could not shake the uneasy suspicion that something was being left unsaid. Jenny was withdrawn. Christian was morose. And that was only a bit more than twenty-four hours ago. Scott shrugged, at a loss to explain the turnabout in his friend's emotions. "I suspect even Christian was moved at last by the spirit of the holiday."

"He should have children. Lots of them. It's clear to the meanest intelligence that he loves them. He'd be such a good father, Scott."

"Darling," Scott said, "when did you become Christian's advocate? And don't say it's the pearls, because I know better. A few weeks ago you were cautioning me that he might not be worth saving."

She glanced at him over her shoulder. "I hope I didn't make him sound as hopeless as all that," she said, frowning faintly.

"And if I did, I suppose it's because I was jealous."

"Jealous? What on earth are you talking about?"

Susan blushed, embarrassed to have admitted something of her fears aloud. She left the bed and drew the gown over her shoulders as she disappeared into their dressing room. "Between the hospital and all the time you were spending with Christian, it seemed as if Amy and I never saw you," she called in to him. "I resented Chris a bit for keeping you so occupied."

"But—"

"I probably shouldn't feel that way," she went on. "After all, I knew the kinds of demands that being a doctor was going to place on you . . . on us. Most often I can accept it, just as I did with Papa when he was alive. Growing up with a doctor for a father, well, you get used to certain things." Susan hung her gown in the chiffonier and unlaced her corsets and petticoats. "So . . . if I sound as if I'm put out with Christian, it's because I'd like to see as much of you as he does." She peeked into the bedroom to see if Scott was listening to her or if he had fallen asleep. His nearness brought her up short. He was standing in the open doorway, one naked shoulder resting against the jamb. Her eyes followed the tapering of his chest hair to where his drawers were resting low on his hips. She smiled a siren's smile. "When I said I wanted to see more of you than Chris, this wasn't quite what I—"

Scott pressed a finger to her lips. "Happy Christmas," he said, drawing off her chemise. He knelt and removed Susan's shoes. Pressing a light kiss to each knee, he rolled her stockings down the taut length of her calves. Pushing those things aside, he stood and took a step backward, admiring the gentle turn of his wife's waist, the curve of her hips, and the lustrous fall of hair that covered her breasts. He brushed aside her hair and smiled wickedly as his gaze lifted to her throat. "Come to bed, darling . . . and wear the pearls."

"Will you be up much longer, Mr. Marshall?" Mrs. B. asked,

tightening the sash on her robe as she peeked in the study. Christian was sitting in his favorite leather armchair, his feet propped on the ottoman. He had a book on his lap but it was closed, and Mrs. Brandywine didn't think he had ever had it opened. His head was resting against the high back of the chair and his eyes were partially closed. "I could stoke the fire for you. It's going to go out shortly."

Christian's faint smile indicated that he was indeed awake. "I'll take care of it," he said, waving her on. "You take yourself off to bed. It's been a long day." There were moments when he thought it would never end. He'd never known a day to drag on so interminably as this one.

"But a merry one," she said, watching him closely. He looked exhausted, much the way he had looked yesterday morning, his complexion gray, his skin drawn taut over the bones of his face.

"Yes," he lied, forcing a deeper smile for her benefit. "Quite merry."

"You were very generous," she said, referring to the gifts of money Christian had given to all his employees. "I know they'd want me to thank you again."

"It's well deserved. I know I haven't . . . been the easiest person to work for."

"No one's complaining."

"Not to my face anyway." Christian lowered his head and picked up his book, opening it. "Good night, Mrs. B. I'll see you in the morning."

When she was gone Christian set the book aside and stoked the fire. He had no intention of returning to his room any time soon. He hadn't slept there last night and thought he wouldn't sleep there again tonight. Though Jenny had returned to her own room, her presence seemed to linger in his, and with it, the memory of what he had done to her. She couldn't be gone from his house quickly enough to suit him.

Yet he shied away from simply turning her out. Scott and

Susan would end up taking her to live with them, and Christian couldn't imagine giving Susan that burden. There was Amy to think of as well. Jenny could hurt the child during one of her nightmares. He had seen the proof of that with Mrs. Brandywine.

Then there was his own staff to consider. They liked Jenny Holland and nothing would sow discontent more quickly than if he were to dismiss her without cause. It didn't seem likely that Jenny was going to give him cause. According to Mrs. B., Jenny was diligent in her duties.

And what of Jenny herself? She wasn't fit to go anywhere without a keeper. That was not a position Christian relished for himself. When he'd told Scott he would let Jenny stay at Marshall House, it had never occurred to him that he would come to regret his words.

Christian turned suddenly, raising his poker slightly as the double doors to the study creaked. When he saw who it was he scowled. "What the hell do you want?"

Jenny had gone pale even before Christian spoke. She had gone out of her way to avoid him yesterday and today, and he was the last person she wanted to see. She immediately began backing out of the room, shutting the doors as she went.

"Come back here!" he snapped.

Jenny froze. Advance or retreat seemed equally impossible. It was the staccato rapping of the poker against the hardwood floor that finally got her to move. She entered the room.

"What's that you have in your hand?" He lifted the poker and pointed to the envelope she was clutching in her fist.

"It's . . . it's my Christmas money," she said, avoiding his pointed gaze.

"For God's sake," he sneered, "are you afraid someone's going to take it from you? Is that why you're carrying it around in that death grip?"

"I . . . no . . . that is, I don't think anyone will take it." She

151

had been going to return it, lay it on his desk and leave it. Jenny nervously smoothed the envelope and slipped it in her apron pocket. "I came for a book," she invented. "I didn't mean to disturb you."

You can't help but disturb me, he almost said. "You didn't come for a book. You were going to return the money, weren't you?"

"I don't . . ." At Christian's hard, cool look, Jenny's shoulders slumped. "Yes, I was going to return your gift."

Christian's hand tightened on the poker. Unaware of how menacing or threatening it sounded, he tapped it repeatedly against the marble apron of the fireplace. "Why?"

"I haven't been here long enough to earn this."

"It's not meant to be earned. It's a gift. That's what one generally gets on Christmas."

She looked down at the floor. "Then your gift was too generous. I, er, I know what some of the other employees received and you gave me far too much."

Christian frowned. "Do you mean to say that you discussed the amount of your gift with other staff?"

"Oh, no," she said quickly, darting a glance at him. "I wouldn't. I didn't. It's just that Mary Margaret and Carrie were talking about how they were going to spend their money, and I realized that you had given me so much more than either of them. It didn't seem right."

Christian leaned the poker against the fireplace and slipped his hands inside the pockets of his quilted smoking jacket. "And what did you think?"

"I thought there must be a mistake."

He shook his head. A lock of copper-streaked hair fell forward. "No mistake."

"Oh." She sucked in her lower lip to keep it from trembling.

"What are you thinking now?" As if he couldn't guess. Christian realized he was becoming quite adept at understanding how her mind worked. He wasn't certain he had any

152

particular liking for the talent.

She sighed softly. "I'm thinking you meant it to be insulting. This money wasn't a gift at all. It's a bribe."

"You think I'm paying you to keep quiet about what happened in my bedchamber. Is that it?"

"Aren't you?" she asked. There was a touch of defiance in her husky voice.

"No. I don't care who you tell. In fact, I'm wondering why you haven't told anyone yet. You've certainly had the opportunity. I left you alone with Mrs. B. and Scott. You could have told either of them that I almost raped you. Why didn't you?"

Jenny made a quarter turn away from Christian. Outside, a street lamp made a pool of yellow light on the snowy sidewalk. She stared at that. "I don't want to be dismissed," she said finally. "I don't have anywhere to go. I imagined you'd send me packing if I said anything so I kept my silence. The money was unnecessary."

"The money was *not* a bribe," he repeated. "And I don't know if I would have dismissed you or not."

She made a small sound in the back of her throat indicating her disbelief. "Of course you'd have let me go. After all, according to you I was the one who lured you into that bed. I was the one who was trying to comfort you. You were simply taking what I offered."

"Isn't that all true?"

Jenny's shoulders stiffened and she crossed her arms in front of her. "You know it's not." She drew in a shallow, calming breath. "If the money wasn't a bribe, then what was it?"

"Talk to Mrs. Brandywine," he said shortly. "She's the one who suggested the amount."

That brought Jenny's head around. "But why—"

"Something about you needing clothes."

After Jenny had withdrawn, Christian slumped into his

153

armchair and kicked the ottoman out of the way. He closed his eyes, pressing a thumb and forefinger to the lids. What in God's name was he supposed to do about Jenny Holland?

Susan came awake by slow degrees, stretching with feline grace. A sleepy glance at the window and the muted sunlight beyond the drapes assured her she had an hour or so before Amy woke. She stifled a yawn with the back of her hand and smiled to herself as she remembered Scott's delicious lovemaking. He'd been fierce and gentle by turns, and Susan had never felt more wanton or adored. She giggled. Happy Christmas indeed.

Warming the soles of her feet against Scott's calves, Susan raised herself on one elbow and studied her husband's angular features. She wondered how long he had been awake or if he had slept at all. There was a small crease between his brows, and his blue eyes were clouded with the strength of his thoughts. He was staring at the patterned ivory paper on the far wall and one corner of his mouth was lifted in a pensive manner. A lock of his fair wheat-colored hair had fallen over his forehead. Susan brushed it back with her fingertips. She continued stroking his forehead even after the hair was out of the way.

"What are you thinking?" she asked.

"Hmmm?"

Susan sighed. Scott was miles away and she doubted very much that he was thinking about their lovemaking. "I've decided that an affair would be just the thing for each of us."

"Hmm-mm."

"There's another man, Scott. Someone I've met only recently, but I know he'd leave his wife if I asked him to. Not that I'd want him to do that. I could be content just having him over a few afternoons each week. Would you mind?"

Scott's frown deepened. He blinked twice and dragged his unfocused stare away from the far wall. "What in the world are you talking about?" he asked, his voice husky.

"It's not important, darling. I was just trying to get your attention." Susan kissed his temple, then fit herself against the hard planes of his body. Her head lay in the curve of his shoulder. "Have you been awake long?"

"No, not long." His arm went around her shoulder. Scott's fingers whispered back and forth along the length of her bare arm. "You?"

"Just a few minutes. For a while there you were adrift with your thoughts. I decided it was time to reel you back in. What were you thinking about?"

"Jenny."

"Oh." Susan considered that. "Should I be jealous?"

"God, no!"

"That's an extremely vehement denial," she pointed out. "Are you certain?"

Scott turned on his wife and kissed her deeply. If that didn't convince her, he thought, nothing would. "Certain," he said, sipping on her rosy lips.

Susan pushed gently at Scott's shoulders. "Hey," she said softly. "I was teasing," Her emerald eyes were faintly apologetic and she cuddled against him again. When they were both comfortable she said, "Tell me about Jenny. Why are you still worried?"

He didn't answer Susan's question directly. "You saw her last night," he said instead. "What did you think?"

"I don't know that I'm qualified to have an opinion. She hardly did more than flit in and out of the dining room while we were eating. Oh, and there was the time she served tea in the parlor while Amy and Christian were cavorting on the floor with the kitten."

"You noticed her then? So did I. What did you see?"

Susan didn't have to think before she answered. Jenny's face was clear in her mind. "Pain," she said. "Withdrawal . . . as if she were terribly hurt and turning away from it."

Scott nodded. "That's what I saw. What was it, do you

155

suppose, that caused her to look that way?"

"I'm sure I don't know."

"I'm sure I don't know either," Scott sighed. "Do you think Christian and I did the right thing by her?"

"If you're really asking me if she belongs in a lunatic ward, then my answer is absolutely not. If you're wondering if she should be staying in Christian's employ, then I'm not certain. You can call me fanciful, Scott, but I think Christian is extremely aware of Jenny Holland."

"Oh?" he prompted. Far from thinking his wife fanciful, Scott was of a similar opinion. Still, he didn't want to feed Susan his thoughts. "Why do you say that?"

"He watches her," she explained simply. "When he thought no one was looking his eyes followed her. When he knew I was looking he made certain that he ignored her. While we were his guests last night I found myself entertaining the notion that Christian was being especially attentive—I don't know, to *prove* something, I suppose."

"To prove something to us?"

"No. He was proving something to Jenny." Susan raised her hands in a helpless gesture. "I really can't explain it any better than that. And don't ask me what he was bent on proving. I haven't any idea. Just as I have no idea why he should want to do it in the first place."

"And Jenny? Is she aware of him, do you think?"

Susan laughed softly. "Oh, darling, do you know any woman who isn't?"

Scott swore under his breath. "I don't like it, Susan. Nothing good can possibly come of it. Jenny's too fragile and, dammit, Christian should know better."

"Scott," she said gently, placing her hand over his heart. "If you feel so strongly about it, why not talk to Christian? Anyway, I merely said that Christian was aware of Jenny, not that he had any intentions of seducing her. She's in his care, after all, and that counts for something with Chris. Credit him with a few gentlemanly instincts."

156

Scott wasn't convinced. "If only we knew more about Jenny," he said, laying his hand over Susan's. "Of her own choice she remains an enigma, and I can't help but think that's part of what makes Christian aware of her." His short laugh was self-mocking. "Now *I* sound fanciful."

"Not really," Susan disagreed. "I don't think you're far off the mark. It's odd, Scott, but I was rather surprised when I first saw Jenny. I kept thinking that I had seen her somewhere before. And recently. That's what made it especially strange to see her tonight."

"Where could you have seen her?"

Susan paused, searching for the right word. "How shall I describe it? Someplace *ordinary*."

"Ordinary? What do you mean?"

"You know, like the butcher's. Or standing in line at the bank or the greengrocer's. That sort of thing. Not likely, is it?"

"No, not likely. Especially not if it was recently. Jenny hasn't been out of Marshall House since Christian took her inside. It's no longer a matter of hiding her. She's the one hiding now, and if *I* realize it, you can be sure Christian knows it as well."

Susan agreed. When Christian wasn't drinking no one was any sharper. The idea that Jenny was hiding from someone or something captured Susan's interest and imagination. She'd have to give it some serious thought. "Then she probably just reminds me of someone. I suppose it'll come to me in time." She yawned sleepily. "Will you talk to Christian?"

He nodded. "If he's not interested in her, then he's going to be offended by what I have to say. He'll probably call me out."

Susan laughed softly. "I never knew two men who enjoyed sparring as much as you do. Sometimes you act like schoolboys."

Scott's grin was sheepish. He rolled toward Susan, partially trapping her under his body. "I just want to lay him out cold once," he said, nuzzling her neck.

"Oh? And what will that prove?"

"It won't prove a thing. But it would give me the chance to operate."

"You still want the lead ball in his leg, don't you?"

He nodded. "I'm going to get it too. Just see if I don't."

"I believe you," she said. Her eyes were soft and her heart had swelled. How dear this man was to her. "I always knew I fell in love with a champion." She would have said more, but Scott's mouth brushed hers and Susan gave herself up to the moment.

"Good day to you, Mr. O'Shea," Jenny said. Her smile was engaging, her expression winsome.

Liam O'Shea tipped his hat as Jenny opened the iron gate securing the Marshall property. His crisp jet-black hair was tousled by the wind. "Miss Holland, isn't it?"

She nodded. "How good you are to remember." She let him close the gate for her and they naturally fell in step together. The wind buffeted them, reddening their cheeks. Jenny tightened her grip on the frog clasp of her gray wool cape. She kept the fur-trimmed hood close about her head so that it hid her face more than framed it.

"I make it my business to remember names and faces," Liam said importantly. "In this neighborhood I have to know who the strangers are. They're up to no good."

"I was a stranger once," she pointed out.

Liam's deep blue eyes danced. He twirled his club with a jaunty air. "Sure, and you were that. But that's before you started feeding me warm crullers."

He made it sound as if she did it all the time, but Jenny had only offered him the braided doughnuts twice; once on Christmas morning and again a few days later. Both times it had been Mrs. Brandywine's idea. The housekeeper's attempts at matchmaking were so obvious and well intentioned that Jenny couldn't take offense.

"Are you going as far as Forty-third Street, Mr. O'Shea?"

Jenny asked, turning her smile on him once more. He was a handsome figure of a man, she thought absently, wondering why she hadn't really noticed it before. He wasn't a tall man, but his broad shoulders stretched the material of his double-breasted coat. The uniform was cinched at his trim waist by a black leather belt and his badge shone brightly from a recent polishing. He wore the standard-issue knee-high black boots, and his stride was filled with confidence. Liam had a wide, open smile and an unruffled demeanor that made him popular with the local aristocracy as well as their staff. Jenny suspected that he kissed the Blarney Stone regularly, but then she never met an Irishman who didn't. It was not the sort of thing she could hold against him. Compliments came as easy to his lips as bitter retorts came to Christian's.

Damn, she swore silently, put out with herself. She didn't want to think about Christian Marshall. She'd managed to stay out of his way since their encounter four days earlier in his study. If only it were so easy to keep him from pressing at the edges of her thoughts. Even now she could hear his voice taunting her. "Shall I make you want me, Jenny Holland? I can, you know." In spite of the cold Jenny felt herself begin to warm from the inside out.

"Are you feeling all right, Miss Holland?" Liam asked.

Jenny blinked. "What? Oh, yes. Yes, I'm fine." She was so warm that she blushed. Let Liam O'Shea make what he wanted to of that. "I didn't hear what you said about Forty-third Street. Are you going that far?"

"Thought you might have missed my answer." He grinned. He smoothed the edges of his handlebar mustache with the tips of his fingers. "Yes, Miss Holland, my beat takes me directly past there. Is that where you're going?"

"Yes," she lied. It was her general direction, not her specific one. "Then you don't mind if I walk with you?"

"Not at all. I'll be pleased to have the company of a pretty colleen like yourself."

And I'll be pleased to have your protection, she answered

159

silently. Jenny knew that where she was going there would be people who'd do everything in their power to see that she was silenced. The criminal denizens of the Five Points didn't have anything on the social elite of upper Manhattan.

Jenny left Liam behind on the corner of Forty-third and Fifth. He had offered to escort her to the servants' entrance at the Vanderstell mansion, but Jenny had declined in what she hoped was a gracious manner. She was thankful Liam was not more persistent since the Vanderstell home was not her destination. The scene could have been very awkward had she shown her face there.

The wind was less biting now that she had turned the corner, but Jenny kept her hood close about her head and her eyes downcast. The soft fur trim tickled her pink cheeks as she watched her feet kick up a spray of snow with each step. Even though she had taken the precaution of wearing woolen mittens and stockings, her fingers and toes tingled from the cold. This unpleasant reminder of what she had already suffered made Jenny more determined to see that justice was done. If she couldn't do that, she thought unhappily, she might very well go mad.

Jenny knew Wilton Reilly was a creature of habit. After a few blocks she turned south to intercept him before he reached home. As soon as she saw him striding along Eighth Avenue, taking his daily constitutional, she would know the time was a few minutes on either side of two-thirty. In the past when she had accompanied him on his walk, she had teased Reilly about his obsession with routine. She had never expected to feel so grateful for it.

Mr. Reilly's brisk walking style didn't allow for wool-gathering or taking in the sights. Those activities were more suited to Sunday afternoons and Central Park. He refused to dwell on anything more thought-provoking than the house-keeper's recent assertion that William Bennington and son were going to hell in a handbasket. Since Reilly agreed, it was hardly a matter to be pondered long. Now his concentration was on the mechanics of walking, shoulders straight, eyes ahead, and arms swinging slightly. His stride was long, purposeful, and quick. He didn't notice Jenny until she stepped squarely in his path.

His first instinct was to tip his bowler, beg the woman's pardon, and continue on his way. It was only when he realized who was standing in front of him that his hand faltered in midair.

"Are you going to strike me, Mr. Reilly?" Jenny asked, her eyes solemn. What she wanted to do was wrap her arms about the older man and never let go. She wanted his protection, his avuncular advice, and his prayers. There had been so many times recently when she was afraid of the course she had set for herself.

"You! My God, it's you!" His voice was not much above a whisper and his usual sangfroid deserted him. He blinked several times as if expecting the woman in front of him to vanish.

"Close your mouth," she teased, resisting the urge to hurl herself into his arms. "You look like a hooked fish." Jenny glanced around. The avenue was virtually deserted, but it was safer if they kept moving. Maintaining Reilly's routine would be important if she were to have even the smallest measure of success. "We should walk."

"I can hardly believe this." He lifted his bowler, scratched his bald pate for a moment, then replaced his hat. "I *don't* believe it. I was so certain . . . that is, we all were so sure that . . ."

"Whatever you thought, you can see it isn't true. But I can understand your surprise. Make no mistake, my being here is something of a miracle. It seems I have a rather odd assortment of guardian angels. Never mind," she added when she caught his puckered frown. "There's no time to explain now."

It was not often that Reilly lost command of a situation, yet now he felt very much at sea. His dark eyes narrowed as he studied Jenny's sweet face. How was it possible that she could

161

still look so innocent, even naive? He hoped that her air of ingenuousness was deceiving, else she would not survive for long. "I can't take this in," he said. "When the others hear . . ."

"No one must know," she said quickly, stilling her panic. "The risk would be enormous. I'm only willing to trust *you*, Mr. Reilly. Can you accept that?"

"Of course," he said without hesitation.

"It will be a burden for you. I'm in need of a great many favors."

"That's of no concern," he replied gravely. "How may I help?"

Jenny felt as if a weight had been lifted. She had cautioned herself against expecting Reilly to assist her, but she realized now how much she had been counting on his help. "There will be risk for you as well. Living in the house as you do, you may come under suspicion."

Reilly snorted derisively. "Allow me to worry about that. Once again, how may I help?"

"I need money. Several hundred dollars will make a good beginning."

Once again Reilly was taken by surprise. His step faltered. "You want me to rob a bank?"

Jenny's breath clouded in the cold air as she laughed. "Oh, Reilly, I believe you have a sense of humor after all. Of course I don't want you to rob a bank. *Any* bank," she added pointedly. "There are some items at the house which I believe you can take without drawing attention to yourself. Selling them will raise the money I need. I've made a list." She reached into a pocket inside her cloak and pulled out a meticulously folded piece of paper. "Here, take this and keep it safe. Don't read it now. The things I've underlined are the ones I think you can take from the house. Some silver pieces, a few items of jewelry, that sort of thing. I've given it a lot of thought and I don't believe they'll be easily missed. The other things listed are items I need you to purchase for me."

162

Tiny white lines appeared at the corners of Reilly's thin mouth as he frowned. "This is all very mysterious. Perhaps too much so. Are you thinking clearly?"

Jenny was taken aback. "Not you too," she said accusingly. "You think me incompetent as well, don't you?"

"Balderdash," he said succinctly. "Don't put words in my mouth. I was trying to interject a note of caution, not comment on your state of mind."

"I'm sorry. It's just that after . . ."

He waved aside her apology. "You don't have to explain."

But Jenny realized that she did. Reilly's understanding of what had happened to her had to be vague at best. He may not have known what had been done to her, but he, like all the members of the staff who had looked in on her from time to time, had thought she was ill. "I can't tell you anything now, but later I promise that we'll talk." She glanced in his direction, her soft doe eyes earnest. "Will you do me this favor without further question?"

He nodded. "Anything you want, but not without question, I'm afraid. For instance, how do I reach you? You haven't even mentioned where you're living or how you're keeping body and soul together."

"And I can't. Not yet. It's better that you know very little." Jenny heard his disdainful sniff and realized she had hurt his feelings again. "Please don't take offense," she said. "I simply don't want to involve you more than I already have. And I must think of the people who are caring for me now. They know so little about me and I intend to keep it that way. I shouldn't want to make my troubles theirs."

"Very well," he said heavily. "I shall respect your wishes, but under protest."

Jenny smiled, confident now that he would not only help her but keep her secret as well. "It won't be possible for us to meet like this anymore but I've arrived at an alternative which I believe will work."

"Go on."

"When you have what I need you'll place a notice in the personal columns of the *Herald*. I will respond in the same manner with further instructions. We can communicate without fear of being caught."

Reilly was not as certain. "I don't see how. Young Mr. Bennington reads those personal columns with religious fervor. If you'll pardon me for speaking so frankly, he's looking for women of . . . of easy virtue, the type who make and keep appointments in their own homes while their husbands are occupied elsewhere."

"I see." Her words were carried away on the wind's back.

"He'd see my name and yours," Reilly went on, "and that would be the end."

"There must be aliases, then." She thought a moment. "What do you think of Butler?"

"Clever," he said dryly. "And yours?"

"Princess."

"Of course." He smiled. "That's very good."

"I'm glad you approve. We're agreed?"

"Yes."

"I must go now," she said, glancing up and seeing that she had accompanied him longer than was her intention. "We're too close to the house. I might be seen." She paused and turned to face him, placing one hand on his forearm. "Thank you, Mr. Reilly. I promise you won't regret this. Someday I'll make it up to you."

His sunken cheeks flushed with ruddy color. "It'll be a pleasure seeing you bring the Benningtons to their knees."

"What makes you think that's my plan?"

Wilton Reilly smiled. "As royalty you can't do anything less."

Stephen Bennington let the gold velvet drapes in the front parlor window fall back. His handsome features were drawn into a taut, thoughtful expression as he turned away from the

164

window. He was still frowning when Reilly entered the house by the front door—a liberty the butler took which invariably struck Stephen on the raw. Why his father insisted on keeping the man employed was beyond Stephen's understanding. It was an old argument they periodically engaged in because it was never resolved. It seemed that William wanted Reilly because most of the Fifth Avenue aristocracy had tried to lure him away at one time or another. His efficiency in running a household was legendary, and there was still a touch of merry old England in his accent that reminded people he had once served dukes and counts. Or so he said. Stephen was inclined to believe otherwise.

Stephen stepped into the hallway and confronted the butler as he was removing his hat and coat. "Who were you speaking to out there, Reilly?"

"Sir?"

"I saw you speaking to someone," Stephen said sharply. "Who was it?"

Not for the first time Reilly thought that young Mr. Bennington was in need of a swift kick in the arse. "I'm sure I don't know, Mr. Stephen," he said politely. "We didn't exchange names."

"Then how was it you came to be speaking?"

Reilly decided to take the offense. "I'm not certain I understand your interest. Is she someone you know?"

The butler's directness took Stephen off guard. "She looked . . . that is, it seemed . . . she reminded me . . ."

"Yes?"

"Never mind." It had only been a brief glimpse, he told himself. His suspicions were unwarranted. He'd only had a tumbler of brandy, but Reilly would have considered him drunk if he had spoken his thoughts aloud. "It's none of your concern." He turned on his heel and retreated into the parlor. "Get me another brandy, Reilly," he said. "And there's no need to mention our exchange to my father. He wouldn't understand."

165

"I'm not certain I understand myself," Reilly said for Stephen's benefit. But he did understand. The Princess had nearly exposed herself this afternoon. She had been wise to think of an alternative way to communicate with him. It was probably a lucky thing that Stephen didn't want to tell his father what he thought he had seen. William Bennington was considerably more cautious than his son, and wouldn't have rested until he was satisfied there was nothing to Stephen's story that a trick of the light or an afternoon of serious drinking couldn't explain.

"Just get me the brandy," Stephen snapped.

"Very good, sir." The butler's mouth bore the hint of a haughty smile as he turned away. Having a hand in Stephen Bennington's comeuppance would be very sweet revenge indeed.

Christian Marshall raked his fingers through his thick hair. "Do you really think I could be interested in her?" he asked Scott. Before his friend could answer he continued. "Susan put you up to this. Trust me, Scott. I don't want Jenny Holland around for a lifetime. Surely it's occurred to you by now that she's hiding here."

"It's occurred to me."

Mrs. Brandywine entered the study with a tray of tea and cakes. When the housekeeper left, Scott helped himself to a cup of tea and wandered over to the window where Christian was standing. "What has she told you?" he asked.

"Hardly anything. And at least one lie that I can name."

"Oh?"

"She said she was Alice Vanderstell's personal maid. She mustn't have realized that I knew Alice has been in the hospital this last year."

"But you let her lie pass."

"Why shouldn't I? I'm sure she thinks she has her reasons. They're unimportant to me."

"Aren't you the least bit curious about her?"

Eaten up with it, he almost said. "Not really."

Scott threw up his hands. "There's no talking to you about this, is there?"

"I'll be sure to tell Susan you did your very best to warn me away from Jenny," Christian said. "I'll also tell her that your concerns are groundless. As long as Jenny Holland stays out from under my feet she can hide here. In fact, I think that Mrs. B. would . . ." Christian stopped when he realized that Scott had ceased to listen to him. He followed the path of his friend's gaze and found himself turning to look out the window. The object of their discussion was standing at the end of the walk in flirtatious conversation with Liam O'Shea. Christian felt an immediate tightening in his gut. When Jenny's hood fell back and revealed the elegant line of her pure profile and the sable richness of her hair, Christian wanted to flatten O'Shea for noticing those things too.

"Should she be outside?" he asked Scott, hoping that he sounded less concerned than he felt.

"I don't see why not. The exercise will do her good."

Christian missed the shrewd glance that Scott darted in his direction because he couldn't take his eyes off Jenny. She was laughing at something Liam said and looked to be hanging on the Irishman's every word. Christian tried to recall if he had ever heard her laugh. He cleared his throat. "She's going to freeze out there. O'Shea should have enough sense to send her inside."

"Jenny doesn't seem to mind. She appears to be enjoying herself. So does . . . what did you say his name is?"

"O'Shea," Christian bit out. "Liam O'Shea."

"Well, Liam O'Shea looks as if he's enjoying himself as well. Jenny could do a lot worse."

Christian made no reply. Jenny had just bid Liam good day and was walking toward the house. The wind or something Liam O'Shea had said had pinkened her cheeks and a smile lingered on her beautiful mouth. Christian had no difficulty remembering what it was like to kiss that mouth. He recalled the soft wet deep kiss with startling clarity and felt the hot tug of desire in his loins. Stepping away from the window, Christian poured himself a cup of tea and wished to God it were whiskey. With what he hoped was complete nonchalance he mused aloud. "I haven't been to Amalie Chatham's place in months. I think I'll arrange to spend New Year's Eve with Maggie Bryant."

Chapter 7

Amalie Chatham was the hostess of one of the most select parlor houses in New York City. Amalie preferred the designation of hostess to madam and parlor house to brothel. In deference to the power she wielded, the gentlemen who visited her establishment were more than willing to help her maintain the illusion of social respectability. The illusion served both the owner and the guests and the relationship had been mutually satisfying for years.

Although Amalie's establishment was not as large or as grandiose in its interior design as her equally famous competitor, The Seven Sisters, Amalie made a reputation for herself by selecting her clientele as carefully as she did her girls. Choosing the men who would grace her salons, and eventually her beds, was done originally out of necessity. Amalie did not have to fill the bedchambers in seven adjoining brownstones as The Sisters did, and she offered only two dozen girls.

Amalie's girls were in some ways a reflection of Amalie herself. Although a number of years past her prime, she still possessed a striking beauty and refinement of features and mannerisms that made one think she belonged in the elite social circles. She cultivated gentlemen friends who held positions of responsibility and power in government, business, and finance. She wore emeralds, furs, and expensive gowns, and thought nothing of attending the theater and opera or driving in Central Park in her elaborately tooled carriage. Amalie liked to be seen in places where other women in her line of business would be thrown out or never admitted. The police did not bother her, it was rumored, because she knew whose pockets to line. No one doubted that the transactions were conducted with an eye for the utmost discretion. Even in Amalie's parlor house it was considered in poor taste to mention the financial side of her hospitality.

The twenty-four girls who boarded in Amalie's establishment on Clinton Place did well if they affected the same air of social superiority. If they did not they were pointed toward Canal Street, where a sailor could have them for fifty cents. Girls did not often leave Amalie's by that route. Although they were charged anywhere from seventy-five to one hundred dollars a week for their room and board, on a single night they could earn enough to make Amalie's rent seem reasonable.

As a whole Amalie's girls were a remarkably diverse lot. It was said that if a man could not find what he wanted among Amalie's collection of femininity, then his tastes did not run to women. Attractive and cultivated, Amalie's boarders were careful listeners and good conversationalists. They knew the social niceties that marked the etiquette of their clientele, and in general they had at least one talent beyond the bedroom to recommend them; some played the piano or harp, others sang. Amalie liked to think her girls would have been as comfortable in the drawing rooms on Fifth Avenue as they were in her private salons.

Jenny Holland didn't know what to expect when she arrived at Amalie Chatham's. There was no sign or red-tinted glass gas lamp to identify the brothel, yet the cab driver who brought Jenny had had no difficulty finding the place. Jenny tried not to think about the odd look the cab driver had given her when she waved him down and announced her destination. She had found herself wanting to explain the circumstances that were

170

bringing her to Amalie's infamous parlor house, but had managed to hold her tongue. After all, she told herself, it wasn't as if *she* were doing anything wrong. It was because of Christian Marshall that she was here.

Jenny was honest enough to concede that there were other factors which contributed to her finally ringing the doorbell at Amalie's. Joe Means and his grooms were celebrating the passing of 1866 in an establishment more modestly priced than Amalie's and in a more dangerous quarter of the city. The Marshall gardener had been drinking steadily since noon, and was now as potted as the plants he nurtured the other 364 days of the year. Mr. Morrisey, the cook's husband and jack-of-all-trades, had surprised his wife by offering to take her to Harry Hill's concert saloon. Mrs. Morrisey, secretly pleased with the opportunity for an evening out, had pretended to be scandalized, and had maintained this posture right up to the moment she linked arms with her husband and walked out the door.

The consequence of so much New Year's Eve revelry was that there were no male employees left at Marshall House when Mrs. Brandywine fell. The housekeeper had gone outside to chase away a stray dog who was whining at the back door, and slipped on the icy flagstones. Jenny found her some twenty minutes after the accident, her right leg bent at an odd angle and the stray dog licking her cold cheek. Carrie and Jenny made a litter to bring her inside while Mary Margaret ran twelve blocks to get Dr. Turner.

Mrs. Brandywine had regained consciousness by the time she was safely and warmly tucked in her own bed, but her pain was enormous, graying her complexion and tightening her skin so that even the dimple in her chin seemed to disappear. Jenny sat by the bed, holding her hand, and waited with ill-disguised impatience for Scott's arrival. She did not require a medical education to know that Mrs. B. had a broken shin bone which would need setting. Instead of passing out again as Jenny hoped she might, Mrs. Brandywine kept calling for Christian.

171

Jenny had come to care too much for the housekeeper to let her wishes go begging. If Mrs. B. wanted Christian, then Jenny would produce him. It was no secret to the staff where he had gone this New Year's Eve. The maids pooled their resources and presented Jenny with cab fare to Amalie's.

Now Jenny's foot tapped impatiently as she waited for some response to her doorbell summons. She saw the cab driver was still watching her curiously and she waved him off.

He shrugged, tipped his top silk hat, and clicked his horses on their way. In more than a dozen years of driving New York aristocracy to Amalie's, she was the first woman he had ever delivered to those doors.

Whatever Jenny had thought she might experience upon ringing the bell, it was not the haughty inspection of her person by an arrogant butler through a grille in the door. To have the grille subsequently slammed shut and the door to remain closed infuriated her. After that rejection Jenny did not bother with the doorbell. She beat her mittened fists against the door.

In the blue salon Amalie Chatham heard the noise and ignored it as long as she thought prudent. Finally she excused herself from her guests and girls and approached John Todd, her butler, bouncer, and occasional lover these past twenty years. She stepped into the foyer and inspected her flame-red hair in the gilt-framed mirror, securing a loose tendril behind her ear. Todd stood behind her, and Amalie's dark green eyes, as glittering as the emeralds she wore, flashed her annoyance. "What is going on out there, Todd? I don't want any trouble tonight of all nights."

"I realize that, Miss Amalie," he said solemnly. Although he had shared her bed more frequently than any other male, John Todd kept his job by virtue of the fact that he did not presume on their relationship. It was important that business this evening proceeded smoothly. Tomorrow, New Year's Day, Amalie would open her doors as if she were no different than any other New York lady and graciously receive gentlemen

172

visitors and serve refreshments from noon until midnight. It was a social tradition followed by another notorious madam, Josephine Woods, and the two hostesses, mimicking the respectability of Mrs. Astor or Mrs. Schermerhorn, competed to see who could receive the most ceremonious calls. John Todd knew that the gentlemen would stay away tomorrow if there was a disturbance there tonight. Josephine, in turn, would be certain to have the most visitors and Amalie would be a bitch for the entire year.

"It's a young lady," Todd said. The lilting strains of the harp in the red parlor could not drown out the pounding at the door.

Amalie's brows lifted. "A young lady? Do you know her?"

"No. And I didn't think it prudent to inquire. I shut the grille and hoped it would be notice enough that she should leave."

"Apparently she did not understand the message or she didn't like it." She put both hands to her head and began massaging her temples. "Get me a headache powder, will you, Mr. Todd? I'll see to the young woman myself. If she's looking for employment, I'll send her to the back door. If she's looking for a particular gentleman, I'll tell her she can find him at Josephine's. That will tweak Josie's nose nicely."

John Todd gave Amalie a brief smile and retreated down the hallway. Amalie walked to the door, smoothed the bodice of her cream satin gown, and slid open the panel behind the grille. She had to stand on tiptoe to clearly see her visitor, but the slight discomfort was forgotten in the wake of her initial shock. This young woman's arrival on her doorstep was perhaps the most fortuitous piece of good luck that Amalie had ever experienced. Her mind was spinning with the possibilities presented and the enormous fortune that could be hers if she were to show discretion as well as ingenuity.

"May I help you?" asked Amalie.

Jenny stopped pounding and took a militant stance, crossing her arms in front of her and thrusting her chin forward. "I have a message to deliver to one of your patrons," she said briskly. "I would like to do so without further delay."

Amalie took immediate exception to her visitor's tone, and compensated for her own anger by answering in a voice that dripped honey. "Just a moment, dearie. I'll let you in." She closed the panel and opened the door, ushering Jenny inside. "Follow me. We'll discuss this in my office."

Following reluctantly, Jenny nonetheless found herself fascinated by her surroundings. She told herself that locating Christian gave her a proper excuse to look in the elegantly appointed parlors but the reality was that she was simply intrigued by what was happening around her.

The parlors were distinguished from one another by the predominant color of their furnishings. They all had velvet carpets, but one was blue, another gold, and still another red. The chairs and sofas were upholstered in matching shades of soft satins and heavy, sumptuous brocades. Crystal chandeliers scattered prisms of light on the gilt-framed mirrors. The paintings on the wall were not vulgar as Jenny expected they might be, but reflected the tastes of someone familiar with fine art. Books and magazines were attractively displayed on small tables among a cluster of lacquered and enameled boxes trimmed in silver and gold.

Ladies in stylish evening dresses, some young, others clearly past the first bloom of youth, yet all of them lovely, were serving champagne to their male guests, entertaining them with an impromptu musicale, or encouraging their conversation. Laughter rose and fell lightly, not intrusively, and the men seemed sublimely content to accept the sounds of amusement as their accolade.

Jenny averted her eyes and hurried her pace as one gentleman, having chosen his lady of pleasure, took her hand and led her toward the staircase and the upper bedchambers. Her cheeks felt uncommonly warm as she stepped into Amalie Chatham's plush, emerald-hued office.

"Won't you please be seated?" Amalie asked graciously. She

174

pointed to one of the twin velvet chairs in front of her desk. "You look half-frozen. May I get you something to drink? A touch of brandy, perhaps? Something to take the edge off the cold?" Without waiting for an answer, Amalie opened her liquor cabinet and poured two drinks.

Jenny hovered for a moment by one of the chairs before she sat down. "Please, Miss Chatham . . . you *are* Miss Chatham, aren't you?" Because Amalie's back was turned, Jenny saw the madam's brief nod and missed her amused, somehow sly smile. "Well, Miss Chatham, I really don't want anything to drink. I'm sure you can understand that only an emergency would have brought me here and I'll be happy to go once I've seen . . ." Jenny broke off as a small snifter of brandy was thrust in her mittened hands. "Really, I don't want—"

"Nonsense," Amalie said in a voice that clearly stated she would not be opposed. "You're shivering and I can't help but think it's partially my fault. Todd shouldn't have left you standing on the stoop that way. Your voice isn't at all what it should be. You sound as if you have the beginnings of a cold already. Go on, drink up. All of it," she added when Jenny merely sipped at the brandy. "Very good. You'll be warmer in no time. Now tell me about this emergency that's brought you out." She took Jenny's empty glass, placed it on the liquor cabinet, then sat behind her desk and warmed her own brandy by cupping the snifter in her palms. "The emergency?" she prompted when her visitor continued to hesitate. "Really, dear, you can't expect that I'm going to allow you to disturb any of our patrons without knowing the nature of your business."

"Oh, I wouldn't have to bother him," Jenny said quickly. "If you'd just let me write the message down, you could give it to him when he's . . . when he's . . . er, quite finished."

"What a quaint way of expressing it," Amalie said dryly. "And how do you think *I* will know when that's occurred? Perhaps you think it merely requires knocking on all the doors and inquiring within. I haven't the least intention of doing

175

anything like that. Now, who is it you want to see and why?"

Jenny opened her mouth to answer, and was startled into silence as the door behind her opened.

Todd poked his head in the door, his eyes raising a question as he saw that Amalie was entertaining the visitor she had sworn to get rid of. "Your headache powders, Miss Chatham."

Excusing herself, Amalie rose gracefully from behind the desk and went to the door. She motioned Todd into the hallway and closed the door behind her, leaving Jenny alone. She whispered hurriedly: "You cannot imagine what has befallen us, Todd! If this is the way the New Year intends to go on, then my fortune is secure. Is William Bennington still here?"

Bewildered by Amalie's leashed, yet intense, excitement, John Todd shook his head. "He left some thirty minutes ago."

Amalie cursed softly. "It's unfortunate, for I'm certain he's the reason our young guest has come here. Stephen hasn't been in, has he?"

"I haven't seen him."

"Just as well. William has a better head on his shoulders."

"What are you talking about, Amalie? Who is she?"

Deep in thought, Amalie ignored Todd's question. "You must find William and bring him here. I've taken the precaution of giving her a powder. Nothing to harm her, you understand, just something to make her drowsy and command her compliance." She winked at Todd. "When the sleepiness passes it will give her the itch, if you take my meaning." She laughed at Todd's startled expression. He wasn't used to her bawdy language outside the confines of her bedroom. "I can get one of the girls to help me put her in a room while you're looking for Bennington."

Todd's dark, satanically winged brows rose nearly to his hairline. "I don't pretend to understand a word of what you're saying. Why in the world would you give her a powder?"

"It's not your concern, Todd. Trust me, I know what I'm doing. It's imperative that we keep her here for now. William wouldn't want to learn that she slipped through our fingers.

176

He'll pay handsomely for the privilege of taking her off our hands. He has a lot of explaining to do. I fancy he'd rather speak his piece to me than to the police."

"You're not making any sense." Todd frowned, worried now by the shrewd glitter in Amalie's emerald eyes. Even her smile was calculating. "Are we holding her for ransom?"

"Don't be melodramatic," Amalie snapped. "Just find Bennington. If you can't do that, then don't bother coming back. Have I made myself clear?"

"As crystal."

"Good." She smiled sweetly and patted Todd's lean cheek lightly. "I have every confidence that you'll be back before we close our doors for the night. That gives you three hours. Don't disappoint me, Mr. Todd. We've had a good arrangement these past years and you've profited nicely. I promise you that won't change if you follow my lead now."

Todd was stung by Amalie blowing hot and cold with him, but he was ever at her service. Her swift mood changes didn't alter his loyalty to her. Besides, he thought, he *had* always profited from her business acumen. This occasion, as odd as it was, was likely to be no different. He glanced up and down the hallway, saw that they were alone, and pressed his lips to the heart of her palm. At another time he would not have dared the liberty, but now, because Amalie clearly needed him for something important, he risked it. Dropping her hand slowly, he held her eyes with his dark ones. "I'll get my coat."

Amalie slipped the headache powder underneath her bodice and escorted Todd to the door. "Come to my room this evening," she said huskily. "I'll be less mysterious with you then." She saw Todd swallow hard in response to the suggestion in her voice and the heat in her eyes. Just knowing that she could still command a man's attention filled Amalie with pride. It was going to be a very good year. She fairly floated along the hallway, humming to herself.

Mere seconds after Amalie Chatham swept into her office she was once again earthbound. Her visitor had disappeared.

177

Amalie cursed heartily, using the gutter language she had learned early in her career. She spun on her heel, eyes darting to every corner of the room, searching out her guest's means of egress. The door which led from the office to Amalie's private suite was slightly ajar. Amalie followed the trail and discovered that Jenny had left the suite by taking a rear exit which led both to the outside or upstairs. Amalie threw open the door to the outside with an angry motion. The dainty footprints were not entirely obliterated by the swirling brush lines formed by the hem of Jenny's cloak.

"Damn her!" Amalie slammed the door shut and leaned against it, catching her breath. Her frustration was only slightly abated by the knowledge that her visitor couldn't have gone far. The powder would be taking effect soon if it hadn't already. The stupid girl was going to freeze to death out in the snow! There was no money to be made in that event. Guided by the purest mercenary instincts, Amalie marched back to her office and out into the hallway to seek some help. It was too late to call back Todd, she decided, but one of her own girls could be trusted to take over for her while she conducted her own search.

Maggie Bryant was coming out of the kitchen carrying a tray of coffee, chocolates, sweet breads, and fruit when she nearly collided with Amalie in the hallway. "What's wrong, Amalie?" she asked. "You look mad as a hatter."

"That's a vulgar expression," Amalie said tartly. Her eyes slid over Maggie's attire, taking in the tightly cinched robe, bare feet, and the tousled disarray of Maggie's curling blond hair, and her pursed lips conveyed her disapproval. Maggie's red velvet robe was modest enough, but Amalie knew better than to suppose that her most widely sought-after boarder was wearing anything beneath it. "You know I don't like you girls using this main hallway when you're not decently dressed. If you want to serve your gentlemen callers something from the kitchen, that's what the rear stairs are for."

On another occasion Maggie might have teased her mentor

for her prudish insistence that the customers were really gentlemen callers. Maggie didn't even care about being taken to task for her manner of dress. Tiresome explanations weren't called for now. Later, when Amalie was more clearly herself, Maggie could explain her reason for using the main hallway. Amalie wouldn't care about the back stairs being icy cold because someone left the rear door open. Maggie couldn't even think who would be so careless. She had used the stairs to go to the kitchen, and when she'd returned to the stairwell with her repast for Christian, the hallway had been bitterly cold. She would have thought the wind was responsible if it hadn't been for the tracks leading away from the house.

"What can I do for you?" asked Maggie. "Is it a headache? Do you want a powder?"

Amalie pressed her bosom. "I have one, but thank you. Who is that tray for? Can you take it to him, then play hostess for me? I need to go out."

"It's for Christian. Normally he would mind very much if I left him in the lurch, but tonight . . . well, it hasn't been a good night for him."

"I hope it was nothing you did or didn't do?" Amalie queried, worried that a customer's complaint might take him elsewhere in the future.

Maggie shook her head. "I don't think so. He was angry when he got here, angry that I was wearing black, angry when he couldn't . . ." She shrugged, shifting the weight of the tray a little. "Let me give this to someone to take to him. I'll borrow something from Dora to wear. That way there won't be any argument from Christian. I'm miffed at him anyway. He had the incredible nerve to call me Jenny. *Me!* Can you believe it? After making such a fuss to see me, he calls me by another woman's name."

"That's all very interesting." Amalie's tone suggested it was anything but. "Don't dawdle, Maggie, I want to leave now. Give that tray to one of the maids and see if you can't find someone else for Mr. Marshall."

Maggie wasn't sure she liked the idea of another girl with Christian, but she recognized that her personal feelings were not the issue. Had the man in question been anyone but Christian Marshall, she wouldn't have blinked an eye at the thought of sharing him. "All right. You go on, Amalie. I'll manage things nicely while you're out." She started to leave, then paused, calling to Amalie over her shoulder. "Where's Mr. Todd?"

"I sent him on an errand. If there's trouble, you're on your own."

Smiling widely, Maggie winked. "Not quite. The police commissioner's visiting Nancy." She gave her head a toss so that her hair fell across her back, and headed for the main stairs. For a few hours at least she could pretend she owned arguably the most famous brothel in the United States.

Maggie found one of the maids aimlessly going through a linen closet. "Leave whatever you were going to do till later," she said imperiously, holding out the tray. "Here, take this to my room and give it to Mr. Marshall with my compliments."

Jenny stopped burying her head in the cupboard once she realized the person addressing her wasn't Amalie. Hiding her cloak and mittens behind a stack of clean sheets, she peeked around the door and forced herself to concentrate on what was being said to her. It wasn't any easy task. Her legs felt leaden, her head was muzzy, and her tongue was thick in her mouth. "Ma'am?" she rasped. "You want something?"

Maggie stamped her foot impatiently. "Take this tray to Mr. Marshall. That's the third door on the left." She frowned when the maid continued to stare at her stupidly. "I don't remember seeing you before. Are you one of the new girls?"

Jenny managed to keep the tray steady, though it sapped her strength to do so. She nodded.

When Maggie stepped closer she could smell brandy on Jenny's breath. "I'm giving you fair warning that Miss Chatham doesn't tolerate drunks, leastways not among the hired help. You'd do well to get rid of the liquor you have stashed in that cupboard before she finds it. I'll give you a second chance. She won't." Her eyes sweeping over Jenny, Maggie conveyed her disgust with an eloquent snort. "You're so drunk now you can hardly stand. That won't do at all, m'girl. Not at all."

Jenny blinked hugely, trying to keep the woman in front of her in focus. Nothing was as it should be, and hadn't been since she set foot in Amalie's parlor house. "Mr. Marshall?"

"Yes," Maggie snapped, pointing a finger in the direction Jenny was supposed to go. "Down there."

"Very well," Jenny said gravely. She started to turn away, hoping to manage the thing without tripping over her own feet. She knew she had no head for liquor, but what she was feeling now was outside the realm of her experience. It was as though she could not direct her body, as if she were no longer the one in command of hands and feet and fingers and toes.

"Just a minute." Maggie stopped her. "What's your name?"

"M'name?"

"Your *name,* you great, stupid girl."

Jenny almost began to giggle. With the portion of her mind that was still functioning rationally, she realized it was probably not in her best interest to point out that she was hardly a great girl when the other woman fairly towered over her. But then Jenny wondered if perhaps she was only seeing it that way. No matter. At the moment she certainly felt stupid so there was no sense in taking exception to the whore's sharp words. "Jenny," she said finally. In spite of her efforts to say it clearly, it sounded like Zhenny even to her own ears.

"Jenny?" Maggie was immediately suspicious. "Is this a joke? Did Christian put you up to this?"

Jenny shook her head, bewildered. "Should I go now?" she asked, trying to be helpful.

Maggie was thoughtful. If she was any judge, then this slip of a girl wasn't precisely to Christian's tastes, but her name did fit the bill. Maggie smiled, thinking that she was about to get a little of her own back. "Oh, yes. You should definitely go now.

And please make certain Mr. Marshall knows your name. Tell him Maggie sent you specially for him."

"But . . ." Jenny was going to say that Mr. Marshall already knew her name, but swallowed the words. "I'll tell him," she said.

Maggie placed her hands on Jenny's shoulders and helped her complete her turn. "That way," she said, giving Jenny a little shove to start her in the right direction.

"Thank you," Jenny said in singsong tones. She gave Maggie a careless grin as she balanced the tray in one hand and twisted the doorknob to Christian's room with the other. She missed the superior, condescending smile Maggie gave her in return.

Christian rolled on his side, propping himself on one elbow as the door opened and closed again. He realized he had fallen asleep during the time Maggie had been gone, but wasn't feeling particularly rested. He rubbed his eyes and stifled a yawn with the back of his hand. "You took your sweet time getting here," he said roughly. The sole light in the room came from the fireplace. Maggie's face and figure were wreathed in shadows.

Looking down at the tray in her hands, Jenny frowned. She searched her memory to find some reason that she should be in Christian Marshall's bedroom. The room itself disoriented her. The ivory curtains she had selected had been replaced by heavy velvet drapes of a deep sapphire shade. They framed the windows and the French doors which led to a small balcony. Gold fringe weighted them down even further. She glanced at the fireplace. The colorful tobacco tins were gone from the mantel and a row of photographic tintypes and a gilt-edged clock had taken their place.

Jenny shook her head, trying to clear it. Her frown deepened as her eyes wandered toward the bed. When had Christian discarded the tester in favor of a brass bed? And why was there a mirror suspended from the ceiling? She had rather liked his canopy.

"This is all very strange," she said finally, walking toward

182

the bed on legs that were no more steady than a newborn colt's. "I think I've brought your breakfast."

"What the hell are you doing here!"

That roar had the effect of collapsing Jenny's legs. She teetered a few seconds before the tray tilted forward and everything slid to the floor. The immediate crash was followed by the tray and finally Jenny herself. She went down with a surprising amount of grace with her legs folded under her Indian-fashion, and her skirt spread like spilled ink around her. Incredibly, the contents of the tray had missed her dress. "Oh, my!" she said, quite unable to control her silly smile. "You're angry, aren't you?"

Words failed Christian. He threw back the comforter and, with no thought for his modesty or Jenny's sensibilities, strode naked from the bed. Hooking one hand under her elbow, he jerked her upright, dragged her toward the door, locked it, then swung her in his arms and carried her back to the bed. All of this was accomplished without any resistance from Jenny—a fact that Christian put down to her being drunk as a sailor in a Bowery saloon. He dropped her on the bed, and found there was a measure of perverse satisfaction in hearing her soft moan. Grabbing the sheet beneath her, Christian yanked it out and wrapped it around his waist. He sat on the edge of the bed, decided he was likely to strangle her if he remained there, got up again, and began pacing the floor.

"I can't begin to imagine what you're doing here," he gritted. "I hope your explanation has the ring of truth, Miss Holland, because I am sorely tempted to beat you black and blue."

His threat made no impact on Jenny. She was staring at her reflection in the mirror overhead. Her eyes were sleepy, her cheeks flushed. The neat coil she had made in her hair was gone. She put one hand to her face, brushing back several strands that lay across her cheek and circled her neck, and wondered what had happened to her pins. The hem of her plain wool gown was raised almost to her knees, but Jenny felt too deliciously lethargic to push it down. She turned this way and that, critically viewing the length of her calves and the curve of her ankles. Nothing there to turn a man's head, she decided. "It's a very odd place to put a looking glass, don't you think?" she asked. "What was wrong with the canopy?"

Her questions brought Christian up short. He stared at her, glowering. "Where in the hell do you think you are?"

"Your room, of course," she said, stretching lazily, still captivated by her reflection. "And don't swear at me, please." She cringed when Christian responded to her request with gutter curses she had only ever heard uttered by madmen and madwomen in the hospital. "Are you quite finished?"

"No," he said, approaching the bed. He sat down on the edge and took Jenny by the upper arms, raising her and shaking her as if she were a rag doll. "Look at me, Jenny Holland. Damn you! Look at me!" Once he had her attention Christian released her abruptly and let her fall back on the mattress. He bent over her, holding her wide, slightly dazed eyes with his own cool, steady stare. "This is not my room," he began roughly. "We're not in my house any longer."

Jenny bit her lower lip, frowning. It could be a trick. That sort of thing had been done to her before. "But you're here . . . and so am I. Didn't I just bring you breakfast?"

Christian shook his head and managed to keep a tight rein on his temper. "No, dammit, you didn't just bring me breakfast!"

"But the tray . . ." She leaned to one side and pointed to the contents that were dashed across the floor. "It isn't kind of you to play with me this way."

Rolling his eyes, Christian demanded, "Why did you follow me to Amalie's and how much did you have to drink to work up the courage?"

Ignoring Christian, Jenny raised her eyes to the mirror overhead and saw that her face was accurately reflecting her complete confusion. She forced herself to concentrate, thinking hard. "Amalie's," she said lowly. "I had forgotten about that. I met her downstairs, but I'm not certain I like her,

184

Mr. Marshall. She was kind enough, I suppose, but not very helpful. Not really. I don't think I like the way she kept staring at me." Jenny's frown deepened. "Why do you think she did that? Stare at me, I mean. It was terribly rude of her."

"Oh, God," Christian sighed. "She was probably taking measure of your potential."

"My potential?"

Christian nodded. Placing one hand on either side of her shoulders, he leaned forward so that he blocked Jenny's view of her reflection. "Hmmm," he said. "Your potential." His head bent lower. "For this."

Surprise was Christian's advantage. Jenny was so startled by the pressure of his mouth against her lips that she didn't struggle. Neither did she offer any encouragement. She held herself very still and let Christian sip and taste the corners of her mouth and draw in her lower lip between his teeth. He bit down very gently. An alien surge of heat blossomed in her middle as his tongue flicked along the soft underside of her lip, bathing the wound he had only pretended to inflict.

Christian raised his head and studied Jenny's serene expression. Her eyes were closed. There was a pale wash of color to her cheeks and her lips were damp and slightly parted. She could have been asleep. "Amalie will want to know that she probably overestimated your potential," he said bitterly, sitting up again. "You can't work in this house and not know how to please a man." Christian's words were at odds with the hot tongues of flame licking at his vitals. He was so hard he hurt. He tried not to think about the unreciprocated ache he felt for Jenny Holland. "Why did you follow me here?" he repeated, wearily raking his fingers through his hair.

Jenny's lashes fluttered and she opened her eyes. She was rather sorry the kiss was over and that bothered her. It didn't seem as if she ought to feel that way, yet she could not help but acknowledge that Christian's kiss had been something more than pleasant. She touched her lips with the tip of her tongue. They were so sensitive she hurriedly pressed them together, denying the frisson of pleasure that threatened to shoot through her. "I don't want to work for Amalie," she said. "I like working for you. Aren't you pleased with my work?"

Christian groaned. There was virtually no hope of getting straight answers. Jenny seemed to be a beat behind his every question. "Yes, Jenny, I'm pleased with your work."

Jenny's smile was lopsided but triumphant. "There! You see! You're a man and I've pleased you. I must have some potential."

Forcing a patience he didn't feel, Christian bit back an angry retort and tried to indulge her drunken logic. "I must have mistaken the matter, then," he said. "You're very good at what you do. But let's forget that now, shall we? Tell me about coming here. Were you already three sheets to the wind when you arrived?"

"Three sheets? I don't know what—"

"Were you drunk when you got here?"

Jenny shook her head, moaning softly as the small motion made her dizzy. "I'm not drunk," she denied. "I only had one glass of . . . I don't remember what it was."

"Brandy. Your mouth tastes like brandy." It was sweet, he wanted to tell her. Her mouth was soft and smooth and silky. He had enjoyed that kiss even if she hadn't. "But I think you had more than one drink."

"I didn't." She saw his skeptical look. "Really, I didn't. Amalie gave me the drink. We were in her office, you see, and I wanted to see you but she wanted to talk and . . ." Jenny's voice trailed off momentarily as she became fascinated by her reflection again. "Oh, it's all very confusing. My head feels so . . . so thick. I don't think I'll drink any more, Mr. Marshall. I used to feel like this before they put me in the hospital. I didn't like it then and . . ." She grew silent once more, worried now. "Are you going to make me go back to the hospital?" she asked suddenly, anxiously.

"No, not if you don't want to go."

"I don't want to," she said quickly. "Ever. I couldn't go

186

back there. I'd never be able to stand it . . . all the screaming . . . the hands . . . touching me. I didn't like it. I was always afraid that . . ." She stirred restlessly, stretching again. She wasn't tired in the least, yet her body felt very heavy and her skin felt too tight for her frame. Collecting her thoughts was difficult. "What's wrong with me, Mr. Marshall?" she asked plaintively. "Why can't I remember things? Why do I feel so strange?"

"What do you feel that's strange, Jenny?" Christian was beginning to have a very good idea what was wrong with her, and he cursed Amalie under his breath. Jenny may very well have had one brandy. Christian could only guess what Amalie might have used to lace it. He leaned closer to her, making her look at him, forcing her to concentrate. "Tell me what you feel."

Jenny caught her lower lip, worrying it. "Light," she said after a moment's thought. "And heavy . . . aching. I feel empty. I want . . . I want *something*."

Christian had no difficulty identifying the something Jenny could not. He'd heard rumors about the drugs Amalie made available for men who made extraordinary demands on themselves and their female partners. Until now he'd never believed it. He cupped Jenny's face, holding her still. "Did Amalie send you up here after she gave you the brandy?"

"No." Jenny's eyes dropped to Christian's mouth. It was a beautiful mouth, she thought. She sighed softly, wishing he would kiss her again. "Someone came to the door and she left her office. I decided to look for you. I didn't want to be alone with her again. Did I tell you I didn't like Amalie?"

"You mentioned that." Christian jerked as Jenny twisted and rubbed her hip against his thigh. "For God's sake, don't do that!"

Jenny wasn't even certain what she had done but she was instantly contrite. "I'm sorry," she murmured. She blew away a strand of hair that had fallen across her mouth. "It's very hot in here, don't you think? We could do without the fire. I'll be

187

sure to tell Mrs. B. that you don't require such a large fire."

"Jenny, we're not in my room," he reminded her.

"Oh," she giggled. "That's right. Mrs. B. asked me to come and fetch you home. And I said I would. Oh, dear. You're glowering at me. Are you angry about that?"

"I'll take it up with Mrs. B. when I see her." Christian believed that he would cheerfully strangle his housekeeper for her interference in his life. Just because Mrs. Brandywine didn't approve of his plans for New Year's Eve was no reason for her to send Jenny after him. He made an effort to stop looking at Jenny as if she were his intended victim. "If Amalie didn't send you up here, who did?"

"I told you. Mrs. B. did. She—"

"That's not what I meant," he interrupted. "How did you get up here? How did you find me?"

"Why didn't you say so?" she asked, her tone accusing. "You have to be clear, Mr. Marshall. It's not easy for me to understand things right now."

Christian marveled at her ability to understate the situation. "Jenny, please answer my question. How did you find me?"

"Maggie showed me your room," she said, making it sound as if it were the most natural explanation in the world. "She told me to take the tray and make sure you know my name is Jenny. But you already know that, don't you? I can't think why she would want to make an issue of it." Jenny drew in a deep breath and asked suddenly, "Will you kiss me, Mr. Marshall? Unless you'd rather not. I wouldn't ask except that . . . well, I don't know why I'm asking. I'm sure I'll be embarrassed once I think about it. If you're afraid I'll get sick again, I'll understand. Only, I don't think I will. I'm not sure how I know that, it just occurred to me and I think it's true. But if you don't want to . . . why are you looking at me like—"

"Jenny."

"Yes, sir?"

"You talk too damn much."

"Oh."

188

"Close your mouth."

She did. Her eyes never wavered from his darkening ones. Christian waited, watching her carefully, judging her readiness. "Now open it," he ordered at last. "Quietly."

Jenny's lips parted on a soft sigh as Christian's mouth settled over hers. The pressure was light, tasting, and made Jenny hunger for something more substantial. Her fingers made a lazy climb up the length of his arms and came to rest on his naked shoulders. His flesh was warm, his muscles taut. As Christian slowly deepened the kiss, exploring the soft underside of her lips with the edge of his tongue, Jenny's palms circled the back of his neck and held him against her. She returned his kiss, matching the darting movements of his tongue because of a need she could not understand or deny. Her own submission frightened her. She wanted and she didn't want. Jenny held onto Christian because he was so solid, so real, and she was very much afraid that letting go would mean the end of her hold on reality.

As Christian stretched out beside Jenny, the sheet around his waist loosened. The covering dipped low over his hips, working its way downward as Jenny arched and twisted in her efforts, not to get away, but to get even closer. He didn't realize the sheet had finally been kicked aside until he felt Jenny stop responding to his kisses. Breathing harshly, he raised his head a fraction and looked at her. Her eyes were open but she wasn't focused on him directly. She was staring at his reflection in the mirror above them.

"Well," he said, watching the rise of color in her cheeks, "now you know why Maggie doesn't have a canopy."

Jenny's reply was stuck in her throat. One of her hands fell away from his neck and trailed down the length of his spine. She watched her inquisitive fingers make the journey and saw the shudder that rippled the length of Christian's naked body. Though Jenny's experience was limited to museum pieces like Renaissance paintings and ancient Greek sculptures, Jenny thought Christian was as perfectly formed as a man could be.

His shoulders were wide, his hips slim. His legs were smooth and bronzed with the light covering of copper-tipped hair. Where they entangled with her legs the contrast between the strength and vulnerability of their positions was startling.

Jenny's skirt hiked higher as she rubbed her leg against him. She wanted to touch the hard curves of his taut buttocks, but her hand froze at the base of his spine. Her fingers trembled as the boldness of her thoughts paralyzed the rest of her.

Christian sensed rather than saw her hesitation, and his loins jerked against her hip, making her feel the hot, hard need she had aroused in him. His mouth silenced the husky gasp that rose in her throat. He took advantage of the invitation of her parted lips and used his tongue to explore and taste her and renew his assault on her senses. One of his hands slipped away from where it had threaded in her hair and slid beneath the hem of her skirt and chemise. His palm moved back and forth along her thigh from knee to hip, learning the shape of her against the curve of his hand.

Feeling light-headed, Jenny pushed weakly at Christian's shoulders. His body was too close to her, enveloping her so that she felt suffocated by his nearness. The kisses he slanted across her mouth took the air from her lungs. The reflection above confused her. The sleepy-eyed wanton who returned her stare was a stranger. The man who partially covered her, the man whose hands were working the buttons at the front of her gown, was equally unfamiliar.

Christian unfastened the first four buttons of Jenny's bodice and drew the dress over her shoulders and partway down her arms. The chemise followed the same path, trailed by the damp path of Christian's mouth. He tasted the delicate line of her collarbone, the hollow of her throat. The warm, steady beat of her pulse in the cord of her neck excited him. His mouth went lower as he tugged at the dress. His tongue whispered across the firm, high curves of her breasts, dipping, teasing, making an ever-widening spiral that finally included the rose-colored aureoles. Hard and puckered, he laved the sensitive skin until

190

the cry that was building in Jenny's throat was released. Groaning himself, Christian's mouth covered her nipple and sucked, feeling the heat that was in her become part of him.

"Mmmm, you really like watching, don't you?" Dora's slender hands closed around the proof that her partner liked the role of the voyeur very much indeed. She began to stroke him, urging a surrendering moan from deep in his chest. His fingers bit into her shoulders as she knelt in front of him. "Close the shutter now, Stephen," she said. "Think about what I'm going to do for you instead."

Stephen Bennington took one long, last look at the shadow-shaded bodies of the man and woman in the other room before he slowly slid the panel closed. Their love play had been exciting. The husky murmurs of their voices had teased him. Just imagining the words they might have exchanged made him grow harder. In his mind's eye he could still see the hot kisses that had been exchanged, the relentless suck of the man's mouth on the whore's breast, the way her hands flittered along the length of her lover's back. Stephen regretted closing the shutter. He wanted to see the whore spread her thighs and accept her randy stallion.

"The woman," he said tightly, trying to control his response to Dora's practiced manipulation. "That wasn't Maggie. Who is she?"

"One of the new maids. That's what Maggie told me anyway." Dora drew back and gazed at Stephen. She thrust out her lower lip in a siren's sultry pout. "Do you want her?"

"Perhaps." He gave a little groan as Dora renewed her efforts. "Keep doing that, m'dear, and I'll never look at anyone else."

Since Stephen Bennington was notorious at Amalie's for never choosing the same girl twice in a row—even on the same night—Dora didn't fool herself into believing his statement carried a grain of commitment.

"And the man?" he asked. The only man he was sure it wasn't was his own father. Stephen had passed William on his way out, a meeting that made both of them uncomfortable in the extreme. Stephen remembered stupidly thanking his father for holding the door open for him. At least Todd and Amalie hadn't been witness to the embarrassing situation. Stephen didn't think he could have tolerated Todd eyeing him through the grille in that supercilious manner that was so much like Wilton Reilly's. Once Stephen was inside, he'd quickly chosen Dora and taken her upstairs. He regretted that his earlier discomfort had made him so hasty. If he had spoken to Amalie when he arrived, she might have seen fit to give him the maid.

"You know I can't tell you who he is," Dora said. Maggie would make certain Amalie gave her her walking papers if she revealed who was rocking the maid in the next room. There was a strict line of confidentiality that had to be upheld, especially with the men who enjoyed watching others. The clientele at Amalie's might meet below stairs, share a joke or a bottle of champagne, even exchange pleasantries, but on the second floor everyone was anonymous. That meant that Christian Marshall would never know he had an audience and Stephen Bennington would never know the male lead in the erotic play.

It was a measure of Maggie's anger, Dora thought, that she permitted anyone to look in on one of her favorite clients. She had always been somewhat guarded where Christian Marshall was concerned. Dora supposed that was over now. Maggie had given him a maid who, as near as Dora could tell, didn't know the first thing about how to handle her man. Christian, on the other hand, seemed to know exactly what to do with the maid. Apparently Maggie hadn't been able to elicit the same response. Poor Maggie. What a blow to her pride that would have been! Bested by one of Amalie's unskilled linen-keepers and sheet-changers!

"Who is he?" Stephen repeated.

Dora smiled slyly. "Why? Do you want him as well?" she teased. She never saw the hand that Stephen raised. The force

192

of the blow to her cheek left her sprawled across the floor.

"Bitch!" Stephen's pale chest heaved with anger. He bent and grabbed Dora's honey-colored hair in his fist, pulling her roughly to her knees, then her feet. She whimpered and leaned against him for support. Stephen discovered that the pathetic sound of her pain and the helplessness of her position were as powerful as one of Amalie's mysteriously potent powders. In the wake of this incredible surge of desire he forgot all about wanting to reopen the panel and see the culmination of the coupling in the adjoining room.

Biting back a sob, Jenny squeezed her eyes shut. Though her body still ached with an emptiness that wanted filling, her mind was clearing by tiny increments. She could no longer watch the things that Christian was doing to her. She could only feel and the feelings were somehow wrong, horribly wrong. Knowing that was not enough to lessen the pleasure.

Her skin was shimmering with heat, tingling with white-hot sparks. They skittered along her arms, her belly, her thighs. When his mouth lifted from her breast there was a brief respite, then his lips pressed their outline to the spot where her heart hammered out an uneven rhythm. Moments later he was raising the tip of her right breast to a stiff point of pleasure with his flicking tongue.

She pushed at his shoulders again, but the protest was too feeble to make an impact on Christian. When she tried to twist away he thought she was arching to fit herself against him. Jenny had to give her objections sound.

"No," she whispered tautly. "Stop. Please stop."

Christian chose to believe he had mistaken what he heard. His fingers urged the bodice of her dress lower.

Jenny found her arms trapped in her gown because of the way Christian was undressing her. She pressed her heels into the mattress and tried to push away, bucking to move him to one side. Her head moved back and forth in negation of what

193

was being done to her. "No! Please, Mr. Marshall. Stop this!"

It was the absurdity of being called Mr. Marshall in a situation of such carnal intimacy that finally commanded Christian's attention. He levered himself away from her, his desire-darkened eyes glittering. "No?" he questioned, his voice dangerously soft. "What are you saying no to?"

Jenny tried to right her gown but Christian stopped her, flinging one arm across her, directly under her breasts. She didn't know where to look. The image in the mirror was appalling. The mixture of rage and wanting in his eyes was frightening. "I don't want you to touch me anymore," she said in a small voice, focusing on a point beyond his shoulder.

"And what makes you think you have a choice?" When she didn't answer, his fingers laced in her hair and tugged lightly, forcing her to arch her neck and connect with his piercing stare. "I asked you something. What makes you think you still have a choice?"

Jenny blinked, wincing as his fingers tightened in her hair. "Don't I?"

"No!" he exploded, his expression hard and unforgiving. "You damn well gave up your rights when you walked in this room! This is a whorehouse and right now you're the whore I choose. Get used to it, Jenny Holland!" He forced her head to one side so she could see the clock on the mantel. "It's almost midnight," he told her harshly. "And I mean this year to go out as I intend for it to go on!"

Chapter 8

Jenny's raw cry of despair was smothered by Christian's hand. He laid his fingers across her lips and turned so that his face was only inches above her. "Don't play at being outraged, Jenny," he whispered darkly. "You've gone too far this time." He waited, watched her swallow all the protests that hovered at the edge of her mind, then slowly let his fingers slide away from her mouth. He cupped the soft underside of her chin while his other hand slipped under her drawers and began pushing them over her hips.

Knowing what was happening to her and being able to do something about it were unrelated events to Jenny. Wherever Christian touched her he was able to urge a response. It didn't seem to matter that she objected with her mind; her body was more than eager to experience Christian's intimate caresses.

The air in the room felt cool on her heated skin as Christian removed her undergarments. Jenny did not look in the mirror because the image she held in her mind's eye was humiliating enough. She wished she could pull up the bodice of her gown to cover her breasts, or yank down the skirt to cover her naked thighs, but her hands remained trapped at her side and she began to feel as if she were being offered up to him. Belatedly she realized that Christian had sensed the sacrificial quality of the act as well and was repulsed by it.

"Oh, no," he said tautly, his mouth against her ear. "I want more than your passive compliance." He removed the dress and chemise so that her arms were free and chuckled lowly, triumphantly, when Jenny's arms went around him of their own accord.

"I don't want . . ." she began softly as Christian's lips pressed kisses to her eyelids. Could he taste the salty tears that welled behind her lashes? "But I . . . *need* . . . I need to be . . ."

"I know." His voice was gentler now. Christian understood Jenny's confusion better than she did. Although her mind was clearer, her body was still a prisoner of Amalie's drug. Christian wished he had a similar excuse for the desire that ruled his actions now. His only defense was that touching Jenny Holland was a powerful addiction in its own right. "Let me help you, Jenny. I can take away the burning."

Was he really asking her for permission now? Moments ago he had furiously overridden her objections, been on the point of raping her, and yet here he was seemingly wanting her approval. Jenny's answer came to her, and she knew then that he had succeeded in doing what he'd promised a week earlier. He had made her want him.

Her hands circled his neck and her fingers threaded in his hair. She pressed lightly drawing him closer, and whispered a single word. "Please."

Jenny's lips were so sensitive to the touch that when Christian's tongue traced a damp line across her upper lip she felt as if she would come out of her skin. The more gentle he was, the worse it was. The burning he promised to ease became more intense. It was only when the pressure of his mouth and hands hardened that she could bear his caresses.

His mouth slanted across hers and she welcomed the bruising force of the kiss. Her reply was equally hungry, equally passionate. His lips touched her face in hard, hurried whisperings. She felt his touch on her temples, her eyes, the bridge of her nose. Her lashes fluttered against his mouth. Her

196

tapered nails scored impermanent crescents in his upper arms. His lips pressed its outline to her cheeks, her jaw, the tender vulnerable spot below her ear. Her mouth was open, her tongue seeking, when his lips returned to hers. Their exploration was no mere tasting now; it was a carnal feast for the senses.

Lips and tongues were not sufficient to convey the wanting that had grown between them. Christian used his entire body to make Jenny aware of the strength of his desire. His hands stroked her, caressing the sensitive underside of her arm from elbow to shoulder. His palms became familiar with the full shape of her breasts, her narrowly tapered waist, the flat plane of her belly. His legs learned the outline of hers, the sole of his foot rubbed her calf.

Jenny's hands flitted along Christian's arms, touched his thighs, the back of his legs. Her knee was bolder, insinuating itself between his legs so she could press herself against him. Her breath caught as he took her wrist and brought her hand to the point where her thighs cradled his. He asked her to touch him. She did.

The hard plane of Christian's abdomen retracted as Jenny's fingers explored the length of his arousal. Her movements were unskilled, cautious, and still infinitely exciting. In a matter of seconds he knew he would lose control if he let her continue. He drew her hand away, raised her wrist to his mouth, and kissed the delicate webbing of blue veins at the back. The soft, little mewling sound at the back of her throat fired Christian's blood. He said her name huskily, kissed her hard, and let his fingers caress her as intimately as she had done to him moments before. They dipped and stroked, preparing her for his entry. She had been hot. Now she was wet.

"Open your eyes, Jenny," he said.

Jenny complied. The hard edge that self-denial had carved in Christian's face was strangely beautiful. Just looking at him heightened her sensitivity to his touch. Her breathing was irregular now. She felt as if she was sipping air, drawing it in in tiny measures with a sibilant sound that was foreign to her.

"Say my name," he said huskily. "I want to hear you say it once."

"Christian."

"Oh, God." He sat back between her parted thighs and slipped his hands beneath her buttocks. Even while her back arched upward, her body clearly wanting him, he felt tension elsewhere as she tried to withdraw from what was happening. "Don't look in the mirror. Look at me. Stay with me, Jenny." Then he guided himself into her.

The carefully measured thrust nearly stripped Christian of control. She was so narrow, so tight. And there was still the barrier. Until now Christian had been able to reject the idea that Jenny could be a virgin. Confronted with the evidence, he'd known it was no longer possible. Then, as she thrust into him, it was no longer true. He was hers, filling her with his rigid, swollen manhood. She was his, accepting the length of him, holding him so perfectly that it seemed they were meant to know each other in just this way.

Jenny felt her body stretching to accommodate Christian's entry. There was pain in the beginning, but it was gone, then forgotten. The ache of wanting returned, the need for something that was just outside the realm of her experience but nearly within her reach.

Clutching Christian's shoulders, Jenny bit down on her lip. "The burning," she whispered. "I still . . ."

"I know," he said, brushing his lips against hers. "Give me a moment. Don't move yet.'

Except for the contractions she could not help, Jenny held herself still. It was the most difficult thing he had asked of her. Waves of heat flooded her body and she wanted to ride the sensation, move with it and against Christian. He filled her, yes, but it was not enough. The tiny beads of perspiration on Christian's forehead, the taut line of his mouth, the dark liquid centers of his normally cool, unaffected eyes made Jenny

198

believe he shared her feeling. He wanted something more as well, and soon they would have it.

"Now, Jenny," he said hoarsely in the manner of a man surrendering to a force greater than himself. "I can't hold . . . wanted you to be ready . . . can't wait."

Neither could Jenny. As Christian's hips ground into hers she abandoned herself to the rhythm he taught her body. She arched, raising herself to meet his thrusts, pulling back each time he withdrew. Their joining was rough and hungry, almost angry with intensity. Her fingers sought purchase among the blankets and, finding them inadequate, she raised her arms above her head and gripped the brass head rails. Her posture was so pagan, so erotically vulnerable, that Christian was nearly undone by her exquisite offering.

Jenny had begun to believe that Christian had lied to her. The burning he had promised to assuage was getting worse, not better. Where their bodies joined the heat was unbearable. Yet gradually Jenny became aware that that was changing. She felt herself being lifted, being urged upward to a place where the fires could be extinguished. Christian was her guide and Jenny followed wherever he led. And the place where he finally brought her made it difficult for Jenny to regret the journey.

Her legs tangled in his, muscles rigid with tension. She rubbed against him, and tight, indrawn breaths gave sound to her quickening excitement. Her head moved from side to side, but not in denial. Her movement captured the increasingly abandoned rhythm of their bodies. The sparks that skittered along her skin were cast off and scattered like stars. Her breasts quivered as Christian thrust into her again and again. She felt him drawing heat from her body as he made her acknowledge the pleasure he could give her. His name became a throaty cry that could not be held back as pure sensation rippled through her. Moments later he joined her, finding his own release and spilling his seed deep into Jenny's womb.

Jenny's white-knuckled grip on the brass rails eased. She drew her hands away slowly, but she made no move to touch

Christian. He was lying on top of her, his heart hammering against his chest. His breath was warm against the curve of her neck, and Jenny could feel the faint brushings of his lips in her hair.

Christian raised himself on one elbow as he withdrew from Jenny. "It's all right," he said, reaching for the sheet that was balled up behind him. "I'm covering both of us now. You can open your eyes again." One corner of his mouth turned up in a reluctant smile as Jenny waited until she felt the sheet across her breasts before she took his suggestion. "Your body is lovely, Jenny. You shouldn't be ashamed of it." If he allowed himself, Christian knew he could become angry just thinking about not being able to paint her.

"I'm not," she said quietly, pointing to the mirror, "but neither am I so vain that I need to admire myself in that."

"You were quite taken with yourself earlier," he told her, reminding her how she had turned and posed, flashing her legs as she took stock of her reflection.

Jenny flushed, knowing that what he said was true. "I don't know why I did that. It must have been the brandy. I've never had it before. I usually only drink wine."

"Brandy's a good deal stronger than that, but it doesn't account for your condition. I'd be willing to wager that Amalie drugged you." Jenny started to sit up but Christian stopped her, placing one hand on her shoulder and pushing her back. He laid his arm across her chest and caressed the side of her neck with his fingertips. "You're quite beautiful, Jenny," he said casually, "and perhaps part of it stems from the fact that you seem so . . . so *unaware* of it. Amalie Chatham, however, is a collector of fine things. In addition to her art and emeralds, her dainty japanned boxes and her Paris gowns, our dear Miss Amalie knows how to choose young women. She has . . . er, scouts scattered over the breadth of this—"

"Pimps," Jenny corrected. "You mean pimps, don't you?"

"Yes, I mean pimps, but I didn't realize you knew the word." He saw her shrug, and knew she would not take the opening to explain herself. "Anyway, Amalie has men who procure women for her. I don't doubt that most of the women come willing, yet I've heard of exceptions. I imagine that Amalie thought herself very fortunate when you presented yourself at her door. Even I might have questioned her sanity if she had just let you slip away."

Jenny swallowed with difficulty. Her mouth was dry. "She wanted me?" she asked incredulously. "For this house? To work for her . . . to . . ." Words failed her. And as she thought of what she had just done with Christian Marshall, she wanted the ground to swallow her up. "My God," she said in a low voice. "I've done it anyway, haven't I?"

"Wait a minute," Christian said, his brows drawing together. "It wasn't—isn't—like that. What happened between us doesn't have a damn thing to do with Amalie or this house."

"Doesn't it?" she challenged, surprising herself with her temerity. "Didn't you say you wanted a whore?"

Christian had known he would eventually regret those words, but he hadn't thought it would be this soon. "Don't make me out as a villain here. I didn't ask for you. Hell, I didn't even know you were here. I was with Maggie, and then you came barging in."

"You knew I'd been drugged!" she accused.

"Not at first I didn't. I thought you were drunk! You were as helpless as a baby and just about as coherent when you staggered in here. It didn't take you long to make yourself available to me!"

Jenny drew in a sharp breath. "That's a lie!"

"Don't fool yourself into believing that. You wanted me!"

"You made certain I did!" she shot back.

"You're damn right! Would you rather have suffered the effects of the drug?"

"Better it than you!"

He ignored her, leaning forward so that his face was closer to hers. His eyes were considerably cooler than they had been a

201

short while ago. "They call it the itch," he said softly. "I've heard that it burns from the inside out, makes a woman so hot that she nearly goes crazy to have a man between her legs. Any man, Jenny. And they tell me the itch doesn't go away without one. You needed me tonight. You'd damn well be climbing the walls right now if I hadn't taken you."

The images he invoked with his husky, implacable voice made Jenny's skin prickle with the heat of embarrassment. "I don't believe you. You're lying to me. It wouldn't have happened that way."

Christian leaned back a little, shrugging. "We'll never know, will we? Unless you want me to ask Amalie for some more of her powder. Care to test what I've heard about the drug against the reality? I suppose I could accommodate you at least once more. Then I'd have to let someone else have you."

Jenny put her hand over her ears. "Stop it! Don't talk about it anymore! I don't want to hear!" When Christian grabbed her wrists and pulled her hands away, she kicked at him. "Leave me alone! I wish I had never come here! I wish Mrs. B. had . . ." Jenny stopped struggling. The anxiety that widened her soft doe eyes was not for herself now. "Mrs. Brandywine!" she whispered. "Oh, dear God, I had forgotten. How could I not have said anything?"

"Jenny?" Christian was still, watching. "What are you talking about? What about Mrs. B.?"

"She asked for you."

"I gathered that," he said dryly, wondering what Jenny's sudden alarm was all about. "You mentioned she sent you."

"Yes, but I never told you why." Jenny yanked away from Christian's grip, and this time he let her go. She sat up, tugging on the sheet as she did so. "She's hurt. She slipped on the icy walk and broke her leg. Mary Margaret went for Dr. Turner while I sat with Mrs. Brandywine. When Mrs. B. started asking for you we—that is, the rest of the staff and I—thought you should know about the accident. But there was no one to come except me."

202

Jenny kept talking as Christian flung off the sheet and jumped out of bed. Unconcerned with his nakedness, he began gathering his clothes, occasionally throwing something of Jenny's in her direction. "I would have told you right away. I *know* I would have if it hadn't been for what Amalie did. I was willing to write out a message, but she was more interested in giving me something to drink."

Christian fastened his drawers, pulling the string tight. "Why in God's name would she drug you if she knew you were here with a message for me?" He wasn't even aware that he had asked the question aloud until Jenny answered.

"But I never had the chance to tell her who the message was for." She frowned, trying to remember. "At least I don't think I did. No, I didn't. We were interrupted and she left and then I did."

"I know," he said caustically. "You didn't like her. You made certain you told me that."

Jenny sat up on her knees, clutching the sheet in front of her. She was making no effort to dress. "Please, Mr. Marshall, I swear I would have told you about Mrs. B. if my head had been clear!"

"I believe you," he said roughly. He pointed to the clothes that were scattered about the bed. "Get dressed now."

Jenny hardly heard him. She was still concentrating on the sequence of events after leaving Amalie's office. "I was already feeling thick-headed and awkward when I went through her suite looking for another exit. I found a way out and got as far as the other side of her hedgerow when I remembered I was supposed to see you. I had forgotten already, you see."

"I *do* see," he said with more patience than he was feeling. "Now will you get dressed?"

"Turn your back."

"What?"

"Turn your back," she repeated.

"Isn't that rather like shutting the stable door after the . . ." He stopped, seeing that she was quite, if absurdly, serious.

203

"Oh, very well." Christian turned away and jammed his legs into his black evening trousers.

Jenny dropped the sheet and pulled her chemise over her head. She sighed, seeing that the wide strap had been torn where it met the scooped neckline. "My cloak and mittens are in the hall linen cupboard," she said, rolling on her stockings. "I hid them behind a stack of sheets."

"Of course." He held up a hand behind him, trying to forestall her explanation. "No, I don't want to hear. I'm sure you had your reasons."

"I did. I didn't want anyone on this floor to suspect I didn't belong. It worked, because when I met Miss Bryant she thought I was one of the maids." She paused and added pointedly, "*Not* one of the whores."

"And she still sent you to me?" Christian couldn't unravel that one until he remembered calling Maggie Jenny. He supposed he was fortunate she hadn't scratched his eyes out for that mistake. "Never mind," he sighed, fastening the studs in his snowy white dress shirt. "I know why she did it. Are you ready yet?"

"Almost." She laced up her black ankle boots, then pulled on her gown. Several of the buttons were missing. The modest collar gaped in a V to a point just above her breasts. Jenny scooted off the bed, holding the material closed with one hand. "I'm dressed. We can go now."

"Wait here. I'll get your cloak."

"And mittens."

"And mittens," he repeated. "I also want to see where Amalie is. It may not be such a simple thing to get you out of here, not if Amalie has decided you're to be one of her girls."

"But I'm not! You wouldn't let her do that, would you?"

Christian's brief glance in Jenny's direction was rife with disgust. "How quickly you've forgotten that I helped you get out of that damnable hospital. Do you really think I'd . . ." He broke off, angry with himself for even bothering to explain. "Forget it. I'll be back in a few minutes." He shrugged into his

204

black swallow-tailed evening coat, unlocked the door, and stepped into the hallway without sparing her another look.

Dora heard the sound of a door opening and closing just as she was escorting Stephen to the main staircase. She prayed it was the maid leaving Maggie's room and not Christian Marshall. Dora did not want to think about the consequences of such a meeting.

She didn't have to think about it. Events just started to unfold, and she was powerless to interfere.

Stephen gripped Dora's arm just above the elbow and squeezed her hard enough to make her wince. "It's Marshall," he said, looking down the hallway over his left shoulder. "*He* had her."

"Oh, God. Don't say anything."

"Come with me," he hissed. "I want to talk to him." Stephen backed up one step, half carrying Dora with him. They began walking down the hall toward her room again.

Christian paused beside the linen cupboard when he saw Stephen Bennington strutting toward him, his arm linked around Dora's with his typical possessiveness. Christian's acquaintance with Stephen was limited to sharing a membership at the Yacht Club, attending some of the same social functions, and the occasional horse race out on Harlem Lane.

In the main he knew only two things about Stephen Bennington. One, the man dressed like a peacock. And two, Stephen had bought his way out of the draft during the war. In the first instance Christian was prepared to be open-minded. Stephen Bennington could dress any way he wished, even if he chose checked short coats, striped trousers, and bold yellow vests, and looked more as if he were wearing an argument than following the dictates of current fashion.

It was the second thing that Christian knew about the man that still had the power to trip Christian's anger. Though there were hundreds, even thousands, of others who had taken the outlet the law gave them and paid someone else to fight in their place, Christian still had no stomach for them in general and

Stephen Bennington in particular.

Christian's hand casually dropped away from the linen cupboard door and he gave a brief nod as Stephen and Dora approached. "Bennington. Miss Dora. Happy New Year." He made to step forward, deciding to go in search of Amalie, but Stephen blocked his path. "Is there some problem?" he asked, looking from Stephen to Dora. Christian did not have to stretch his powers of observation to conclude that young Bennington had drunk beyond his tolerance and that Dora was uncharacteristically nervous. He also did not miss the beginnings of a bruise on Dora's cheek and the faint swelling below her eye.

"No," said Stephen, pinching Dora's dimpled elbow to keep her quiet. "No problem."

"Then perhaps you'd move out of my way?"

Stephen wavered slightly on his feet, and it was Dora who actually steadied him. "In a moment. I was wondering about the high-stepper I saw go into Maggie's room earlier. Couldn't help but notice you just came from there, so I thought I'd ask about the girl. Is she available now?"

Dora was relieved that Stephen had had the presence of mind to lie about how he'd actually seen the girl. She relaxed a little.

"She may be," Christian said indifferently, "though you'll have to find her yourself. She left the room before I did."

Stephen's mouth turned down at the corners, betraying his disappointment. "Damn it. She looked to be an exquisite bit of tenderloin. Did you have her and Maggie together?"

Christian saw Dora blanch at the crudeness of Stephen's expression and his question. Her presence, and the fact that Bennington was obviously drunk, kept Christian from putting Stephen face down on the carpet. "If you'll excuse me," he said. "I am looking for Amalie."

Dora gathered her courage and pulled Stephen to one side so Christian could pass. "Amalie isn't here now," she told him. "She and Mr. Todd both had to step out. Maggie's the hostess

206

in Amalie's place."

That further explained why Maggie hadn't returned to her own room, Christian thought, and also why Dora was having to put up with Bennington. Todd would have shown him the door for striking one of Amalie's girls.

Stephen smirked, chuckling under his breath. "So you didn't have them both." He winked at Dora. "Somehow I knew that."

Christian let that comment pass, supposing that Stephen was recommending he try a *ménage à trois*. "Dora, would you like me to escort young Bennington here to the door?"

"Now see here, Marshall," Stephen snapped, drawing back his shoulders and throwing out his chest. "You don't have any right to—"

"It's all right, Mr. Marshall," Dora said, trying to keep the peace. "Stephen was on his way out when he saw you. He just wanted to know about the girl." She made another attempt to urge Stephen along, but he pulled away from her. Dora immediately dropped her hands to her sides and stepped backward.

"Look, Bennington," Christian said, "I already told you that if you're interested in the girl you'll have to find her. I don't know where she is. Now, if you'll both excuse me, since I can't see Amalie, I'm going to get my coat and take my leave." Christian turned to go, and was stopped by Stephen laying a hand on his shoulder. "What the hell do you want now, Bennington?" he asked wearily, glancing back.

"This, you bastard." He drove his fist into Christian's jaw, sending Christian sprawling against the wall.

Christian realized he had seriously overestimated Stephen's drunken state or underestimated his stupidity. He straightened and cupped his jaw, nursing it. "Before I set you on your ass," Christian gritted, "suppose you tell me what that was for." He motioned Dora out of the way as he and Stephen began to circle one another. "I don't kid myself that it's because of the girl."

"Not because of the girl," Stephen confirmed. "At least not

that one." He made a jab with his right that Christian ducked easily. "Your interference cost me a . . ." Stephen broke off, distracted by the sound of voices on the back stairwell, all of which he recognized. Dammit, he thought, not now. Not when he was prepared to give Christian Marshall a small portion of what he deserved for ruining his life. He threw out another wild punch, and took a blow to his gut instead. Winded, he doubled over, backing up against the wall. Gaslight flickered as one of the glass lamps was knocked askew. "I should kill you for what you did," he said, sucking in his breath. "If it hadn't been for you I would be—"

"That's quite enough, Stephen," William Bennington broke in as he entered the hallway from the rear. "You've said more than you need to." Father and son exchanged equally hard, narrow-eyed stares before Stephen looked away. William took off his silk top hat and put it under his arm. He made a slight bow to Christian, acknowledging his presence. "My son will make a formal apology when he's sober."

"That's not necessary," said Christian. He spoke to William but his attention was on the entourage that the elder Bennington had with him. Mr. Todd was behind William, just off his right shoulder, and beside him were Amalie and Maggie. Everyone but Maggie was still wearing cloaks, mufflers, and gloves. From the flakes of snow on their shoulders and hats, Christian could see they had only just come indoors. Amalie's cloak was damp at the bottom where it had apparently brushed through at least one drift. Christian tried to picture Amalie tramping through the snow and couldn't. The notion did not fit the role she had chosen for herself.

Maggie was fidgeting with her hair, a sign that she was worried about something. Amalie's smile was forced. Only Mr. Todd was looking pleased with himself. Christian found the entire confrontation odd rather than alarming.

"I disagree," William said, loosening the wool scarf around his neck. "You will have your apology." He gave his hat and scarf to Todd. "Take these, please, then see that my son is

208

escorted to my carriage. Send him home. I'll take a cab."

Todd nodded after glancing in Amalie's direction for approval. "Very good, sir." He broke away from the others. "Mr. Stephen? This way, please. Miss Dora? I'm certain your presence is required in the red parlor."

Stephen stumbled a little as he pushed away from the wall, but brushed off Todd's hand when the older man offered his assistance. Mustering what dignity he could, he took Dora's arm instead.

Christian waited until the trio had disappeared down the main staircase before he spoke. "I'm certain Stephen will appreciate your timely intervention come morning. I honestly can't say that I feel the same way." He moved his lower jaw back and forth, shaking out the stiffness. "I was on the point of smashing his pretty nose."

"I saw that," William said gravely. "My son can be impulsive, but I've not known him to be so belligerent. Chalk it up to the high spirits of the holiday, youthful exuberance, and a touch more to drink than he can handle gracefully.

"My thoughts exactly," Christian said. He wasn't sure any of those reasons were sufficient to explain Stephen's animosity. Stephen had been on the verge of making himself clear when his father had interrupted. Christian regretted not knowing more than he regretted missing the chance to flatten the younger Bennington. "Now, if you'll excuse me, before Stephen stopped me I was going back to get my coat."

"Maggie," Amalie said sweetly, stepping around William. "Please get Mr. Marshall's coat for him."

What the hell was going on? Christian wondered. His eyes darted to all members of the trio trying to divine their purpose. "That's all right, Maggie. I can get it myself."

"It's no bother," Amalie said, speaking to Maggie.

Thinking of Jenny's safety, Christian's mind worked furiously. "If you don't mind, Amalie, I'd rather not worry that my money's being lifted. I'll get my coat myself."

The insult struck home. Amalie's cheeks flamed with color.

"My girls do *not* steal!"

"Oh?" Christian asked coolly, raising one brow. "Then no one told the little light-fingers that Maggie pawned off on me earlier. I caught her going through my pockets while she thought I was asleep. When she realized I was watching her, she ran off. That's not the sort of treatment I expect in your house, Amalie. I considered chasing her, but decided I'd let you handle it. I doubt I would be as fair-minded as I know you'll be. I was on my way to find you when Stephen accosted me." He started walking to Maggie's room. "My experience tonight speaks for itself," he said. "I'll get my own belongings."

"A light-fingers!" William snarled at Amalie. "You told me it was . . ." He stopped, seeing that Christian was taking in his every word. "Excuse us, Marshall," he said abruptly, taking Amalie by the elbow. "Amalie. Your office. Now."

Amalie's mouth opened and closed but nothing came out. The frown between her brows creased her forehead, making her look every bit of her fifty years. Her dark, glittering eyes narrowed on Maggie, and she was satisfied when the other woman recoiled slightly. Amalie had to blame someone for this turn of events and Maggie was the most useful target. Her skirts rustled noisily as she broke free of William's grip and turned on her heel. Without a word to anyone she stalked toward the back staircase, her chin thrust forward aggressively. William followed, his long, hurried stride speaking eloquently of his impatience and anger.

When they were alone in the corridor Christian rounded on Maggie. "Would you please tell me what in God's name is going on here tonight?" he whispered harshly. His fingers raked his hair. "And don't give me crap about it being the high spirits of the holiday!"

Maggie's sea-green eyes glistened with tears. "Do you think anyone's told me anything?" she fairly wailed. "Oh, God, Christian, I think I'm in so much trouble! Amalie was furious when she came back and found out I sent that girl to your room. How was I supposed to know she wasn't one of the maids? She looked like one. I couldn't have known she was a thief!" She sniffed inelegantly, searched for a handkerchief, and when she couldn't find one, plucked Christian's out of his vest pocket. "I had no idea that anything like that was going on until you mentioned it! I thought the girl was drunk, but she must have been faking it as a way to cover for herself. I even warned her not to let Amalie see her!" Maggie blew her nose hard. "How could I have let her take me in that way! Amalie's going to send me to Canal Street, Christian. I just know she is."

"I seriously doubt that."

Maggie folded the handkerchief and dabbed at her eyes. "You didn't see how angry Amalie was when she came back here. Mr. Todd and Mr. Bennington were waiting for her in her office. They were all there only a few minutes before Amalie called me in and asked me if I had seen that girl. I think Amalie must have suspected that Jenny girl was a thief."

"Why do you say that?"

"Because that's why Amalie left the house—to look for her. Amalie wouldn't have done that if she hadn't good reason."

Christian believed that as well, but unlike Maggie, he knew more about the nature of Amalie's real interest in Jenny. "What does Mr. Bennington have to do with any of this?"

"How should I know? Perhaps that little witch stole from him earlier this evening. It wouldn't surprise me if Mr. Todd brought him back to identify the bitch." She raised her eyes beseechingly. "What am I going to do, Christian? What if Amalie tells me to pack my bags?"

"You'll land on your feet, Maggie," Christian said emotionlessly. "Cats like you always do."

Maggie's mottled cheeks suffused with color. "You really are a bastard, aren't you?"

He shrugged carelessly. "That's what they say."

Angered by his indifference to her fears, Maggie balled up both hands and pushed hard at Christian's chest. "Damn you! This is more your fault than mine! If you'd been a real man

211

tonight, with a real man's appetites, I wouldn't have sent that bitch to you."

Christian caught Maggie by the wrists and squeezed so hard that her fingers unfolded. The handkerchief dropped to the floor. He released her as suddenly as he had grabbed her, then brushed himself off, straightening his vest and jacket. "I'm sorely bored with being accosted this evening. Don't try digging your talons in me again. Ever." A muscle ticked in his lean cheek. "As for having a real man's appetites, I think you know the problem was with the menu, not my hunger."

Maggie sucked in her full lower lip at Christian's scathing tone. She knew she had gone too far, but an apology stuck in her throat. She took refuge in self-righteous rage. No man had found her lacking before—including Christian!

Before Christian knew what she was doing, Maggie had swept past him and thrown open the door to her room. He reached out to stop her, and found himself clutching at air as she flounced angrily toward the unmade bed. Christian held his breath, waiting for the inevitable explosion once she spotted Jenny.

"Get your coat and get the hell out of here," she snapped, yanking pins from her hair. She tossed them on the bedside table and sat down on the bed, shaking out her fine, silky blond hair. The glance she darted in the mirror above her vanity assured her she looked magnificent even if Christian couldn't appreciate it. She wished she could call back what she had said about his appetites. Christian Marshall was one of the few men she actually enjoyed in her bed. "What are you waiting for?" she said instead. "Come in, then get out."

Releasing his breath slowly, Christian limped across the room to get his coat. Where the hell was Jenny? Under the bed? In the wardrobe? God, he hoped not. He considered looking behind Maggie's dressing screen, but couldn't think of a way to do it without rousing her suspicions. It was only when he reached the coat and hat hooks that Christian understood Jenny was no longer in the room. His eyes quickly scanned the

212

French door and saw the latch had been thrown back. There was no place she could be but out on Maggie's postage-stamp balcony. At least she had had the sense to wear his coat.

"Where is it?" Maggie demanded, seeing Christian's hand waver above the empty brass and porcelain coat peg. "You obviously didn't hang it there."

"I could have sworn I did," he said, affecting puzzlement. He searched the room, pretending to look for it. "I must have left it downstairs," he said finally. "Good evening, Maggie. I won't say that it's been a pleasure."

"Good riddance!" She kicked at the tray that was still resting on the floor. Her cherished oriental carpet was littered with the tray's contents. "Jesus, Christian! Look at this mess!" A bit of melted chocolate stuck to the toe of her shoe. She grabbed one corner of the sheet she was sitting on to wipe it away. "I swear if I ever see her again, I'll kick her all the way to the Bowery where she belongs!"

His mouth twitched at this further evidence of Maggie's helpless anger. "It appears she was no better a pickpocket than she was a maid." He started to go, but Maggie's choked scream rooted him once more.

"Ooooh!" She held up the sheet, snapping it so Christian could see it clearly. Spots of dried blood darkened the material. "You found out what she was good for, didn't you? On my bed! You took the little trollop on my bed!"

The set of Christian's mouth was grim as he took the sheet from Maggie's trembling hands. He balled it up and pitched it into the corner of the room. "Isn't that exactly what you had in mind when you sent her in here? And I think trollop hardly applies. The blood speaks for itself."

Maggie sneered. "That's easily faked. I've done it often enough for gentlemen who like to pretend that sort of thing. I didn't know you were one of them. Imagine Christian Marshall's tastes running to virgins." She laughed, but the sound held no humor. "I had no idea. You should have said something. I could have been more accommodating." She

213

reached out and held Christian by his jacket sleeve when he turned to go. "Just a moment. You never paid up. Put your money on the vanity. You owe me at least for my time."

Christian reached for the money clip discreetly tucked away in the lining of his jacket. He peeled off some bills and threw them on the bed. "For your time and hers," he said. "You pimped her, Maggie. You deserve something for that."

"Bastard!" she screamed as Christian walked away. She scrambled off the bed and knelt on the floor. Picking up an unbroken china saucer, Maggie flung it at Christian's head. He ducked out the door moments before it shattered against the wood.

In the hallway Christian quickly retrieved Jenny's cloak and mittens, folding the cloak over his arm so it might be mistaken for his own coat. He hurried down the stairs and out the front door, and the frigid wind immediately tousled his hair. The strains of treacly sweet harp music and warbling soprano voices finally behind him, Christian kicked up snow dust as he rounded the corner of Amalie's brownstone. He had no difficulty finding Maggie's balcony. It was the only one with a shivering female leaning over the iron railing.

Lights from inside the house illuminated the lawn. Christian had to stand very close to the house to avoid being seen by anyone happening to glance out one of the parlor windows.

"Can you jump?" he called up to her in as loud a whisper as he thought safe.

Jenny was afraid to answer for fear of Maggie hearing her, although the noise from inside the room hadn't abated much since Christian left. Maggie was still swearing and throwing things. The vanity mirror had been the last item to go.

"Never mind," he said as it was brought home to him why she didn't respond. "Just climb over the railing and lower yourself down. I'll catch you."

Madman! Did he think she was part spider?

"Jenny! Do it! There's no other way!"

She wished she could prove Christian wrong, but if there

214

had been another way down she would have already taken it. Grasping the railing with fingers that were growing numb with cold, Jenny carefully raised first one leg, then the other, over the side. Her skirt was a nuisance, getting caught on one of the iron curls that decorated the railing. She yanked at the material impatiently. When she tore it, setting herself free, she also lost her balance. Her feet slipped on the edge of the icy balcony and her grip on the railing loosened. It took all her willpower and every bit of courage she had not to scream as she fell.

Christian heard her scrambling for purchase before he actually saw that she was in trouble. He jumped away from the house and blocked Jenny's fall with his own body. They both tumbled in the snow, winded by the force of their contact with each other and the ground. As soon as Christian was able he dragged Jenny into the shadow of the balcony.

"Are you all right?" he asked, his own breathing harsh.

She nodded, swallowing air in great gulps. "I—I'm fine. Please, Mr. Marshall, can we go home now?"

"Yes, we can go." She had sounded so childlike in her request that Christian was beginning to feel paternal. He didn't like it much. "The sooner, the better. Here, take your mittens and cloak and give me my coat." When they were done trading garments, Christian took Jenny's hand and helped her to her feet. "Keep low past the windows. At the corner of the house I want you to start walking away as quickly as you can. I'll hail a cab and pick you up in a few minutes."

"But . . ."

Christian sighed. "No arguments. I don't think we can risk being seen together. If you knew how many people were interested in your whereabouts, you wouldn't bother me with questions."

Jenny had a very good idea of not just how many wanted her, but who they were. She did exactly as Christian asked.

*   *   *

William Bennington leaned back in the emerald velvet chair opposite Amalie's desk. He raised a glass of champagne to his lips. He could feel the bubbles burst against his mustache as he drank. The alcohol was just what he needed to wet his parched throat. There had been a few moments upstairs when William didn't have enough saliva to spit. His cobalt-blue eyes bored into Amalie's green ones and remained there until she had the grace to look away first.

"You should be embarrassed," he said sharply, twirling the stem of his glass. "What you tried to perpetrate tonight was nothing short of blackmail, and don't think I didn't know it from the beginning! I wouldn't have returned here at all if that leg-breaker of yours hadn't been so insistent."

"Don't take that tone with me, Bennington. I saw how you listened to what I had to say. I didn't hear you denying it could be true when I confronted you in this office. Now that she's disappeared you're carrying a different tune."

"You stumbled upon a petty thief who looked a lot like—"

"Not 'a lot' like her," Amalie interrupted vehemently. "*Exactly* like her. Of course I thought there had been some mistake."

"And immediately jumped to the conclusion that somehow it meant money in your hands. I don't begin to pretend to understand how your mind works, Amalie, but I know you overstepped your bounds this time. That girl—what did Maggie say her name was?"

"Jenny."

"Jenny, then, had a clever little scheme going for her. I think you realize now that's all it was. I don't care *who* she looked like." He finished his champagne. "I have to admire her panache. She marches right up to your front door, announces she's got a message for someone, manages to get herself upstairs, and proceeds to rob your clientele. I shouldn't be at all surprised if your business falls off a little after this incident."

"I don't know that anyone was robbed," Amalie snapped.

"Marshall said she fled when he caught her in the act."

"Count yourself fortunate if that's true."

"Are you going to speak of this to others?" she asked.

"Give me one reason why I shouldn't. I can't get over the fact that you thought you could turn a fortune on my grief."

"Hah!" Amalie threw her head back in a scornful gesture. "I don't believe for a moment that you felt grief at her passing. Neither you, nor Stephen. Especially not Stephen. He told more than one of my girls that she was a family embarrassment. The way he tells it she was quite out of her head at the end."

William had always suspected his son had a loose tongue. He'd confirmed it earlier when he witnessed Stephen's confrontation with Christian Marshall, and Amalie had confirmed it again. "Believe what you like, Amalie. I don't know who you saw here this evening, but I assure you it wasn't my daughter!"

Amalie laughed. "Oh, that's rich."

"If you're splitting hairs, she was my stepdaughter."

"I'd think you'd be happy about that. If she was as mad as Stephen said she was, then you don't have to worry that the same thing might befall your . . ." She broke off as the door opened a crack. "What is it, Mr. Todd?"

"I just wanted to know if Mr. Bennington wanted me to get a cab for him."

William set his glass on Amalie's desk and stood. "That's all right, I'm going now. Don't trouble yourself." When Todd slipped back into the hallway, William braced his arms against the desk and leaned forward threateningly. "If I ever hear that you're trying to stir trouble like this again, I'll make certain you're shut down, Amalie. Don't think you're so powerful that you can cross me and get away with it. No one likes the stink of blackmail, especially not the people whose favor you court. Keep out of things that don't concern you, Miss Chatham, and after the holiday come around to the bank and make a withdrawal."

217

"Are you serious?" she asked incredulously. "You don't want my money in your bank? I know there's been trouble since Caroline Van Dyke's death was made public. With no marriage you need—"

"You didn't let me finish. Take everything except one hundred thousand dollars." He ignored Amalie's gasp. "That's what your erroneous assumptions and greed have cost you this evening. Just a word—*one word*—from you about this to anyone and I'll have your business as well." He straightened, watching her closely while he combed his beard with his fingertips. "I can find my own way out, Amalie." He smiled pleasantly. "Happy New Year."

Amalie held herself stiffly until he was gone, then she sank back in her chair, thoroughly exhausted by the night's events. She had been so *sure*. How could she have made such an incredible mistake, shown such poor judgment? Plucking the headache powder from where she had stuffed it in her bodice, Amalie tore the packet open slowly.

"Get me a glass of water, will you, Mr. Todd?" she asked when he let himself into her office.

Todd brought the water in from her private kitchen and held it out to her. "You don't look well. Would you like a massage?"

She nodded. "Just my neck and shoulders." She dropped the powder into the water, made a grimace, and drank it down in one long swallow. Setting the glass down, Amalie leaned forward so Todd could get behind her. His massive hands could have crushed her neck, yet his touch was infinitely gentle, probing her tension spots with just the right amount of pressure.

"William swears that girl was not his stepdaughter," she said at last.

"Do you believe him?"

Amalie felt as if Todd had just taken a weight from her shoulders. Trust him to be the one person who would not make her doubt herself. "Do you know, John Todd," she said quietly, her eyes hardening as she considered her next move,

"I don't think I do."

The cab ride home was silent. Except for Christian's terse instructions to tuck her feet under his thigh to keep her toes warm, he and Jenny didn't exchange a word. He helped her down from the carriage, paid the cab driver, then hurried up the walk alone, leaving Jenny to follow in his wake.

Mary Margaret opened the front door to them, taking Christian's coat as he shrugged out of it. "Dr. Turner's with her now," she said. "She won't let anyone but you help him set her leg. You'd better go up right away." Mary Margaret's heart went out to him as he turned from her, his face ashen, and began mounting the stairs two at a time. "Poor man," she said under her breath. "What a time he's had of it. Him and Mrs. B., just like this, they are." She held up two crossed fingers to show Jenny. "And what took you so long? Sure, and we've been waiting on pins and needles for you to return. Dr. Turner was ready to go to Amalie's himself after the pair of you. I thought of sending Liam to get you, but he's not on duty this evening."

Thank God for that. "It's a long story," Jenny said wearily, still looking at where Christian had disappeared in the upper hallway. She unhooked the frog clasp at the throat of her cloak and slipped it off her shoulders. It wasn't until she heard Mary Margaret's gasp that she remembered the gaping neckline of her gown and the torn hem.

"Sweet Jesus, Mary, and Joseph," the maid said, eyes bulging. She crossed herself quickly. "What happened to you?"

"It's nothing," Jenny said, drawing the cloak around her again.

"Nothing! Did someone at Amalie's mistake you for a—"

"Something like that."

"Oh, my!"

"I'd rather not talk about it, if you don't mind. In fact, I'd like to go to bed. Now that Mr. Marshall's with Mrs. B. I suppose that will be all right, don't you?"

Mary Margaret nodded. She stepped past Jenny and locked the front door. "Go on, Jenny. Just a quick check with Dr. Turner and I'm soon for bed myself. I wonder if I should turn down the bed in Mr. Marshall's room. Add coals to the fire?" She turned around and saw she was talking to the air. Jenny was already climbing the stairs. Her progress was slow, almost painful, and her hand didn't glide up the polished bannister as it normally might. Instead, Jenny held it in the manner of someone needing its support. Mary Margaret turned back the lamps in the entrance hall and followed a few minutes later, her fiery brows drawn together in a thoughtful pose.

Chapter 9

"Would you like anything else?" Jenny asked her patient. "Another cup of tea? Mrs. Morrisey made crullers this morning."

Mrs. B. snorted, pursing her lips. The expression was at odds with her cherubic features. "Stop trying to coax a better humor from me with food and drink. I'm heartily sick of this bed, this room, and Mrs. Morrisey's crullers. Feed them to Liam O'Shea or that stray dog everyone thinks I don't know you've taken in." She wrinkled her nose sourly. "And if I have one more cup of tea I'll float away."

"Oh, my. You *are* determined to be cranky today." Jenny bent over the bed and adjusted the pillows behind Mrs. B.'s back and head, not letting the housekeeper see her amused smile. It was easy enough to understand Mrs. Brandywine's ill humor. Being a virtual prisoner in one's bed for two weeks, and knowing there were at least four weeks yet to come, was bound to try a person's patience. Jenny gave Mrs. B.'s splinted leg a cursory glance and saw her ankle was swollen. Dr. Turner had cautioned Jenny to look for signs like that and correct them immediately. "Let's elevate that leg a little, shall we?"

"*You* elevate it," Mrs. B. grumbled. "*I* can't move it."

"Are the splints really as heavy as they look?"

Mrs. B. glanced down at her injured leg. It was resting

outside the covers that were tucked around her elsewhere. The wooden splints went from her ankle to just above the knee, and they were kept in place by a bandage that spiraled up her leg. The thing was stiff and cumbersome, but it did exactly what it was meant to do—keep her leg immobile. "Damn plaguey thing! I thought Dr. Turner was building a house around my leg."

Jenny smiled as she gently nudged a pillow under Mrs. B.'s foot. She readjusted the housekeeper's nightgown so that part of the splint was covered by the ruffled hem. "You sound just like Mr. Marshall when you talk that way."

Mrs. B. affected an injured air. "There's no cause to insult me. Where is he anyway? I haven't seen him at all today."

"He's gone to the office at *The Chronicle*."

"Again? That's every day this week."

"I think so." Jenny shrugged. She kept her hands busy rearranging items on the luncheon tray she had set across Mrs. B.'s lap. "He doesn't confide his plans to me, you know. Not that what he does is any concern of mine. And frankly, even if it were, I don't have the interest nor the time to inquire." She and Christian had never spoken about the night at Amalie's. She had asked no questions about the confrontations in the hallway outside Maggie's room. To do so would have raised other questions, other memories. Christian had never volunteered any information. Except for the occasional watchful glance he cast in her direction, Christian seemed to have put New Year's Eve out of his mind.

"Stop that," Mrs. B. said, pointing to Jenny's fluttering hands. "And take the tray away. I'm not hungry."

Jenny put the tray on the nightstand and picked up the book that was lying there. "Would you like me to read to you?" she asked, thumbing through the pages to find where they had stopped the day before.

"Put that down and stop trying to change the subject."

"I wasn't aware that's what I was doing," she said, replacing the book.

"Hhhmmph. It's my leg I injured, not my brain. I see how things are between the two of you. Perhaps I even see it more clearly than I did before, now that I've got nothing to do but speculate."

"Then allow me to suggest you take up knitting or letter-writing or needlepoint," Jenny said dryly.

A glimmer of a smile crossed Mrs. B.'s lips. She touched her forefinger to the dimple in her chin, striking a thoughtful pose. "Mr. Marshall's never taken this much interest in *The Chronicle* before. Once or twice a week is usually all he would devote to actually going down to Printing House Square. Of course he always did a lot for the paper in other ways, but I've never known him to be so active in its daily operation."

"You don't know that's what he's doing now," Jenny countered. "Just because he goes there doesn't mean that he's necessarily doing anything. He could be sitting at his desk twiddling his thumbs."

"That's what speculation is, m'dear. I'm merely *supposing* what he may be doing." She raised her eyes innocently. "For all I know his interest in the paper is secondary to his desire to get out of this house."

Jenny fought a battle with herself not to respond to that comment—and lost. "What makes you say that?"

"Because—and this is fact, not my overworked imagination—the two of you were avoiding one another before my accident, and it's gotten worse since. With your new responsibilities because of my injury, it's inevitable that you'd see more of Mr. Marshall. He's corrected the situation by spending most of his time away from here. Now, you tell me, Jenny. Fact or fancy?"

"You'll have to ask Mr. Marshall," she replied evasively. "I'm sure I don't know why he does the things he does."

"What happened the night you went to Amalie's?" she pressed. "Mary Margaret told me what you looked like when you came—"

"Mary Margaret had no business mentioning that to you."

223

"Did Mr. Marshall do something to you that—"

"Stop it!" she snapped, agitated. There was silence for a long moment. Jenny's shoulders slumped and her eyes fell away from Mrs. B.'s startled countenance. "I'm sorry," she said softly. "I shouldn't have spoken to you like that. I just don't want to talk about it, not about that night anyway."

"I should be begging your pardon."

Jenny shook her head. "No, I understand that you're concerned about him."

"About you as well. But that doesn't excuse my prying."

Jenny walked to the window and parted the drapes. She cleared a small circle on one of the frosted panes with her fingertips. Her breath clouded the spot almost immediately. "I worry about him too," she said finally, her voice whisper soft. "Do you know he rarely laughs? Or smiles? He seems so strong, as if nothing touches him, but I've seen such pain in his eyes. I think he must always be hurting." She turned a little, resting her shoulder and the crown of her head against the window. "I don't mean his leg. That wound doesn't bother him overmuch. But here"—she touched her heart—"here he has a hole in his soul." Jenny's smile mocked her own wandering thoughts. "Fact or fancy?"

"Fact," Mrs. B. said quietly. Her gray eyes misted over as she studied Jenny's face. She saw innocence . . . and wisdom. How well this woman-child understood Christian. "The hole hasn't always been there," she continued. "It was carved out during the war."

"I think I knew that." She hesitated. Finally: "He lost everyone, didn't he?"

"Eventually. First it was Braden at Bull Run. Two years later David fell at Gettysburg. By all accounts, not twenty yards from where Christian stood." Mrs. B. absently fingered the lace on the neckline of her nightgown, remembering how it had been when Christian returned home, hollow-eyed and bitter. The self-recriminations, the blame, had started then.

"In a way, Mrs. Marshall was another casualty of the war.

ACCEPT YOUR **FREE GIFT** *AND EXPERIENCE MORE OF THE PASSION AND ADVENTURE YOU LIKE IN A HISTORICAL ROMANCE*

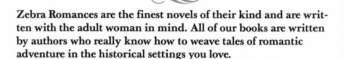

Get a Free
Zebra
Historical
Romance

*a $3.95
value*

There were hundreds of wounded coming into the hospitals every day. She volunteered her services when it would have been just as acceptable to start a drive for funds or supplies. But that wasn't Cathy's way. She and Christian were so much alike in that regard, always in the thick of things. Dreamers. Romantics. Having lost two sons already, and another one wounded, made her even more determined to see that the sacrifices had not been in vain. When cholera swept the wards it made no allowance for what the Marshalls had already suffered. Cathy died here at home, a few days after she contracted the disease."

"Christian was here then?"

"Hmm-mm. September '63 it was, two months after Gettysburg. He never left her. Stayed with her right until the moment she was buried, then without a word to anyone of his intentions, he packed his things and went back to the fighting."

"But his leg!"

"He could get around well enough by then. The Army was glad to have him back and Christian . . . well, Christian needed to be there. He and his father could barely be civil to one another at that time. Harrison spent nearly all his time at the paper, rallying support for the war, writing special pieces himself, editing the copy, editorializing about the necessity of conscription. With so many men off to fight, his reponsibilities were almost endless.

"Christian didn't always agree with Harrison's politics, but more than that he resented his father for spending hours away from Cathy when she needed him. Harrison was at *The Chronicle* when his wife died. Christian didn't want to forgive his father that, so he left." Mrs. Brandywine sighed softly, shaking her head from side to side. "All her life Cathy was the peacemaker between her husband and her second-born. She used to confide in me, wondering if she would ever see the day they stood aligned. She never did. Her death drove them apart."

"They never reconciled? Even after the war?"

"Especially not after the war. Oh, Harrison tried in his own fashion, helped Dr. Turner's efforts wherever he could. He wanted Christian involved with the paper, but that had always been the main bone of contention between them. Christian was so withdrawn and angry in those days. He didn't understand that Harrison was grieving too, that throwing himself into his work was the only way he knew how to go on. They needed each other so much then and neither of them knew how to make the first move. Harrison died in his office at *The Chronicle* seven months ago. It was a stroke. Christian was at one of the clubs, drinking and playing cards, when it happened."

"Oh, God."

"It was never a question of them not loving one another," she went on. "There was no doubt about that. It was the *liking* that created the problems."

"I think I understand," said Jenny. "Perhaps they were more alike than anyone suspected. Mr. Marshall sounds determined, opinionated, and forceful, even a little overbearing."

"Are you talking about father or son?"

"My point exactly. You can't tell the difference." She pushed away from the window and approached the bed. "Wasn't there another brother? What happened to him?"

Mrs. Brandywine nodded. "The baby. Logan. Mrs. Marshall never knew about her youngest." Mrs. B. took a slow breath to compose herself. "We think he died in Georgia, in Andersonville Prison. There was never any official word from the government—North or South. The last letter we received from him said only that capture was imminent. Like Christian, he was a scout."

"A spy, you mean?"

"I suppose you could call it that. He actually worked for Mathew Brady."

"Logan was a *photographer?*"

Mrs. Brandywine was surprised that Jenny knew what Brady

226

did. For herself, Mrs. B. would have never heard of him if it hadn't been for his associations with Logan and Christian. "You know of Mr. Brady?"

"I'm familiar with his photographs, some of them anyway. There was an exhibition in . . ." She caught herself. Jenny couldn't say where she saw the photographs because the housekeeper would never believe her, and if she did . . . well, that would prove equally complicated to explain. "The war never seemed quite real to me until I saw his work. It's an astonishing accomplishment to have chronicled the entire conflict."

The derisive snort that came from the open doorway had Jenny spinning around. Christian was leaning against the doorjamb, eyeing her critically, disdain lifting one corner of his mouth. His arms were crossed in front of his chest and there was a folded newspaper under one arm. He looked as if he had been standing there for some time. The only evidence to the contrary was the fact that Mrs. Brandywine would have seen him first and she was clearly as startled by his appearance as Jenny.

"Brady always took more credit than was his due. It practically took an Act of Congress to get him out of his Washington studio during the war."

"But I've seen his pictures," Jenny protested. What was Christian doing home in the middle of the day? Didn't he have something better to do than interrupt other people's conversations?

"You've seen what his money financed. Any man who worked for Brady had to give up credit for the photographs he took. Brady's name was assigned to everything. Good photographers, men like Tim O'Sullivan and Alex Gardner, left him and struck out on their own because of Brady's unwillingness to let them use their own names."

"Did you?"

"Leave him?" He shook his head. "No, I never worked for him. It was a commercial venture to Brady. He had an idea that

227

the photos would make him a fortune after the war. He didn't anticipate that so many people would want to forget that it ever happened."

Christian realized that his voice was becoming a little heated and that Jenny was looking at him oddly. He shrugged, feigning indifference. "Besides, lugging a hundred pounds of equipment to each new site, like some damn camp follower, wasn't for me. I did it occasionally, when I thought it was important to have a perfect record of the enemy's layout, but mostly I sketched whatever the commanders needed to see. It was quicker, infinitely more convenient, and I never had to worry that the sunlight would fail me."

Christian took the newspaper from under his arm and tapped it lightly against his thigh. "Logan, on the other hand"—he looked from Jenny to Mrs. Brandywine—"you *were* telling her about Logan before I got here, weren't you?"

Mrs. B. nodded and Jenny, watching Christian, was disappointed that his expression remained inscrutable. She couldn't tell whether or not he resented them discussing his brother.

"As I was saying, Logan was fascinated by photography. He'd take the equipment anywhere, no matter how difficult it was, just to prove it could be done. Setting up his tent behind enemy lines was not the wisest thing Logan ever did."

"That's how he was captured?" she asked.

Christian nodded. "Eventually, yes. But not the first half dozen or so times he did it."

"How incredible," Jenny breathed softly.

"He's dead," Christian said quellingly. "Don't romanticize his exploits. It belittles everything he was trying to accomplish. Enemy lines, cannon placement, field positions were incidental to what he was doing. Scouting was part of the job, so he did it. But Logan wanted to show the war as it really was, a great yawning shadow of death. Ugly, bloody, fields riddled with corpses, and . . ." He stopped, realizing he was speaking as much for himself as he was for his brother, perhaps more so.

228

In Jenny's eyes he saw the truth and sensed that she knew it too. "Anyway, he's dead," he said heavily. "Because of Brady's rules I can only guess which pictures Logan might have taken. It's part of what's been lost."

"I'm sorry."

Christian found it odd that her words did not seem inadequate. They were the same words so many others had spoken to him, and he had never found any comfort in them. Yet when Jenny said them, he felt as if she were healing a festering wound. That she could have such an effect on him reminded Christian how truly vulnerable he was. He did not want to think about that. His hand tightened on the paper he held and he shored up his defenses.

He stepped away from the door and walked to Mrs. B.'s bed, choosing the side opposite Jenny. "I decided to come home for lunch," he said. "Here, I brought you this."

Mrs. Brandywine did not have to be hit over the head with the paper to know that the earlier subject was now closed. Still, she thought with a touch of satisfaction, it was the first time Christian had strung more than two sentences together about the war since Braden died. Perhaps things were finally beginning to change for the better. She took the newspaper from him and unfolded it. "Why, Christian, this is *The Herald*. What are you thinking of bringing it in here?"

He gave a short laugh, leaning over the bed to tug on her nightcap. "Don't even try to pretend you haven't been reading this on the sly. Since you've been bedridden there have been more copies of this paper circulating the house than circulate the corner of Broadway and Ann Street where Bennet publishes the damn thing!"

Mrs. B. dismissed that. "You're exaggerating."

"All right," he allowed. "But just a little." He eased himself down on the bed, careful not to disturb Mrs. Brandywine's leg. "Whose head should I have for bringing it to you in the first place?" The tray that Jenny was lifting from the table clattered as it slipped through her nervous fingers. Christian knew precisely how to interpret that event. "Never mind. She's as good as admitted it herself."

"Stop teasing her," Mrs. B. advised. "She'll leave you high and dry, and with me laid up you'll be in a fine mess. Who'd see to the particulars of running this white elephant? Mary Margaret? Mrs. Morrisey? Hah! I see you take my point." She smoothed the paper over her lap. "In any event, this is a fine paper. It offers a wonderful variety of news."

"It offers a wide variety of gossip, you mean. Disguised as news."

"The paper's views are interesting."

"They wouldn't know an opinion at *The Herald* if it crawled onto the editorial page," he said bluntly. "No one over there believes in them. They think everyone is as cynical as they are."

Mrs. B. gave Christian a sharp look. "They could be right," she said pointedly.

"Touché."

She smiled. "Well, their foreign correspondents are quite good. Almost as good as those young men who work for you," she added loyally.

"It's too late for flattery. Go on," he prompted. "Open it up. I know what you're dying to read." He glanced up at Jenny just a beat too slow to catch the anxious light that had come to her deep brown eyes. "Will you have Mrs. Morrisey prepare me something for luncheon and bring it here?" he asked. "I don't have long. I'd rather stay with Mrs. Brandywine."

The corners of the housekeeper's eyes crinkled as her mouth bowed upward with sheepish pleasure. She took her wire-rimmed spectacles from the nearby table and slipped them on. "That's because you like to read the personal ads too," she said, snapping open the paper. "I don't believe for a moment you're interested in my company."

"Then you'd be wrong."

"Flatterer."

The exchange of lively banter went on long after Jenny had

left the room. Neither of them noticed that the peach blush in her cheeks had faded once she realized they were going to read the personals together, and they didn't pay much attention to her later when she returned with Christian's lunch and left again.

"Here's an interesting one," Mrs. B. said, taking a finger sandwich from Christian's plate. "Listen. *'Velvet Dress—can see you Friday morning; impossible afternoon. Write or telegraph at once. Jerome.'* Do you suppose Velvet Dress is married?"

"Probably. But Jerome's not, otherwise he wouldn't have used his own name."

"He's deeply in love with her, I'll wager. And she's unhappily married. Her husband wed her for her money and treats her poorly."

Christian blinked widely, amused by Mrs. B.'s romantic turn. "Do you always make up stories about the people who place these ads?"

"Not always," she sniffed. "Sometimes it's only too plain what they're all about. Here, for example. *'Miss Ruthie Wilver, formerly of Milton's on Lexington Avenue, invites all gentlemen friends to call on her at Gertie's on West 27th Street.'* Mrs. B.'s lips puckered in disapproval. "The hussy. It's ads like that that make this page a city scandal."

"And boosts *The Herald*'s circulation a hundredfold. You have to admire Bennett's head for business. He knows what sells papers." Christian took a sip of coffee. "Besides, is there really so much difference between Velvet Dress and Miss Ruthie Wilver? Our mysterious velvet lady is probably cuckolding the husband she married for *his* money. Jerome is just one in a string of, umm, companions that she's caused to become infatuated with her."

"Hmmmph. I don't believe it for a second." Mrs. B. pushed her glasses back up on her nose. "This is cryptic. *'Princess. All things required moved to new location. Arrangements in order. See Smith. Next? Butler.'* What do you suppose that all means? I've been trying to decide about this pair for weeks now."

Christian set down his coffee cup and put his empty tray aside. "Let me see that one," he said. Mrs. B. gave him the paper, and he skimmed it a few moments before he found the ad buried in the middle of the second column. "It is fairly obscure," he agreed, puzzling over it. No, he was thinking. *No!* It was simply some sort of queer coincidence. It was just because he was so damned *aware* of her that he'd even think of Jenny in connection with this. "You say you've been wondering about the Princess and Butler for a while now?"

"Hmm-mm." She took back the paper. "They've been writing back and forth since—I'm not sure—I think it's been since after Christmas."

"Aaah," he said, raising both brows and pointing an accusing finger at her. "Then you've been smuggling this paper in longer than I thought. A turncoat in my own home."

"Actually I had sworn off the paper, but it's difficult to give up, especially when others enjoy it so. Jenny started bringing it back in. She finds it as amusing as I do."

"Then you sometimes read it together?"

She nodded. "My eyes tire easily and the print's so small, you see. It's a good way to pass the time, creating stories about the people."

"Hmmm. And do you have one about the Princess?"

"Why do you keep calling her *the* Princess?" she asked, drawing off her spectacles and collapsing the thin wire stems. "It's just Princess. That's all Butler ever calls her. Jenny does the same thing as you. Odd, isn't it? I never think of calling her that."

If Christian had been swallowing anything but air he would have choked. He still had to clear his throat before he could speak. Jenny had been the Princess on the lunatic ward. He had spoken without thinking. "I wasn't even aware of it."

"That's what Jenny said too." Mrs. Brandywine placed her glasses on the table and rubbed her eyes, missing Christian's startled look. "I think Princess started sending messages first," she went on. "They were all strange. I suppose that's

232

what makes them so interesting. I shouldn't be surprised if Jenny and I aren't the only ones trying to decipher what they mean."

Christian slid off the bed and stood up, taking his tray. "It's a peculiar pastime. Perhaps you should take up knitting."

Mrs. Brandywine laid her head back against the pillows. Yawning sleepily, she shooed Christian away. "Go on with you. You're the second one today to suggest that."

Christian went. There was no need to ask who the other person was. Apparently he and Jenny Holland were of a singular mind on some issues.

Christian didn't return to *The Chronicle* after lunch. Instead he went to the old site of Phineas T. Barnum's Museum on Broadway and Ann. Newly completed and fashioned in the modern French style, the white-marbled building housed all the energies of *The New York Herald*.

He hadn't given a thought to the possibility he would be recognized, but that was indeed the case. There was an awed hush that came over each center of activity he passed on his way to the manager's office. Word traveled from mail clerks to printers to copy editors to reporters, and by the time Christian reached his destination, Frank Vollrath had his door open and a chair cleared for his guest.

Frank held out his hand to Christian. "I hope you aren't here to see Old Man Bennett. He hasn't set foot in this office for months now. Turning everything over to his son now."

"Lord, no. I told everyone I met that I wanted to see some back copies of the paper. They kept pointing me here."

Frank chuckled, tugging at his untidy eyebrows. "They probably think you're a spy." He ushered Christian in. "Give me a minute. I'll send someone for the issues. How many and how far back?"

"One copy of each edition you've published since Christmas."

233

If Frank thought it was an odd request from the publisher of a rival newspaper, he didn't show it. "All right." His voice bellowed into the outer room, rapping out Christian's request. One young man leaped away from his desk and practically tripped over his own feet in his rush to get the papers. Frank turned back to Christian. "New kid," he said, rolling his eyes. "They're so damn eager they get in the way. You want to take them with you or read them here? I can find someplace private for you."

"I'll take them." He accepted Frank's offer of a cup of coffee while he waited. "Tell me something, Frank. If I wanted to put an ad in *The Herald*'s personal columns, who would I see?"

"Hell, see my city editor," he joked. "If *you* placed an ad with us, that would be big news. Aren't you getting enough coverage in our social columns?"

"Very amusing," Christian said dryly. "Why don't you come work for *The Chronicle*?"

"Just so you can fire me? Not on your life. Besides, serving under your command in '64 was enough."

"You were a lousy soldier," Christian said matter-of-factly. "Now, about those personal ads?"

"Second floor. There's always someone at the desk during business hours to take the ad. It can also be done by mail. We have half a dozen clerks who do nothing but sort mail for the personals."

"Do you keep a record of who places the announcements?"

Frank shook his head. "Part of the appeal is anonymity if that's what the person wants." He held up his hands innocently. "No questions from us. Strictly cash transactions, no credit or billing."

"But if someone came in here personally to send a notice through your paper, there'd be a clerk in the ad office who would take care of them, right? I mean, someone on *The Herald* has to read the announcement and set the price, don't they?"

"True, and I think I know what you're getting at, but I'm

going to tell you right now that if you're hoping to identify someone coming in here, your chances are very slim. The clerks are overworked and fairly jaded about what they do. They don't read the ads so much anymore for content. They count up the words, give the cost, take the money, and say, 'Who's next?' The sheer volume of people in and out of that office every day, most of them new faces, would make it difficult for them to single out any one person."

Frank saw Christian's disappointment before it was veiled behind his hooded lids. He looked past his visitor's shoulder and crooked his finger at the young man who had just appeared in the doorway. "Give them to Mr. Marshall," he said.

Christian took the stack of neatly bundled papers and laid them on the floor by his chair. He waited for the young man to leave before he spoke again. "What if it's someone who places a notice more than once?"

"Do you mean if it runs for several days?"

"No, I'm talking about the person who keeps up a dialogue with someone else using *The Herald* as the medium."

Frank's thick mustache skewed to one side as he became thoughtful. "Your chances for identification improve, of course, but I think you'll find that most people who carry on a conversation through our paper deal with us by mail. I have to tell you, Christian, you've aroused my curiosity. Can you tell me what you're looking for? Or whom?"

"Just some information," he said carelessly.

"Are you thinking of competing for our ad business over at *The Chronicle*?"

"I might be," he said, enjoying seeing Frank's eyes bulge in astonishment. He picked up the stack of papers by the twine handle and stood. "Give Bennett my regards."

"Father or son?"

"Either one. But make sure you tell the old man I said I preferred the architecture on this lot before Barnum's Museum burnt down."

235

"Hell, that'd get me fired."

Christian's smile was sly. "I know."

"Did you go out this afternoon, m'dear?" asked Mrs. Brandywine.

Jenny nodded, fussing with Mrs. B.'s pillows. "How did you know?"

"There's still a bloom in your cheeks. I can always tell when you've been out. I'm glad to see you're doing it more often. It's good for you." She sighed longingly and pushed away the lap tray with her dinner only half eaten. "Tell me what it's like outside. Where you go . . . what you do."

"Oh, stop it, Mrs. B." Jenny laughed, covering her uneasiness. She wasn't about to explain that she had been to *The Herald* this afternoon, or that she placed what she hoped would be her last announcement to Reilly. "One would think you've spent the whole of your life in this bed. Take a look out the window. You can see for yourself that it's flurrying again and that in another five minutes or so it will be pitch black out."

The housekeeper's smile was as wistful as a young girl's. "The ball will be up in the Park," she said.

"The what?"

"The ball will be up in the Park," she repeated, frowning slightly as she studied Jenny's blank expression. "Sometimes I don't think you're from around here. The Park is *Central* Park, and everyone knows when the ball's up it means that the pond at Fifty-ninth Street and the lake north of the Mall are frozen over."

"Oh." She removed Mrs. B.'s tray, picked up a brush, and began running it through the older woman's pale hair. "Apparently everyone doesn't know it. I was born here and I've never heard it put that way."

"But you've been ice-skating there," the housekeeper prompted.

236

"Well, no. But I've been skating before. Lots of times. When I was in . . ." She caught herself in time to keep from blurting out where she had learned to skate. "When I was interested in that sort of thing," she corrected herself, affecting a superior tone, "I was told I had quite a flair for it."

Mrs. B. laughed. She had never heard Jenny sound so immodest. "Then you should go to the lake sometime. Mary Margaret and Carrie do. It would be good for you to join them."

"I don't have money for skates," she said, hoping that would end the subject.

"You can rent them."

"I don't have money to rent them." She tugged a little harder than she meant to on Mrs. B.'s hair, and the housekeeper winced. "I'm sorry," Jenny offered quickly. She set down the brush and began plaiting Mrs. B.'s waist-length hair. Jenny realized the only way to keep Mrs. Brandywine from probing into her personal affairs was to lead the conversation where she wanted it to go.

"You know, Mrs. B.," she said thoughtfully, "I've been wondering about something Mr. Marshall said today."

"What's that?"

"About sketching during the war. Even if he was only drawing pictures for the military, he must have had some talent. I mean, there had to be a reason they gave him that position."

Mrs. Brandywine was rendered speechless for a moment, her gray eyes half as wide as silver dollars. Finally she sputtered, "Do you mean to tell me you've been living under his roof for these past six weeks and you don't even know who Christian Marshall is?"

"He's the owner and publisher of *The Chronicle*," she said simply.

"Oh, my dear, dear child." Mrs. Brandywine threw up her hands and raised her eyes heavenward. "Hasn't anyone told you . . . mentioned . . . Oh, but of course they wouldn't, would they? It's been so long since he *has*, you see. Still, most

237

of us can remember what it was like before. How he would work! Disappearing into that studio for hours on end . . . making us all think we'd seen the last of him . . . it was really quite something."

Jenny was just as bewildered as she had been moments before. "What are you talking about?"

Mrs. B.'s hands fluttered back to her lap and smoothed the lawn fabric of her nightgown. "Mr. Marshall's an artist, Jenny. An exceptional one, if the truth be known." Her mouth flattened into a thin line for a moment. "And it used to be widely known. Such promise that boy had! Still has, I should think, if he'd pick up a brush again. Won't, though. As far as I know, he hasn't been in his studio in months. And it was months after the time before that. I keep it tidied for him, just hoping that one time I'll go in there and find something moved or smell the noxious odor of paint, but that never happens. I don't suspect it ever will."

"An artist," Jenny said softly, thinking of Christian's beautifully shaped hands, the lean fingers, the touch that was reverent, exploring, and set her skin tingling with heat. Then she thought of his eyes, the cool aquamarine eyes that could be remote, shuttered, and somehow alert and watchful. He was always assessing. What did he see with those eyes now? she wondered.

"Not just that," Mrs. B. continued, warming to her subject. "Before the war he designed Colonel McAllister's country home in Washington Heights and Newling's palace in the Adirondacks. Joliet's restaurant on Broadway is his work and so is the St. Mark Hotel. And he hadn't reached his twenty-sixth year when those plans were put down!"

"He does none of it anymore?" asked Jenny. "No painting? No designing?"

"Nothing."

Jenny considered that in silence for several moments. "I saw sketches," she said finally, her brows drawn together above her soft doe eyes. "I had forgotten until now. There was a

238

leather notebook in the pocket of Mr. Marshall's coat. Remember? I was wearing his coat when I first came here. I found the notebook during the journey. There were sketches in it . . . of me. They were hideous." She shuddered as a chill skittered down her spine. "Or rather *I* was hideous. I had no trouble recognizing myself." Jenny's laugh was self-mocking. "I was half out of my mind with cold and fever by then, and do you know I was still vain enough to throw that book away? I couldn't bear it that there should be a record of how I looked."

Jenny wound Mrs. B.'s plaited hair into a coil and secured it with a few pins at the nape of her neck. She helped the housekeeper adjust her nightcap so that it framed her round face attractively. "You, on the other hand, are looking quite pretty. Perhaps Mr. Marshall could be inspired to paint your portrait."

Mrs. B. blushed. "You're a flatterer, Jenny Holland. If you ever saw the women Mr. Marshall painted, you'd know he wouldn't be interested in me. Still, thank you for the compliment."

Jenny bent down and kissed Mrs. B.'s warm cheek. "I wasn't flattering you. It's the truth, but I'd be interested in seeing some of Mr. Marshall's work. Are there any paintings here in the house?"

"Only in his studio. Whatever was hanging came down. The Astors have a few pieces. And the Bennetts and the Vanderstells. People like that. Friends of the family."

"Well, since I'm not likely to be invited to Mrs. Astor's for tea and a private viewing, where is Mr. Marshall's studio?"

"On the fourth floor in the north wing. His mother had part of the attic converted for him before he ever went abroad to study. Nothing terribly fancy or he wouldn't have accepted it. When he came back he just stayed there, then the war came, and . . ." Mrs. B. took good measure of what she saw in Jenny's complacent expression. "Oh, no," she objected. "I'm not giving you my permission to go up there."

"You don't have to give me your permission. Just tell me

239

where the key is."

"No."

"I'll tidy the place as you did."

"No. Mr. Marshall would be furious. He only lets *me* up there, and that's because he knows I'm not prying into his things."

"I wouldn't be prying," she said, affronted. "I won't move anything. Everything will be just as you left it the last time. I promise."

Mrs. Brandywine was skeptical and it showed. "Why is it so important?"

"I have an interest, that's all." Because she had lain in his arms, she could have said. She had let him inside her and sometimes now, in the surreal moments between waking and sleeping, she could feel him inside her again, driving his body into hers, filling her, and there was nothing that had ever happened to her, or would happen again, that touched what he had made her feel. And in the aftermath, as he had beforehand, Christian Marshall remained a stranger.

"You'll find the key in Mr. Marshall's desk. The one in his room, not his study. If he discovers you've been up there, you'd better be prepared to tell him I sent you there to clean."

"I can tell him that," she smiled. "But let's hope he doesn't ask you. You're the one who's not a very good liar."

Mrs. Brandywine was already regretting giving in to Jenny before the younger woman was out of the room. Then she was gone and it was too late to undo what had already been done.

The steps leading up to Christian's studio were so narrow that two people could not have mounted them abreast. The dull blue wallpaper was scarred by the corners of furniture and crates that had been forced through the passage. There was a worn and dusty runner contouring the stairs. It was held in place by iron rods. The hem of Jenny's skirt scattered dust motes and cleared a few cobwebs as she climbed the stairs. She carried her lamp in both hands, holding it out at arm's length to shower light in front of her. Every time she heard a sound she paused and listened carefully. It wasn't the thought of Christian coming upon her that worried her. Jenny was much more concerned with mice.

At the top of the stairs she stopped and unlocked a second door. Knowing that she'd probably be damned for her own curiosity and quite unable to curb it, Jenny stepped inside.

The studio was much larger than she had expected. Three, perhaps even four rooms the size of the main parlor could have fit into it. The mansard roof of the house meant the interior walls of the attic did not slant away at an angle that made most of the space useless. Almost every part of the studio could be walked in without bending one's head.

There were three skylights, none of which were of any use now. Even if it hadn't already been dark out, they were covered with several inches of snow. There were also two windowed alcoves on opposite sides of the studio which brought in natural light during the daytime; one caught the dawn, the other sunset. Below the curtainless mullioned windows were built-in storage benches, their lids thickly padded and covered with blue velvet to make a comfortable seat. Jenny lit two more lamps with hers and continued exploring.

The room was too large to be heated properly, even when the fireplaces off the twin chimneys were blazing. It was a measure of her curiosity that Jenny didn't take much notice of the cold or the way her breath clouded in front of her as she examined Christian's array of clutter.

There were tables with dried palettes of paint on them. Brushes of every conceivable composition and size were scattered across the top. Most of them were ruined now because they had been left there with paint still thick on their tips. Jenny picked one up and pressed it to the tabletop. The bristles, brittle with paint, snapped as if they were threads of spun glass.

Jenny realized Mrs. Brandywine had found some things

241

impossible to tidy. The palettes and brushes, once brilliant with colors, were dulled now by a thin film of dust. She had to use her imagination to recognize vermillion and emerald and magenta and sapphire and cinnamon and ginger and rose. She blinked back salty tears, grieving for Christian and the colors he had buried here.

She found rough plans for homes that would never be finished, designs for an observatory, a theater, and, of all things, an ice cream parlor. Jenny impatiently swiped at a tear. No one could accuse Christian of pandering to the wealthy. An ice cream parlor!

Wandering the room, Jenny ran her hand lightly along the curved backs of the settees and chaise-longues, touched the uppermost rungs on the ladderback chairs and ran her knuckles down the ribbed cover of the rolltop desk. Sheets that by their relatively white condition showed signs of a recent airing shrouded all the furniture save the iron-railed bed and the desk. It seemed to Jenny that Christian must have eaten, breathed, and slept with his work. How could he have given it up?

The photographic equipment was an unexpected find. Was it Christian's or Logan's? she wondered. There were several brassbound cameras of different makes and quality, the heaviest being about twenty-one pounds, the lightest at least ten. To Jenny's eye they all appeared to be in good condition, and probably were all in working order. She found two boxes packed with lenses, another packed with chemicals that hadn't been opened, and three cases filled with a dozen glass plates each.

"It's like finding gold," she whispered aloud, her voice echoing strangely in the room. "God, how much farther along I'd be if only I'd known this was here." Reluctantly she tore herself away from the equipment. The temptation to make use of it was so great that her hands shook. "You're not a thief, Jenny," she reminded herself. "Not yet, anyway."

She glanced around again, wondering what had been used for a darkroom. She saw a door off to her left that she had supposed led to the storage section of the garret. Now she noticed the placard hanging from the doorknob saying, *Keep out*. Jenny turned it over. *Stay out*. How typically Christian, she thought, amused. He didn't want anyone interfering with his darkroom, whether he was working inside or not. She peeked in the room just long enough to assure herself she hadn't mistaken its purpose. The watertight glass baths arranged side by side on the waist-high bench and the rows of dark amber chemical bottles told her that she hadn't. Jenny sucked in her breath and turned to confront the thing that had brought her to the attic in the first place.

Christian's paintings were everywhere. Stacked five and six deep, leaning against the walls, they lined the perimeter of the spacious room. Although Jenny had been drawn to them the moment she walked through the door, she was equally wary of looking through them. She wouldn't have thought twice about viewing them in a gallery or in someone's private collection, but now, seeing them like this, posed awkwardly and carelessly in the cold confines of Christian's studio, Jenny was reminded they weren't on exhibition. This was Christian's privacy she was invading. It was more than dust she was stirring. It was the past.

All the paintings were turned to the wall; none of the canvases faced her. Perhaps a tenth were actually in elaborate gilt-edged frames; dozens and dozens of others remained stretched on the same lightweight wooden stays that Christian had once set on his easel. The city's hot, humid summers and bone-chilling winters had done considerable damage already. Most of the paintings were badly warped.

Jenny's eye caught the dates scrawled on the backs of several of them and she used that as her beginning point, hoping that Christian—or Mrs. Brandywine—had organized the paintings in some sort of chronological order. Jenny bit her lip, hesitating. How much did she really want to know?

She started with 1855.

*   *   *

Christian noticed the light coming from one of the attic windows when he was still two blocks west of the house. At first he didn't think much of it, shrugging it off as Mrs. Brandywine doing her seasonal cleaning. Then he remembered Mrs. B.'s condition and the lateness of the hour. She hadn't dragged herself to the fourth floor twenty minutes before ten just to polish his studio.

Christian warned himself not to jump to conclusions. There could be a number of explanations. The only one he would accept, however, was a burglar. A stranger in his studio was fine with him. He was likely to kill someone he knew.

Digging his heels into Liberty's flanks, Christian urged his horse home at a faster pace. He left Liberty with Joe Means, raced up the same slippery flagstones that had felled Mrs. B., and dropped the stack of *Herald* dailies that he'd had neither the time nor the courage to read earlier in his study. From the middle drawer of his desk he removed an ivory-handled Remington revolver, from another drawer, the bullets. The weight of the gun was too familiar in his hand. His palm began to sweat. With a last glance at the clock on the mantel, he began mounting the stairs.

He knew he wasn't dealing with a burglar when he went to his bedroom and found his attic key missing. He debated whether to leave the gun behind. In the end he decided to keep it. It would serve her right if he used it, he thought, for in his mind there was only one person he knew foolish enough to be in his studio.

There was not a lot of satisfaction in being right.

Jenny Holland was sitting on one of the sheet-covered settees, facing the door. She was bundled in two thick blankets she had pulled from the bed and blowing on her fingertips to keep them warm. Her breath came in short harsh sobs, and her long lashes were spiked from tears that rolled slowly over her cheeks. The area around her, the settee, the floor, her lap, was littered with hundreds of sketches he had made during the war.

Not only had she been through his paintings, he realized,

glancing around the room to see the wreckage she had created, but she had found the sketches as well.

"Damn you!" He slammed the door shut behind him. "God *damn* you!"

Jenny's head jerked up. The sketches on her lap scattered. Her face went ashen as she confronted the terrible fury in Christian's bitterly icy eyes. Her mouth went dry when she saw what Christian held in his hand.

Christian's long, slightly uneven stride carried him to Jenny's side in seconds. His left hand wound in the thick coil of hair at the nape of her neck. He yanked her to her feet as if she weighed no more than the kitten he had once likened her to. Jerking her head back, exposing her throat, Christian pressed the cold barrel of the revolver under the delicate curve of her jaw. "God, I want to hurt you," he bit out, holding her wide, terrified eyes captive with the strength of his narrow stare. "Do you understand? I want to *hurt* you!"

Jenny's voice was almost inaudible. "I know. In your place I'd feel—"

His left hand tightened in her hair so that she gasped with pain. "Don't patronize me! You can't begin to *know* how I feel." He lowered the gun slowly, watching her face all the while. Finally he tossed it on the settee. He wanted to shake her. Instead he found himself forcing her on tiptoe, raising her face to his. Her mouth was slightly parted, her lips wet. Christian's mouth covered hers punishingly. The kiss went on. And on. Desire stirred in him. He raised his head and captured her eyes with his own. "Or what I'm feeling now," he said menacingly. "Shall I show you?"

Jenny's hoarse scream was never heard beyond the walls of the studio as Christian half dragged, half carried her to the bed. "No! Oh, God, no! Don't do this—" She clawed at him, kicked at him, but her heavy wool gown and the blankets impeded her attack. She was pushed down on the bed and given no opportunity to scramble out of the way as his body followed hers.

His hands were in her hair, his fingers threaded painfully in the dark sable strands. He cupped the back of her head, keeping her immobile while his weight rested heavily across her body. His forearms pinned her and his uninjured leg was thrown across both of hers. His eyes held hers briefly, then dropped to her mouth. Her quick breathing, timid and tremulous as it was, still had the effect of pressing her breasts to his chest. He knew the shape of her intimately.

The kiss he slanted across her mouth was hungry and angry. His lips were hard and hurtful, grinding. His tongue speared her mouth, raping it. It was a tasting, and an assault. If he heard her whimper, it had no effect on him. The pressure of his mouth bruised Jenny's lips while his tongue made them damp.

Christian's fingers unwound from her hair. His breathing was ragged as he lifted his head. Jenny immediately turned her face to one side and stared at the wall, ignoring his rasping command to look at him. She bit her own lip as she felt his hands slide to the collar of her dress. She thought he was going to rip her gown. He didn't. Christian reared back and threw up her skirt and petticoat.

With the heavy folds of her gown bunched around her waist, Jenny began kicking wildly. She felt his fingers slip under the drawstring waist of her cotton drawers. She sucked in her abdomen, trying to get away from his touch, and pushed at his wrists. When she couldn't move him, when her undergarments began to be pulled inexorably over her hips, Jenny loosened her grip on Christian's wrists and clawed at his face. She bloodied his cheek on her first swipe.

"Bitch!" Christian touched his face with his fingertips, tracing the path she had scored in his cheek. Drawing his hand away, he stared at the blood for several seconds, then slowly raised his arm to backhand Jenny.

Jenny couldn't look away now. She stared at him, not defiantly, but pityingly, facing the potential blow squarely. It never came. Christian lowered his hand instead, grabbed Jenny by her hips, and twisted her so that she lay on her stomach. Her struggles were futile now. She could beat against the feather

246

tick, but not against Christian. He tore at her drawers, smacking at her hands as she tried to protect herself.

"I'm not going to beat you," he growled, releasing her long enough to open the button fly on his trousers. "I have . . ." He paused, slipping his hands under her hips and raising her toward him. ". . . .something else in mind."

Jenny felt him taking position behind her, grinding his hips against the cleft of her thighs. The heat and rigid hardness of him were pressed to her skin. The throbbing outline of him was a violation. Jenny lunged for the iron rails at the head of the bed, trying to flatten herself. She missed, her fingertips slid over the cold, curved rails and clutched at the air. Christian's curse was expressive of his intent.

"Please," she begged, twisting sideways just as he would have entered her. Her eyes were dry, what tears she had left were clogged in her throat. She stared at him, dark eyes darting, searching his face for some sign that he was vulnerable to something she could say or do. "I'm sorry, Mr. Marshall. I'm *sorry!*"

It wasn't her apology that stopped him, or even the incongruity of being addressed by his surname. It was the bleak, ruined whisper that was Jenny's voice, the reminder of earlier tortures she had suffered, that made an impact on Christian.

He sucked in his breath on a harsh sob and pushed Jenny from him, rolling away at the same time. He lay face down on the tick, his face buried in the crook of his arm.

Jenny scrambled to a sitting position, covering her naked thighs and legs with her skirt. Her torn drawers lay on the floor by the bed. She looked away from them quickly, then sat very still as Christian sat up, threw his legs over the opposite side of the bed, and righted his own clothes.

"Why aren't you running, Jenny Holland?" Christian demanded, keeping his back to her. His thumb and forefinger were pressed to his eyelids. "Why aren't you running as fast and as far as you can?"

"Am I still in danger?" she asked quietly.

Christian shifted, half turning toward her. He lowered his hand. His face was drawn, haggard. Anger lingered in the taut line of his mouth and in the cool aquamarine lights of his eyes. "Don't you understand?" he asked roughly, his narrow glance darting over her. "Don't you have any idea? As long as you're under this roof you'll be in danger from me! I can't keep my hands off you. I want you all the time. I wake up hard thinking about you under me, your legs wrapped around me, your breasts taut and swollen from my hands, my mouth! I ache from wanting you. Don't mistake this for some passionate declaraton of love," he added tersely. "I could more easily despise you than love you! What I want from you is strictly carnal pleasure. Don't try to make it pretty in your own mind. I assure you it's not pretty in mine."

Lightning quick, Christian reached across the bed and slipped his hand around the side of Jenny's neck, exerting just enough pressure to force her back down to the mattress. He readjusted his own position so that his head was directly above hers. Only his hand touched her, and it seemed to her that she remained unmoving through the strength of his will alone.

"You see how it is, Jenny?" he asked. "I still want you. And it's not going to stop until I have you, and probably not even then. I'll want you again and again . . . and again. You're like a *need* with me." He paused, waiting for a response from her. When it didn't come, he gave her a small shake. "Damn you! Say something! Tell me you'll stop pushing your way into my life, into my thoughts! Promise you'll stop following me with those wounded eyes of yours!"

"I—I'm not certain th-that I can," she stammered. "I—I've never known anyone like you before."

"You've never *known* anyone before me," he said in a low voice. His thumb touched her swollen lips. He remembered how soft they had been under his. She was so fragile, so very delicate. Christian knew he was going to destroy her rather than let her open him up to more pain. "Be my mistress."

248

Jenny couldn't think for a moment. Her lips parted on the sound of her question. "What?"

His thumb continued to trace the sensitive line of her lower lip. "I want you to become my mistress. You'll be available to me whenever I choose, for whatever I choose. I'll give you jewels, gowns, furs . . . anything you want in exchange for the right to have you in my bed, open to me . . . your hands, your mouth there for me . . . for *me!*"

Jenny returned his stare unblinkingly. "I don't want those things you said," she whispered. "But there is something . . ."

Christian's smile was almost triumphant. He knew she had a price. He knew she could be bought. "What is it?"

"My portrait," she said. "I want you to paint me. *That's* what you must do to have me as your mistress."

Christian recoiled from her. "No!"

"Then no."

"What?"

"Then my answer is no. I'll leave in the morning." She sat up, but didn't leave the bed. With deliberate, economic motions Jenny began to unbutton the bodice of her gown. When it was loose enough she pulled on the hem of her dress and eased it over her head. The strap of her chemise fell over her shoulder when she dropped her gown on the floor. Soft sable strands of her hair whispered along her collarbone and across the neckline of her chemise. The room was cold and Jenny's nipples pressed their rigid outline against the thin fabric.

"I thought you said . . ." Christian began, watching her with growing confusion. The ache in his loins was painful now.

"I did," she said steadily. "I meant it as well. I won't be your mistress and I'll be gone tomorrow, but you're not the only one who needs. Tonight we'll exchange payment in kind."

Chapter 10

Christian decided it was possibly the most brazen proposal he had ever received. This was the woman he thought of as a fragile and delicate spirit? He could only stare at her incredulously.

Jenny unlaced her shoes and kicked them off. "Don't mistake this for a declaration of love," she said calmly, rolling down her stockings. She buried her feet beneath the goose-down comforter. "All I want from you is . . . how did you phrase it? Oh, yes . . . carnal pleasure."

A muscle worked in Christian's lean jaw as his own ugly statements were impassively hurled back at him. She was watching him through the long, heavy fan of her lashes, her head tilted to one side. A sigh parted her lips, and her hand paused in the act of lowering her chemise strap. Her thumb made a light pass across her collarbone, drawing Christian's eyes.

"That's what you said, isn't it?" she asked softly. "Not to make it pretty? Well, I'm not."

Christian's eyes darkened with desire, but remnants of his old anger remained, directed at himself this time. He should have told her that when he was with her, when his body joined hers and the sensations of their loving were shuddering through him, it was so exquisite, so beautiful that it frightened him. He didn't believe he had done anything in his life to deserve the kind of pleasure he had experienced with her. But he couldn't tell her that. He couldn't expose himself to Jenny Holland. She already knew too much about him.

"Christian?" She said his name with a whisper-soft huskiness. "Should I go now?"

He shook his head, reaching for her wrist. "But perhaps we should go to my room," he said lowly. "It's too cold for you here."

"Warm me."

"Oh, God, Jenny Holland," Christian groaned, tugging on her wrist so that the gap between them was narrowed. "I will. I *will*." His palms stroked her arms from wrist to shoulder, suffusing her skin with heat, but it was his mouth on her lips and his tender, tasting caress that warmed her from the inside out.

The embers of desire were buried deep and faintly lit, but Christian found them, nurtured them, and brought out the fiery response that Jenny wanted to know again. He brushed her mouth lightly, teasing her with gentle kisses at the corners of her lips until she opened her mouth and asked for something more. The tip of his tongue made a damp outline of her lips, traced the ridged barrier of her teeth, and finally dipped into her mouth deeply and took up the sweet battle with hers.

He kissed her temples. The dark strands of her hair tickled his mouth. There was nothing more fragrant, more alluring than Jenny Holland's sable, soft hair. Christian found it difficult not to tell her that. He rubbed his cheek against her instead, back and forth, awash in the silky cascade that was Jenny's hair. His teeth caught the lobe of her ear. He tugged and heard the tiny catch in her breathing. "Sweet Jenny," he whispered just before his tongue followed the whorl of her ear.

Christian's mouth touched Jenny's brows, her eyelids, the delicate line of her pared nose. He kissed the faint hollows just below her cheekbones, the tip of her chin, the exposed line of her throat as she arched it beneath him. Her pulse beat warmly against his mouth.

There were words exchanged, hurriedly whispered instructions that substituted for other words, other phrases neither of them dared to think, let alone say aloud.

"Help me with this," he said, fingering the neckline of her chemise.

"Later: "Your shirt. Take it off."

When they were naked: "Put your hand there."

"There?" she asked.

"Yes," he said, sucking in his breath. *"Yes."*

The goose-down comforter covered them from head to toe. "This must be what a cocoon is like," she said, pressing herself against the length of his body.

"Do you want to be a butterfly?" His fingertips slid up the soft skin of her inner thigh.

"Yes."

"Then spread your . . . wings, Jenny."

Christian's breath was hot against her neck. His mouth moved to her breasts. They were sensitive from the earlier manipulations of his hands. He took one coral-tipped peak in his lips and tugged. He could almost feel the cord of fire that snapped in a whiplike fashion from her breasts to the core of her pleasure. Her thighs opened to him and his fingers found her, exploring, stroking. She held him tightly, placing her mouth against his shoulder so that he could feel the murmurs of her desiring against his flesh.

Her hips bucked as he continued to caress her with his fingertips. Her heels dug into the tick. Christian could feel her nails in his back, her palms sliding along the length of his taut skin from shoulder to buttocks. Her knuckles brushed his thighs. She cradled him with the heat of her body. Her legs entwined with his so that he knew the long, lithe shape of them.

"Invite me inside," he said throatily, grinding his hips against her.

Jenny's hand traveled down his chest, flickered across the

253

hard tips of his nipples, then followed the narrowing path of hair past his flat belly and lower still, until her hand curled around his throbbing arousal. She guided him into her.

There was no holding back then. Christian drove himself deeply, feeling her contract all around him. "Did I hurt you?" he asked, levering himself up on elbows. He couldn't see her face in the darkness of their cocoon.

"No." She touched his cheek. "This is what I want. You. Inside me. Does wanting you like this make me a—"

Christian stopped her. Ducking his head, he had no trouble finding her mouth with his. "Ssshh," he whispered against her lips. "No talking. Just feel, Jenny. Just feel."

It was not a difficult order to obey. Christian began moving inside her, slow, deep thrusts that raised slender threads of tension in her arms and legs.

Jenny moved against him, sounding her pleasure in sharp little gasps that, had she but known it, excited Christian as much as her fingers curling into the hair at the nape of his neck. Their passion mounted as they made their payment in kind, bartering kisses, caresses, touches, and tastes until the sensations between them became too great to sustain.

There was a shared cry as tension melted, making their limbs liquid and lazy. They were awash in sensual pleasure, everything they felt in that moment so clearly defined the very endings of their nerves seemed to sparkle with heat and light.

Christian was a long time moving away from her. She did not seem to mind that he stayed inside her or that he remained partially aroused. Jenny just held him, her long, slender arms a gentle chain around his waist. The back of his hand traced the curve of her hip.

"We should go downstairs," he said.

"No. Let's stay here."

"All right."

Silence settled between them, and Christian thought Jenny had fallen asleep until she said his name. "What is it?" he asked.

254

"Do you ever still think I'm mad?"

"No."

"Never?"

"Never."

"Thank you for that," she said softly. Jenny rested her head on his shoulder. "If I were someone else . . . someone—I don't know—someone in the upper crust . . . would you still have asked me to be your mistress?"

"Meaning, I suppose, that you think if you were the daughter of some wealthy society matron I could be induced to offer marriage. Well, nothing, not even an outraged father with a gold-plated shotgun, could make me offer—"

Jenny placed her index finger over his mouth. "You don't know what I was thinking," she said, amused. "Would you still have asked me to be your mistress?"

"Yes," he bit out. "Now what did that prove?"

"That I'm not merely a convenience to you because I happen to live under your roof. That you'd want me in the same way if I came to you on a silver platter."

Christian's brows pulled together in a thoughtful frown. "And that's all right with you? You wouldn't want to be anything but my mistress?"

Jenny laughed quietly. "Have you forgotten? I don't even want to be that."

"But—"

She shook her head, cutting him off as her hair rubbed against his shoulder. "That's not what tonight is about. It's about goodbye."

Christian didn't believe her, but he didn't tell her that. The surest way to force her out the door, he thought, was to tell her he knew she was bluffing. He had every intention of keeping her with him until he decided their odd, but infinitely satisfying, relationship was at an end.

"I want you again," he said, hating the edge of despair he heard in his voice. It mocked him, warning him that he might not know her as well as he thought. "Now."

"All right," she said.

Their lovemaking was like a punishment now. It did not have the hard, brutal selfishness that Christian had tried to force on Jenny when he found her in the studio, but it had a certain wild fierceness to it that was more like the animal coupling he had professed to want.

Their touching was greedy, their caresses clumsy with need. The force with which he claimed Jenny left her breathless. His mouth was hard on hers. His teeth nipped at her throat, her shoulder, the tips of her breasts. He left tiny bruises where the hard, humid suck of his mouth caught her flesh. She left crescent brands on his skin with the tapered ends of her nails.

She wound her legs around him, and he was so deep inside her that she thought he must be touching her womb. Her willow-slender body was supple under the sinewy strength of his. "Christian," she said, "I can't . . . no more—"

"Yes, you can. Just a little higher . . . feel it, Jenny?"

She felt it. She felt him. The sensation and Christian were one and the same. She was enveloped by the shattering tension and her body shuddered against him. Christian went rigid as her pleasure swept from her into him and it seemed they were no longer individuals but shared a singular identity.

After their ragged breathing had calmed they fell asleep in one another's arms. Christian woke several times during the night, and each time he reached for Jenny she was there. Still, in the morning she was gone.

Christian arrived on Scott Turner's doorstep just as Susan and Amy were sitting down to breakfast. He was carrying the stack of *Herald* dailies under his arm. He stamped his feet to brush off the snow as Susan opened the door to him.

"Christian!" She couldn't mask her surprise. "Come in, come in! God, it's cold out there this morning!" Susan shut the door briskly as an eddy of snow and wind whirled through the entranceway. "Scott's not here," she told him. "He's already gone to the hospital. If it's something medical, then . . ."

Christian shook his head. "That's all right. There's no emergency. I can talk to him later. Mostly I came to see you. I need your help."

"My help?" Susan was astonished.

"You, er, don't mind, do you?"

"Mind? No, of course I don't mind. I'll do whatever I can." Her smile was friendly as she held out her hand for Christian's coat, hat, and muffler. She watched him transfer the stack of papers from one hand to the other as he shrugged out of his coat. "Does it have something to do with those?" she asked, pointing to the papers. She hung up his garments in the entrance hall, looking at him expectantly.

"Hmm-mm. Is there someplace I can put them?"

"Come on into the dining room. Amy and I were just going to have breakfast. Would you like to join us?"

"A cup of coffee would be fine." He dropped the papers on one corner of the table as Amy slid off her chair to clutch at his legs. "Good morning, brat," he said, ruffling her strawberry-blond curls. "How's the kitten? Muffin, isn't it?"

Susan wasn't fooled by Christian's gentleness with Amy. She saw the strain about his mouth and eyes, the forced smile and drawn skin, and realized that only something of extreme urgency could have brought him around this early in the morning. Sliding a cup of coffee in his direction, Susan broke into her daughter's excited conversation concerning the kitten. "Amy, why don't you eat breakfast in the kitchen with Mrs. Adams? I bet she'll let you give Muffin a saucer of milk yourself."

That caught Amy's attention. She wiggled out of Christian's grip with such alacrity that both adults laughed.

Susan shut the door to the dining room. "What's happened, Christian? Is it Mrs. B.?"

"No," he said quickly. "No, she's fine." He pulled back a chair and sat down, folding his hands around the steaming mug of coffee to warm them. "It's Jenny. She left me

257

this morning."

"She's gone?" Susan's green eyes clouded and she sank slowly into her seat. She hadn't missed Christian's phrasing. Jenny hadn't merely left. She had left *him*. Interesting . . . and troubling. "But where could she possibly go? I wasn't aware that she had anyone."

"I think she might," he said slowly. "I'm not certain, but there might be someone who's waiting for her."

"Christian, maybe you'd better start this story closer to the beginning." She saw him balk at the idea, his mouth flattening grimly. "All right then," she said, retreating a little, "begin with where you think she is. I know you probably think Scott tells me everything, but he doesn't. I've never heard him even hint that Jenny had family or friends."

"I don't think she's ever said that she has. That's just it, Susan. Jenny's told us precious little about herself—next to nothing, in fact. What Scott and I know is mainly supposition, and Scott's ideas are so fanciful they're almost ludicrous. I mean, if she were *really* held in that lunatic ward against her will, why hasn't she ever said anything about it? Don't you think that's strange?"

Susan shrugged. "Perhaps she's afraid to talk about the ugliness of her experience. I should think you'd be able to sympathize with her there." She held up her hands, palms outward. "Sorry. I couldn't help myself. No more pointed thrusts, I promise."

Christian nodded, accepting her apology. "Have you ever heard Scott call her the Princess?"

"Yes. He mentioned it was her name on the ward. It was one of the incongruencies that intrigued him."

"I know." He motioned to the newspapers. "Do you read *The Herald*? The personal columns?"

"Sometimes," she admitted a trifle sheepishly.

"Recently?"

"No."

"Well, someone's been placing notices in there and signing

258

them Princess."

"Oh, Christian." Susan laughed, shaking her head. "You can't possibly think that—"

"I do," he said firmly. "And even if I didn't, I'd still have to investigate it. There's no other lead, you see. If I can't find her through this, then she's lost to me."

Susan's heart went out to him. This was a Christian Marshall others rarely got to see. "You want her back?" she asked.

Christian was startled momentarily. "No . . . I don't know." He looked past Susan's shoulder. One of his early paintings hung on the wall. It was a still life and not a particularly good one, but Susan had liked the colors and the way he had used light to make the apples look as if they were ripening even as you looked at them. That painting was supposed to be in his studio with the others, but when Susan discovered he was removing them from the walls of Marshall House she had begged one from him. "I want to know she's safe," he said. He thought of Jenny and how he would tilt her head to one side and use light along the curve of her neck and shoulder to show the translucent quality of her skin. Her lips would be glistening, ripening. He would paint desiring in her eyes.

"Do you love her, Christian?" Susan asked boldly, watching him closely.

Christian's aquamarine eyes dropped away from the painting. "No, Susan, I don't love her. That would be . . ." His voice trailed off. "No, I don't love her."

He believed it even if Susan found just cause to doubt. She didn't argue, though. "What is it you want me to do?"

Christian stripped away the twine that bound the stack of papers. "I have three weeks' worth of papers here. That's several thousand personal notices. I need help going through them. I want to find every reference to Princess or Butler. That's who Princess writes to. In yesterday's paper there was a reference by Butler to a location. I'm hoping the specific site was mentioned in an earlier ad." From his jacket pocket he took out the notice from yesterday's *Herald* and showed it to

Susan. "This is all I have to go on."

Susan read it aloud. *"Princess. All things required moved to new location. Arrangements in order. See Smith. Next? Butler."* Her eyes were doubtful. "You could be right, I suppose. There may be an address in these earlier editions. I assume that 'Next?' means Butler is awaiting further instructions."

"That's what I thought. I'm going to pick up the paper for the next several days to see if there's anything in there."

"And Smith?"

"I don't have any idea."

"What arrangements, I wonder?"

"I'm hoping that will become clearer once we find the other notices. Mrs. B. mentioned there were others detailing some sort of list."

Susan pushed her plate of cold eggs and bacon to one side and rolled up the long sleeves of her russet day gown. "I detest newsprint on my clothes," she explained when Christian regarded her action questioningly.

"Oh, I thought you were getting ready to do some scrubbing."

"Hand me some of those papers," she said in businesslike tones. "The sooner we start, the sooner we'll know something."

Christian and Susan read steadily right up until luncheon. The reading was tiresome to their eyes, which was precisely the reason Christian hadn't asked for Mrs. Brandywine's help. He didn't even know if his housekeeper realized Jenny was gone yet. He'd left the house without a word to anyone himself.

"What do we have so far?" he asked as Mrs. Adams brought them hot bowls of spiced tomato soup and slices of freshly baked bread. Christian leaned back in his chair and allowed Amy onto his lap. He tucked a linen napkin into the collar of her dress.

Susan rubbed her eyes, then stifled a yawn with the back of her hand. "What we have doesn't amount to much yet," she told him. She fingered through the clippings near her placemat. "'*Butler. Contact printing frame. Rack. Stu will know. Princess.*' And: '*Princess. Need funds. Items on original list expensive. Suggestions? Butler.*'" Susan buttered a slice of bread and passed it to her daughter. "Don't dribble on Uncle Christian, dear," she said absently. "Here, Christian, this one is interesting. '*Butler. Watch Ruby R. Sterling—Princess.*' I have to admit that I'm no closer to understanding than I was when we started."

"I'm not either," he said reluctantly. "Let's break after lunch. I'll pick up today's *Herald* and see if anyone in the office where they take the ads remembers Jenny. I'm told that it's not likely." He ducked his head then, concentrating on his lunch and Amy, and hid his despair from Susan.

Scott Turner recognized William MacCauley's shuffle before the attendant tapped him on the shoulder. "What is it, William?" he asked, removing his stethoscope. "Can't you see I'm busy with a patient?"

"Dr. Morgan wants to see you in his office."

Scott hid his agitation and readjusted the sheet about his patient's chest. "When?"

"I think he means now."

"You're doing much better, Mr. Reid," Scott said, ignoring William for the time being. "Your fever's down since yesterday. I expect it will be normal by morning. A few days' observation for the chest pains you've had and then we'll release you. The attendant will be around soon with your medication." Scott smiled encouragingly at the older man and patted him lightly on the wrist. "I'll be back this afternoon to see you." He stood up, taking his leather bag from the neighboring empty bed. "Excuse me, Mr. Reid, but you heard William. I'm in demand."

Scott was in the hallway before his scowl showed. He pushed back a fallen lock of wheat-colored hair and snapped at MacCauley. "This had better be good. I don't have time for administrative meetings in the middle of morning rounds."

William MacCauley shrugged and shuffled and kept his mouth shut.

Scott was further irritated when he was kept cooling his heels in Morgan's outer office. According to the hospital administrator's secretary, Dr. Morgan was busy with some important benefactors.

"Oh, for God's sake," Scott muttered. "At least tell him I'm here, Porter. MacCauley said Dr. Morgan wanted to see me right away."

Charles Porter's thin lips pursed tightly. "He'll see you when the Benningtons are gone," he repeated.

"The Benningtons? Those are the benefactors?"

Porter nodded, tidying the stack of papers on his desk.

Scott sat down in a brown leather armchair and stretched his legs in front of him. "I wasn't aware they contributed to the hospital," he said casually. How odd, he thought. If Christian hadn't related the peculiar events that had occurred at Amalie's on New Year's Eve, Scott realized he wouldn't have given a second thought to the Benningtons visiting the hospital. Not that it meant anything anyway, he cautioned himself. He likened it to the experience of learning a new word, then suddenly seeing the word everywhere. It wasn't the best analogy, since Scott had known of the Benningtons before Christian ever mentioned them.

He and Susan had their account at First Hancock Savings and Trust, where William Bennington was president and Stephen sat on the board of directors. Scott was still considering taking his money out of the bank. It didn't sit well with him that Stephen was a hothead and his father appeared to have private dealings with Amalie Chatham. The conclusion that Scott and Christian had finally drawn from the incident was that Amalie had wanted Jenny for her stable and that the senior Bennington was an interested customer—until he believed Christian's story about Jenny being a thief. Apparently William Bennington wanted a whore he didn't have to worry would steal him blind. On the other hand, Stephen's unprovoked attack on Christian remained a mystery. Neither Scott nor Christian could make anything of it, and Stephen's tersely worded apology sent round a few days after the New Year did not shed any light on the matter.

Scott had actually been more interested in Jenny's resourcefulness in the situation than in Christian's account of events in the hallway. Jenny Holland was clearly a remarkable young woman, and Scott was increasingly convinced that his original thoughts concerning her commitment to the lunatic ward were not so very far off the mark. It was unfortunate, he thought, that Christian remained unconvinced.

"Have they been donors long?" Scott asked when Porter failed to respond to his first overture. The secretary was looking extremely uncomfortable, Scott decided.

Porter's voice was staccato, impatient, and hushed. "Since October," he rapped out. "And you didn't hear me say a word. Not a word, you understand? They're *anonymous.*"

"Oh, I see," Scott said dryly. "No social recognition for their goodwill, just greasing heaven's gate a little."

"Must you be so—" He broke off as Dr. Morgan's office door opened and the Benningtons stepped out. "You can go in now, Dr. Turner," he said, rising from behind his desk to escort Stephen and William from the building.

Scott grimaced at Porter's fawning. He went into Morgan's office unaware that both Benningtons had paused in their leaving to give him a second, interested look.

Dr. Morgan was standing at the tall, curtainless windows directly behind his desk. The morning sun was reflected off the film of macassar oil Morgan used to slick back his hair. The middle part was arrow straight, much like Morgan's posture. When he heard Scott's entrance he turned away from the window. He was frowning. His brows were like sooty thumbprints above his eyes. A deep crease connected them. "Dr. Turner," he said stiffly by way of a greeting.

"Dr. Morgan."

This brief exchange was as much as Horatio Morgan allowed for amenities. He went directly to the point of the meeting. "Do you remember that Jane Doe patient we treated a number of weeks ago? Well, it's recently come to my attention that perhaps Dr. Glenn was mistaken in his identity of the body that was found . . ."

Scott barely heard the rest of Morgan's statement. He was slowly shutting the office door and thinking it was going to be a very, *very* long day.

Christian, Susan, and Scott had their chairs pulled in a semicircle around the fireplace. Except for an occasional popping ember, the parlor was quiet. Christian's toes nudged the brick apron. He held Muffin in his lap and his fingertips idly stroked the kitten's calico fur. Susan's hand was interlocked with Scott's. Occasionally she squeezed it. Scott held his sleeping daughter, his chin resting in the cap of her curls, his expression thoughtful.

"I keep wondering where Dr. Morgan came by his information," Scott said, breaking the heavy silence as he mulled over the interview again.

"Does it really matter?" Christian asked.

"No, I suppose not. Someone from the hospital could have seen her on one of her walks to *The Herald*. If the number of clippings are any indication, then she was out of the house quite a bit in the last few weeks."

"We still don't know that Jenny *is* Princess," Susan reminded her husband. "Christian couldn't find anyone at *The Herald* who could confirm his suspicions. No one remembered Jenny, and there's no clue as to the identity of this Butler person. You gentlemen are assuming Butler is a man, but there's absolutely no evidence to support that."

"There's precious little evidence to support anything," Christian said dully. "What do we know except that she's gone and that Dr. Morgan's suddenly concerned that his Jane Doe is alive?" Christian put the kitten on the floor and leaned forward in his chair, resting his chin on his folded hands. "Does Morgan really think I know something about Jane Doe?"

Scott nodded. "There were no direct accusations, but the good doctor was definitely pumping me for information about you. I suppose I was foolish to think that our doctor-patient relationship would never come to his attention. Glenn probably mentioned that I was in your home the same evening that Jenny escaped. Remember? Susan sent him over when he showed up here."

Susan grimaced. "What a dear you are to bring that error to my attention—again," she said pointedly.

Scott had the grace to look guilty. "Sorry, darling."

"It's not important now," Christian interjected. "I'm far more concerned about Morgan's general interest in Jenny. It doesn't make sense that he'd show so much interest in a Jane Doe."

"Haven't I been saying that all along?" Scott asked the room at large.

"Yes, dear," Susan soothed, patting the back of his hand. "You've been telling us from the beginning that she's a somebody. I think even Christian is coming around to that point of view. I know your conversation with Dr. Morgan has made me a believer. But the question now is which somebody is she?" Susan's lower lip was thrust forward as she sighed wearily. "I wish I could remember where I've seen her before. I can't help but think that—"

"You've seen Jenny before?" Christian interrupted.

Susan nodded. "Hmm-mm. But it's no good asking me about the incident. I can't place it. I told Scott it was someplace quite ordinary. I mean, where do we go that's not ordinary? Scott doesn't even like taking a box at the theater for the season."

This time it was Scott who grimaced. "What a dear you are to bring that to my attention—again," he said pointedly.

Christian cut off Susan's reply. "Someplace ordinary," he

mused. "Like an ice cream parlor? A store?"

"Yes," Susan said. "Exactly like that. But it's no good, Christian. I haven't been able to recall the incident in enough detail. I think Jenny must simply remind me of someone else."

"There *is* no one else like her," Christian said firmly. He stood, missing the knowing looks that Susan and Scott exchanged behind his back. He stretched, arching his back and throwing his arms wide, and walked to the table where Susan had put the clippings. The notices they had spent all morning and late afternoon collecting were pasted to a sheet of writing paper so they couldn't be scattered. Susan had been inspired to arrange them in chronological order and number them. She thought organization might help. It didn't. The ads Princess had placed remained an enigma. "I'm going to look at the notices again," he said. "The answer has to be in here."

Susan groaned softly. "I *can't* look at them one more time. Scott, why don't you help Christian? You haven't spent as many hours with them as we have. You're still fresh."

"Always," he leered playfully.

"Oh, stop that. Let me have Amy. I'll take her up to bed, and after she's settled I'll make us all a strong pot of coffee."

Scott gave his wife a peck on her proffered cheek, then joined Christian at the table. Neither of the men sat down. They leaned over the table, supporting themselves on their elbows, and scooted the paper back and forth between them.

1. *Butler. Contact printing frame. Rack. Stu will know. Princess.*

2. *Princess. Need Funds. Items on original list expensive. Suggestions? Butler.*

3. *Butler. Watch Ruby R. Sterling—Princess.*

4. *Butler. Potassium iodide. Ferrous sulfate. Potassium cyanide. Stu will know. Princess.*

5. *Princess. Need delivery address. Butler.*

6. *Butler. Found ideal location. Please secure for me. Gospel Hotel. And he rose, and immediately took up the pallet and*

266

went out before them all; so that they were all amazed and glorified God, saying "We never saw anything like this!" Princess.

7. *Princess. All things required moved to new location. Arrangements in order. See Smith. Next? Butler.*

8. *Butler. Meet me afternoon Friday or Saturday. Princess.*

Scott blew air through his lips and made clicking noises with his tongue. He was a loud thinker. "Who is this Stewart fellow?" he asked after several minutes of blustery thought. "And what the hell does he know that we don't?"

"Don't swear," Christian cautioned. "Susan will come back down here and blame me for your fall from grace." He pushed the paper to Scott. "Where do you see Stewart?" he asked.

"Right here." He pointed to the line in numbers one and four which mentioned Stu. "Stu is short for Stewart, isn't it?"

"Possibly, but I don't think so in this case. I think the Princess is referring to something else. These chemicals she mentions have given me an idea. I don't know why I didn't see it earlier. Do you know what they're used for?"

"Poison?"

Christian's mouth skewed to one side as he gave his friend a dry glance. "This is Jenny Holland we're probably talking about, Scott. Try to keep that in mind. I don't think she's planning a murder."

"Well then? What are they used for?"

"They're all chemical agents in the wet-plate process."

"Speak English, please."

"Photography," Christian clarified. "They're chemicals used to develop pictures." His words quickened as he became excited by his own idea. "Potassium iodide is the chemical that's added to collodion. Don't frown, Scott, I can explain. Collodion is rather like a glue of sorts, a thick fluid that's poured over the glass plates photographers use to take pictures. When it dries it forms a remarkably tough, transparent, and colorless skin. The collodion becomes the film that holds a photographic image."

267

"I see," Scott said slowly. His expression was doubtful. "I think. I've never done any photography."

"After the collodion is set," Christian continued, "but before it's actually dry, the plate is sensitized in a bath of silver nitrate."

"And the chemical reaction makes light-sensitive silver iodide," Scott said, the fog beginning to clear.

"Exactly. The light-sensitive plate is placed in the camera and the exposure is made. The Princess didn't ask for silver nitrate, so I think we can assume that she already had access to some or that it was an item on the original list that Butler mentions in number two. The other chemicals she wants— ferrous sulfate and potassium cyanide—are used after the plate has been exposed. The ferrous sulfate is the standard developer and potassium cyanide is used to fix the image. This is followed by a wash of water."

"That's all very interesting. But who is Stewart?"

"Not Stewart. Stu. As in studio. She was obviously concerned that Butler wouldn't understand what she required, so she recommended talking to someone at a photographic studio. Anyone there could explain to Butler precisely what she was asking for. That's what she's talking about when she mentions the contact printing frame and rack. The printing frame is what holds the negative to the paper and the rack is for holding the frames in the sunlight for exposure."

"So, the Princess is interested in photography."

"I'd say it's more than an interest. She seems quite serious about it. Perhaps she's a professional photographer."

"Do you still think it's Jenny we're talking about?" asked Scott.

Christian nodded briefly. "I'm more convinced than ever. I overheard a brief part of a conversation between Mrs. B. and Jenny. Jenny was talking about Mathew Brady's work. She was obviously familiar with it. Admittedly it's a slim connection, but I think it's worth noting." Christian's mouth turned up in a faint smile. He spared a glance in Scott's direction. "You once told me that Jenny was very clever, probably more clever than either or both of us. If these ads don't point that out, then I don't know what does."

"The truth is, they're probably *too* damn clever. What does this mean?" Scott pointed to numbers two and three. "Butler is short of funds and asks for suggestions. Princess tells him to watch Ruby R. Sterling. I'm afraid that Ruby R. Sterling sounds like the moniker of a madam, Christian. In fact, I'd wager if we asked around, we'd discover Ruby R. is exactly that type of person."

Christian was spared answering by Susan's return to the parlor. She placed a tray on the table and began pouring coffee for each of them. "I can hardly believe what I was hearing, Scott. I had a great-aunt named Ruby and she was definitely not a madam."

Scott's smile was rueful as he accepted his cup of coffee. "It was just a suggestion. It seems to me that we have to toss around some possibilities here or we're unlikely to hit on what the Princess was talking about."

"Actually, I do have an idea," Susan said. "It occurred to me when I heard you say the words aloud. I think when Butler asked for suggestions, the Princess's reply tells what to sell. A watch. A ruby r., which is probably a ring. And sterling, which I take to mean silver."

Christian grabbed Susan by the waist, lifted her a few inches off the floor, and kissed her full on the mouth. "You're brilliant!"

She blushed prettily and smiled archly at her husband. "Do you see, Scott? I am brilliant."

"I never doubted it," Scott said gallantly. "Christian, would you stop fondling my wife?"

Embarrassment warmed Christian's cheeks and he released Susan so quickly that Scott laughed. "All right," he said, serious again. He stabbed at the clippings with his forefinger. "Susan's explanation makes sense, but we still don't know where the Princess is. It seems as if Butler had no difficulty understanding her message. He asks for a delivery address and she provides him with one. A few days later he replies that everything has been sent there. I think we can assume that when she asks Butler to meet her, she is referring to the address in number six."

Above the lip of her coffee cup Susan frowned. "I don't know any Gospel Hotel. Do either of you?"

Both men shook their head. "It occurred to me that it might be a place for indigents to get a hot meal and roof over their head for the night," Scott said. "Aren't there some missions in the Bowery or the Five Points?"

"There probably are," Christian said. "But I can't imagine that one needs to secure a room there. That's what the Princess asked Butler to do for her. And do you really suppose a mission would accept delivery of photographic equipment or that she would refer to it as an ideal location? It seems to me that the Princess is talking about more permanent lodging."

"What about this verse?" asked Susan. "I assume it's from the Bible, but what is it supposed to mean?"

Scott shrugged. "I don't recognize it, but I'll get our Bible." He left the parlor and returned a few moments later with it. Placing it on the table, Scott began to thumb through it. "Old or New Testament?"

"New," said Susan. "I think it's talking about a healing. Perhap you'll find something in John."

"Gospels!" Scott and Christian spoke at the same time, excitement in their voices. Scott's fingers turned the pages rapidly.

Christian raked his copper-streaked hair. "I can't believe how incredibly dull-witted I've been! Matthew, Mark, Luke, and John," he explained to Susan, who was frowning in his direction. "It's St. Mark! It has to be the St. Mark Hotel that she's talking about! There are no hotels named after the others."

Scott's eyes were skimming the text of the Gospel according to St. Mark. "This could take me forever," he sighed.

"That's what the concordance is for," Susan said gently. She nudged the heavy Bible away from her husband and slid it in front of herself. "Give me a moment. 'Pallet' would seem to be the word to look up." Ignoring the expectant, anxious expressions of Christian and Scott, Susan took her time examining the concordance. Moments later she raised her head, smiling triumphantly. "Here it is, the Book of Mark, Chapter Two, Verse Twelve." She read it aloud. When she was finished her smile faded. "I still don't understand. What does the Princess mean by it?"

"I don't think she means anything by it," said Christian. "It's not the content that's important to her. It's the placement. Don't you see? Chapter *Two*, Verse *Twelve*. 212. That's the room she asked Butler to get for her. Actually, it's a suite of rooms. I know every inch of that hotel, and the Princess requested a corner suite. If she had wanted something else she would have simply chosen a different chapter and verse."

"How clever," Susan said admiringly.

"Yes." Christian's voice and expression was dry. "She's clever."

"Well, Christian," said Scott. "It seems that you know where the Princess can be found. What do you do now?"

Christian folded the paper with the clippings pasted to it and put it in his vest pocket. "I wait, of course," he said.

"Wait?"

He nodded. "Until Friday or Saturday afternoon, when Butler meets the Princess. It will rather be like killing two birds with one stone. I'll know if Jenny is the Princess and if Butler is her lover." But how will I stand it if it's true?

It was late when Jenny finally arrived at the St. Mark Hotel. Most of the day had been spent brooding. Had she done the right thing leaving Marshall House? Was she certain she could go through with her plans? What if she were caught? At

271

different times during the day she had been absolutely paralyzed with fear. If Christian had appeared during her aimless wandering around the frozen pond at Central Park, Jenny would have flung herself in his arms and begged him to let her be his mistress. But of course he hadn't, and Jenny believed she had come too far to cry surrender. She had to go on.

Jenny's feet hardly made a sound crossing the wide lobby of the St. Mark. The polished mahogany paneling reflected her passing from the glass-enclosed entranceway to the registry desk. The candle-lighted chandeliers burnished her hair. She tried not to think that Christian Marshall had designed this building. She hadn't known that when she'd first realized the location of the St. Mark was perfect for her purposes. It shouldn't make any difference to her now, yet it did. Jenny felt as if she were still surrounded by him, as if she had never left the protective circle of his arms. It was not the clean break she had envisioned when she left him.

"I believe you have a suite reserved for me," she told the desk clerk.

"The name, miss?" he inquired politely, frowning at Jenny over the rim of his glasses. Her manner of dress was not precisely shabby, but it certainly did not speak to the kind of money that most guests of the hotel had.

"Mrs.," she corrected. "Smith. A friend made the arrangements for me. I was told everything would be taken care of when I got here."

The clerk ran his finger up and down the hotel's log book. "Are you Mrs. Carlton Smith or Mrs. Norris Smith?"

"Which one is Room 212?" she asked.

The clerk looked at Jenny oddly, but answered nonetheless. "Mrs. Carlton Smith," he said.

"Then that's who I am," she answered sweetly. Jenny slid a one-dollar note across the surface of the desk. Until she reached her suite it was all the money she had. She hoped it was enough. "May I count on your discretion, Mr.—?"

"Hughes," the clerk said, pocketing the bill. "Henry Hughes. And you may certainly depend on me, Mrs. Smith." He turned his back, found the key to Room 212, and faced Jenny again. He leaned around across the counter, whispering conspiratorially as he passed her the key. "Will there be many gentleman callers, ma'am?"

Jenny wasn't surprised that he thought she was a prostitute. What other kind of woman didn't know what name she had been registered under? *Smith,* she thought disgustedly, shaking her head as she climbed the stairs to the second floor. Reilly should have been more imaginative with her alias or more specific about which Smith. Now the clerk would expect to have his pockets lined periodically just to keep his silence. The owners of the St. Mark probably frowned on a prostitute setting up business in one of their suites.

Jenny rolled her eyes. She wondered if Hughes had been on duty when Reilly had brought in all the photographic equipment. She hoped he had been. That would give the little toady something to think about!

William Bennington's disgusted expression was directed at his son. "Put down that paper and listen to me," he directed sourly.

Behind his copy of *The Herald* Stephen's brows rose slightly. His tired reply came from behind the paper. "I've heard every word, Father, and I fail to see where it's leading. I thought our visit this morning to Dr. Morgan settled things. You told him your concerns and he said he'd look into the matter. If you thought it was so damn important to do something, why did you wait this long to go to Morgan?"

William yanked the newspaper out of Stephen's hands. He crumpled it up angrily and threw it into the fire. "I waited," he gritted out, "because I thought Amalie's suspicions were without substance. What am I supposed to believe when a madam whore like Amalie tells me that she thinks she's seen

273

my stepdaughter? We had Morgan's assurances that she was dead. Of course I believed Morgan."

Stephen wasn't looking at his father. He was watching the newspaper go up in flames. "I anticipate the blame for this being laid squarely on my shoulders, and, frankly, I won't accept it. If you had told me earlier about your conversation with Amalie, I would have mentioned the incident with Reilly on the walk in front of this house. You didn't and I didn't. When you did, I did. It's that simple. Amalie thought she saw her. So did I."

"Yes, but you saw her first. Days before she showed up at Amalie's. If you'd said something then, I would have taken Amalie more seriously."

"I *thought* I saw her. Hell, it could have been anybody. I told you I didn't get a good look. And Reilly. He's a cool one. Never blinked an eye when I asked him about it. I'd had a few drinks." Stephen shrugged. "As I said, I'm not sure who it was. It just reminded me of her."

William walked away from his son and took up a position by the fireplace. He picked up the drink he had left on the mantel and took a swallow. "If she's alive, what's she doing? Why hasn't she come here?"

Stephen glanced sharply at William, his cobalt-blue eyes narrowed assessingly. "Do you really think she'd come back here? We'd have to have her committed all over again. She knows that."

"Damn her!" William muttered under his breath. "Why couldn't she just have cooperated? Why did she have to be so damn outspoken when it came to your marriage plans? My God, things could have been so simple if you had been able to marry Caroline." He tossed back the rest of his drink. "Well, that's over now. We have to have a plan, Stephen. We have to find her. I don't think we can trust Morgan to help us. He might go through the motions, follow the leads we gave him, but he'll deny to his last breath that he ever knew who his Jane Doe patient really was."

"*You'll* have to have a plan, Father," Stephen said, rising from his chair. "*I* have commitments this evening. Maggie is waiting for me at Amalie's and I don't want to be late. Anyway, I think the person you should be damning is Christian Marshall. If he hadn't gone back into the treatment room for a story, she would never have gotten out, and we wouldn't be having this conversation. You shouldn't have interfered at Amalie's when I wanted to lay him out. He deserved that at least."

"Perhaps. But he also would have deserved an explanation for your actions. And that, Stephen, is precisely what he cannot have. It's still unclear to me what his involvement in all this is."

"What do you mean?" Stephen's interest was piqued. "Except for his inadvertent interference at the hospital, how is he involved?"

William thrust his hands in his pockets. His angular features sharpened as he pushed out his lower jaw. "Weren't you paying attention when I spoke to Morgan? Doesn't the coincidence strike you as odd? And don't ask what coincidence. I'm talking about Marshall's presence at Amalie's New Year's Eve."

"There's nothing strange about that. I've seen him there before. He's usually with Maggie."

"Yes, yes," William said impatiently. "But that's not my point. This New Year's Eve he began his night with Maggie and ended up with another woman entirely. Maggie said she was a maid. Marshall said she was a thief. You saw her through the peep and said she was a whore. *And Amalie Chatham swears she's my stepdaughter!*" He found a cigar in his pocket, bit off the end, and spit it into the fire. "If Amalie's right, then you saw Marshall bedding your sister!"

"Stepsister," Stephen corrected. "Let's not forget there's no blood between us."

William waved aside Stephen's interruption. "Don't you see? You might not have recognized her that night, but

Marshall surely would have known who was straddling his thighs. How could he have been that close to her and not realized that his whore was the Jane Doe patient from the hospital?"

"Then that means Amalie was mistaken in her identification. That really makes the most sense to me, Father," Stephen said, gathering his coat and hat. "If you had seen what that whore was doing to Christian Marshall and what he was doing to her, you wouldn't think twice about it being my dear, *dear* stepsister. In all the time I knew her she was not precisely warm to the idea of a man between her legs."

"Arrogant pup," William said after his son was out of earshot. "It was *you* she didn't want between her legs." He lighted his cigar and puffed on it thoughtfully. William believed he knew what had to be done even if Stephen didn't. Vigilance was required, and the person to start with was the one closest to the family. William Reilly.

Stephen shuddered his pleasure into Maggie Bryant, then rolled off her and onto his back. He stared at her in the mirror, his narrow smile one of complete satisfaction. "You were hot tonight," he said.

Maggie's fingers touched the tips of her aroused breasts and she shivered slightly, then stretched with feline grace. She turned on her hip and rested one slender arm on Stephen's chest. "You were rather, ummm, energetic yourself this evening. Quite fierce actually."

He had been thinking about his stepsister, wondering if his father had been right. Had she really been the one spreading her legs for Christian Marshall? It didn't seem possible. She was such a cold bitch around him. Sometimes her manner put Stephen off, other times it was all he could do to keep from throwing up her frilly petticoats and burying himself inside her. He doubted she'd be so cold then. Just thinking about it made him grow hard again. He drew Maggie's hand to his loins

276

and showed her what he wanted. When her hand wasn't enough he told her to use her mouth.

Stephen watched her in the mirror. Maggie glided over his chest, teasing him with hungry kisses. Her soft hair caressed his flesh. He stopped thinking it was Maggie who was giving him this pleasure. Instead he envisioned another woman, one with wide doe eyes and sable brown hair. It was to that woman that Stephen Bennington gave his seed.

It didn't matter to Maggie who Stephen thought she was. Amalie had given her explicit instructions. Satisfy young Bennington, then get him to talk about his stepsister. Maggie accepted Amalie's orders without questioning them. She knew that remaining at Amalie's parlor house hung in the balance. If she was successful with Stephen, then her future was secure. Maggie was confident she would know so much about Stephen's family when she was through that Amalie would positively be bored with all the information. Getting Stephen to talk had to be less difficult than pleasing him—and that had certainly been easy enough this evening. He was in rare form.

Moving so that her lips brushed his ear and her breath was warm against his skin, Maggie told him that.

Chapter 11

"I didn't think you were ever going to get here," Jenny said, letting Wilton Reilly into the spacious sitting room of her suite. "When you didn't come yesterday I began to worry."

"You said Friday or Saturday." He removed his coat and gave it to Jenny. He dropped his hat and scarf on the three-legged table by the door. "I really did try to be here yesterday, but there were some problems."

Jenny paused in hanging up the coat. "Problems? You mean household problems, don't you?"

The butler shook his head and his dark eyes conveyed sympathy. "I'm afraid not. Mr. Bennington's hired someone to follow me."

Jenny's lips parted, but there was no sound to her astonishment. She quickly hung the coat and folded her arms around her middle to hide the trembling of her hands. "How do you know?" she asked.

"The same way I know most things that happen in that house," he said. "One of the maids overheard Mr. William giving the man his instructions. She came to me right away. Of course Martha doesn't understand the exact nature of what she heard, and I didn't enlighten her. I told her that Mr. William was looking for an excuse to let me go. That satisfied her."

The suite was not cold, but Jenny shivered nonetheless. She

sank slowly into an upholstered rocker while Reilly took a seat on the gilded chair opposite her. Jenny's toes pushed against the red and gray patterned carpet so that her chair moved back and forth gently. The winter sunlight came through the sheer ivory curtains and parted drapes and touched the curve of Jenny's cheek. She tilted her head to one side so she could feel its warmth more fully. Pointing to the low table between them, Jenny offered her guest the refreshments she had ordered from the hotel dining room.

"Nothing for me," she said when Reilly looked at her expectantly as he poured his own tea. "Who is this man my stepfather's hired?"

"No one to worry about. He's just a cop trying to pick up some extra money."

"A cop?" Jenny found it difficult to swallow. "Someone local?"

"Yes. I don't think Mr. William realizes I already say hello to Liam O'Shea two or three times a week while I'm out walking. O'Shea apparently didn't mention that he's acquainted with me. He wouldn't have been given the job otherwise. What's the matter? You don't look well." Reilly set down his cup and leaned forward anxiously. "Can I get you something?" When Jenny shook her head, Reilly's thin lips flattened in disapproval. "It's obvious that you're upset. I hope you don't think that I would be so foolish as to allow O'Shea to follow me here. That's precisely why I didn't come yesterday. I couldn't get rid of him."

"And today?"

"I surprised him by changing my routine. I took a hack. He couldn't follow."

"Be careful, Mr. Reilly. Liam O'Shea knows me."

Reilly frowned. "How can that be? You were so rarely out of the house, and then you went to the hospital. How could he possibly know you? He hasn't been assigned to our area for very long."

"Just a minute," Jenny said, raising her hand. "I don't think

280

I understand something. Did you and the rest of the staff know I was in the hospital?"

"Well, yes," he drawled a trifle uncertainly. "Mr. William told us you were at New York Hospital. We weren't allowed to visit, of course."

"Of course," Jenny said slowly, anger flashing in her eyes. "That's because I wasn't there. My stepfather had me committed to Jennings . . . the lunatic ward."

The butler paled. "He wanted us to believe that you were mad, but when the last doctors came and you were carried out, he only explained that you were seriously ill. A fever, they told us. Said you would have better care in the hospital. It never occurred to us that he was having you committed. We wouldn't have stood for it!"

"Don't you think he knew that?" Jenny asked softly. She reached out to touch the butler's hand, laying her fingers across his white-knuckled fist to thank him for his faith in her. "When I escaped they let it out that I had died." She withdrew her hand. "I've been staying with some very kind people who know next to nothing about me, Mr. Reilly. I met Liam O'Shea while I was living there."

"Then you've been living somewhere near Fifth Avenue, north of Thirty-fifth Street. That's the approximate area O'Shea walks."

"I think you missed your calling," she said, smiling faintly. "You should have been a detective."

"You're not going to tell me who you were with, are you?"

"No," she said firmly. "No, I'm not. I've left him . . . them." She corrected herself as soon as she realized her error, but it was not quick enough. The butler's raised eyebrows warned her he had heard. "Please, Mr. Reilly, I want to keep it all separate. It's as if I've had two lives."

"What about Liam O'Shea?" he asked. "You said he knows you."

"But not as William Bennington's stepdaughter. Only as Jenny Holland. He thinks I'm a maid."

281

"Jenny Holland," he mused, raising his eyes to hers. The look he gave her was cautionary. "Don't be so clever that you set a trap for yourself."

"I've been careful," she said defensively.

"Not careful enough. Haven't you wondered why Mr. William has O'Shea at my back?" Briefly he told her about the encounter with Stephen after his first meeting with Jenny. "I won't be able to come here often. The risk would be too great. If you require my assistance, then you'll have to let me know through *The Herald*."

"I don't think I want to do that anymore. I'm not as confident about the method as I used to be." Jenny found it difficult to talk. Her thoughts were spinning wildly. It frightened her that Stephen suspected he had seen her with Reilly. Then there was the incident at Amalie's in which she had almost been exposed. Jut the memory of standing on the other side of Maggie's door listening to the conversation in the hallway gave Jenny chills. Even now it was hard for her to believe she had been within a few feet of Stephen and William Bennington. Only Christian's quickly constructed lies and Maggie's balcony had saved her from being discovered.

Jenny poured herself a cup of tea. "It would be better if you wrote to me here. Get a box at the post office and let me know the number. I'll contact you that way. Then we don't have to worry that Stephen or William will open your mail." She sipped her tea slowly. "There's something else you should know, Mr. Reilly. My stepfather may have more than Stephen's suspicions to go on." Her voice dropped to a throaty whisper as she related the events of New Year's Eve. She told the butler everything except Christian's name and what had occurred between them. That was a private memory she kept for herself.

Reilly listened to Jenny's tale and his consternation grew. At the end of her tale he was shaking his head from side to side and rubbing the bald spot on the top of his head. "I don't like it," he said. "Don't like it at all. I don't know what you made of it, but it seems clear to me that Amalie Chatham thought she recognized you."

"Once I thought about it that's what I concluded as well. But how, Mr. Reilly? I've never met Amalie before in my life."

"I should say not," he said stiffly. "The tart."

Smiling faintly, Jenny set her cup of tea on the table. "I see you have no more of an idea than I do. Never mind. It doesn't really matter any longer. I can't think that it's very important. I'm not likely to meet her again."

Reilly's agreement was offered reluctantly. "Is your equipment satisfactory?" he asked, changing the subject. "Do you have everything you need?"

She nodded. "I've gone through everything and it's all there—exactly what I wanted. You're quite marvelous, do you know that?" The ruddy color that flushed the butler's cheeks caused Jenny to laugh softly. "I mean it, Mr. Reilly. I wouldn't be able to set on this course without you."

"Don't remind me. I'm not certain I want to be responsible for whatever it is you've been scheming."

"You're not responsible," she said firmly.

The butler snorted lightly, his dark eyes skeptical. "That's not the way I see it," he said in a voice brooking no argument. He glanced at the pendulum clock noisily ticking away on the opposite wall. "I regret I can't stay longer and talk sense to you." He sighed. "It would probably be a waste of my breath. You were always softhearted and headstrong." His palms pushed against his knees as he stood. "Are there other items you require?"

"I have all the equipment I need," she said. "But I would be grateful if you'd send some items from my wardrobe here. I only have two dresses, a few undergarments, and one pair of shoes. The extra money my employer gave me at Christmas time was spent on a cloak and mittens. I'm afraid I didn't budget it very well." Her smile was rueful. "Having to worry about money has proved to be a humbling experience. And now that the night clerk thinks I'm a prostitute, I'll have to have some funds set aside just to keep him quiet."

Reilly blinked hugely. The bald crown of his head turned bright red. "What in God's name are you talking about? What would ever lead him to that conclusion?"

"Well, for one thing I arrived with virtually no belongings. For another, I didn't know under what name I had been registered. I asked for Smith but there were two. Then I simply asked for Room 212. That made the clerk suspicious."

"Just a minute," Reilly said, frowning. "Didn't the ad say C. Smith?"

"Yes, but as I said, there were two. I didn't know which one I was."

Reilly shook his head, trying to clear it. "I don't think I understand the problem. Who was the other Smith?"

"Mrs. Norris Smith, I think."

"Then why were you confused? You were supposed to be C. Smith."

"But . . ." She paused and tried to make sense of their conversation. "Oh, you meant *C.* Smith, not *see* Smith." She laughed when she saw Reilly was still completely bewildered. "Never mind. It's not important." She slipped her arm through his and escorted him to the door. Reilly opened it and they stepped out into the carpeted hallway. "I appreciate you coming this afternoon, Mr. Reilly," Jenny said gravely. "You've been very good to me. I won't forget this. I promise." Impulsively she stood on tiptoe and kissed the butler's cheek.

Embarrassed and not a little moved, Reilly cleared his throat. "I only hope I don't regret it. You know how to get around this old man's heart."

Jenny helped Reilly into his coat. "Not so old," she said, surveying him critically from head to toe. "You're still a fine figure." Jenny realized she was reluctant to see him go. She would be alone again and lonely. "You won't forget the clothes?"

"No. You'll have them within the week." He reached in his pocket, withdrew some bills, and thrust them at Jenny. "For you," he said gruffly.

"But you already left me money."

"It's not enough." He raised his hand and cut off her argument. "Don't argue. We both know you'll be needing this." He wrapped his scarf about his neck, adding a roguish flourish as he tossed one fringed end over his shoulder. "Besides, it rather makes me feel like Robin Hood."

Jenny smiled, relieved that it wasn't his own money that Reilly had forced into her hands. She wondered what he had stolen and sold to come by it. "That's all right then. As long as you can give me this, you're welcome to anything I have." Jenny lingered in the hallway until Reilly turned the corridor toward the stairs. Once he was gone she couldn't find an excuse to stay outside her suite. Slipping inside, she promised herself that she wouldn't dwell on thoughts of Christian Marshall—at least not for more than an hour or so.

Christian Marshall bent to pick up the hat he had purposely dropped on the stairs. Wilton Reilly passed him and continued on his way without a glance in Christian's direction. Christian paused a beat, then followed. Once outside the hotel Reilly hailed a hack. Joe Means, who had been waiting for Christian with the carriage, took up a leisurely pursuit at his employer's curt order. Joe wanted to know if Christian had found Jenny Holland, but one brief glance at Christian's tense, shuttered expression warned Joe that questions would be unwelcome.

Christian sat back on the leather cushions of the open carriage and unfolded a blanket over his legs. He raised his scarf over the lower part of his face to ward off the bitterly cold wind. Trusting Joe to maintain sight of the hack, Christian let his thoughts wander back to the bits of conversation he had overheard.

The stairway had not proved to be the most advantageous of positions, but Christian, familiar with every inch of the hotel, knew his options were limited. Friday morning, in anticipation of Butler's arrival, Christian had tried to rent a suite near 212, only to discover they were all occupied. He returned in the afternoon with a sketchbook and pencils and used the excuse that he was looking into some design problems to gain access to the upper floors. Once the clerks at the St. Mark realized who Christian Marshall was, they were eager to assist him in any way they could. They found nothing odd about the fact that he spent most of the afternoon hovering about the second floor lobby and dining room or pacing the stairway between the first and third floors. The intensity of his expression, the perpetual tightness of his mouth as he studied the structure and made sketch after sketch led them to believe the St. Mark was in imminent danger of collapsing. It was rather remarkable that the rumor never circulated beyond the registration desk. It was less surprising that no one summoned enough courage to ask Christian Marshall himself. His thoughts on Jenny Holland, he was particularly unapproachable.

On Saturday his mood was not improved. He arrived at the St. Mark knowing that if Butler did not appear he would have to go to Room 212 himself. The suite was registered to a Mrs. Carlton Smith. See Smith. C. Smith. Christian recognized the connection immediately and could not accept it as coincidence. Jenny had to be there. He was certain of it. If only he were so certain that he wanted to see her. Each time a door on the north wing of the second floor opened, Christian found himself tensing with equal parts dread and anticipation. Never were any of the people who stepped into the hallway his Jenny. *His* Jenny. He heard himself think it but did not let himself think of the ramifications.

Christian had to know about Butler first. He was disappointed when the man—and Christian knew in his gut that it was going to be a man—didn't appear at the St. Mark on Friday. It was clearly a case of being careful what one wished for, because when Butler arrived and the door to 212 opened to him, Christian was devastated.

Jenny's sweet, husky voice had carried as far as the stairs.

"When you didn't come yesterday I began to worry." Christian didn't remember what the man had replied—indeed, if he had said anything at all. Jenny's words echoed in his ears. There was affection in her voice, a touch of anxiousness that was reserved for someone she cared about. Christian was unfamiliar with the jealousy that raged through him. For a moment he thought he was going to be sick. Then he collected himself and concentrated on thinking rationally. Butler was an older man, balding, rail thin, staid, and severe. There was nothing about the man that reminded Christian of Jenny, but he didn't rule out the possibility that Butler could be a relative. Far from ruling it out, he clung to it. During the half hour that Butler was in Jenny's suite Christian constructed a half-dozen scenarios that explained their relationship. He was an uncle twice removed or a second cousin. Christian even allowed himself to go so far as supposing that Butler was a longtime friend of the family, a mentor, or an old business associate.

Then Butler left the suite and Christian heard Jenny's throaty voice again. *"I appreciate your coming, Mr. Reilly."* The man's name wasn't Butler, it was Reilly. Butler was Reilly just as Jenny was Princess. The subterfuge grated on Christian's nerves. He was weary of wondering about Jenny's secrets and equally tired of her clever little games. *"You've been very good to me."* He wished he hadn't heard that. *"Not so old. You're still a fine figure."* What the hell had she meant by that? A muscle worked in Christian's cheek as he gave his imagination free rein. In his mind's eye he saw Jenny undressing for Reilly, then undressing him. He saw her lying back on the bed, raising her arms, beckoning her lover with her smile, her eyes. *"As long as you can give me this, you're welcome to anything I have."* Reilly had given her money. Christian hadn't seen the transaction in the hallway but he knew what had happened. *"You're welcome to anything I have."* It would be a long time before he forgot she had said that. *"Anything I have. Anything."* A long, long time.

She isn't a whore, Christian told himself. Wasn't. She *wasn't* a whore. Perhaps he had made her one at Amalie's. *"You're welcome to anything I have."* In Christian's foul mood he could think of only one thing Jenny had to give. He wondered if she had taken photographs. Jenny Holland was probably setting up a very interesting studio inside her suite.

"Do you have the hack in sight?" Christian demanded, leaning forward and shaking Joe by the sleeve.

"That's the hack a few carriages ahead of us, sir. Your man's changed cabs three times now."

Christian realized how far afield his mind had been wandering. He wasn't aware of what Reilly had been doing. "Do you think he suspects we're following him?"

"Can't say for certain, Mr. Marshall. But it doesn't look that way. He's not trying to elude us."

Christian thought it over, but didn't understand if his quarry was using method or madness. "Where are we?"

"We're coming up on Forty-second."

"What in God's name are we doing so far uptown?"

Joe knew a rhetorical question when he heard one. Since he was merely following orders as well as the cab, he remained silent.

Christian slumped back into his seat, crossing his arms in front of his chest. His mother would have said he was pouting. His father would have said he was spoiling for a fight. They both would have been right. At the moment Christian had the temperament of a ten-year-old and he refused to give it up.

"The hack driver's pulling up, sir," said Joe.

"Proceed slowly," Christian instructed. "I just want to see where Reilly goes."

Joe did as he was told. He and Christian both watched the man alight from the cab, pay the driver, then cross to the other side of the street in long, hurried strides.

"Damn it," muttered Christian. "Can you follow him without drawing attention to us?"

Joe nodded confidently. He drove north a half block, then swung the carriage around while Christian kept his eye on

288

Reilly. The man they were following never noticed them. When Reilly stopped in front of one of the massive private palaces along the avenue and opened the iron gates as if he owned the property, Joe's eyes widened a little. "Does he live there?" Joe asked, turning in his seat so Christian could hear him. "I thought that's where the Benningtons live." As he spoke Reilly sprinted up the front steps, paused briefly to catch his breath beside one of the Corinthian columns flanking the main entrance, then disappeared inside the door.

"Good day t'you, Mr. Marshall. Joe." Liam O'Shea lifted the brim of his hat with the rounded tip of his club, offering them a jaunty salute. "Right brisk day it is," he said. He matched his stride to Christian's slow-moving carriage.

Christian lowered his scarf. His smile was polite and indifferent. He did not want to engage O'Shea in conversation.

Liam accepted Christian's coolness philosophically. He was more comfortable talking to Joe Means than he was conversing with one of the Avenoodles anyway. "How is Mrs. B. doing, Joe?"

"She's chompin' at the bit. Wants to be up and about."

"I can understand that. Tell her I want the same. No one else thinks to offer crullers unless she puts them up to it."

Joe chuckled. "I'll tell her."

"Haven't seen Miss Holland lately."

"No, she left," Joe said smoothly.

"Oh. I'm sorry to hear that. Sure, and I'll miss the colleen. Enjoyed our walks together." He shrugged, swinging his club in rhythm with his stride. "Will you give Mary Margaret a message for me?"

Joe risked a glance back at Christian and saw that his employer was impatient to be gone. "Come by yourself with it," said Joe.

"That's just it. I can't." Liam stopped as they reached the end of the block. He used his club to point over his shoulder at the mansion behind them. "I've gotten myself a special assignment. I'm doing some work—private—supplementing the pay, as it were. I won't be able to take her—"

"You're working for the Benningtons?" Christian interrupted. He gave Joe a sharp gesture with his hand indicating he should halt the carriage.

"Can't really say that, Mr. Marshall." Liam rocked on his heels, his hands behind his back. His stance was self-important and proud. He'd gotten Mr. Marshall's attention. "Sure, and if I did a bit of detective work for you, you'd not want it bandied about. You'd want the arrangement private and confidential."

What Christian wanted was to bloody O'Shea's face until he had his answers. He was forced to give up his childish emotionality and take another approach. "The thing of it is, O'Shea, I'm looking for someone to do exactly that sort of work. I was thinking of going to the Pinkerton Agency, but I really haven't made up my mind yet. Perhaps if you told me what sort of thing it is you're doing for the Benningtons, I'd know whether or not you're suited to what I need."

Liam glanced up and down the street. He was on his own time now—well, really Mr. Bennington's time—but it couldn't hurt to talk to Mr. Marshall for a while. After all, Mr. Reilly was back in the house and it was unlikely he would go anywhere soon. With the exception of his cab ride this afternoon, the butler was fairly predictable. Liam wasn't overly concerned about losing Reilly's trail earlier. He knew the cabbie who brought Reilly back. Later today he'd find where he picked the butler up. O'Shea's smile radiated confidence.

"I'd be pleased to tell you what I can, Mr. Marshall," Liam said. "But not right here in front of the house. Wouldn't be good."

Christian took the hint. "Then perhaps you'll accept a ride. I'm going home. We can talk on the way."

Liam stamped his feet, ridding them of clumps of snow and ice, and hopped into the carriage. "What sort of work is it that you have in mind?" he asked, accepting the blanket that Christian offered him. He laid it over his legs as the carriage rolled forward.

"It would be personal," he said slowly, trying to think of something that O'Shea would accept. "Nothing for *The Chronicle.* I imagine your work with Bennington has something to do with the bank."

"No, no," Liam said quickly. "Nothing of the sort."

"Then I should see Stephen for a reference," he prompted.

Liam shook his head, rolling one tip of his mustache between his thumb and forefinger. "His father. But I don't have Mr. Bennington's information for him yet. If you talk to him now he won't be able to give you a good estimate of my ability."

"That's all right. I suppose I can trust that he wouldn't have hired you if he hadn't made inquiries of his own."

"True enough," Liam said. "He was satisfied."

Christian nodded. Outwardly he appeared relaxed, although beneath the blanket his hands were tensely gripping his knees. "I just don't know," he said, pretending to vacillate. "I'm convinced the job I have in mind for you is of a delicate nature." He lowered his voice to a confidential tenor. "I believe the woman I'm currently seeing is having an affair with another man," he said, only to realize as he heard the invented words that they were true. "A married man. If it's true, naturally I'd decide against offering marriage. I'd want you to watch her . . . see where she goes, who she meets. Have you ever done any work of this sort before?"

"Except for the mark being a woman it's the same thing I'm doing for Mr. Bennington."

"Then you're following a man?" he asked lowly. "A business associate?"

"An employee."

Christian took an inspired stab at the man's identity. "The butler?" O'Shea didn't have to answer. His face gave him away. "You're following Mr. Reilly?"

"But how—"

"Joe knows him," he lied, hoping his driver would support him.

As if on cue Joe glanced over his shoulder and nodded.

"I heard Joe call to him," Christian continued.

Liam wondered how he had missed that exchange. It probably happened while he was concentrating on the hack Reilly arrived in. "I see. I don't suppose it matters that you know," he said, his discomfort evident. "I didn't really tell you."

"No, you didn't. And I'm sure that if I had talked to William he would have confided the nature of your job to me." Like hell. "Don't give it another thought. If you worked for me I'm sure I could count on your discretion. But tell me, I'm very interested in how you work. Does Mr. Reilly know you were following him?"

Liam glanced at Joe's back. "If Joe knows the man I really shouldn't—"

"Don't worry about me, Liam," Joe said, turning his head. "I ain't likely to say anything. Can't say that I know him all that well or like him any better." Above Liam's head Joe winked at Christian, joining the conspiracy.

Liam's hesitation was brief. He was eager to convince Christian Marshall that he could handle another assignment. His chest expanded as he sat up a bit straighter. "No, Reilly doesn't suspect anything. He couldn't. I've been very careful. That's my nature when it comes to matters like these."

Not careful enough, Christian thought. Reilly had changed cabs three times. The man knew something. "What is it that you're trying to find out?"

"I'm not really certain," Liam admitted reluctantly. "Mr. Bennington's secretive. I suspect it has something to do with thefts. That's what these cases usually are. The owners believe a valuable retainer is stealing from them, but don't want to lose the employee if they're wrong. Situations like that are better handled without a lot of fuss." He pointed to himself. "That's why Bennington hired me. I'm just supposed to document the butler's movements. Find out where he goes, who he sees. Exactly what you have in mind."

Christian ignored Liam's prompting. "And have you?

Documented his movements, I mean? Really, this is fascinating," he encouraged, hoping O'Shea would rise to the bait. "Today, for instance, where did he go?"

Liam cleared his throat and his eyes darted away from Christian's probing ones. "Can't tell you that," he answered. "Wouldn't be right, would it, what with me not having the chance to tell Mr. Bennington yet."

Christian's stiff fingers relaxed their grip. He knew O'Shea was putting him off because he didn't have the answer. Apparently the cop had lost sight of his man. That relieved Christian. Jenny was not implicated in whatever the butler was doing. Or was it the butler who was not yet implicated in whatever scheme Jenny was plotting? The truth of it was, everything concerning Jenny Holland was a puzzle that made Christian's head ache. Except for the fact that there was no liquor in his house—a matter easily remedied—Christian couldn't think of one reason why he shouldn't crack open a bottle of whiskey when he arrived home.

"You're right, of course," said Christian. "You can't tell me. But if it's a matter of theft, as you suspect, then it's likely the man is meeting someone who would help him get rid of the stolen items."

"Certainly." Liam was standing on firm ground again. "We call them fences."

"Yes, I've heard of that." But Reilly wasn't carrying anything when he went to Jenny's room. And the butler had given Jenny money, not the other way around. Something didn't fit. Why wasn't he surprised? he thought dryly. "It sounds like a very interesting case. Do you know, there may be a story in it for the paper. Not now, of course, not while you're working on it, and we certainly wouldn't use any real names, but it could have some story potential."

"I don't know about that," Liam said uneasily. "The commissioner frowns on his men picking up extra work."

"Then the city should pay them better," Christian countered. "Let me think about it. I won't talk to my city

293

editor without speaking to you first." Christian threw back the blanket as Joe brought the carriage to a stop in front of Marshall House. "Joe can take you wherever you want to go," he said, jumping to the sidewalk. "It's been a pleasure talking to you, O'Shea."

Liam tugged on his mustache, frowning. "What about the personal matter you mentioned to me?"

"I haven't decided yet. Frankly, I'm not certain she's worth all the trouble. If she wants this other man, then maybe I should just let her have him."

"But I thought you didn't really know if she was seeing this other fellow. Isn't that what you wanted me to find out?"

Christian leaned against the carriage and crooked his finger, getting Liam to bend his head closer. "Just between us, O'Shea, I know. I've always known. The question is how badly do I want to catch them at it? Then there's the other man's family. Perhaps they don't deserve the scandal this would cause."

"That's considerate of you."

Christian thought so too. Since he was creating the story he felt he could afford to be magnanimous. He pushed away from the carriage, raising his hand and waving Joe off. "I'll remind Mrs. Morrisey and Mary Margaret about the crullers," he called. Christian turned away, bowing his head and hunching his shoulders against the wind. He started up the sidewalk to the house, limping noticeably because his leg was stiff. "Damn it, Jenny Holland, what have you got yourself involved in?" His words were carried away so quickly that Christian wasn't sure he had spoken his thoughts aloud.

Jenny unfolded the paper that had arrived at the same time as her evening meal. The first thing she noticed was that it was *The Chronicle*. She had asked for *The Times*. The second thing she noticed was the date. March 9, 1867. She stared at it for a long moment, unaware of her drawn-out sigh. Eight weeks had passed since she'd left Christian Marshall. Eight interminably long weeks. How much longer would it be before she'd stop marking time by her aloneness? Jenny cautioned herself that it had to end. Lately she'd been making herself sick over it. Without looking in a mirror she knew she was losing weight. The gowns that Reilly had packed and sent to her didn't fit the same way they had even a few weeks ago.

Jenny picked at her dinner while she read the paper. Once she scraped off the sauce she found the whitefish to be palatable. The asparagus was tough and stringy, but the rice was buttered and seasoned exactly to her liking. She ate all of the rice, left the asparagus, and forced down half the fish because she remembered breakfast hadn't stayed down and she hadn't ordered any lunch.

Nothing in *The Chronicle* caught Jenny's interest. She read the front page perfunctorily, but didn't go to the inner pages to follow up on the stories. The obituaries received a cursory glance. The editorial page had no contributions from Christian, so Jenny passed it over. She didn't care what anyone else had to say. The society pages were filled with accounts of the latest dinner gala at Delmonico's. Everything from the menu to the guest list was printed. Jenny glanced over the latter. William and Stephen had been there. So had Christian.

She refolded the paper and tossed it on the opposite chair with an angry flourish. It was probably too much to hope that they had choked on their littleneck clams or spilled a magnum of Moët et Chandon all over their hostess. That at least would have been interesting.

When the young waiter from the hotel dining room came to collect Jenny's tray, she found herself engaging him in conversation just because she was so anxious to hear a voice other than her own. When she realized how she was prattling on and how he was misinterpreting her interest, she showed him the door.

Jenny realized the managers of the St. Mark didn't know quite what to make of her. Since Reilly's visit nearly eight weeks ago there were no gentlemen callers. None. The night clerk had stopped hinting about his hush money once he understood that no guests meant Jenny wasn't a prostitute. There were those on staff who thought she was ill; others thought she was merely peculiar. They all agreed she was a recluse.

Except for an occasional evening stroll, Jenny rarely left her suite. The St. Mark Hotel offered family-style dining, which meant guests were seated twenty or even thirty to a table. It would have been difficult *not* to become acquainted with at least a few of the 500 people staying in the hotel. Jenny avoided the elegant dining room for just that reason. She also avoided the lobby, reading rooms, and parlors. Any time of the day one could find loungers in those areas, but just before the dinner hour they held such a crush of registered guests and visitors that it was inevitable that some of the crowd would spill out onto Broadway.

From the windows in her second-floor suite Jenny would often watch the throng until it disappeared, accommodated at last by the splendor that was the St. Mark. As lonely as she sometimes was, Jenny still never experienced the least desire to be part of that crowd. The astonishing press of people actually frightened her.

Jenny traveled the length of her sitting room several times, going from the door to the large bowed windows by a number of different routes. Sometimes she went to the right of the chaise, other times to the left. She would stop in front of the unlighted fireplace and rest her shoulder against the mantel, studiously avoiding her reflection in the gilt-framed mirror above it while she fidgeted with her hair. She would pause in front of one of the registers which brought the centrally heated air to her suite and warm her perpetually cold hands and feet. She fingered the fringed drapes with one hand while the other pressed a skeletal imprint onto the frosted window panes.

She moved slowly, without purpose or deliberation, wandering rather than pacing. Jenny thought she could fool herself into believing she wasn't agitated. It didn't work. For all the peace of mind she had she might as well have been frantically tracing and retracing her steps until the carpet was worn shiny.

The evening was cold, but Jenny made no allowance for it as she stepped out onto the balcony from her bedroom. She breathed deeply, welcoming the chill that filled her lungs and cleared her brain. Resting one hip against the iron railing, her arms folded under her breasts, Jenny looked directly across the lamplighted street. Her bedroom balcony doors did not open onto Broadway, so she was not looking past the heavily trafficked thoroughfare. Her view wasn't distracted by the steady promenade of fashionably dressed women and their formally attired escorts on their way to the theater. Flakes of snow glittered in the gaslight, not jewels. Around the corner from where she stood there was no end to the parade of carriages, horsecars, coaches, and sleighs. If it hadn't been for the bells, the occasional crack of a whip, and the rise and fall of laughter, Jenny might well have forgotten how close she was to the heart of the city.

Half as wide as Broadway, the street Jenny faced was silent in contrast. It wasn't deserted, just serene. Drivers quieted their horses. People didn't laugh as loudly. Jenny really didn't notice the calm that enveloped the street. As she stared at the building opposite her, Jenny felt and heard the steady thrumming of her heart to the exclusion of everything else.

The First Hancock Savings and Trust was a large, imposing brownstone built some twenty years before the St. Mark Hotel. The actual banking institution went back nearly forty years before that. It was a highly respected house of finance, counting a dozen of the richest families in New York among the depositors and investors. Under the direction of the Van Dyke family it had never failed, never even faltered. In sixty years there had never been a hint that The Trust was anything but sound. There were rumors alleging something to the contrary now. Jenny knew that because she had started them.

The rumors were not without foundation. Jenny was not so vindictive that she would have set the stage for a panic without sound evidence. She had heard and overheard more than enough conversations between her stepfather and his son to know that The Trust was skirting the edge of complete ruin. William had approved a number of large loans during the war that were never going to be repaid. By themselves those loans could not have toppled The Trust, but when they were followed by William Bennington's poor investments, made in haste to recover the anticipated losses, the situation had been altered dramatically. In addition, William and his son were taking depositors and interest funds directly from the bank and making personal investments in real estate, anticipating the steady northward move of the city would drive up prices. There was a very good chance that they might achieve the individual wealth they craved and believed was their due, but it was coming at the expense ot thousands of small depositors in The Trust.

The problem was proving it.

Jenny had cautiously begun circulating stories about the bank's problems a few weeks after she'd first realized what William and Stephen were doing. That had been in August. She had had to go carefully, dropping hints as if she were unaware of what she was doing, as if she didn't understand the complete consequences of her apparent indiscretions.

Looking back, perhaps it was true that she hadn't understood about the consequences. She had hoped for more than talk about a changing of the bank's officers. Jenny had counted on action and it had never happened. Now, each day from her balcony, she watched William Bennington enter the bank. Minutes later he would appear in his office, safe, smug, and secure behind his desk. This was proof enough to Jenny that no one was going to oust her stepfather from his position as president; this was proof that she had failed to arouse real concern about either William or Stephen.

She had not failed, however, in arousing the Benningtons' concerns. It had not taken William long to identify the source of the rumors. Once he had he had not hesitated to take action. The consequence that Jenny hadn't foreseen was the treatment room at Jennings Memorial.

Sometimes Jenny wondered if she would have acted any differently had she known how her stepfather would respond. She supposed that the answer to that lay in the fact that she was still pursuing him, this time with more cunning and stealth. She wasn't going to rely on the bank's officers to do what needed to be done. Jenny was going to provide the proof and offer it publicly if she had to. She planned to see that William and Stephen Bennington were exposed on the front pages of *The Chronicle*, *The Herald*, and *The Times*.

The execution of her plan was more difficult than she had anticipated, and Jenny was more thoroughly discouraged than she had been in weeks. She had chosen her suite at the St. Mark because it offered the best view of William Bennington's office at The Savings and Trust. When she asked Reilly to reserve the room for her, she had in mind being able to watch her stepfather come and go from the bank. Jenny wanted to renew her familiarity with William's routine. She wanted to show people that on some of the occasions when William and Stephen worked together in the office, both of them left with more than the evening paper folded under their arms.

Secured between the pages of one of the dailies were hundreds, sometimes thousands, of dollars that belonged in the bank's safe. At least that was how Jenny thought they were removing the money. She couldn't make an accusation until she was certain. If she was wrong, William and Stephen would see that she was committed somewhere for the rest of her life. There would be no second chance at escape.

Jenny wasn't certain when she first hit upon the idea of photographing William and Stephen in the act of stealing, but the more she thought on it, the more the scheme appealed to her. A photograph would provide incontrovertible proof of the theft. It would convince where she could not, and Jenny became determined to see the plan through regardless of the risk to herself.

Jenny's interest in photography dated back several years. Although the profession was dominated by men, it was the general opinion of polite society that here at last was a pastime perfectly suitable for females. It required a deft touch, a good eye, and in most cases, an abundance of patience—all of which were considered innate characteristics of women. Of course it also involved the use of complex equipment and chemicals and demanded attention to scientific factors like exposure time and reflection density, but it was believed women could eventually master photography in spite of the scientific nature of the hobby.

Jenny Holland had never been aware that she wasn't supposed to learn quickly or learn well. When photography was introduced in her Paris boarding school by the head-master, Jenny was immediately fascinated. What was supposed to have been a pleasant pastime became something very different in Jenny's skillful hands. Touring the Continent with the other young ladies, Jenny carried more equipment in her trunks than clothes. She shocked her classmates by photo-graphing most everything that caught her eye, then developing the pictures in a portable darkroom which consisted of nothing more than a rack for the chemical baths covered by a large black horse blanket.

Most often when Jenny was involved in this pursuit, her classmates took great pains to avoid her. Half hidden beneath her makeshift tent, Jenny bore less resemblance to a young woman of some social consequence than she did to an ostrich with its head buried in the sand. It was scandal enough that Gilliard's Seminary for Young Ladies had accepted an American into their exclusive fold, without having to acknowledge the woman photographer was one of their entourage. Her eccentricities were tolerated only because she was vulgarly wealthy. The Seminary for Young Ladies toured Amsterdam, Venice, Athens, and Rome, but it was Jenny who gave them a permanent record of their trip. It was only when they returned to Paris that Jenny's efforts were appreciated.

Jenny reflected on the risks she had taken during that tour. She had fallen into a canal in Venice while trying to set up her tripod. Grave, solemn Monsieur Gilliard had jumped in after her while his wife fainted from sheer mortification. Madame Gilliard had been revived with smelling salts, and Jenny had saved the headmaster because the well-intentioned hero couldn't swim a stroke. There had also been a mishap in the Alps involving a narrow rocky ledge and a nest of baby birds. And then there was the incident in Amsterdam with the windmill when she had saved her camera but not her dignity.

It had all been high adventure then, Jenny thought. What she was doing now was not. Sometimes the enormity of what she was undertaking paralyzed her. She was desperately afraid of the consequences of her actions.

Looking across the street at her stepfather's office, Jenny felt the return of her earlier frustration and despair. The distance from her hotel room to The Trust was greater than she had first thought. The lenses for her camera, even the ones she had specially ordered after taking the suite, were not powerful enough to see clearly into William Bennington's sanctuary. Even though William's desk was set at an angle to the large, full-story window, Jenny's view was often obscured by the reflection of sunlight on the glass panes. On the occasions when she managed to coordinate light angles, exposure time, and the proper lens, the best pictures she obtained were still lacking the clarity she needed. The person behind the desk could have been anyone.

There was an additional problem that Jenny had not anticipated. When Stephen and his father were together both men tended to argue on their feet. That meant movement and movement was the bane of Jenny's work. The exposure time required by the wet-plate process demanded that the subjects remain still. That was not difficult if the photographer's target was stationary. In all of Jenny's pictures First Hancock

301

Savings and Trust was beautifully detailed. The street, however, always seemed to be empty because the carriages and passersby moved too quickly to be captured on the collodion film. When William and Stephen moved around the office their images were lost to the camera's eye. The best she achieved was a blur, suggesting activity but certainly not providing the evidence she required.

Daily it was being brought home to Jenny that she would have to get closer if she was going to achieve success. How that could be accomplished still eluded her. She wasn't hopeful that a solution to her problem existed, and on some days, such as today, when she was feeling particularly sorry for herself, she didn't even care.

An icy blast of wind swept past the balcony and fluttered the hem of Jenny's gown. She felt the cold air trapped under her skirts and shivered violently in response. Except for possibly contracting pneumonia, there was nothing that could be accomplished out on the balcony. Jenny stepped back inside, locking the double doors behind her.

The St. Mark boasted more than the luxury of central heating. In designing the hotel, Christian Marshall had incorporated the best features of other popular guest palaces such as the Fifth Avenue Hotel and the Metropolitan. In addition to the perpendicular railway which cautiously and sometimes crankily lifted patrons from the lobby to any one of the other seven floors, the St. Mark suites also had the convenience of private bathing rooms. To Jenny's way of thinking, it was heaven. During her tour of Europe she had seen nothing to rival the ingenuity and innovation that were the trademark of America, and no city in the United States embraced comfort and convenience like New York.

She ran warm water for her bath, filling the oak-rimmed copper tub less than halfway. For Jenny the luxury of soaking shoulder deep in scented water was still offset by the memories of the treatment room.

A dressing room adjoined the bath, and here Jenny changed her clothes, slipping into the satin wrapper that Reilly had sent in the trunk of garments. The leaf green robe, which Jenny purchased in a Paris salon at a price that had even shocked her, was supposed to have been a gift for her mother. Lillian Bennington never saw it.

As soon as the first word of her mother's illness reached her, Jenny left France, but she still harbored guilt that she had not done so earlier. She had arrived in New York two weeks after her mother was buried. Standing over her mother's grave, flanked by the stepfather and stepbrother she had only just met, Jenny convinced herself she should never have left her mother at all. How different things might have been.

Jenny wrapped her hair in a towel, laid her robe over the back of a chair, and slid into the tub. Her fingers and toes tingled briefly as the numbing cold disappeared. She leaned back, resting her head against the rim, and remembered her mother's surprisingly practical, farsighted reaction to the first secession of states from the Union. Anticipating war, Lillian arranged for her daughter to attend school in Paris on the eve of Lincoln's election. By the time of his inauguration Jenny was already on her way to France.

In hindsight Jenny sometimes questioned her mother's motives in packing her off. At the time it seemed as if Lillian's anxiousness was directly related to the dangers that would necessarily accompany war. To anyone who would listen, Lillian expressed her belief that the Rebels would be parading up Fifth Avenue before Lincoln mustered an army. It was inevitable that Jenny would come to share her mother's fear. When she was placed on the boat for Europe Jenny cried because her mother was staying, not because she herself was going.

Her doubts began to surface shortly after her arrival in Paris. In the second letter she received from home Lillian announced her intention to remarry. By the third letter it was a

303

fait accompli.

Jenny squeezed warm water from a sponge onto her shoulders. She smiled faintly. *Fait accompli.* It was a pretty expression, but it didn't soften the bitter anger Jenny felt at the time. She wasn't so young then that she didn't realize her mother had been conducting an affair with William Bennington for months. Jenny had never been introduced to the man, which is why she never took account of the whisperings among the servants. She was naively confident that Lillian would not be seriously interested in another man. It was less than a year since her husband's death. A social escort was sometimes required, and that was perfectly acceptable, but a husband? Jenny still had difficulty believing Lillian had married William Bennington. Then it had hurt deeply and terribly. Jenny felt betrayed for herself and for her father.

Lillian's marriage became the excuse Jenny never thought she would need to stay in Europe. By the time the war in the States was over, Jenny had been on her own for more than a year. She remained in Paris against her mother's wishes, establishing her independence by renting a home and hiring a companion instead of going to live with distant relatives in Amsterdam. There was a vague threat about stopping the flow of money from New York to Paris, but Jenny knew better than to suppose it was serious. She suspected it was William Bennington's way of reminding her that until she turned twenty-one he controlled her finances. Jenny didn't think her mother would let him cut her off. Up until the time of Lillian's illness she was right.

In June Jenny learned of her mother's heart condition from Mr. Reilly. From her family's lawyer she learned that her quarterly allowance had been stopped. Jenny could have borrowed money to secure her passage to New York, but she was too proud and too angry. In order to return home Jenny sold most of her clothes and all of her photographic equipment. She gave away her collection of photographs to friends who had expressed an interest in them, not caring if she had any reminders of the years she had spent away from her mother.

All during the Atlantic crossing Jenny imagined her first meeting with William Bennington. She planned to spit in his eye, and regretted it didn't happen that way. When Jenny was greeted with the unexpected news of her mother's death she fainted.

God, but that had been humiliating, Jenny thought. At the moment when she had wanted to be poised and self-assured, she had demonstrated to William and Stephen that she was emotionally fragile. How they had turned that to their advantage!

She rose from the tub, dried herself off, and shrugged into the wrapper that had unleashed so many unhappy memories. Taking the towel off her head, Jenny shook out her hair and untangled the curling ends with her fingertips. The humidity in the bathroom caused short, dark tendrils to cling damply to the nape of her neck and her temples. She pressed the towel to her face, held it there long enough to dam the tears that welled in her eyes, then tossed it on the floor.

The tears angered her. She hated the weepiness that had become so much a part of her life of late. She needed to be strong. Instead she felt uncertain, vulnerable, and more often than not, helpless. Jenny was very much afraid she would fail. The treatment room of Jennings Memorial haunted her.

She firmly pushed those thoughts to the back of her mind. Padding barefoot from the dressing room, Jenny pulled back the covers on her bed to warm them. She knew she was still too restless to sleep comfortably. In the last two weeks it had become necessary for Jenny to thoroughly exhaust herself before she could fall asleep. Just as she had on every other night, Jenny hoped that if she reviewed her photographs some solution would come to her. She left her bedchamber and started across the parlor, heading for her darkroom on the opposite side.

Jenny had only traveled a short distance when a movement near the fireplace caught her eye. Her head swiveled in the direction of the movement and she stopped abruptly, her dark eyes widening when she saw who was standing at one end of the mantel.

Instinct alone brought a hoarse scream to Jenny's throat.

Chapter 12

The sketchbook under Christian's arm dropped to the floor as he stepped away from the mantel. Loose papers scattered. He didn't notice. His first concern was for Jenny.

"I didn't mean to frighten you," he said softly. His approach was hesitant, anxious. He stopped when Jenny held out her hand, palm up. "I'm, er, I'm sorry. I shouldn't have come in. I realize that now. But there wasn't any answer at the door when I knocked and I got worried, so I used the key the clerk gave me and I . . . Jenny? Are you all right? Oh, God, Jenny, don't faint. Are you going to fai—"

Christian leaped forward and caught Jenny just before she hit the floor. He didn't make any attempt to carry her into the bedroom. For several minutes he simply held her, enfolding her in the circle of his arms and breathing in the fragrant scent of her hair. "I'm sorry, Jenny," he whispered, rocking her lightly. Soft strands of her hair tickled his mouth as he spoke. "Wake up and you can damn well tell me to go straight to hell."

"Don't swear at me," she said. She couldn't help smiling when Christian's response was to hug her more tightly. Her arms crept around his neck and she buried her face in the curve of his shoulder. "Are you really here? I'm not dreaming?"

"I'm really here." He got to his feet slowly, bringing her with him. His hands supported her back, then gradually drifted to her hips. The curves of her body seemed to be made to fit the angles of his. "Did you dream of me?" he asked. The words seemed to be drawn out of him reluctantly. There was a certain awed quality to his voice that would have been understandable had he been a green youth. Christian hadn't been a green youth since his twelfth year when Mary McCleod invited him into the tack room. Jenny made him feel eleven. His aquamarine eyes caressed her face, finally settling on the rose curve of her lips. "Did you?" he asked again.

"Daydreams," she said. "Night dreams. I couldn't seem to help it."

Her honesty undid him. Her honesty *and* the tip of her tongue, which peeped out to wet her upper lip. Christian's soft groan accompanied the lowering of his head. His mouth pressed its hard outline against Jenny's mouth. He was too starved for the taste of her to begin lightly. It was all he could do to keep from devouring her.

Jenny knew she wasn't thinking clearly. Christian's presence was never conducive to rational thought, but his kisses turned her inside out. His lips touched the corners of her eyes. She felt him at her temples, her jaw, her neck. His tongue pushed its way into her mouth, tracing the ridge of her teeth, thrusting deeply in an erotic rhythm that drew Jenny closer and shattered the last fragile bastion of her common sense.

She had questions for him. What was he doing here? How had he found her? It was just that at the moment she didn't care about the answers.

Jenny's hunger matched Christian's. Her hands slipped beneath the coat he had unbuttoned but not bothered to remove. Her fingers fumbled with his shirt studs, plucking them out so she could feel his warm skin beneath her palms. Her head twisted beneath his and her mouth pressed kisses to the hard line of his jaw. Jenny's teeth nipped his ear lobe, dragging a throaty growl from Christian that in turn started a frisson of heat in Jenny's spine. It was like that. He touched, she responded, then the act of giving and receiving reversed and they simply reveled in shared desire.

Christian let go of Jenny long enough to shrug out of his coat. When he held her again it was to lift her in his arms. She was everything womanly, yet she was cradled against him like a trusting child. It was then that Christian knew he couldn't deceive her. She had a right to know exactly what he wanted from her.

Instead of carrying her to the bedroom Christian walked across the parlor to where the sketchbook had fallen. He set Jenny on the chaise, and when she would have held him by his shirt, he kissed her quickly, hard, then pried her fingers free. Her dazed, darkening eyes almost made him change his mind. Wanting her made him ache.

"I want you to see these," he said, raising the sketchbook and thrusting it into her hands. It was hard to talk around the tightness in his throat. He gathered the scattered sheets of paper and placed them on top of the book. "These as well. You have to decide if they're enough for a beginning."

Jenny's hands were shaking. She knew what she held.

"It's not my best work," Christian went on apologetically as Jenny began to slowly sift through the sketches. "My model . . . she left me and . . . and I had to rely on memory. I thought I knew every line and curve of her face yet there were times—"

Jenny raised her eyes to Christian's anxious ones, cutting him off. "Your memory played you false," she said. "You've made this woman seem beautiful."

"So she is." He was looking at Jenny, not at the sketches in her hands.

"I'm not."

"Not always. But mostly . . . yes. Yes, you are." His eyes weren't cool or dispassionate. They glistened with a transparent veil of tears. "And Jenny, you saw my sketches from the war . . . somehow you sensed what they were to me. You knew I thought I would never draw anything beautiful again."

Jenny dropped her head quickly as her cheeks flushed. She

309

continued leafing through the drawings and tried not to think of herself as the model. It was difficult. A part of her could not help but be flattered by the way Christian viewed her.

Christian's work was astonishing for its clarity. The lines were pure, each stroke of his pen deft. He captured Jenny's profile in a single line. The eye followed the curve of her face from forehead to chin in one continuous motion. The tilt of her chin suggested a regal bearing. The hint of a dimple at the corner of her mouth suggested a sly cleverness.

Jenny filled the sketchbook in a variety of poses. Christian had captured her amused and bemused. He was uncannily accurate when it came to recreating the emotions that flitted across Jenny's face. He caught uncertainty, happiness, confusion, conceit, anger, fear, passion, and joy. Sometimes she stared out from the page, her eyes bright with laughter. In other sketches Christian recalled more solemn times when Jenny's eyes expressed thoughtfulness and a certain haunted distance from the casual observer.

Pale washes of color had been added to some of the sketches. The hue in her cheeks was rose, her lips a shade darker. The rich texture of her hair was suggested with colors ranging from cocoa to chestnut. Her complexion was translucent, glowing.

Jenny worried her lower lip as she studied the sketches. They were disturbing because of what they revealed to Jenny about herself. She had not expected to feel this exposed by Christian's work. She wasn't aware that he had watched her so closely or perhaps knew her so well. It was disconcerting to think that he might know more about her character than she knew herself.

Jenny collected the loose pages of drawings, straightened them, and slid them inside the sketchbook. She closed it and laid it aside, then raised her eyes to Christian. His anxiousness was not readily apparent now. He had become guarded in anticipation of her rejection. His cool glance was shuttered, the planes of his face austerely set. His copper-streaked hair reflected the gaslight. The line of his mouth was no longer

310

sensuous; it was grim.

"You don't like them," he accused roughly.

"It doesn't matter if I like them or not," she said. "That was never part of the condition I laid down. But as it happens, I like them very much. Your talent has matured."

Christian relaxed a little. "It's not the portrait you wanted."

"No, it's not. But these sketches are so much more. I don't care about a formal portrait. I never did. I only wanted you to use your gift again."

"I'm going to do the portrait anyway. I want to."

"All right."

"You'll pose for me?"

"Yes."

"It's going to be a nude."

The brief spark of humor in Christian's eyes gave him away. "Liar," Jenny said. "But it wouldn't matter. I'd do that for you as well."

"You would?"

"Hmmm." Jenny slid off the chaise and knelt on the floor in front of Christian. Her arms circled his neck and she applied just enough pressure at his nape to get him to lower his head. Her lips parted. Her breath caressed his mouth. "You're not going to regret taking me as your mistress," she whispered.

Christian was regretting that he had not made himself more clear. He no longer wanted a mistress. But as Jenny's soft lips pressed his hungrily, Christian put aside his intentions to ask her to marry him. He would save his proposal for later, when she was lying against him, her body damp, her fragrance musky. At the moment the question of marriage did not seem important. He only wanted to love her.

"Let me take you to bed," he said. His words were spaced around the kisses that Jenny continued to tease him with. Christian's palms slid up and down her back, sometimes coming forward just enough that his thumbs brushed the sensitive undersides of her breasts. For a while the satin wrapper had been cool beneath his hands; now Christian could feel Jenny's heat. Her wanting excited him. "Bed," he said again, his voice husky.

Jenny shook her head. "Right here." Using her foot, she impatiently pushed the low table out of the way. When the carpet was cleared she leaned back, clutching Christian by the shoulders so that he followed her and blanketed her with his body.

"Right here," he echoed, surrendering. The bed suddenly seemed very far away and quite unnecessary. Christian buried his fingers in Jenny's thick hair, cupping the back of her head. The kiss he leveled on her mouth was almost violent with need. It had been too long an abstinence to go gently now.

Jenny felt the same way. Eagerness made her fingers clumsy as she helped Christian out of his clothes. She laughed uneasily as she realized how apparent it was that she wanted him.

"I'm flattered," Christian said softly, stilling her hands as they made to remove his trousers. He released her wrists and her hands drifted lower, cupping his arousal. "Very flattered."

She smiled. Her eyes were dark, her skin flushed. She felt him tug on the sash of her robe, and the leaf green satin whispered across her flesh as he peeled it away. He kissed the curve of her shoulder as it was exposed. His fingertips stroked her breasts.

Ridding himself of the rest of his clothes, Christian lay on his side and pulled Jenny close. Their legs tangled. He was hard against her belly. His hands cupped her bottom, and she moved against him sinuously while her arms circled his back. He could feel the swollen points of her nipples against his chest.

Jenny rolled onto her back, opening herself to Christian without any prompting. It was she who urged him to take her, and even though she was ready for him, she still gasped at the strength of his first thrust.

Christian held himself motionless inside her. He swore under his breath. "I hurt you." There was an accusation in his tone but it was meant for himself and not Jenny.

"No . . . that is, it's all right." Her eyes pleaded with the

312

ones already distancing themselves from her. She felt him begin to withdraw. Jenny's legs curved around him, stubbornly holding him to her. "Don't you dare leave me, Christian Marshall. I want this. I want you."

He basked in the warmth of her husky voice. "Show me," he said. He slipped his arms under her shoulders, supporting her while he rolled onto his back. Her legs unwound so that she straddled him. Christian's hands drifted over her breasts and rib cage as she slowly sat up. The bemused, startled look in her eyes made Christian ache all the more. He had forgotten how innocent she really was. "Show me, Jenny."

Jenny felt Christian's hands on her thighs. He pressed, lifting her slightly so that it was she who moved around him. "Oh!"

"Oh," he repeated, mocking her softly.

"But—"

Christian wasn't interested in objections, not when the tight warm fist of her body was contracting all around him. "Go ahead, Jenny. You take me."

Jenny moved experimentally, raising and lowering herself slowly, controlling the sensations, measuring the depth of each thrust. She leaned forward. Her hair spilled around her shoulders like a dark curtain. Her breasts were offered to Christian's roaming hands. His knuckles brushed her nipples. As if snapped by a thread of fire, Jenny's hips jerked in reaction and she moaned softly.

"That's it," Christian encouraged tautly as Jenny deepened her thrusts. "Just like that." He kissed her hotly when she bent over him. His hands were like liquid heat on her flesh, massaging her back, caressing her breasts. As she continued to move over him, finding the rhythm that suited her pleasure, Christian's fingers slipped between her thighs and stroked her intimately. He shared her growing excitement, liking the small sounds of desiring he could coax from her.

Jenny raised herself up and looked down at the place where Christian's hand moved against her. Watching him took her

313

breath away. Her back arched, drawing Christian's eyes to the graceful line of her neck and the tautly swollen curves of her breasts. She commanded all of Christian's attention as she abandoned herself to his touch.

Christian heard his name as Jenny's pleasure peaked. He liked hearing her say it. There was a tiny catch between the syllables as she sipped the air. "Oh, Jenny," he said. "Come here." His hands spanned her waist, held her tightly as he twisted, then he was driving into her hard, stroking her until she cried out again and they shared pleasure this time, their senses shattering within moments of one another.

Jenny's breath was ragged, almost as harsh as Christian's. Her hand rested on his chest and beneath her palm she could feel his heart pounding. "I may never move," she said after more than a minute of silence. She wanted to cuddle, to hold and be held. Christian seemed willing to oblige her. "Never ever."

"It could be awkward." His fingers sifted through the soft, silky strands of her hair. When she turned her head, nuzzling against him, Christian kissed her full on the mouth. The kiss lingered. And lingered. "On the other hand . . ."

She laughed, turning away so that his lips brushed her cheek. "I should be furious with you," she said, reaching for her robe. She started to sit up, intending to put on the robe, but Christian stopped her.

"Don't bother. I'll only take it off you again." His eyes held hers, making sure she knew he meant it. "Let's go to bed."

Jenny let the robe slide through her fingers. "Let's."

Once they were in bed, under the covers, and warming one another with the soles of their feet and the palms of their hands, Christian asked Jenny why she should be furious with him.

"You can't think of a reason?" she asked, quieting in the circle of his embrace.

"I could probably think of several, but I'm not going to list them for you. What if they're reasons you hadn't thought of?"

"There's that," she said dryly, acknowledging his point. "I should be mad at you for coming in here uninvited. You scared me."

"I apologized for that. I knew you were in here, but when you didn't answer I thought something had happened. I let myself in only to realize that you were in the bath. I could hear you splashing. It was agony waiting for you. I kept thinking about you, what you looked—"

"Good," she said, cutting him off before he was carried away with his own imagination. "You deserved to be tortured."

"I was. Never more so than when you fainted. *That* frightened the hell out of me."

"It was silly. I don't know why it happened."

"You've lost weight. A brisk wind would send you flying. Haven't you been eating?"

"Of course I eat . . . when I remember."

"I thought so. Mrs. B. will want to fatten you up."

"Mrs. B.?"

"Yes," said Christian. "When you come home with me. She's getting around with only a cane now. The stairs are difficult for her, so we converted the yellow parlor on the first floor into a bedroom. She's still a mother hen, watching over me, wanting to watch over you. She knows I planned to see you tonight and she knows why."

Jenny's eyes widened. "You told Mrs. Brandywine that you were coming here to . . . to—"

Christian placed his forefinger across Jenny's lips, silencing her. "To ask you to be my wife."

"Your wife?" Jenny jerked away. She sat up, clutching the sheet to her chest. "What are you talking about? Is that what you meant about me going home with you and Mrs. B. fattening me up? Do you expect me to *live* with you?"

Now Christian sat up, his back stiff against the headboard. The play of light and shadow made the angles of his face seem more severe than they really were. "Jesus! You make it sound as pleasant as contracting a disease. I'm talking about marriage, Jenny, not the plague. Of course I expect my wife to live with me."

"And you expect me to be your wife," she said, snapping her fingers. "Just like that."

"Is there something I'm not understanding?" he asked, throwing up his hands and giving her a sharp glance.

"Obviously."

"Then explain it to me."

"Have you forgotten? The bargain we struck was for me to be your mistress, not your wife."

"I don't care about the damn bargain." It was all he could do to keep from shaking her. "That's not what this is all about and you know it. What do you have against being my wife?"

Realizing she was coming perilously close to shouting, Jenny lowered her voice. "Except for the fact that I don't want a husband, I don't have anything against being your wife."

Christian's voice sank as well. "Then it's not me you object to, just marriage."

"Marriage is all right," she offered, "but not for me. As to the other, how could you think I objected to you? That doesn't make any sense, Christian. What was that all about in the other room, then?"

His cool eyes snapped at her. "Animal coupling?"

Jenny looked away, hurt by his vulgarity. "You had better leave," she said quietly. "I don't think I want you here any longer."

"Hell, Jenny, you know I didn't mean that."

"Do I?"

Christian leaned toward her, brushing back the heavy lock of hair that had fallen over Jenny's shoulder. He felt her flinch slightly, but his hand remained at her neck, curving around her nape. She couldn't avoid his thumb as it passed along the line of her jaw, lifting her face to his. "You know me better than anyone, Jenny, better than anyone's ever known me. You know when I'm hurt, when I'm frightened. Even when I only show you anger you know about the other things I'm feeling,

316

the deeper things that I want to keep buried. Is it any wonder that I worked so hard to keep you at a distance? You scared the hell out of me."

His thumb continued to stroke her jaw. He felt her lean her cheek toward him, unconsciously asking him not to stop the caress. "You were unexpected and I was unprepared. Almost from the beginning I suspected you were dangerous, but I underestimated your impact. You didn't hammer away at me, yet I always knew you were around. So gentle, Jenny. Gentle *and* relentless. Like a spring rain. I couldn't seem to stop you . . . I didn't always know if I wanted to.

"You made your presence felt in my room, then in my house. I'd ask who put out the fresh flowers in my study and the answer would be Jenny. Who was making old Mrs. Morrisey laugh? Jenny. Where did the new drapes come from? Oh, Jenny found them, someone would say. How did this copy of *The Herald* get here? Jenny bought it. Who was going to care for Mrs. B.? Jenny would, I was told.

"You were the answer to everything. Until I met you I never knew anyone so unobtrusive who was also impossible to ignore. I warned you to stay out of my way, then was angry when you did. I cursed you for being in my bed, then wouldn't let you go. Are you really going to tell me you didn't suspect what was happening, Jenny?"

"I suspected," she replied, edging toward him. "But it's not the same as knowing. I still don't know, Christian, and I won't say the words for you so you can merely confirm them. I want to hear them from you."

"But I asked you to marry me," he defended himself.

She ignored that. "Say them," she repeated.

"Dammit, Jenny," he growled softly, feeling as if he were being pushed to the wall. He caught the sweet fragrance of her hair. "I . . ."

"Yes?"

"I love you."

She launched herself into his arms, smothering his face with kisses. Her lips touched the corners of his eyes, his mouth. Laughing, she trailed kisses along the underside of his jaw and across his brow. Her mouth brushed his cheeks, his temples, and pressed a smile into the thick softness of his hair.

Christian felt the dampness of her cheeks as she pressed her face to his. He took her gently by the shoulders and drew her back, searching her face. She didn't even try to blink back the tears that welled in her dark eyes. They fell freely, silently, at odds with her tender, serene smile. "Oh, God, Jenny Holland, I love you." Holding her close, he kissed away the tears.

Jenny quieted in Christian's arms. She laid her head against his shoulder and he rocked her. The tears dried up but the smile remained. She closed her eyes and he kissed her spiky lashes.

"Jenny?"

"Mmmm?"

"You're still not going to marry me, are you?"

"No. But that doesn't mean I don't love you. I do, you know. I had a hint it was happening on Christmas Day. Remember? The Turners came to dinner and you romped on the floor with Amy and that kitten you bought her."

"I was trying to tell you that I didn't mean those things I said earlier about disliking children and cats . . . and the other ugly things I hurled at your head."

"I didn't realize that at first. I thought you were doing it to be spiteful. But I kept thinking about it, and it seemed to me that perhaps you didn't know any other way to make amends. I wanted to believe that you were trying to say you were sorry. That was the first inkling I had that I could love you."

Jenny laid her palm on Christian's chest, just above the steady beat of his heart. "I've known it with certainty since the night I went uninvited to your studio. I looked at your paintings, your plans, and I felt something for your work. But when I looked at your sketches from the war I felt something for the artist. It wasn't pity, Christian. No matter what you thought at the time it was never pity. What I felt was more of a

318

sadness, an ache in my soul that I thought you must share. I knew then that I loved you. I couldn't have hurt so deeply if I didn't love you."

"But you left me."

She nodded. The ends of her hair tickled his arm. "It was time," she said simply. "But you found me anyway."

"You didn't make it easy."

"You shouldn't have found me at all," she said seriously. "I wasn't playing a children's game of hide-and-seek. How did you know I was living here?"

"*The Herald*. I saw the personal columns."

"I see," she said, frowning. She sat up a little straighter, opened her eyes, and swiped at them with the corner of the sheet. "Who else knows?"

"Susan and Scott—because they helped me decipher the Princess's enigmatic messages to Butler. And Joe Means because he brought me round in the carriage when I was first trying to get a glimpse of the man."

"You saw him?" she asked incredulously. "You saw Mr. . . ." She stopped short of giving Reilly's real name. "—Mr. Butler?"

"It's no good, Jenny. I know who he is. His name is Wilton Reilly and he's the head of staff at the Bennington residence. I know who you are as well, and I can only think that it has everything to do with your reason for not wanting to marry me."

It was all Jenny could do not to bolt out of Christian's arms. She knew he had to have felt her stiffen. "What do you mean?"

"Do you really think I care about you being a housemaid?" he asked. "I don't know why you didn't tell me at the outset that you worked for the Benningtons. It's them you're afraid of, isn't it? That's why you spun me the tale about working as a companion to old Alice Vanderstell. You were afraid someone might go to the Benningtons and tell them where you were."

Jenny eased herself out of Christian's arms. She couldn't

319

talk to him when she was so close. More correctly, she couldn't lie to him at such close quarters. She tucked the rumpled sheet around herself, securing one corner between her breasts. "How did you draw all these conclusions?" she asked, skirting the truth.

Christian stretched out, leaning back on his elbows. He appeared more at ease than he really was. It was difficult to watch Jenny and pretend he didn't know she was still spinning tales to him. The trouble was, he didn't know the truth either. In the past two months he and Scott and Susan had tested several theories and found all of them wanting in one way or another. What he had related to Jenny was simply the conclusion they'd agreed was the least objectionable.

"I followed Mr. Reilly when he left you. He—"

"But he's only been here once . . . eight weeks ago. Do you mean you've known I was here all that time?"

"Yes," he said without apology. "I said you didn't make it easy to find you, but it wasn't impossible either." Christian's smile was faintly wicked. "And I was determined."

"But you never—"

He anticipated her question. "I didn't come to see you because I wasn't ready. There was the matter of your portrait, don't forget. You set the terms. Once I knew you were safe I had to decide what I was willing to do in order to have you again. I began sketching out of spite, to prove something to you. In the end I did the drawings out of love and proved something to myself."

Jenny blinked rapidly, damming the tears that came so easily to the surface now. She pointed to her eyes as salty droplets fell anyway and apologized, "Happy tears." Picking up a pillow, she held it pressed to her chest and brushed her damp cheeks against the white cotton case. "Tell me about Mr. Reilly," she said, swallowing the lump in her throat. "You started to tell me you followed him from here."

Christian nodded. His eyes darted over Jenny's ashen face. He believed her when she said the tears were happy ones, but

320

he couldn't help thinking that she was hiding something else. There were pale, violet shadows under her eyes; the skin of her face was stretched taut. He had already acknowledged her weight loss, and now he saw how fragile her wrists were as she clutched the pillow. Compared to Jane Doe of the treatment room, Jenny's health was robust. But when Christian thought back to the last time he had seen her, he knew she was ill now.

"Christian?"

"What? Oh . . . sorry. I was thinking about something else." He gathered the threads of his wits. "Joe and I followed Reilly back to the Benningtons. Your friend changed hacks three times."

"He suspected he was being followed."

"True, but not by me. He thought O'Shea might spot him."

"You know about Liam?' she asked, astonished.

"Before I met O'Shea in front of the Benningtons," he began in a caustic tone, "the only thing I knew about him was that you enjoyed his company on your daily walks."

"Christian! You were jealous!"

"You don't have to sound so pleased about it," he said testily. He pretended to ignore her girlish giggle, but it warmed him just to know that he could make her laugh, even if she was laughing at him. "Anyway, I found out that O'Shea had been hired by William Bennington to follow Reilly."

"Who told you that?"

"O'Shea did. But he didn't know precisely what he was looking for. He thought it might have something to do with thefts within the house."

"Thefts?" Was it possible her stepfather had actually missed the items Reilly was stealing for her? "You mean Mr. Bennington thought Reilly was guilty of stealing?"

"No," Christian denied. "I mean O'Shea thought that's why he had been hired. William never really confided in him, except to say that O'Shea was to track the butler whenever he left the house." Under the blanket Christian absently massaged his leg. "I never really accepted O'Shea's theory. It seemed to me that Bennington was using Reilly to find you."

Jenny's mouth was very dry. She couldn't swallow. "Why would you think that?" she rasped.

"Several things," he allowed casually. "There were a number of events which when viewed separately seem to have no bearing on you, yet Scott and I finally realized it was rather like not being able to see the forest for the trees."

Jenny bit her lower lip. "I wish you hadn't involved Dr. Turner."

"That's an odd request considering he's been involved since the beginning. If it hadn't been for him . . ." Christian let Jenny finish the sentence for herself. "Susan as well. She's the one who actually pointed out the forest."

Jenny sighed. "Perhaps you'd better explain about this forest. I'm sure I don't understand."

Christian doubted that. He could almost see Jenny's mind working furiously as she tried to recall events that would have connected her to the Benningtons. "I'm sure you haven't forgotten New Year's Eve," he said, raising one brow. "No? I thought not. And you know I'm not referring to what happened *in* Maggie's room. I'm talking about what went on afterwards, out in the hallway. Tell me, when did you run to the balcony and hide? When you heard Stephen, or when his father arrived?"

She shrugged, refusing to answer, and clutched the pillow closer to her chest.

"It doesn't matter," said Christian. "I was just curious. I never gave it a thought when it happened. It didn't occur to me then that you might actually know either of the Benningtons. I had pretty much concluded that you hid because of Amalie's intentions. Now I realize that was only part of it." Christian stuffed a pillow behind the small of his back and the headboard. He crossed his arms in front of him and regarded Jenny thoughtfully. "The day after you left me, while I was at Susan's enlisting her help, Scott was called to Dr. Morgan's office." The stillness that settled about Jenny was that of a

322

cornered fawn. Christian wanted to reach for her but he suspected she would bolt. Instead he ticked off the next points on his fingers. "William and Stephen were leaving the office as he went in. From Morgan's secretary Scott found out they were large contributors to the hospital trust and had been since October. When Scott finally spoke to Morgan he was informed that there was a possibility that the Jane Doe patient was still alive."

Jenny blinked once and continued to stare steadily at Christian. Inside, her stomach heaved.

"Odd, isn't it?" Christian asked. "The Benningtons again. And benefactors to Jennings Memorial since October? Once Scott really thought about it, that struck him as odd as well. Jane Doe arrived at Jennings only a few weeks after the Benningtons became philanthropists. The Benningtons are not noted for philanthropy, by the way."

"I'd heard that," Jenny said, for want of anything better to say.

"And finally there was Mr. Reilly, who brought us round to the Benningtons again. Those events were the trees. As Susan said, 'Bennington seems to be the name of the forest.' Would you agree?"

Jenny's eyes darted away. "I might."

"And what if I tell you this? I know, for instance, that you have some sort of photographic studio set up in here. I assume it's in the other bedroom."

"*Assume?*" she snapped waspishly. "Don't you mean you explored it while I was in my bath?"

Christian simply went on as if she hadn't spoken. "I also know that directly across the street from you is First Hancock Savings and Trust. Interesting, don't you think, that William Bennington is the president of that bank?" He felt the full force of Jenny's anger as she glared at him. He sighed. "Jenny? Can't you trust me at all? Aren't you going to tell me what it is you're doing?"

Her mouth flattened mutinously.

323

"I see," he said, disappointed. "I hadn't realized how selfish you were."

Jenny was too shocked by that pronouncement to say anything for a moment. Finally she asked, "What do you mean?"

Now Christian shrugged carelessly, affecting an indifference he didn't feel. "Just that you're the worst kind of giver—the one who won't take anything in return."

"One doesn't do favors with the expectation of receiving," she said a shade piously as if reciting something from a catechism. "It's not right."

"I'm not talking about anything so paltry as doing favors," he said impatiently. "That doesn't begin to describe what you've done for me. And I'm not talking about expectations. It's one thing not to expect anything in return, quite another to refuse something when it's offered. That's what makes you selfish. You get pleasure from giving, but you won't let me have the same pleasure."

"Whatever I did, I did because I love you."

"Damn—darn it, Jenny! What the—heck do you think I'm doing it for?" He rubbed his temples, shaking his head at the same time. "God! Listen to me! I can't believe I'm talking like . . ." He stopped because Jenny was in his arms again, laughing and crying and kissing him as she'd done when he'd first said he loved her. Christian didn't understand, but he accepted his good fortune and wrapped his arms around her. "Jenny . . . Jenny . . . let me help you. I *want* to help. Don't turn me out."

"Just hold me," she said, curving her body against his and quieting in his arms. Her fingers fiddled with the knot between her breasts. "Hold me. That will help for now."

So Christian held her. He stroked her back, his fingers sifted through her hair. And he waited for Jenny to confide in him. Occasionally he glanced down at her, just to make certain she hadn't fallen asleep. He kissed her forehead and her lashes fluttered. He saw he had managed to interrupt her thoughts.

324

and raise a smile.

"I still don't want to get married," she said.

"All right." For now, he added silently.

"I have to stay here. I need to be near the bank."

"Are you going to tell me why?"

"William Bennington and his son are stealing from it."

"You're certain?"

"Yes."

Christian heard the conviction in Jenny's voice and believed her. He nodded thoughtfully. "There were rumors about the bank a while back. Nothing about embezzlement, just about The Trust not being as sound as it should be."

"It wasn't a rumor. It was—*is*—true. But the embezzlement is only a small part of it. Apparently Mr. Bennington made a number of bad investments as the war drew to an end."

"How do you know this?"

"How does anyone in service know anything?" she asked airily, hating the fact that she was still lying to him. "We listen at doors."

"I take it you were caught?"

"Yes."

"And drugged?"

"I think so. I'm not certain what was done to me, only that it was done gradually. I didn't know I had been found out, you see. I didn't suspect what was being done to me until it was too late. I was told I was going mad and there were days when I believed it."

"Didn't the other servants suspect? Mr. Reilly?"

"I was fairly, umm, isolated from the others. Mr. Bennington made it seem as though he cared about the welfare of his staff. He hired a special attendant for me and Dr. Morgan visited several times. Eventually I was taken away. The staff was told I was going to the city hospital. Instead I was taken to a cellar lodging room somewhere in The Five Points. I don't really remember much about that . . . I could have been there hours or days. I was completely delirious by then."

Jenny was thankful for Christian's closeness now. She needed his warmth, his acceptance. "Some men took me to Jennings."

"Dead Rabbits."

"That's what I was told. I could never identify them."

"It's just as well. They'd kill you if they thought you could." He laid his hand on her bare shoulder as she shivered. "I'm sorry. I shouldn't have said that."

"No, it's all right. It's nothing that I haven't already thought of. I never understood why Mr. Bennington didn't have me killed then." But she *had* understood. Jenny knew precisely why she hadn't been murdered for what she had overheard, yet it was part of what she wanted to keep from Christian.

"It would appear to have been the expedient thing to do," Christian said, thinking it over. "Maybe he intended for you to die while you were in Jennings."

"Perhaps." Jenny knew differently. If the treatments had actually killed her it would have been an accident, the result of Dr. Glenn's zeal and the attendants' ineptitude. William hadn't wanted her dead then, though Jenny thought he had probably changed his mind by now. "But you and Dr. Turner saw that it didn't happen." Jenny ran her palm along Christian's forearm. Her fingers intertwined with his. "I don't know what Dr. Turner ever saw that made him suspect I was sane," she said wonderingly. "He only saw me briefly, and I didn't even know my own name then. After Dr. Glenn started treating me, I knew it was only a matter of time before I ended up like the others on the ward."

She was probably right, Christian thought, remembering Jenny as he had first seen her. She had been near the edge of madness. His fingers squeezed hers. "Why haven't you gone to the police with your story?"

Jenny raised her head just long enough to give Christian an eyeful of amazement. "I can't believe you asked me that," she said. "This is New York, Christian. Mr. Bennington doesn't buy cops. He owns their superiors. Going to the police would

326

e like signing my own commitment papers to Jennings. I'd as oon kill myself."

Christian didn't comment on her last statement, but he new he wouldn't forget it either. "So the police are out. What loes that leave?"

"Can't you guess? You're one of them."

He thought about that for almost a minute, then he swore oftly under his breath. "You mean the newspaper, don't you? 'hat's where you want to take your story."

Jenny nodded. "I don't know how else to get a fair hearing. As far as I know the city's papers are still independent. They're he one place where Mr. Bennington has no influence."

"All right," Christian said. "I'll take the story to *The Chronicle*. We'll print it."

"I knew you were going to be difficult," she sighed.

He frowned, his brows drawing together. "Difficult? I thought I was doing exactly what you wanted. *The Chronicle* will run the story. Front page. Unlike Bennington, the paper's he only place I *do* have some influence."

"No commissioners in your pockets?" she teased. "No politicians?"

Christian looked down at himself. "No pockets."

Jenny giggled, raised his hand to her lips, and kissed his knuckles. "I realize you're eager to help, Christian, but until I have proof there's no story. Print what I'm telling you without proof and the courts will see that Mr. Bennington owns your paper."

"Perhaps," he said. "Perhaps not. Innuendo could do a lot of damage to Bennington. *The Herald* wields a lot of power that way. There may be a way to present the story without giving Bennington the opportunity to file a libel suit."

"No," she said firmly. "That's not the way I want to do it. And that's not the reputation *The Chronicle* has. Or *The Times*. Even *The Herald* wouldn't take this story. If Mr. Bennington had committed a social peccadillo, that would be different. But this is more than being caught with his pants down at Amalie

Chatham's. This involves The Trust's reputation as a financial institution and the safety of thousands of depositors' money. I want proof, Christian. I want this to go from the papers to the courts and I want so much proof that my—that Mr Bennington can't buy his way clear of the evidence."

"How do you propose we get it?"

"We? You mean you're really going to help me?"

Christian sighed. "Of course I am."

"Even after what you've heard?"

"Especially after what I've heard."

Jenny released Christian's hand and scooted across the bed, dragging the sheet with her. She crooked a finger, indicating he should follow as she put her legs over the side of the bed.

"Where are we going?" he asked, hitching a blanket around his middle. "And am I dressed appropriately?"

She laughed. "You're fine. Come on. I want to show you my darkroom." Jenny paused long enough in the parlor to shed her sheet and slip into her satin wrapper. Christian kept his blanket.

He whistled softly when Jenny opened the door to the spare bedroom. "This is quite something," he said appreciatively. He leaned against the doorjamb and surveyed the room while Jenny lit a lamp. In the corner to his left was a tripod, about five feet high. Another was set up near the window with a brassbound camera already attached to it. The black blanket a photographer had to wear over his head when he took his picture was lying on the floor beside the tripod. The nightstand to the left of the bed was crowded with bottles of chemicals, a couple of glass funnels, and a discarded lens. There was also another camera, this one a double-extension model with long, tapered leather bellows for an extended range of focusing movements.

The bedroom was Jenny's studio as well as her darkroom. Christian was doubly impressed when he saw where she was developing her pictures. Jenny had removed the mattress from the four-poster. It sagged against one wall. The bed's pale yellow canopy lay over it. The four-poster now supported what looked to be an old army tent, or rather two old army tents sewn together.

Christian pushed away from the door and went right to the bed. He lifted the flap at the foot and peered inside, then motioned Jenny to bring the lamp closer. He took it from her and stepped over the bed frame to get inside the darkroom.

Jenny had set a table against the headboard. On it were trays for the chemical baths. Parallel to the table, but several feet above it, hung a yellow pane of glass. Christian pointed to it. "Is that how you filter the light when you're working?" he asked.

"Hmm-mm. I can set a dimly lit lamp on it and don't have to worry that my pictures will be exposed. It gives me enough light to see by, but doesn't destroy the photographs."

He nodded. He had something similar in his darkroom. "When did you become interested in photography?" he asked, hunkering down in front of the table. He found a stack of albumen-treated paper, a case of lenses, and a hatbox partially filled with pictures she had already developed. He raised the hatbox. "May I?"

"Certainly, but you'll be able to see them better if we go in the parlor. There's more light there."

Christian agreed. Jenny sat in the large overstuffed armchair, her feet curled under her, while Christian sat on the floor and leaned back against the chair. Jenny's tapered nails lightly scratched his neck while he bent his head over the photographs. "Tell me how you come to know so much about photography," he repeated.

Jenny was hoping he would forget that he had ever asked. Here were dangerous waters. "I read some things," she said. That was true.

"Oh? What?"

"*The Silver Sunbeam* for one. It's a technical manual."

"I'm familiar with it." He was making piles of the photographs, sorting them according to clarity. "What else?"

"Le Moniteur de la Photographie. Tijdschrift voor Photographie." She pronounced the titles of both journals with careless ease.

"Those are periodicals, Jenny."

"So?"

"So? They're foreign periodicals. The first one is French. And if I'm not mistaken, the second is Dutch. You read both those languages?"

Jenny was furious with herself. She'd let her guard down because he'd asked the questions so casually, as if he were only making small talk to fill a void. Christian's focus seemed to be elsewhere, more on the pictures than on her. "I didn't actually read them myself," she lied. "Mr. Bennington's cook is French. The housekeeper is Dutch. You'd be surprised how many people are interested in photography these days."

Christian's murmured reply was strictly noncommittal. He would have been very interested to hear about a cook and housekeeper who could afford to have foreign periodicals posted to them in New York when so many English journals were available. Jenny was spinning another tale. Rather than pin her to the wall with it, Christian simply filed it away. "The equipment you accumulated didn't come cheaply," he said. "Where did you get the money?"

She wasn't going to let herself be trapped again. "I think you already know the answer to that. You read the personal columns."

"Watch Ruby R. Sterling," he said.

"Yes."

"So Reilly *is* stealing from Bennington."

"Just some items that won't be missed. I'm fairly certain of that. I wouldn't have asked Mr. Reilly to risk being found out on my behalf."

Christian finished sorting. He set the hatbox aside, picked up the first pile of photographs, and flicked through them. "What is Reilly to you?" he asked.

"A friend."

"That's all?"

Jenny tugged on the end of Christian's hair. She could hardly believe what she was hearing and astonishment was rife in her tone. "Are you suggesting there's something more between us?"

"It occurred to me. I was just around the corner in the hallway when he met you here. You told him he was still a fine figure of a man. He gave you money. You said—and I quote—'As long as you can give me this, you're welcome to anything I have.'"

"My God, Christian. I don't even remember the conversation and you're repeating it back to me verbatim. You must have been disturbed by it."

"Disturbed?" He put down the pictures in his hand and picked up another set of prints. "That's a rather mild way of putting it. I contemplated murder."

"Mine?"

He shook his head. "I still wanted you too badly. No, I thought about killing *him.*"

Jenny leaned forward and kissed the crown of Christian's head. "Mr. Reilly is a dear, dear friend. He's the one person I knew from my other life that I thought I could trust. As far as I know I was right. He's kept my secret. We correspond by mail now, though infrequently. I'm still concerned that Liam might find me through Mr. Reilly."

"Don't worry about O'Shea. He's occupied with another case."

"How do you know?"

"I hired him."

"You did? To do what?"

"To keep William Bennington from ever finding you." He turned his head and slanted Jenny a boyish grin. "Liam O'Shea's services didn't come cheaply, but since he's the only cop I have on my payroll, I can afford to make certain he stays loyal to me."

331

Chapter 13

Jenny couldn't think of anything to say for several moments. As she sat in silence, withdrawing from Christian, his grin faded. He put the pictures aside and stood up.

"It's not the end of the world," he told her. "O'Shea's a trustworthy man in his own fashion."

"If his loyalty can be bought, no man is trustworthy. What if Mr. Bennington offers him more money?"

"Why should he?" Christian countered. "William doesn't know that O'Shea is leaving details out of his report on Reilly. Specifically, he's not telling Bennington about the post office box that your friend rented or about the occasional letter he receives there. I don't think you realize how quickly Bennington could have nailed Mr. Reilly to the wall with that information."

"Mr. Reilly wouldn't have betrayed me."

Christian laughed shortly, without humor. "After your experiences with the Benningtons I don't know how you can still be naive. Anyone can be forced to talk, Jenny. Anyone, that is, who values his own life. If William Bennington found a way to have a perfectly sane woman drugged and committed to Jennings, don't you think he could manage to get an address from Reilly?"

"If that's true, then why hasn't he done it already?"

"I thought that was obvious. He's just not certain that Reilly can really lead him to you. He doesn't want to raise suspicions with false accusations. But if he had evidence from O'Shea that Reilly was contacting you, then it would only be a matter of time before Bennington found you."

Jenny adjusted her position as Christian rested his hip on the rounded arm of her chair. "Does Mr. O'Shea know where I am?"

"No. He's being paid by me *not* to know—or learn—certain things. In his own mind I think he believes I'm after Bennington in connection with a story for the paper. That was less true when I hired Liam, but now that I know what you want to do, his theory may turn out to have a grain of truth." Christian put his arm across Jenny's shoulder and nudged her so that her head fell against him. His fingers played in the softness of her hair. "Am I forgiven?"

"I suppose."

"How generous of you," he said wryly.

"Oh, Christian, you know I forgive you. It's just that I thought I had planned better. I didn't know I needed protection."

"It's not as if I put a guard on you."

"I know," she sighed, discouraged. "But I thought I was being careful, you see, and now I realize that I'm neither cautious nor clever. I've been here for eight weeks and I still don't have the evidence I need. I seem to need protection and answers, but I don't like this feeling of being dependent."

"That's been made very clear to me today," he said. Above her he was smiling, but when she glanced up at him suspiciously, he was looking grave. "Tell me about your photographs. What is it that you want them to show?"

"Besides details of the hideous ornamentation on that brownstone, you mean?"

He chuckled. "Yes. I'm assuming your interest in The Trust is not strictly architectural."

"It's not." Jenny slid off the chair and onto the floor. She

334

picked up the last set of pictures Christian had and passed each one on to Christian after she had looked at it. "This one's not too bad. See? That's my—er—that's Mr. Bennington behind his desk."

"It is? William or Stephen?"

"Why, it's William."

"You're sure?"

Jenny took back the picture and tossed it into the hatbox. "If you can't tell, then it's no good." She looked at the next one. "Here. You can see the safe. It's open. That's a newspaper Mr. Bennington has spread across his desk."

"It looks like a blotter. Where's William?"

"He's bending in front of the safe."

"He is?"

Jenny took back that picture as well. "Look at this one. What do you see?"

"Someone . . . Stephen, I think . . . sitting on the edge of his father's desk. That's William behind the desk. What are they doing? Playing cards?"

"Christian!" Jenny fairly wailed his name, she was so upset. "Can't you see that it's money they're handling? It's spread all over the desk. And that's a newspaper under it. They fold up the paper with the money inside and Stephen walks out with it. William spends the next twenty minutes or so going over the account books to make certain everything tallies."

"They look like they're playing cards, Jenny," Christian said heavily, aware of her disappointment. "It may not be what I'd want the president of my bank to do on business time, but as far as I know, it's not illegal."

"You know they're not playing cards."

"I know it because you're telling me. Your pictures aren't clear enough. I don't know of a lens that's been made that will do what you want it to do. You can't have it both ways. If you keep your distance, your pictures won't have enough clarity. If you go closer, you'll be sacrificing your safety."

Jenny knew he was right. She had come to the same conclusions herself. Yet for some reason it angered her that Christian was pointing them out to her. She began pitching the photographs into the hatbox. "I need help," she snapped. "Not a recital of what I already know to be true. Oh, dammit, I'm crying again." She knuckled her eyes impatiently, then continued tossing the prints with quick, angry motions. She felt Christian's hands on her shoulders and she shrugged him off. "No! Leave me alone. I want to be m-miserable right n-now. I'm-m enjoying this."

Christian let her go. "Of course you are. I don't know why I didn't realize it right away."

"D-don't make f-fun of me!" Jenny shoved the hatbox away from her. It tipped, spilling the photographs. "There! See what you've made me do!" She began to sob harder, uncontrollably. She couldn't wipe away the tears as fast as they were coming now. "What's wr-wrong with m-me?" she asked plaintively. "Wh-why is this h-happening?"

Christian caught her by the elbow as she started to go after the spilled pictures. "Leave them."

"B-but—"

"Leave them." This time he didn't let Jenny shake him off. He stood and brought Jenny with him, swinging her into his arms. Surprised as she was, she still didn't stop crying. "I'm putting you to bed, and you're going to stay there until I bring Scott here . . . and then you're going to do exactly what he tells you." He pushed open the door to her bedroom with his foot. "And if that means staying in bed for the next year, you'll do that as well."

The stern look Christian gave her kept Jenny quiet, but as soon as he set her on the bed, she bolted in the direction of the bathroom. Christian followed, waited until she was through being sick, then wiped her face with a cool cloth and gave her a glass of water to drink. He helped her to her feet, held her while she continued to weep softly, then, seeing no end to it, led her back to bed.

"I'm going for Scott now," he said. "Any objections?"

Jenny shook her head. She hiccupped. "You sh-should get dressed f-first, though."

He kissed her on her wet cheek and tucked the blankets around her. "Thank you. I'll do that." He held the image of her pathetic, watery smile the entire way to Scott's and back again.

"It's no good pacing," Susan said as Christian started his fourth tour of Jenny's parlor. "Sit down, have some tea, and see if Scott hasn't finished examining Jenny by the time you've finished it." Susan poured a cup of tea for Christian in anticipation of him cooperating. After a brief hesitation, he did. Susan sighed with relief. She tried to recall a time when she had seen Christian as agitated as he was now. She couldn't. Even when Jenny disappeared, he'd managed to hold himself together because he'd had a direction, a purpose. He was helpless now and hating it. As soon as she'd seen him tonight Susan knew something was very wrong. She'd offered to come along as much for Christian's support as to keep him out of Scott's way while Jenny was examined.

Susan passed a cup of tea to Christian. "What are those?" she asked, pointing to Jenny's photographs that were still scattered on the floor.

"Jenny's been taking pictures."

"Could I look at them?"

Christian nodded. "You may as well. I was going to drag you and Scott into this anyway. I think together we could solve Jenny's problem."

"Oh?" She reached for the hatbox, shoved the pictures inside, and placed it on her lap. "What problem is that?" she asked, sifting through the photographs.

"Later. When Scott's here as well. He may not want to involve you."

Susan snorted lightly. "As if he'd have a say in the matter."

Christian's eyes warmed for a moment. "You sound like Jenny."

337

"I'll take that as a compliment." She continued to study the photographs, taking her time with each one as she tried to understand what it was that Jenny was doing. While she looked at them, Christian finished his tea and took to pacing the floor again. He was too occupied in his own thoughts to notice the stillness that had settled over Susan. As for Susan, she said nothing about what she had seen in the photographs, nothing about the fact that she had finally recalled where she'd first seen Jenny Holland.

Christian did give Scott his full attention when he entered the parlor. Susan set the pictures aside. "Well?" they asked simultaneously.

Scott put his bag down on a table and raked back the lock of hair that had fallen over his forehead. "I've given her something to help her sleep," he said. "She's resting now. May I have some tea, Susan?" He sat down beside her while she poured. He could feel Christian's gaze boring through the top of his head. Scott took a large swallow of hot tea before he went on. "Jenny's thoroughly exhausted, Christian. I'd say her weight's down about ten pounds and, to borrow a trite phrase, she's as weak as a kitten. Weaker, actually. Whatever it is that she's doing—and she said you'd explain—she's done with as far as I'm concerned."

"She agreed to that?" asked Christian, surprised.

"It's not a matter of whether she agrees or not, Christian," he barked, causing Susan to recoil at his vehemence. "I'm her doctor and I say she's done with it."

"Scott," Susan said gently. "What's wrong?"

"Nothing."

Christian's eyes frosted over; fear made his voice cold and stilted and barely audible. "Just how sick is she, Scott? Is Jenny going to die?"

Scott's head jerked upward and he took full measure of Christian's ashen face. Damn Jenny for putting him in this position, he thought miserably. "No," he said sharply. Then more quietly: "No, she's not going to die. It's not pneumonia

338

or the influenza. She's worried herself into a near collapse, but it's nothing that rest and regular meals won't take care of."

"You're certain?"

Scott met Christian's suspicious gaze squarely and lied through his teeth. "I'm certain." He finished his tea. "Now tell me what it is that Jenny's been doing here. It seems to me that it has some bearing on her present state of mind."

Christian eased himself into the rocker opposite Susan and Scott. "Show him the photographs, Susan. I'll explain." While Scott and Susan reviewed the pictures together Christian went over everything Jenny had told him. He pointed out technical problems with the prints as well, showing them where Jenny had made mistakes with exposure time and in developing the image. "Her work is actually quite skillful," he told them, "but the problems are technical, well beyond the solutions that would come with continued trial and error. She can't get the proof she needs at this distance. We have to take the cameras into the bank."

"Of course," Scott said agreeably. "We'll ask William and Stephen to pose in front of the open safe, preferably with their pockets overflowing with treasury notes."

"Oh, Scott," Susan chided. "I'm sure if Christian is suggesting we take the cameras into the bank, then he knows how we're going to do it without raising suspicions."

Christian smiled, appreciative of Susan's confidence even though it was underserved. "As a matter of fact, Susan, nothing's occurred to me yet." He picked up one of the pictures and studied it, rocking back and forth gently. "But something will . . . I know it."

Amalie Chatham's excitement was a near-tangible thing. She drew Mr. Todd out of the blue parlor and down the hallway to her office and suite. "Tell me again," she said once they were alone. "You really found her?"

John Todd nodded. He took off his coat and tossed it over the

339

back of a chair. Crystals of ice melted in his hair. "You wer
right, Amalie. Christian Marshall was the key. After all thi
time of following him and getting nowhere, I thought you ha
to be mistaken about him. But tonight"—he whistled softly i
appreciation of Amalie's quick wits—"tonight your suspicion
were confirmed. She's registered as Mrs. Carlton Smith, Roon
212 at the St. Mark. That's how Marshall asked for her. He go
the room key and—"

"He didn't see you?"

"No. I'm sure of it."

"Did you see her?"

"Well . . . no," he admitted reluctantly. "That is, no
exactly."

Amalie's excitement vanished so quickly it might never have
been. Her emerald eyes flashed. "What do you mean, 'no
exactly'? Did you or didn't you see her?"

"No."

Amalie flounced to the sideboard, poured herself a drink.
then rounded on John Todd. "Then how do you know who
Marshall was seeing?" she demanded. "It could have been
anyone! My God, Todd, you shouldn't have come back here
without making certain. Otherwise what good was it having
Maggie wheedle information out of young Bennington?
Finally, I hear something that I think has merit—namely that
William's stepdaughter was actually committed to Jennings
and that she left through the apparent negligence of Christian
Mar—"

Todd held out his hand. "Don't go on, Amalie. I don't want
to hear any more. I'm convinced that Marshall met Bennington's stepdaughter this evening. Look at this and decide for
yourself." He picked up his coat, drew a sheet of paper out of
one of the pockets, and unfolded it. He didn't take it to Amalie;
he made her come to him for it. "Marshall dropped this when
he was crossing the lobby."

Amalie stared at the sketch. Her mouth slackened, then
finally opened in astonishment. "It's her! She's the one!"

"I know! What's more, I took the sketch to the desk clerk after Marshall went upstairs. He had no difficulty identifying her. According to him she's Mrs. Carlton Smith, Room 212."

"I don't care what she's calling herself these days. I know who she is, Mr. Todd, and you know how to find her. William Bennington is going to regret trying to turn the tables on me!"

"How are you feeling this morning?" Christian asked, setting a breakfast tray across Jenny's lap.

"The same as I did yesterday, and the day before that, *and* the day before that," she answered crossly. She picked up a piece of dry toast and nibbled on the end of it. Her churning stomach settled a little. "Really, Christian, it's been almost two weeks. Don't you think Scott's being a trifle ridiculous, confining me to bed this way?"

"I didn't get any sympathy when he did the same thing to me."

"That was different. You were pie-faced for longer than I've been ill."

"So I was."

Jenny moved her legs over so that Christian could sit on the edge of the bed. She couldn't fault the care he'd given her these past ten days. He made certain she ate, saw that she napped, read to her, entertained her with stories about growing up in Marshall House, and promised her that he was working on the problem of the Benningtons and The Trust.

She believed him. As she began to recover her strength, Christian asked her countless questions about William Bennington's routine. He wrote everything down, leaving nothing to memory. He knew that there were only two days a month when the Benningtons were likely to take any money—the days when the safe swelled with funds for local payrolls. They never wrote drafts, but always dealt with cash, and it appeared they worked together. Most of what Jenny knew about the thefts came from overheard conversations, but she had observed enough since moving to the St. Mark to understand what was going on in William's office, even when she couldn't see the events clearly. Eventually she satisfied all of Christian's questions and concerns. However, she was never privy to what ideas he was entertaining. As far as Jenny knew, Christian still hadn't come up with a way to solve the technical problems.

"Eat something," he prompted, gently pushing the piece of toast toward her mouth again. "When Scott left you in my charge I promised not to let you waste away."

"That's hardly likely to happen." She took a bite of toast. "Are you going to paint today?"

"No." He glanced out the window of her bedroom. "Too cloudy today. I doubt if it will clear. You should have agreed to come back to my house, Jenny. Then I wouldn't have all these problems with the light. Of course you'd probably freeze in my studio," he admitted after a thoughtful pause. "I don't think spring is coming this year. I hear they're still skating in the Park."

Jenny sighed. She would have liked to have gone there with Christian. "May I see the portrait?"

"No. Not until it's finished." It was the same answer he had given her since he'd begun. His easel sat in one corner of Jenny's bedroom, covered with a sheet. His paints and palette and brushes were scattered on a table which he had hopelessly damaged with spatterings of color. "It's one of the best things I've ever done," he offered, hoping to put her mind at ease.

"So you say. If I had my way you wouldn't be painting me at all right now. Why you would want to paint someone with sallow skin, shadows under her eyes, and a bony chin is beyond me. Wait until I fill out a little more."

"I'm filling you out as I go along," he promised gravely, fighting a smile. "It's an artist's prerogative."

Jenny gave him an arch look, then pointed to her tray. "Take this away, please. I can't eat anything else."

Christian eyed the remains of her breakfast skeptically.

"Shall I order something else from the kitchen?"

"No. I'm really not hungry this morning."

"All right." He stood and picked up the tray. "I'm taking this back and then I'm getting a paper. Don't go farther than the bathing room."

Jenny promised she wouldn't and she kept her promise. As soon as Christian was gone she threw back the covers and darted for the porcelain bowl sink in the bathroom. When she was finished being sick she cleaned her teeth and went back to bed. Later, at lunch, when Christian commented on her ravenous appetite, Jenny didn't enlighten him as to the reason.

Susan Turner finished tucking in the covers around her daughter and stepped back from the bed. So peaceful, she thought, as Amy's eyelashes fluttered closed. Behind her she heard Scott come into the room. Susan put a finger to her lips, gesturing him to be quiet, then waited for him in the hallway while he kissed Amy good night.

Susan hooked her arm in her husband's as they walked down the stairs. "Mrs. Adams kept your dinner warm. Yankee pot roast, parsley potatoes, and sweet butter carrots. It was very good when Amy and I ate two hours ago. I can't vouch for the meal now; neither can Mrs. Adams."

His wife's not-so-subtle reproof didn't go unnoticed by Scott. "Dr. Morgan called me in again," he said by way of explanation for his late arrival. "Just as I was leaving. I also went by the St. Mark to examine Jenny."

"How is she?"

"Much better. I'm very pleased with the recovery she's made. In fact, Christian's taking her out tonight for some fresh air. They're going up to the Park. This will probably be the last week for skating."

"Jenny's going to skate?"

"No, of course not." He looked at Susan as if she were mad for even posing the question. "She's going to watch. All

343

bundled up, I might add. It's time for her to get out of that hotel room; she's the last person who needs to be confined and restricted."

Susan didn't say anything, but a frown played at the corners of her mouth. She wished that Jenny would agree to go back to Marshall House. "I'll get your dinner," she said. "You can tell me about Dr. Morgan while you eat."

Scott didn't get around to talking about Morgan until he was almost through with his meal. In spite of Susan's interest she let him skirt the subject until she brought out dessert.

He forked a piece of the apple pie and held it out to Susan. She shook her head. Scott shrugged and plopped it in his own mouth. "Morgan wanted what he always wants—to know if I'd learn anything about Jane Doe. He asked about Christian. Apparently he's heard rumors that Christian's taken up residence at the St. Mark with a married woman."

"Dear God," Susan sighed. "I was afraid that would happen. Christian never has accepted his own notoriety. I wouldn't be surprised if there was some mention of his liaison in *The Herald.* Worse, *The Chronicle.* He's endangering Jenny by staying there with her. She can't be anonymous if he's not. Sooner or later, because of Christian, someone is going to express an interest in Mrs. Carlton Smith."

Scott put down his fork and reached across the corner of the table to touch his wife's wrist. This was no idle concern she was expressing. "Susan? What's this all about? Don't you think Jenny's safe going to the Park tonight?"

"Yes . . . no . . . I don't know, Scott. I suppose if she's agreeable to leaving, then she must think it's all right. It's night, after all." With her free hand she fingered the pearls at her neck as if they were worry beads. "But then she's never really gone anywhere with Christian. She doesn't know what a stir he can cause just walking across the St. Mark lobby."

"You're exaggerating," Scott said. "Christian doesn't draw attention to himself."

"He doesn't have to. People just notice him."

344

"Perhaps," he conceded reluctantly, "but that doesn't mean they know who he is."

"Only one person has to," she reminded him. "Just one. And that one person says, 'Who is that striking woman on Christian Marshall's arm?'"

"Do you really think anyone has the answer to that question?"

"Someone will. We can't know how long it will take, Scott, but eventually someone's going to see her and *know* she's not Mrs. Carlton Smith."

"So? It's not as if they'll *know* she's Jenny Holland either. For God's sake, Susan, she was a maid at the Benningtons'. Why would anyone remember her?"

"I did," Susan said softly. "So did Alice Vanderstell."

"What are you talking about?"

Susan laid her hand over Scott's. "Can we go to the hotel?" she asked, ignoring Scott's question. "Please? Mrs. Adams can stay here with Amy. It's important I see Christian. I should have told him as soon as I realized but I—"

"Realized? Realized what?"

But Susan was already on her feet, pulling Scott along. "If we hurry, maybe we can stop them before they leave the hotel."

"Are you warm enough?" Christian asked. "I should have told Joe to bring the closed carriage."

Under the fur rug, Jenny snuggled against Christian. Her hands were clasped inside the wonderfully soft ermine muff he had bought for her at A.T. Stewart's. She raised it to her face and rubbed her cheek on it. "I'm warm," she said, smiling as the fur tickled her lips. "And I'm glad you sent for this carriage. It's beautiful out tonight. I can't think of a better place to be."

"You can't?" he asked, pretending disappointment.

"I'm not the one who insisted you spend every night on the mattress in my studio," she said tartly. "I wanted you

345

with me."

"Do you still?"

Jenny slipped one hand out of the muff and raised it to Christian's cheek. "Still," she said. "Always."

He kissed the back of her hand, turned it over, and kissed the heart of her palm. It was such an unexpectedly romantic gesture that Jenny fell in love all over again.

All the way along Broadway up to Fifty-ninth Street their carriage passed omnibuses and horsecars filled with people determined to make the best of the unexpectedly long, bitterly cold winter. Flags were raised on all the transports indicating the pond and lake were still frozen. Christian asked Joe to take them north of the Mall to the lake so Jenny would be able to sit in the comfort of either Beach or Terrace House and watch the skaters. When they arrived, however, Jenny didn't want to go inside. She dug her heels in and refused to go anywhere save in the direction of the lake shore.

"Have you always been so stubborn?" he sighed.

"Always." The frozen lake sparkled under calcium light posts. Skaters of both sexes, rich and poor and middle class, darted across the ice. A five-piece band played on a snowbank near Beach House. Out on the ice the skaters, novice and experts alike, responded to the rhythm. It was a spectacle filled with radiant color and glitter. The scene reminded Jenny less of skating on the canals in Amsterdam and more of the resort she had visited in Switzerland. She came dangerously close to blurting out her observation. "Papa said I was born stubborn," she said a shade wistfully instead. "I expected people to do as I wanted. He said it was the crown that made me that way."

Christian's interest was captured immediately. He knew so little of Jenny's background and what he had heard often only increased his skepticism. "The crown?"

"Hmmm. Oh, look!" She pointed at a trio of skaters who were racing across the ice, each of them clutching a mug of frosty ale. None of them spilled a drop.

"I'm full of admiration," he said dryly. He urged her along,

346

afraid if they stood too long in one place she would get cold. "Tell me about the crown."

"It's really nothing. Just a birthmark that Papa insisted was shaped like a crown. I've never even seen it. It's on my head somewhere, buried underneath my hair, but then I didn't have much hair when I was born so Papa saw it quite clearly."

"And he called you the Princess."

Jenny nodded. "Silly, isn't it?"

Christian's reply was noncommittal. How had Alice Vanderstell known about the pet name? Vanderstells were money. Jenny Holland was not. The discrepancy made Christian wonder again about the clothes in Jenny's wardrobe. When he had asked her about them, she had only said that Reilly had sent them. He had accepted that answer, not really noticing then what he noticed now.

Beneath Jenny's cloak she wore a green crinoline dress with white undersleeves. The skirt had five wide flounces and a tight, high-necked bodice. He hadn't been thinking about the quality of the tailoring or the fineness of the material when she had modeled it for him earlier. Then he'd been more interested in the way she looked inside it. The deep emerald color made her eyes seem darker and somehow brighter at the same time. She had looked so exquisite that he'd wanted to suggest they stay right where they were. Perhaps it would have been better if they had. He might never have raised these questions now.

Unaware of the thoughts her comments had provoked, Jenny allowed Christian to turn them back toward Beach House. Her silent compliance was the only admission she made about beginning to feel the cold. She adjusted the hood of her cape, keeping the fur trim close to her face. Every time they passed other people closely, Jenny averted her eyes. Since leaving the hotel she'd been uncomfortably aware of the stares that Christian occasionally elicited. The risk seemed small when compared to her desire to spend time with him away from the St. Mark or Marshall House. Here, in the Park, among hundreds of other courting couples, she could pretend he was

347

courting her. It was a thought that warmed her.

"Did you skate here when you were a boy?" she asked.

"No. Sometimes the river would freeze. We'd skate there." He pointed to the refreshment stand. "Would you like something warm to drink?"

Jenny shook her head. "I'm fine. Who's we?"

"My brothers and me." There was a rasp to his voice that the sudden emotion evoked. He could still hear the sound of his brothers' laughter as they chased flat stones on the ice with brooms. "The ice broke under Logan once," he told her. "God, we were scared. He was clutching the edge of the ice, crying for us to help him. Braden and David and I were so afraid, all we could do was jump up and down and scream for help. It's a wonder the ice didn't break under us as well." He shook his head, a small smile of amusement playing about his mouth. "Lord, but we were idiots."

"What happened?"

"We finally remembered what to do. We made a chain with our bodies and pulled Logan out, then took turns carrying him home on our backs. As I recall we got the thrashing of our lives."

"Even Logan?"

"No. He got pneumonia."

Jenny and Christian entered the spacious sitting room at Beach House and found empty chairs near the stone fireplace. Among the crowd of people were matronly chaperones who kept an eagle eye on their charges. Hand-holding was frowned upon. Public kissing could cause a scandal. Still, Jenny saw several couples easing toward the shadowed corners who looked as if they were willing to take the risk.

"Tell me about Logan," she said. "How did he become interested in photography?"

Christian tugged on the back of Jenny's hood. It fell, uncovering her hair. The firelight burnished wisps of sable at her temples. He wondered about the crown again. The Princess. Yes, she was that. "Logan? Actually I was interested first. After the ice accident, when he was bedridden, I showed him how to make pinhole cameras. He thought it was magic. When he realized it wasn't, he was hooked."

"Do you still regret teaching him?"

"I don't think so, not anymore. I used to tell myself that if I hadn't had the interest, then he wouldn't have either. Logan was like a shadow. Oh, he did the things Braden and David did too, but he was most firmly attached to me. When the war began and I went, Logan joined up with Brady as a photographer's assistant. He was seventeen. Then some of Brady's men left to work under their own name and Logan finally got his chance to be in the thick of things." Christian leaned forward and stared at the fire for a moment. Then he gave Jenny a sideways glance. "I've finally come to realize that Logan made choices, just as we all did. I didn't kill him."

Jenny's small gasp didn't carry farther than Christian's ears. "Of course you didn't kill him," she said. "Did you really think that you had?"

He nodded, straightening. He stretched out his legs and crossed them at the ankles. "Most days I did. I felt the same way about David. I watched him fall at Gettysburg. It was one of the few times I set up a camera. He was posing for a picture we planned to send home. A Rebel sniper caught him in the chest. They told me later I threw myself into the fray, cutting down Rebs left and right. I took a bullet in the leg and got a medal for valor. Jesus, they said I was a hero. Like hell. I was just trying to get my brother back."

Jenny's heart went out to him. In the background the tinny carnival-like music of the Park band played on, at odds with Christian's poignant revelations.

"I even blamed myself for Braden's death. Father didn't want him to go because he was needed at the paper. I was a more likely candidate to represent the Marshalls on the battlefield."

"What a horrible way of putting it. You make yourself sound expendable."

"It's the truth," he said, shrugging. "Or at least that's how I thought of it then. The trouble was, I had my own doubts about the rightness of the war. I didn't feel as strongly as the rest of my family about the South's secession. Braden knew that. He went in spite of Father's objections. He died in the very first battle."

Jenny's hand rested on Christian's forearm. She squeezed his wrist lightly because she could think of nothing to say.

Christian's shook his head, shedding his maudlin thoughts as if they were a second skin. In truth, for years they had been just that. Whiskey had never freed him. Jenny had. "I'm sorry, I hadn't meant to go on. You're very restful, Jenny. I almost forgot where we were. The next time you ask about Logan and photography we'll leave the discussion at pinhole cameras."

Jenny opened her mouth to reply, then closed it abruptly, frowning at Christian. His brow was drawn together and his eyes had become distant, gazing at a point beyond Jenny's shoulder. Jenny turned to see if anyone was standing behind her. No one was. Puzzled, she looked back at Christian. Suddenly the shuttered look left his cool eyes and he took Jenny's breath away with the smile that turned on her.

"You inspire genius, Jenny!" He took her by the elbow and drew her to her feet.

"I do?" she asked, bewildered. Christian was fairly dragging her across the floor toward the door, making no effort to shorten his stride. His limp didn't impede him at all. Breathlessly she asked, "Where are we going?"

"To the carriage. Then home. I can't wait to show you!" Just beyond the steps of Beach House Christian stopped, lifted her, and kissed her full on the mouth. "I've figured it out, Jenny! I know how to get a camera into the bank. God, it's so simple! All this time . . . right in front of us."

His excitement was infectious. She laughed giddily. He kissed her again. "Let's go," she whispered. "People are staring."

He wanted to say, "Let them," but resisted. Christian

released her reluctantly, straightened the hood over her hair, and led her to where Joe was waiting with the carriage.

Stephen Bennington excused himself from his escort abruptly. Embarrassed by his churlish behavior, young Sylvie Andrews looked to her chaperone for an answer. Sylvie had quite accepted the fact that she would never keep and hold a man for her looks alone, but she had hoped the size of her fortune would keep a worldly man like Stephen Bennington at her side for at least the length of one evening.

Bobbing and weaving among the squeeze of people, Stephen caught sight of Christian just as he was entering his carriage. When Christian sat down Stephen could see the woman who huddled next to him. He quickened his pace, still not believing his eyes.

Jenny saw him a moment before Christian did. Inside the muff her hands pressed together in white-knuckled prayer. Stephen was upon them before Christian recovered his surprise and could tell Joe to go.

"Marshall," Stephen said. He raised his hand to tip his hat and realized he had lost it during the chase.

"Bennington." Christian's cool eyes were watchful. When Stephen's seemingly polite interest rested on Jenny, Christian's stare turned piercing.

"You're the very last person I expected to see here tonight," he said to Jenny. "No doubt you could say the same of me."

Jenny made no reply.

"Don't you think it's time you came home, Caroline? I imagine you think this latest escapade of yours has been a lark, but how long do you think it can continue? The madness is certain to rise again."

"Caroline?" Christian asked. "What does he mean, Jenny?"

Stephen laughed while Jenny continued to sit there mutely. "She's been calling herself Jenny, has she? I'm not familiar with that name. Sometimes it was Anna or Grace. Once she called herself Marie."

Tears glittered in Jenny's eyes. Her glare called him a liar.

"Let's go home, Caroline. We can take care of you there."
He reached over the side of the carriage and brushed Jenny's
shoulder with his fingertips. She recoiled violently.

Christian stood. "Take your hands off her, Bennington. I
swear I'll kill you if you touch her again."

"Your concern's misplaced." Still, Stephen removed his
hand. "Caroline's family." He glanced back at Jenny. "Haven't
you told him that?"

Christian felt as if he had been hit. His glance also went to
Jenny. "What's he saying, Jenny? Are you related to him?"

"Tell him, Caro."

Jenny felt the pressure of both their stares. Her throat was
so raw and aching from unshed tears that speaking was painful.
"I'm Caroline Van Dyke, Christian. Stephen's my stepbrother."

"And?" Stephen prompted.

"And my fiancé."

"There you have it, my friend," Stephen said. "Caro's
coming with me. This ends the frantic search we've been
conducting for her."

"I'm not your friend," Christian said coldly. Inside he was
reeling from Jenny's double blow. "And Jenny's not going
anywhere with you. Not unless she wants to."

That he could even think she would want to go with Stephen
filled Jenny with dread. "No," she said almost inaudibly. "I
want to stay with you. It's not all been a lie, Christian." The
eyes she raised to him were pleading.

Christian sat down and placed a proprietal arm about
Jenny's slim shoulders. "You heard my wife, Bennington.
She's staying with me."

Stephen was rendered speechless for a moment. The
handsome, finely drawn aristocratic features sagged briefly in
astonishment. "Your wife! But that's . . . that's not possible!
She was engaged to me!"

"Good use of the past tense," Christian said with light
sarcasm. "She *was* engaged to you. She *is* married to me." He
nudged Joe, who was sitting with his back turned, pretending

not to hear anything but prepared to leave at a moment's notice. "Good evening, Stephen."

"Wait!" Stephen gathered his wits just as the carriage rolled forward. "She can't be married to you!" he called after them. "You didn't even know who she was! It's not legal! I tell you, it's not legal!" Belatedly he realized he was drawing unwelcome attention with his shouting. He dropped the fist he had unconsciously raised and took several deep breaths. Raking his fingers through his ash-blond hair, Stephen ducked his head against the curious stares and retraced his steps back to Beach House. It occurred to him that he should probably break off with Sylvie now that Caroline was undeniably alive. There was no question but that he intended to have her.

The ride back to the St. Mark was very much like the ride home from Amalie's on New Year's Eve. Neither Christian nor Jenny spoke. To Joe's way of thinking it was like driving a hearse. He was glad when they reached the hotel.

Scott and Susan were waiting in the lobby. They did not have to be told that something was wrong. Christian's expression was stony; Jenny looked as if she would shatter. "We're coming with you," Scott said firmly, not waiting for an invitation. "Susan has something she wants to tell you."

Christian shrugged. "Suit yourself. The three of you go on up. I'm going to the bar first."

The sadness in Jenny's eyes deepened. "Chris—"

"Nothing from you," he said, cutting her off. "Nothing."

Jenny raised the hem of her skirt and darted up the wide staircase. Her hands were shaking so badly when she reached her door that she couldn't insert the key. Susan took it from her. "Let me," she said gently.

"Perhaps you should go to bed, Jenny," Scott said once they were inside. He took her cloak, then Susan's.

"No. I want to wait for Christian." She sat in the rocker. "I'm afraid neither of us is going to be good company." She missed the look that passed between Susan and Scott at her understatement. "Perhaps you'll want to visit some other time."

"Jenny," Susan said, "if you weren't so upset, you'd realize we'd hardly be making a social call at this hour. It's after ten."

Jenny glanced at the pendulum clock. "So it is. Is something wrong then? Your little girl—"

"Is fine. We came about you. Where are your photographs?"

"In the bedroom." She pointed to the door on the right. "They're still in the hatbox."

"May I?" asked Susan. "I want to show you something." At Jenny's assent Susan got the hatbox. She sat down beside her husband on the chaise and sorted through the photographs. "Here. It's this one." She showed it to Scott, who studied it for a moment and finally nodded. Then Susan passed it to Jenny.

Jenny gave the picture a cursory glance, then looked at Susan. "I don't understand. What is it that I'm supposed to see?"

"On the wall behind Mr. Bennington's desk. Don't you know what that is?"

She looked at the print again. "I suppose it's a painting." She shrugged. She traced part of the photograph with her forefinger. "This looks like part of a frame. Gilt-edged, I think. From the size suggested here, it would be rather large." She gave the picture back to Susan. "Obviously it means something to you, but honestly, I don't know what it is. I've never seen it clearly. The angle's all wrong."

"I believe that you've never seen this painting in Bennington's office," Susan said. "But you're familiar with the portrait. You must be. You posed for it."

Jenny's mouth parted slightly but no sound came out. She took back the photograph and studied it again.

"You won't be able to tell anything from it," Susan said. "I—"

Christian opened the door to the suite. He was followed by a waiter carrying a tray. It held four cups, a silver creamer and

354

sugar bowl, and a silver coffee urn. Christian took the tray, set it down on the table between Susan and Jenny, then dismissed the waiter. He pulled the overstuffed armchair closer to the table and began to serve. "It's going to be a long night," he said. "I thought a clear head was in order."

"That was cruel," Susan said, accepting the cup that Christian offered her. "You know what we thought when you said you were going to the bar."

"I can't be held accountable for your assumptions," he countered. "The hotel's dining room is closed. The bar's the only place to get coffee at this time of night. Scott? Do you want a cup?"

Scott nodded. "Still, Christian, Susan's right. You deliberately let us believe you were going to get drunk."

"I still may." He passed a cup to Scott, then Jenny. "But, please, go on with your conversation. I'm sorry I interrupted."

Susan started to speak but Jenny cut her off. "Susan was just explaining how she came to realize I'm Caroline Van Dyke." She passed Christian the photograph, ignoring the starts of surprise that rattled the Turners' coffee cups. "If you've never been in my stepfather's office, then you wouldn't know from this picture that it's my portrait hanging behind his desk. I didn't know it myself. But apparently Susan's been there and she remembered. Is that right, Susan?"

"Yes. There was a problem with our account. I went to see Mr. Bennington personally to straighten it out. I wasn't with him long and I didn't study the portrait, but I had to have been aware of it to remember it now."

Christian looked at Susan over the rim of his coffee cup. "You always said you thought Jenny was familiar. It seems you met her at the bank." He tossed the photograph on the table. "How long have you known?"

"Since the night I saw the photographs," Susan admitted uncomfortably.

"I see. I wish you would have said something then."

"I thought it was Jenny's secret to keep or divulge."

355

Jenny set down her cup and saucer on the table. Hard. "Stop it. All of you. You're talking as if I weren't in the room. Christian, I'm sorry that you had to learn the truth the way you did—perhaps it would have been more palatable coming from Susan rather than Stephen—but that's the only other way you would have learned it. I wouldn't have told you if I had had a choice—for all the reasons that you're showing me now."

"Well," he drawled, raising an eyebrow, "I apologize for being a little upset at what I've heard this evening. I can't think why it should bother me to confront a man tonight who is both your stepbrother and your fiancé. I suppose I should be rejoicing in the revelation of your true identity. After all, I was willing to marry a housemaid. What a stroke of luck that she's worth twenty million."

"Twenty-five," Jenny said softly.

"Twenty-five, then." He laughed shortly, humorlessly, and turned his attention to Scott and Susan. "That's an adequate dowry, don't you think?"

"Christian." Scott said his friend's name injecting a note of caution. He didn't understand half of the exchange between Christian and Jenny but he knew better than to jump to more conclusions. "Perhaps we'd better listen to Jenny's side."

Christian leaned back in his chair. "By all means. Go on, Jenny—or would you prefer Caroline? Or Caro?"

His sarcasm stung Jenny, but her composure held. "I understand that you're too hurt to make explanations easy for me," she said. "But I hope you can find it within yourself to give me a fair hearing."

Ruddy color tinged Christian's cheeks. Trust Jenny to make him see he was behaving like an ass. "I'm listening," he said. Although he gave the impression of being bored, at least the bitterness and bite had gone out of his voice.

Jenny spoke primarily to Susan and Scott, with occasional glances at Christian. She told them first of the encounter in the Park with Stephen Bennington. "I told Christian that Stephen was my fiancé because that's what Stephen wanted me to say. I thought giving in would just shut him up. I should have known better. The truth is a little more complicated than Stephen would have wanted anyone to understand. It's true that we were engaged for a very short period of time, but I cried off before there was a formal announcement. A few directors at the bank knew, and that's about all. I don't think Stephen ever informed them I didn't intend to go through with the marriage.

"The portrait that you saw, Susan, was one I sat for while we were engaged. That would have been in late July . . . just after I returned from Europe." Jenny paused, realizing by the confusion of her audience that she was explaining herself badly. "I think I should start at a different point," she said. "Perhaps it would help if you knew about my father."

"We all know Charles Van Dyke by reputation," Scott told her. "His financial success was not something that could be hidden."

"True," Jenny replied. "But he was also a very private man, a family man. He was not as attracted to the social rounds as my mother. He was much more comfortable in his own home, he used to say. So why should he want to dress to the nines?" She smiled at the memory of her father's blustering. "Papa enjoyed talking like that. He'd puff out his chest, prepare for a fiery oration, then something silly would come out of his mouth and we'd all end up laughing."

Christian was sitting up a little straighter now. He had set his cup and saucer on the arm of his chair and allowed his coffee to grow cold.

Jenny didn't really notice Christian's attentiveness. She went on, creating the fabric of the tale with the threads of her memories. "Papa often let Mother go to the theater or parties with other men as escorts. Although I didn't know it at the time, William Bennington was one of those men. He was a widower, a man with business dealings with my father, and I suppose Papa thought it was a perfectly acceptable arrangement. If there was a scandal at the time I wasn't aware of it. My

357

existence was very insular in those days—not so much different than it has been recently.

"At that time, however, the protection was provided by my father. He wasn't as indulgent as you might imagine. He might have called me the Princess when I was being mule-headed and demanding, but that didn't mean he gave in to me. In our home he was always king. More often, he called me Jenny. Just to keep me common, he'd say. Mother never used it. She thought it was silly when I already had a perfectly good name. Actually it was a corruption of my middle name, which is also my mother's maiden name."

Scott's cup clattered as he set it down. "Jennings," he said softly as realization struck. "Lillian Jennings. My God, I never realized . . . your grandfather . . ."

"Hmmm. My mother's father. I'm sure his name is all over that hospital, though I never had occasion to see it. Ironic, isn't it, that I should be committed to the hospital my grandfather endowed." Jenny's smile was derisive. "And it doesn't end there, Dr. Turner. The madwoman who sometimes shared my cell? She's my godmother."

Chapter 14

"Alice Vanderstell!" Scott's brows had risen nearly to his hairline. "Alice is your godmother!"

His astonishment brought a real smile to Jenny's lips. "The Vanderstells were close friends of my father. The families are distantly related and there was a certain pride they shared in their Dutch roots."

"That's why she called you the Princess then," Christian said, leaning forward. He rested his elbows on his knees. "She really did recognize you. And of course she would have known about the birthmark and the pet name if she stood at your baptism."

Jenny nodded and explained the origin of the name to Scott and Susan. "But I'm getting ahead of myself again." She poured herself more coffee and sipped it before she went on. "I hope I've made you understand that my father and I were very close. I loved my mother, and yet I didn't know her very well. But Papa was as much friend as he was parent and mentor. I was just fifteen when he was killed in a train accident on his way home from Washington." Jenny's voice dropped to a husky whisper and she stared at her shifting reflection in the coffee cup. "I didn't accept the loss very well. That's the first time I met Dr. Morgan. My mother called him to treat me when I didn't recover from my father's death as quickly as she thought I should. He wasn't overseeing the entire hospital in those days. His responsibility was the lunatic ward."

"Were you committed?" asked Scott.

"No. Mother kept me at home and Dr. Morgan came a few times. He brought this . . . this *thing* . . . and they'd strap me to it and it would spin . . ." Her voice trailed off as the memory threatened to choke her. Composing herself, she continued, relating her mother's decision to send her abroad and the arrival of William and Stephen Bennington in her life. "I returned to New York too late. Mama was already dead and William was in control. It was awhile before I understood how manipulative my stepfather was and that Stephen was very nearly his equal." Her cheeks flushed as she began to relate her relationship with her stepbrother. "Initially I was flattered by Stephen's attentions. There was never any brother-sister familiarity to contend with. He was a very attractive man and I rather liked to think that he could be interested in me. It hadn't occurred to me yet that the size of my fortune was more appealing than I was. Only weeks after I returned, we became engaged."

She stood up, placed her cup on the mantel, and leaned her shoulder against it. She crossed her arms in front of her waist, hugging herself. "I chanced upon a conversation between William and Stephen and learned more than I ever wanted to know about their plans. It should have been obvious to the meanest intelligence that they wanted to continue to control my money. If I married Stephen, they could retain their hold even after I was twenty-one."

"Not necessarily," Christian said. "There are laws in this state to protect your wealth. It wouldn't become the property of your husband."

Jenny shook her head. "My father loved me, Christian, but he never considered for a moment that I was capable of managing my own wealth. His will is very specific in that regard. I could inherit the money at twenty-one, but I had to appoint not one, but *three* advisors to oversee it. At twenty-five, after four years of their tutelage, my father granted that I could dismiss them."

"I take it those conditions were if you remained single."

"That's right. But should I marry anytime before I'm twenty-five, the money becomes my husband's property. My father was extremely clear on that account. There's no breaking the will; it's perfectly legal."

"What happened once you broke the engagement?" asked Scott.

"I became ill."

"You were drugged?"

"Yes, I think so. I have to believe that, don't you see? The alternative is that I was going mad—just as they said I was. They had two motives for removing me. One, they wanted to stop the rumors about their management of the bank. Two, they wanted control of the money again. You see, I'd turned twenty-one but I hadn't yet named the trustees. If I remained secluded because of my illness, I wouldn't be expected to make the appointments; they would be made for me by the board at the bank."

"William and Stephen?" asked Susan. "Would they have been named?"

"William, certainly. I don't know about Stephen. The important thing here is that the executor position was now going to be a shared responsibility among three people. William didn't really want that. His ultimate aim in sending me to the hospital was to keep me firmly under this thumb until I agreed to marry Stephen.

"I doubt if even Dr. Morgan understood that. William had him treat me at home in the beginning—I think my stepfather was aware of what happened to me when Papa died. It was clever of him to use Morgan again. I had already established a history with the good doctor. After a few visits I was brought to Jennings by way of the Five Points. The one thing William didn't want was for me to die."

"It's not that I want it either," said Scott, "but wouldn't it

361

have solved William's problems?''

Jenny shook her head. "He'd have murdered me himself if he thought it would have gotten him the money. The truth is, he's better off with me alive. If I die before my twenty-fifth year and have no husband, my fortune goes to private city charities.''

"But shouldn't some of your money already be going to charities?'' Susan asked. "After all, Caroline Van Dyke was declared dead.''

"I know,'' Jenny said. "Mrs. B. read her obituary to me. The next step is to set up a foundation for distributing the money. That will take six months or so because I'm sure William is putting up a struggle to see that he remains at the head of it. I hope to have the proof I need before he or Stephen is named director. Basically my fortune is in escrow right now. No one can touch it until the foundation is established. That's why William is taking so much from the bank. People think he has a lot of personal wealth, but he doesn't. Even with what my mother left him when she died, he couldn't maintain the mansion for more than a few years. Actually, unless he buys the house he'll have to move out. It's part of the twenty-five million.''

"What do we do now?'' Scott asked. "Stephen knows you're alive. Will he still want to marry you?''

"I don't know.'' She rubbed her upper arms, shivering slightly. "William may decide it's too late for that. They may choose mur—''

"Don't even think it, Jenny,'' Christian interrupted. "It's not even a possibility. In the morning I'm taking you back to Marshall House, where I know you'll be safe. According to the information you gave me, William and Stephen are likely to take funds from the bank again on the 31st. If your appearance doesn't alter their routine, then we have six days to make our plans.''

In spite of Christian's positive tone, Scott wasn't encouraged. "Six days? We've been working on the bank problem for two weeks now, and Jenny wrestled with it for two months before that. What can we do in six days?"

Christian started to answer, but he stopped himself midsentence. Jenny was sucking in a yawn and trying to hide it behind the hand pressed to her mouth. "We'll talk tomorrow," he said, pointing quickly to Jenny.

"Tomorrow? Oh, but . . . oh. I see. All right. Yes, we'll talk tomorrow."

Jenny's yawn changed to a sleepy, apologetic smile. "You don't have to leave on my account. I'd like to hear Christian's plan."

Three voices answered in unison. "Tomorrow."

Christian followed Susan and Scott down to the lobby to say good night. When he returned to the suite the only lamp that was burning was in Jenny's bedroom. He found her there, curled on her side under the covers. She wasn't sleeping. Her eyes were open and she was staring at the balcony doors, deep in thought. He paused in the doorway, uncertain. When she glanced in his direction he asked, "Am I welcome here?"

"Do you want to be?"

He nodded. "Very much so."

"Then come in."

Christian walked over to the bed. His hand brushed the edge of the mattress. His lean fingers looked dark against the white counterpane. "And here?" he asked.

In answer, Jenny moved more toward the middle of the bed and made room for Christian.

He stripped off his clothes, lifted the covers, and slid in beside Jenny. Their knees bumped, and it was Christian who quickly retracted, putting space between them. By slipping his arm under a pillow he raised his head slightly, keeping him level with Jenny. "I was a perfect ass earlier this evening," he said.

"I know."

Christian smiled. "Yes, I'm certain you do. What I'm trying to do is apologize."

"Don't try. Do it."

"I'm sorry. You would have had every right to throw me out. Susan and Scott would have helped you."

Jenny's eyes remained grave. "I haven't yet agreed to go with you tomorrow, Christian. Don't assume my cooperation."

Christian went very still. He couldn't believe what he was hearing. "Jenny." He said her name cajolingly, as if she were not to be taken seriously.

She sat up. "*Now* I'm throwing you out," she said. "Or I can leave." She threw back the covers and started to scoot toward the far side of the bed.

"Jenny, what the . . ." Christian didn't know what to do. He grabbed her wrist, and when she tried to shake him off he held her fast. "Tell me what I've done."

Jenny yanked at her nightshift, covering her legs as Christian used his superior strength to pull her close again. "You're no different than the others," she said bitterly.

"What others? What are you talking about?"

She stared up at him, blinking rapidly. Her fatigue had faded in response to her anger. "Control," she bit out. "You're controlling. First my father. Then William and Stephen. In Jennings it was the attendants. They did what they wanted anywhere, anytime. They were always in control. Always."

Christian released her wrist, but he didn't move away. Neither did Jenny.

"It's the same with you," she said, imploring him to understand. "I'm so afraid for you, darling. You won't even consider the possibility that something might happen to me."

He didn't want to hear this. Now it was Christian who sat up and turned away. He felt Jenny's hand alight on his shoulder as she knelt behind him. "I won't let anything happen to you," he said roughly, his throat tight. "I *won't*."

"You may not be able to prevent it," she said. Her arms slid around him from the back and she rested her cheek against his hair. "And you'll blame yourself anyway. I know you will . . . and it won't have been your fault. Just like it wasn't

364

your fault that Braden or David or Logan died. You're not responsible for your mother's death, nor your father's. It *happened*. There's no good explanation . . . no fairness in it."

Jenny heard him suck in his breath as his shoulders heaved once. She could feel the ache of his unshed tears as if they were her own. She held him. Her eyes burned. Long minutes went by before she spoke again. "I want to be with you, Christian, but of my own choice. Can you accept that? Can you accept that you can't determine or control everything that happens to me?"

Christian laid his hands over Jenny's and turned his head slightly. Her lips brushed his ear. "Never stop loving me, Jenny," he said lowly. "I can accept anything but the thought of you not loving me."

"You'll never have to accept that," she said, drawing him down on the bed. She kissed the corners of his eyes and tasted the damp, salty traces of his tears. Her mouth hovered above his. "I love you, Christian Marshall. That's not going to change."

Christian believed her. "I don't mean to be a perfect ass," he said.

"I know."

His hands curved against Jenny's waist. "I wanted to smash Stephen Bennington's face tonight."

Jenny adjusted her position, resting her head on Christian's shoulder. "I didn't love him. For a while I pretended that I did, but I was engaged to him because I didn't know what else to do . . . and being in love seemed a convenient solution." Jenny's fingertips were a light caress across the hard plane of Christian's abdomen. "You understand, don't you? Why I didn't tell you who I was?"

"I understand. You were afraid to trust anyone—even me. Especially me."

"It was more than that," she admitted. "I *enjoyed* being Jenny Holland. People accepted her."

"The only difference between Jenny and Caroline is the size

of the fortune."

Jenny considered that for several moments. She pressed back another yawn. "It's something to think about it, isn't it?"

"May I suggest sleeping on it instead?"

Jenny thought it was a very good suggestion. She allowed fatigue to claim her, and fell asleep long before Christian permitted himself the same luxury.

Christian felt as though he'd only been asleep minutes when he was wakened abruptly. At first he thought the noise had come from the outer room. He stilled, his ear cocked toward the door, hardly daring to breathe. When the sound came again he realized it was beside him.

"Jenny?" Except for a low, aching whimper she didn't stir. Christian reached for the bedside lamp, lighted it, and replaced it on the table. As he turned on his side light fell over his shoulder and beyond, caressing Jenny's face. Beneath her heavily lashed lids her eyes were moving rapidly. Her mouth was slightly parted. There were tiny beads of perspiration glistening above the curve of her upper lip.

Without warning Jenny's left leg shot out. Her foot caught Christian on the shin. He cursed softly, not because of his pain, but because of hers. He could only imagine what dreams were torturing her; she had actually lived a nightmare.

Christian placed one hand on Jenny's shoulder. He shook her gently and said her name again. Her face contorted. He recognized the anguish. He'd seen it in the treatment room as she was being forced under water. Jenny was right when she said there were events over which he had no control, but in Christian's mind this didn't qualify as one of them. He could spare her the remainder of the nightmare.

Brushing aside a strand of hair that had fallen across her cheek, Christian said her name forcefully, compelling her to join him in wakefulness. Jenny's eyes were deep wells of darkness when they opened, unfocused and startled. She felt a flutter in her heart and heard the shortness of her own breathing. There was a moment of panic that disappeared as soon as she realized Christian was with her.

"Was I sleepwalking?" she asked.

"No."

"Just a nightmare then."

Christian did not mistake the relief he heard in her voice. "Do you remember any of it?"

"No."

He got out of bed and padded naked to the bathing room. He tossed a towel over his shoulder and wet a fresh cloth. When he returned to Jenny he washed the visible traces of her nightmare away. His touch was gentle, his very presence soothing.

"I'm going to have a baby, Christian."

Christian's expression didn't change. He patted her face with the towel, then he dropped it and the cloth over the side of the bed.

"Aren't you going to say anything?"

He propped himself on an elbow. The back of his fingers caressed her cheek while his eyes remained cool, fathomless pools of marine blue.

Jenny suddenly realized why he wasn't saying anything. "You already knew, didn't you? Scott told you, after he promised me he wouldn't!"

"No, Scott didn't tell me. Were you afraid I'd insist on marriage? Perhaps even force it if I knew?"

"Yes."

"But I didn't, did I? And I've known almost as long as you and Scott have."

"You have?"

"Hmmm. Would you like to see your portrait, Jenny?"

"Now? But you said it wasn't finished."

"It's not. But then neither are you." He grinned, levered himself away from her. "Not quite. I make it to be another six months give or take a week. Is that about right?"

She nodded.

"I thought so." He wrapped the fallen towel around his hips, went to the easel, and turned it around, stripping away the sheet. "I warned you I was filling you out."

Jenny gasped softly at what he revealed. No words came to mind to express what she felt in that moment. Awe kept her silent.

She had no real sense that she was looking at herself. What she saw was a young woman, obviously pregnant, sitting in a rocker with her back to a mullioned window. A penumbra of light haloed her hair. Her face was partially shadowed but there was a suggestion of ineffable peace in the smile that hovered about her lips. One hand rested on the arm of the rocker. The other rested on her swollen belly. She wore a plain cotton shift. No lace. No ornamentation of any kind. There was purity in the simplicity of the shift, grace in the woman's pose, and earthiness in her condition. Christian's brush strokes were soft. The colors blended at the edges, diffusing the light so that it seemed to come from the canvas as if it existed there independently of the sun.

Christian watched Jenny closely, gauging her reaction. He followed every expression that crossed her face and knew that she wasn't displeased. He covered the painting and turned it away. "I knew when I began painting you that something was different. I couldn't even identify what it was at first . . . just a difference. Then the picture began to take shape and it was as if my hand were disengaged from my eyes. When I looked at what I had sketched . . . when I saw . . . I knew then it was true. So many things fell into place after that. Your sickness that you struggled to hide, the weight loss. Your crying."

"My fainting," she added.

"That too. God, you scared me that night." He returned to bed, sliding under the covers she held up for him. "You didn't know yourself until then, did you?"

She shook her head, her smile sheepish. "I was so hopelessly ignorant," she sighed. "Scott had to tell me. It was a relief to know there was nothing wrong with me. The crying was the worst part of it. Sometimes there was no rhyme or reason to it.

Scott says it's not all that unusual, that after my body gets used to being pregnant I won't be a watering pot." Jenny's forefinger trailed across Christian's lower lip. Her expression became serious. "I like the painting, Christian. I like it very much. You honor me . . . and our child."

Christian's head lowered. He touched Jenny's mouth with his own. They shared the first sparklings of heat. Jenny's lips parted and Christian caught her sigh. Her mouth was warm, sweet, and his kiss was tender and tasting.

She removed her nightshift, pulling it over her head. For a moment she was embarrassed by Christian's frank, almost impersonal assessment as he looked for changes in her body. But then passion flared in his eyes and Jenny forgot about embarrassment. Whatever changes there were, real or imagined, met with his approval. Most definitely. She removed the towel from his hips and regarded him as openly as he had regarded her. Oh, yes. There were changes and there were *changes*.

They did not exchange many words. It was unnecessary. Their bodies spoke for them. Jenny had only to move a certain way, lean into Christian, arch her throat, or shift her weight for Christian to know what she wanted and to respond to her need with the touch of his hand or the caress of his mouth. Christian welcomed Jenny's exploration. Her lips were damp, velvet soft, and they made an erotic sucking sound each time they touched his flesh.

Christian's knuckles brushed the undersides of her breasts. They were so achingly sensitive to his lightest touch that he went slowly, gently, until that too became a form of such exquisite torture that Jenny begged for his mouth. His tongue laved her nipples while her fingers curled in his hair and her breath grew increasingly ragged.

His mouth returned to Jenny's and he kissed her deeply, silencing the short gasps that gave sound to her pleasure. Jenny's hands slipped away from Christian's hair, first bunching in his shoulder, later skimming the length of his spine. He arched, grinding his hips against her. She moved too, cradling him so her skin felt the hot pressure of his arousal.

Jenny kicked at the sheet that had become tangled in their legs. The barrier between their flesh was unwelcome. Jenny wanted to feel the contrasting strength and texture of Christian's legs against hers. They changed positions and Christian was under Jenny. She moved over him, touching her lips to his mouth, his chin, trailing kisses along his neck and collarbone. Her forefinger traced the outline of his chest muscles, and she felt him suck in his breath as her mouth dipped over his navel and her tongue made a damp, tickling foray. She moved lower. And lower still. She heard him say her name, and the sound of it was husky encouragement as she began to pleasure him with her mouth.

Christian's strong fingers pressed white against the mattress. The liquid heat of Jenny's mouth fired his loins. He withstood the loving assault as long as he could before dragging her away. He made her endure the full measure of equal pleasure in return, parting her legs so he could stroke the hot, moist flesh that was at the center of her excitement. He lifted her legs and brought them over his shoulders. Her heels dug into his back as Christian's probing caress lashed at her senses.

Jenny was a willing captive to all that Christian did to her, all that he made her feel. Yet there was no sense that she was surrendering anything. Nothing was given that wasn't given freely. Christian was as deeply held by the spell that Jenny cast. It wasn't a word that brought him inside her, but a look. The desire that darkened her eyes to polished onyx was not to be ignored. He held himself still inside her while she adjusted to the hard length of him, then he almost dared her to be the first to move.

It was not a challenge she cared to take up. She arched beneath him and he couldn't help but respond. He stroked her slowly until it was no longer possible to continue that way. The elemental need they shared demanded shorter, harder thrusts, and even though Christian wanted to draw out the pleasure

370

just shy of forever, he gave in to the more basic, quickening rhythms that were the prelude to loving's end.

Jenny clutched him for purchase as pleasure rippled through her. She bit her lower lip until Christian's mouth slanted across hers, hot and hungry. Their mouths were touching as he shuddered against her. They exchanged hurried whispers that spoke of their joy, desire, and love.

Afterwards there was little to say. Their bodies curved together. Christian's arm rested under the soft fullness of Jenny's breasts and his warm breath parted light strands of her hair. Their breathing calmed in unison and they fell asleep within minutes of each other.

They woke up making love. It was an odd experience as they came to awareness together. Their eyes, which had a sleepy sort of desiring in them, cleared and widened as they exchanged startled glances. "Oh, my," said Jenny. The hard evidence of Christian's desire was buried deep within her. "Oh, God," said Christian. He closed his eyes a moment and tried not to think of how tightly she held him. "I'm sorry," he said, and started to withdraw. "I'm not," she said, and trapped him with her legs. After a moment she eased up slightly and said innocently, "Unless you don't want to . . ." Christian chuckled softly. "Like hell."

"Do you want to come with me?" Christian asked. He picked up a sweet roll from the breakfast tray he had ordered and took a bite. He was ravenously hungry and made no secret of it or the reason. It was his third roll.

Amused, Jenny smoothed a linen napkin over her lap and poured herself a cup of tea. It was early yet; outside daybreak was gray. "I think I'll stay here and finish packing some things."

"You don't mind being alone?"

371

"It's only until you bring Joe back from Marshall House with the carriage," she reminded him. "How long can that take? Besides, the Benningtons don't know where I am. I'm not worried about Stephen showing up here in the short time you're gone. And if you're really concerned, you can always send someone around to Marshall House with a message."

"I thought of that," Christian admitted. "But besides the carriage, there are some things I want from the attic. I can get exactly what I need if I go myself."

"From the attic? What could you possibly want?"

"Hatboxes." He plopped the last bit of roll in his mouth, stood, and gave Jenny a sticky kiss on her cheek. "Don't pack any of your chemicals, the baths, or your paper," he told her as he put on his coat. "We'll need those things here if we're going to develop the pictures quickly. The tripods, cameras, and glass plates can all go to Marshall House."

"You're not making any sense. How are we going to take pictures without a camera?"

"Oh, we'll have a camera," he said, winking at her as he opened the door. "It just won't look like one."

"Beast!" she called over her shoulder. "You're enjoying the mystery. Don't you dare leave without telling me what you're plotting."

"I'll be back in an hour or so," he said. "See if you can figure it out." He shut the door, but even in the hallway he could hear the string of colorful curses Jenny hurled at his head. He laughed. She could be quite inventive with her language when she wanted to be.

Jenny set down her cup and tossed her napkin onto the tray. "Go ahead and laugh, Mr. Marshall," she murmured. "But I'll have the answer by the time you return. Just see if I don't." Jenny stood up, rolled back the sleeves of the plain blue-gray dress she wore, and prepared to organize the darkroom. She'd only gotten halfway there when there was a knock at the door to the suite. "Hah!" she called, spying Christian's key on the table by the tray. "I shouldn't let you back in." She picked up

372

the key, intending to dangle it in front of him, perhaps even make him give up the answer to the hatbox mystery for it. She opened the door a crack. "Did you forget some—"

John Todd shouldered his way into the suite. Jenny was no match for his speed or his strength. She was caught unprepared, and her scream was more of a harsh, breathy outpouring of air. She had no hope that it was heard. It was only as John Todd was laying a chloroform-soaked handkerchief across her mouth and nose that Jenny identified her assailant. Losing consciousness, she remembered the eyes that looked down at her as the same ones that had studied her from behind the grille at Amalie Chatham's parlor house.

Christian stood in front of Room 212 and patted down his pockets. "I forgot my key, Joe."

"Maybe it's open," Joe said. He dropped the strap of the large reed hamper he had been dragging behind him and reached around Christian, giving the door a nudge. "See? I thought it was ajar."

"Hmm. It shouldn't have been." He pushed it open wider. "Jenny? I'm back. Bring in the hamper, Joe. Put it in her studio. We'll take the hatboxes out later." Christian poked his head in the bedroom. "Jenny?" The door to the bathing room was closed. He crossed the room and knocked lightly. When there was no answer he opened it. She wasn't there. Neither was she in the dressing room. "Joe? Is she in the studio?"

"No, sir," Joe called back. "Not in the tent either."

Christian went back to the parlor and seconds later Joe joined him. "Dammit, where can she have gone?"

Joe shifted the weight of his lean, wiry frame from one foot to the other. He fiddled with the curling tip of his mustache while he waited for direction from Christian.

Christian went in the studio, looked around, then did the same in the bedroom. "She hasn't even packed anything. That's what she stayed behind to do." He raked back his hair, puzzled. His eyes went to the brass and porcelain pegs where her cloak was hanging. "She must be in the hotel somewhere. She didn't take a wrap." That relieved him. "We might as well start packing. She'll probably be here soon."

But after half an hour Jenny still did not appear. Christian sent Joe to the dining and reading rooms to see if she was there. At the same time he went to the front desk to make inquiries. They both returned to the suite without any information.

Just inside the room Joe bent and picked up a scrap of linen from the floor. He looked at it, saw the initial J embroidered on one corner, and tossed it to Christian. "This fancy bit of lace isn't mine," he said. "Belongs with Jenny's things. She dropped it."

Christian gave it a superficial glance, then stuffed it in his vest pocket. He opened his mouth to say something, stopped, and his brow creased. He drew out the handkerchief slowly and looked at it again, then at Joe. "Jenny's not really Jenny, remember? You heard what she said last night. She's Caroline Van Dyke. This isn't hers."

Joe wasn't certain what Christian was getting at. "Well, sir, it ain't mine. I don't care for lace and the perfume ain't to my liking either."

"It's pungent, isn't it?"

"Don't know from pungent. It stinks."

Christian laughed shortly, raising the handkerchief to his nose. He inhaled and his laughter died. "It's not perfume, Joe. It's chloroform."

"Sir?"

"Chloroform. The stuff surgeons use to knock out a patient."

"You're sure?"

"I smelled enough of it during the war." He put the handkerchief away again, but this time in his pants pocket.

"What does it mean, Mr. Marshall?" But he knew. Jenny was gone. A shiver went through him when he saw the murderous light in Christian's eyes. Joe knew then the owner

374

of the handkerchief was going to die.

Christian found Jenny's key to the suite. Joe waited for him in the hallway while Christian locked the door. They went to the front desk together. Using pages from the registration book, Christian quickly sketched the faces of four men. The clerk was able to identify both William and Stephen Bennington, but only because they sometimes came into the hotel for lunch or dinner. He also recognized Wilton Reilly and swore he hadn't seen the man for months. The sketch of Liam O'Shea meant nothing to him.

Discouraged, Christian thanked the man for his help, tore out the sketches, and stuffed them in his pocket. He motioned Joe Means to follow him. They went outside to the carriage, where they sat for several minutes, neither of them having the slightest inclination to move.

"Don't understand it, Mr. Marshall," Joe said. "If none of those men took her, then who did? And how did they leave with her?"

"It's a certainty they didn't go through the lobby. I would imagine a service staircase and entrance was used. As to your other question . . . I have no idea who actually abducted Jenny, but it seems clear to me that the Benningtons are behind it."

"Is that where we're going, then? To the Benningtons?"

Christian nodded, the set of his mouth grim. "We'll begin there," he said. "So help me, Joe, if they've hurt her in any way I'll . . ." He let the rest of the threat go unspoken. Joe Means filled in his own ending.

Christian was shown to the breakfast room at the Bennington mansion by a skittish housemaid. Her odd, nervous behavior attracted Christian's attention, and the absence of Wilton Reilly prompted him to ask after the butler. He wasn't surprised to discover that both his observations were connected. According to the maid, Wilton Reilly had been dismissed the previous evening.

"Has he left yet?" Christian asked.

"No, sir. He's packing now."

"Ask him to wait for me in my carriage." Christian thought he could use Reilly's help. Jenny had trusted the man, and Christian realized he could do worse than trust someone who had befriended Jenny. "I may have a position for him."

The maid's lips parted in surprise and her eyes widened fractionally. She could hardly believe what she was hearing. It was an amazing turn of events, and it served the Benningtons right for what they'd put Mr. Reilly through last night. "Oh, yes . . . yes, sir!" She opened the door to the breakfast room, forgetting in her excitement to announce Christian.

Christian walked in boldly. "Don't bother getting up," he said to the two startled occupants. "You'll be wanting to get to the bank, William, so I won't take much of your time. Tell me where Jenny—where *Caroline* is—and I'll leave you alone."

It was Stephen who reacted. He threw down his paper and his chin thrust forward aggressively. "Get out of here, Marshall," he said, coming to his feet. When Christian didn't move, Stephen called for the butler. "Reilly! Show this man—"

"He doesn't work for you," Christian said calmly.

"What?"

"The maid told me you dismissed Mr. Reilly. Had you forgotten?"

He had. Ruddy color exposed Stephen's embarrassment, and he took a threatening step toward Christian. "I'll show you out myself."

Christian's lip curled derisively. "Show or throw?"

William Bennington's fork clattered to his plate. "Stephen, sit down," he snapped, annoyed by his son's behavior. "What's this all about, Marshall?"

"I told you. I only want to know where Caroline is."

"She left you?" asked William. "Stephen seemed to think after seeing her last evening that she wasn't happy. It would be

376

in keeping with Caroline's rather bizarre manner to leave without a word."

"You know damn well she didn't leave me. Not of her own free will. What have you done with her, Bennington? I want Jenny back."

"Jenny? Oh, yes. Stephen mentioned that was the name she was using." William poured himself a cup of tea, walked to the sideboard, and added a small measure of whiskey. His entire demeanor suggested calm indifference to Christian's questions and concerns. He returned to his chair and regarded Christian with a shuttered glance, giving nothing of his thoughts away. "My son also said that you had married her. It won't wash, you know. Even if it's true, which I seriously doubt, the marriage can be annulled. Caroline's mental state is such that she can't be held accountable for her actions."

Some of Christian's confidence faded, though he managed not to show it. Williams's reaction confused him. It wasn't at all what he had expected. He began to wonder if he was mistaken about William's involvement. "I didn't come here to discuss my marriage," he said coldly.

"Why you've come here doesn't matter to me," said William. His cobalt-blue eyes were hard, his sharp, aristocratic features predatory. "In truth, you've spared me a visit to your home. I had planned to call on you today and bring Caroline home myself." He set down his cup. "I don't know what your initial interest in Caroline was, or even how your paths crossed. Frankly, I don't care. I'm telling you now that your relationship with my stepdaughter is at an end. She's fragile, Marshall, dangerously unbalanced, and I have doctors who will support what I'm telling you. If she's left you, then you should consider yourself fortunate and leave the task of finding her to Stephen and me."

Christian listened to what William had to say and dismissed all of it. "I want to search the house and grounds," he said. "I can do it with your permission or without it. Either way I'm going to do it. I *will* find Jenny."

Stephen looked at his father, not believing that William would permit Christian to carry out his outrageous threat. "Father?"

William shrugged. "He's obviously unbalanced as well," he said. "You can search if you like, Marshall, but I hope you won't be difficult when the police arrive."

From the open doorway Wilton Reilly spoke. "The police won't be necessary, Mr. Bennington. Mr. Marshall and I are leaving now."

Christian glanced over his shoulder and saw the butler. "I told the maid to have you wait in the carriage if you want a position," he said. "I don't need you here."

"Uppity bastard," muttered Stephen, glaring at Reilly. "You're welcome to him, Marshall."

Reilly ignored Stephen and spoke directly to Christian. "Miss Van Dyke's not here, sir," he said with great dignity. "I would know if she were. More to the point, neither Mr. William nor Stephen know where she is. That is the reason I was dismissed. I would not reveal her whereabouts."

For a moment Christian was hopeful, then he realized that Reilly did not know where Jenny was now, only where she had been. "Very well." He turned on his heel. "Let's go. We'll talk in the carriage."

"What in God's name was that about, Stephen?" William demanded harshly after Christian's and Reilly's departure. "Did you tell me everything that happened last night at the lake?"

Stephen's face darkened with fury. He was not a child to be chastised. "You think I know something about Caroline's disappearance. That's why you were bluffing. To protect me! You could have saved your breath. I don't know where the hell Caroline's gone to, and I don't need your protection."

"You should have followed them after they left the Park."

"And leave Sylvie at Beach House? Besides, I went to Marshall's later, just as I told you, and neither Christian nor Caroline were there."

378

"So the housekeeper said," William sneered. "Do you really think she'd tell you anything?"

"I saw the carriage return to the house," Stephen reminded his father. "The driver was alone. I couldn't have known when they left the Park that they wouldn't be returning to Marshall's home."

"You couldn't. You *couldn't*. Tell me, Stephen, what is it that you *can* do? Can you grasp the situation we have here? Marshall thinks we have Caroline, and we know we don't. She's disappeared again, and that can only mean trouble for us. Dammit, Stephen, Caroline Van Dyke can ruin everything we've been working for! There's no telling what she's already said to Marshall."

"She's mad, remember? You said it yourself. We have doctors to support us. Morgan and Glenn will make certain no one listens to her ravings. You're exaggerating the threat to us."

William shook his head. "I want her found and I want her locked away where she can't escape and where she won't be listened to. When that's done I'll believe we're safe from her accusations." William stood and leaned forward, bracing his arms on the table. He looked down his nose at his son. "Take care of it, Stephen. Understand? I want you to take care of it. Hire help if you must but for God's sake, *do* something."

"And when I find her? What then?"

"Haven't you been listening? I told you. We'll commit her again." He caught Stephen's loose-limbed shrug. "Do you have an objection to that?"

"None," he said. "But you're the one who's been suggesting that Caroline is so dangerous. I don't know why you hesitate to resolve this problem with a more permanent solution."

"A more permanent solution?"

Stephen said nothing. His eyebrows lifted slightly and he continued to stare at his father.

William stared back. Finally he said, "Use your judgment."

379

Stephen's eyes followed William as he walked away from the table and out of the room. Once his father was gone he reached in his pocket and extracted a business card. Amalie Chatham's name was engraved in ornate, flowery script on one side. He turned it over. The handwriting was sharp and spared no ink for extraneous flourishes. The card had been delivered in a plain white envelope. According to the maid who gave it to him, someone had slipped it under the front door.

Stephen read the message twice. "Use your judgment," his father had said. And he had. When he chose not to tell William about the message, and when he gave nothing away to Christian Marshall. "Take care of it," his father had said. And he would. Perhaps he and Amalie Chatham could strike a bargain that would prove lucrative to both of them. She had Caroline Van Dyke and he had access to more money than Amalie ever dreamed of.

Chapter 15

Jenny recognized the room she was in almost immediately upon waking. It was Maggie's and Maggie was noticeably absent. The woman who sat at the vanity, her back turned to the mirror, was Amalie Chatham. John Todd stood by the balcony doors, and behind him the brass handles were chained.

Jenny sat up slowly. Her mouth was dry and her tongue felt thick. She tried to wet her lips and couldn't. The cool and heavy weight on her left wrist caused Jenny to look at her hand. She nearly gagged at the sight of the iron manacle. A chain secured her to the bedpost. She closed her eyes and pressed her free hand to her temple, massaging the violent pain that suddenly stabbed her there.

Jenny could feel Amalie's reflected stare and it made her skin crawl. She had been left very little in the way of dignity. Shackled like an animal, she had also had her gown, shoes, and stockings removed. The shift she wore was a modest covering by Amalie's standards, but not by Jenny's. She shook her head, releasing the heavy fall of her dark hair so that it covered her shoulders and filled in the expanse of flesh above her bodice neckline. Still, she felt vulnerable to the eyes of her captors. Jenny forced herself to look at Amalie and pretend she wasn't afraid for herself or for her child.

"She's awake," Amalie said to John Todd. "You can wait in

the hallway. I'd rather speak to her alone. If I need anything I'll knock on the door."

John Todd gave Amalie a curt nod and crossed the room. At the door he paused. "If Stephen Bennington comes?" he asked. His dark eyes darted to the concealed panel.

"Show him to the bedroom next door. He can see her from there. I'll decide how close he can get after I've talked to him." When Todd was gone, Amalie turned her attention to Jenny. "Do you remember who I am?" she asked bluntly. Her voice was cold and her emerald eyes were as flat as bottle glass.

Jenny's head dipped slightly to show that she did indeed remember.

"Good. Perhaps fewer explanations will be required." Amalie pointed to the marble-topped bedside table. "There's water for you. Champagne, if you wish it." She saw Jenny eye the refreshments warily. "None of it's drugged. I don't think that's necessary now, do you?"

The chain rattled as Jenny stretched toward the table. She poured herself a glass of water, drank it greedily, and poured another. She sipped the second glass, but even when she knew her throat was soothed enough to speak, she said nothing.

"I recognized you right from the beginning." Amalie went on, seeing that she had Jenny's full attention. "When you came here that first night, I realized who you were. There's a portrait of you in your stepfather's office at The Trust. Did you know I bank there? I have for years. Even when your father was alive I kept my money at the Hancock Trust. Charles Van Dyke managed investments for me as well. My arrangement with William has been less profitable, but not excessively so. I was willing to stay with The Trust even when I heard rumors that affairs there were not, shall we say, quite aboveboard.

"Then I saw you. Rather odd, that. According to the papers and Stephen's loose tongue you were dead. Yet there you were, right on my doorstep." Amalie approached the bed, but only came close enough to pour herself a glass of champagne. "Once I recovered from the shock of seeing you, it occurred to me

382

that your business here had to be related to your stepfather. I don't know that I really considered what your intentions were, but it truly never came to me that you were here to see anyone but William." She shrugged, studying her champagne in the firelight. "He said you were dead. Obviously you weren't. I thought there was some money to be made from that inconsistency."

Jenny's fingers tightened on her water glass. "Whatever you thought you could get from William or Stephen—I'll pay you more."

"If only that were true," Amalie sighed. She went back to the vanity, sat down, and primped in front of the mirror a moment before turning to face Jenny again. "I can't depend on that. I know something of the nature of your father's will. Stephen again, I'm afraid. He can't seem to help from talking when he's amorously occupied. My understanding is that since you're unmarried and over twenty-one, your estate must be entrusted to three managers. I think it's unlikely that they'll want to give me so much as a penny. No, I'm afraid that won't work. I shall have to depend on Stephen or William to line my pockets."

"Christian Marshall will pay."

"Christian Marshall will kill me," Amalie said. There was a flicker of emotion in her eyes, quickly shuttered. "I don't think it would be best to apply there for funds. Anyway, the Benningtons owe me. William has one hundred thousand dollars of my money. I want it back and more."

"How did you find me?"

"A bit of luck. Common sense. I suspected that there was some connection between you and Mr. Marshall. John Todd followed Marshall. It took time but"—she waved her hand expansively, indicating Jenny's presence in the room—"you're here now. We've known for two weeks where you were, but Mr. Todd had to wait until Christian left you alone. Mr. Todd tells me he thinks you were ill. Is that so?"

Jenny's lips flattened mutinously. Amalie's solicitousness

was as absurd as it was unwelcome.

"No matter," Amalie said when she saw Jenny was not going to answer. "You're probably wondering what's to become of you. Or are you? I can't quite make you out. Stephen's told several of my girls in the past that you've taken fits before." Amalie touched the side of her head with her forefinger. "Something lacking with your mental faculties, he says. Is that so?"

"Oh, I'm absolutely mad," Jenny said solemnly. "If I weren't chained like a rabid dog, I'd show you exactly what you have to fear from me."

Amalie gave a small start, her eyes narrowing as she studied Jenny and tried to make out what it was that her captive was really saying. "There's no sense in you being difficult. I won't tolerate it. You would be pathetically easy to drug. Keep that in mind, please."

Jenny knew that she would. There was the baby to think of.

"I've sent a note round to Stephen." Amalie sipped her champagne. "I thought he might be easier to deal with than his father."

"Stephen is no one's fool," Jenny said.

"I'll keep that in mind," Amalie said dryly. "I'm expecting your stepbrother soon. I'm sorry. Perhaps you prefer to think of him as your fiancé."

"I prefer not to think of him at all."

Amalie permitted herself a small, husky chuckle. "Under the circumstances, that's understandable." Her smile faltered, then faded. "I really don't know what Stephen will want to do with you. For what it's worth, I won't let him have you cheaply."

Jenny ignored that. "Christian will find me," she said instead. "For what it's worth . . . he *will* kill you."

Amalie set her glass down and stood. "There will be something for you to eat later. I'd advise against screaming or trying to draw attention to yourself in some other manner. There's no one in the house this time of day who will come to your aid. My girls know better than to interfere in my business. Also, I won't hesitate to gag you or put you in the fruit cellar. You'd be much less comfortable there, but I leave the choice up to you." She gathered a good measure of her gown in one fist and turned on her heel. The satin fabric rustled noisily. Without a backward glance, as though confident of Jenny's cooperation, Amalie left the room.

Stephen quietly closed the panel which allowed him to view Jenny. He turned, leaned casually against the wall, and studied Amalie. She was looking very composed and confident. John Todd's presence in the room was a contributing factor to her self-assurance.

"She seems well," he said.

"She's only been here a few hours and she's being well cared for," Amalie told him.

"What has she said?"

"Very little."

"What have you told her?"

"Again, very little. She knows I'm negotiating with you."

"Oh? Is that what we're doing?"

"I hope so," said Amalie. "I'd like to come to some sort of agreement today."

Stephen's cobalt-blue eyes were dark and unfathomable. "What is it you want, Amalie? And why come to me and not my father?"

"Your father and I had a falling out." She smiled coolly. "I think you know precisely what I want. I want quite a lot of it actually. There's a matter of a hundred thousand that your father stole from my account."

Stephen whistled softly under his breath, showing his surprise. "Father never mentioned that. A hundred thousand? That's a great deal of money. I don't know if I can get it for you."

Amalie laughed softly. Even John Todd smiled. "I'm not

sure you understand. That's *my* money. Once you give me that we'll be even. Whatever figure we arrive at for Miss Van Dyke is in addition to the one hundred thousand."

"I'll have to think about that, Amalie," Stephen said calmly. "You may want to reconsider yourself . . . say twenty-five cents on the dollar. You could recover a quarter of your money."

Amalie remembered what Jenny had said. Stephen was no one's fool. Well, neither was she. "I'll make certain the right people know she's alive, Stephen. I can name three gentlemen on your board of directors who call on this house. Your fiancée will do the rest. I think she has quite a story to tell. I haven't learned it all, but I can."

"Caroline won't keep quiet about your part in this. You won't get any money at all if you take that route, Amalie."

"Perhaps not, but I'll have my pound of flesh. I can live with that." She paused a beat. "Can you or your father?"

Since it was Bennington flesh that Amalie would take, Stephen had to reconsider his position. "If I pay you, what then?"

"Then it's over. I look the other way. So does Mr. Todd. You can take your fiancée from the house . . . dead or alive."

"What makes you think I'd want her dead?"

Amalie's head tilted to one side and she raised her hands, palms upward. "Just a passing thought. It occurred to me that you might be able to get your hands on her money through the Van Dyke Foundation."

"I could have all her money if I marry her."

"It would be better if she were to die in an accident soon after the wedding," Amalie said shrewdly, speaking Stephen's thoughts aloud. "But we digress. To wed her, you must have her, and to have her, you must meet my price. I understand that the Van Dyke estate is valued in excess of twenty million dollars. Don't shake your head at me, Stephen. That's the figure you quoted to Maggie not so long ago. Caroline is yours for nine hundred thousand." She ignored the hiss of Stephen's angry, indrawn breath. "That's in addition to the one hundred thousand. You owe me—"

"One million," he said tersely. "Your demand is outrageous. I won't pay it, Amalie."

"Why don't you think on it," she said politely. "There's no real hurry. I can be patient, oh, for three days or so. And I won't even charge you anything for her care."

Stephen took a threatening step toward Amalie, but stopped when he saw John Todd draw a derringer from beneath his jacket. Helpless and hating it, Stephen thrust his fists into his pockets. He would not come to Amalie's again without a weapon. "I can't get any money for you before Wednesday. And there's no possibility that I'll be able to bring anything near what you've asked for."

"Think on it, Stephen. I'll accept real-estate deeds transferred to my name. Jewelry is nice. I want cash as well, but I'm prepared to be somewhat flexible. Get back to me in seventy-two hours with your answer. I won't do anything at all until then."

Stephen's jaw went rigid. He glared at Amalie, then at the gun John Todd had leveled at his chest. He stalked out of the room, slamming the door behind him.

"How do you think that went, John?" Amalie asked when Stephen's footsteps receded in the hallway.

Mr. Todd put away the gun. He put his arm around Amalie's shoulders and kissed her on the cheek. "Very well," he said. "I think that went very well."

For the purposes of demonstration and explanation Christian gathered everyone in Jenny's suite at the St. Mark. Mrs. Brandywine was there, sitting in the rocker with her ivory-knobbed cane resting at an angle on her wide lap. Wilton Reilly sat in the overstuffed armchair. His fingers tapped gently against brass tacks that dotted the curve of the arm. Occasionally his glance would dart solicitously to Mrs.

Brandywine, but she had yet to spare him more than a tight-lipped smile. Susan Turner shared the chaise with Liam O'Shea. Christian had invited the cop because Liam had shown he could be trusted and Christian suspected he would genuinely care what happened to Jenny Holland. Discovering that she was really Caroline Van Dyke had briefly set him back on his heels, but Liam decided he could like her in spite of her fortune. That announcement, delivered in Liam's musical brogue, was responsible for the only smile the group had shared.

Scott had brought in a chair from the bedroom. He was sitting on it backwards, straddling the seat and resting his folded arms across the rococo curves at the back. His chin pressed against the back of his hand. His features were grave, solemn with thought.

Christian stood by the fireplace. He was leaning against the wall and his hands were thrust deeply into the pockets of his black frock coat. A gaslight not far from his head brightened strands of copper in his dark hair. The tight set of his mouth caused a muscle in his cheek to tick as regularly as the pendulum clock.

Except for the beribboned hatboxes which occupied chairs, tabletops, and the mantelpiece, the room was exactly the way Jenny left it. Susan was fingering the handkerchief, running her thumb across the delicately embroidered J.

"It doesn't mean anything to me," she said finally. "It must belong to someone the Benningtons hired."

Liam O'Shea shook his head. "Not to be contradictin' you, ma'am, but I think I'd know if the Benningtons hired someone to do this. They never knew Jenny—er, Miss Van Dyke—was stayin' here."

"It's still Jenny," Christian told the cop. "I agree with him, Susan. I don't think William or Stephen is responsible for this."

"Who else has a motive?" asked Scott.

Mr. Reilly stopped drumming his fingers momentarily.

"Perhaps someone who knows how important the Princess is to the Benningtons. That's what we have to hope for, isn't it? If no one contacts the Benningtons about Miss Caroline, then our chances of finding her are almost nil."

Christian supposed it had to be said, but he didn't like hearing it. "Mr. Reilly is right," he admitted reluctantly. "No one has made any demands on me for ransom and it's been some ten hours since she was abducted. No messages have been delivered here or to my home. I have to assume that whoever took Jenny plans to contact the Benningtons. It seems someone besides ourselves knows that Jenny is Caroline Van Dyke."

Scott nodded. "Perhaps the Benningtons have already learned something since this morning."

"I hope so," said Christian. "In part, that's the reason I've asked all of you to come here. We have to keep Stephen and William in sight on the assumption they *will* learn something—if they haven't already. I'm proposing teams. Mr. O'Shea and Joe Means will share responsibility for Stephen. Mr. Reilly, Mrs. Brandywine, and I will watch William."

"Me?" squeaked Mrs. Brandywine. "Christian, you know I want to help, but there's my leg to consider."

"That's why you'll be staying here, Mrs. B.," he told her. "You'll be able to watch William while he's at the bank. Mr. Reilly or I will be your legs."

The housekeeper smiled widely, satisfied with her contribution to the plan. "I'll be happy to do that," she said.

Scott's brows raised slightly. "What about me?"

"Keep to your routine, or rather your lack of routine, at the hospital. Jennings is the best place for you to be. If Jenny's taken there, or if Morgan or Glenn are called to treat her, I'm confident you'll find out about it."

Susan twisted a cloth-covered button on her bodice. "It seems you've thought of everything," she told Christian a shade wistfully. "Is there nothing at all that I can do?"

Christian pushed away from the wall and reached for the

hatbox on the mantel. Without moving it, he straightened the section of black velvet ribbon at the front of the box. "There's something *only* you can do," he said.

Susan sat up straighter, her eyes eager. Out of the corner of her eyes she saw her husband frown. She avoided looking in his direction. "What is it?"

"I promised Jenny that she would get her evidence on William and Stephen," he said quietly. "No matter what happens, I plan to keep that promise. She placed herself at risk any number of times because it was important to her that the Benningtons be stopped. I think I know how to stop them, but I find I can't do it all myself."

"Is this going to be dangerous for Susan?" Scott demanded.

Susan's lips pursed to one side and she rolled her eyes. "Do you really think Christian would let me do something the least bit dangerous?" She turned back to Christian. "Go on. I'm listening."

"I want you to take the pictures of William and Stephen," said Christian.

Scott jerked upright. "Now just a minute—"

"Will you please let Christian explain?" Susan said, cutting off her husband. "I suppose it has something to do with all these hatboxes." She pointed to them in a sweeping gesture. "Do you have a camera in each of them?"

"In a way," Christian said. "The hatbox *is* the camera. A pinhole camera." He glanced at the clock, then walked to the box resting on the table between the group and adjusted the ribbon on the front of it. "Jenny and I were talking about my brother Logan last night . . ." Christian stopped, collecting his thoughts. It was nearly impossible to believe that twenty-four hours ago he and Jenny had been together. "And that's when I realized that a pinhole camera was the answer. The photograph will be coarse, not as sharp as if we were using a lens, but with a little luck we'll get something that will identify William and Stephen for the thieves they are."

Susan held up one hand, palm outward. "I know very little about photography, Christian. We have a stereoscope at home for looking at pictures, but I know next to nothing about the technical end. How does one take a picture with a hatbox? Er, which side do you aim?"

One corner of Christian's mouth turned up in a faintly amused smile. "The side with the pinhole." He went to a third hatbox and adjusted the ribbon, covering the nearly invisible hole. "It works very simply," he said. "I could have used any type of box as long as it could be made light-tight. I chose a common hatbox because it wouldn't call attention to itself if carried into the bank. The ribbon helps secure the lid against stray rays of light entering, and it serves the additional purpose of providing a shutter for the lens."

"I thought you said this doesn't have a lens," said Scott.

"It doesn't. Not really. It has a pinhole which allows light to enter. The light rays will produce an image on the photographic paper I've secured to the opposite inside wall of the box." Christian looked at the blank faces of his audience and realized they only had a vague idea of what he was talking about. "Take my word for it, all right?"

They nodded in unison.

"I've painted the inside of all these boxes with a flat black paint. That stops the light rays coming through the pinhole from bouncing in all directions and fogging the paper. As I said, the ribbon acts as a shutter . . . an eyelid, if you will, and keeps the light out until you're ready to expose the paper to your subject. While we've been sitting here I've been experimenting with the exposure time. That's why I set up a number of hatboxes. I uncovered the pinholes when you sat down and I've been covering them up again at different intervals. The light in here is not so different from the light in the bank. I'll do some more bracketing of the exposure tomorrow as well. There will be some adjustments for daylight because William has that large window in his office. If it's a bright day the exposure time

391

will be shorter."

"Do you mean you've been taking our picture?" asked Scott.

Christian nodded. He covered the last pinhole. "And I have to say that you've all been cooperative. One of the problems with using a pinhole camera is that the exposure time is longer than if we were using a lens. I've made exposures from four to fifteen minutes. That can be a long time for a person to sit relatively still, but you've all pretty much done that. There's no way of knowing if William and Stephen will be so cooperative, but we have to get lucky sometime, don't we?"

"But they're not going to be stealing the money right in front of me," Susan said. "I'm not certain I understand how this is going to be done."

"I'll admit that the odds aren't in our favor. Not that it's risky," he said quickly, to assure Scott. "Timing is everything. We know the day they're likely to take the money. Because of the payroll schedule we even know the approximate hour when the safe is filled. From this room we can see almost all the activity. The increase in guards will let us know that a transfer of funds is going to take place. According to Jenny, William and Stephen are skimming the cream. In order to catch them at it Susan will go into the office on our signal, just minutes before we think they're preparing to take the money. She'll play the dissatisfied customer and make enough noise so that William *has* to listen to her." He went on for several minutes, explaining in detail what it was that Susan would do. When he finished he looked at them expectantly. "Well?"

There was a long silence. "I suppose it could work," Scott said reluctantly. "I'd feel better if I could see what sort of pictures these damn hatboxes are going to take. There's no sense in Susan doing any of this if we can't depend on getting a good photograph."

Susan opened her mouth to protest, then thought better of it. Scott was right. They had to know there was at least some hope that the picture would be sharp enough to show what

392

was happening.

"Give me twenty minutes," Christian said. He collected the hatboxes and disappeared into Jenny's studio and darkroom. It was actually thirty-five minutes before he returned. He passed the photographs around one at a time. The first one was underexposed. The next, overexposed. But two others, exposed to the light for intermediate periods of time, were clear enough to identify everyone in the room. One was sharp enough to detail the buttons on Susan's bodice. Because of the way Christian had secured the light-sensitive paper to the curve of the hatbox, the photographs gave a panoramic view of the room. The objects that had remained unmoving throughout the exposure time were clearer beyond anyone's expectations.

"Well?" Christian asked again, collecting the prints.

This time there were no objections.

All things considered, Jenny supposed she was being treated well. The only people she saw were Amalie and John Todd. In the three days Jenny had been at the parlor house, the door to her room was never opened by anyone but the madam and her bodyguard and lover. It seemed no one else had any interest in what was going on in Maggie's room.

Amalie visited Jenny frequently. Her polite inquiries into her captive's health grated on Jenny's nerves, yet Jenny pretended not to be bothered by the questions. She pretended not to be bothered by anything that was said or done to her, and discovered that her nonchalance served to make both Amalie and John Todd nervous. Jenny's calm defiance underscored her conviction that Christian Marshall would find her.

Nights were the most difficult. Jenny's sleep was troubled. She woke often only to discover that she had been fighting the manacle that kept her chained to the bed. Her wrist was chafed and swollen from her battle, and her waking mind told her what her sleeping mind refused to believe—there was no escaping this iron bracelet.

Amalie examined Jenny's wrist impassively and ordered John Todd to bring some ointment for it. "You should have said something," she told Jenny. "It hasn't been my intention to harm you."

It was late in the evening on the third day of Jenny's confinement. In the circumstances, Amalie's statement struck her as extremely funny. Jenny was only peripherally aware that her laughter had an edge of hysteria. She withdrew her hand from Amalie's grasp and cradled it against her chest, manacle as well. Her eyes were accusing. "You're going to let Stephen kill me," she said lowly.

Amalie rose from the edge of the bed. "That's nonsense," she snapped. "Stephen's here now and, believe me, what he's interested in won't kill you." Ignoring Jenny's harsh, indrawn breath, Amalie crossed the room to the dressing screen. She disappeared behind it for a few seconds, then reappeared dragging Maggie's wooden tub with her. "He's met my price," she said matter-of-factly. "In your place I'd be flattered. Your fiancé has gone to great lengths to have you. Not many women can say they really know how much a man wants them, but there's no doubt about Stephen. He's proved it by agreeing to my terms."

Jenny was hardly listening to Amalie. She was staring at the tub which Amalie had brought to the side of the bed. Her throat had constricted the moment she realized her captor's intention.

"One million," Amalie went on. "Can you imagine that he thinks you're worth so much? I suppose you could say that in a way the money's yours, but Stephen doesn't think like that. He believes it's *his* pockets I'm picking." She chattered away while she filled the tub with water from the adjoining bathing room, hardly aware of Jenny's withdrawal. "Did you hear that, Stephen?" she asked, staring pointedly at the cleverly concealed panel where Stephen was watching from the next bedroom. "But it's not his money, is it, Caroline? You'll have

394

to settle that with Stephen yourself, dearie. After you're married."

Even Amalie's last statement did not rouse a response from Jenny. She watched the last bucket of water being poured into the tub in frozen silence. Amalie added a few drops of attar of roses to the water. The sweet, cloying fragrance made Jenny's uneven breathing more pronounced.

John Todd walked into the room then, and his attention was immediately caught by Jenny's distress. He shut the door behind him and crossed the room quickly, tossing Amalie the ointment. "What's wrong with her?" he demanded, watching Jenny closely from the foot of the bed. He was beginning to regret his part in Amalie's plan, but he didn't dare tell Amalie that. The truth was that he felt sorry for Jenny. Her complete helplessness moved him in ways he had never anticipated. It was a constant struggle to keep from releasing her, and he knew he was in Amalie's scheme over his head.

Todd's tone forced Amalie to really notice Jenny. Her forehead creased as her brows drew together. "I don't know," she was forced to admit. "She wasn't like this a few minutes ago."

Their conversation, conducted as if she weren't present, brought Jenny back to the present. Her troubled glance darted from Amalie to John. "I won't get in there," she said huskily, forcing the words past the tightness in her throat. "I won't."

Amalie threw up her hands, her frown fading. "My Lord! You gave us a scare for a moment." She turned to John. "She must be shy about bathing in front of you. Why don't you wait with Stephen? I'll call if I need you."

When John Todd was gone, Amalie sat on the bed again and took Jenny's wrist. She smoothed the salve on Jenny's chafed skin, then put the medicine away. "There," she said briskly. "That's better. It's not so painful now, is it? Do you need help getting into the tub? The chain will reach that far."

"I won't." Jenny drew her knees up to her chest. The hem of her shift covered her toes. "I told you I won't."

"This is ridiculous," Amalie said. "Of course you will. I told you Stephen's here. He's waiting to be with you and it's only fitting that you're made ready for him. Is it because he's watching you now?"

"Stephen can see me? Now?"

"Haven't you been listening to me?" She pointed to the opposite wall. "Just beyond there, in the next room. The opening is difficult to see, but then that's the idea. The occupants of this room never know when they're being watched. You and Mr. Marshall never knew, did you? Stephen told me earlier tonight that he saw you New Year's Eve. Remember? Maggie gave you this room."

Jenny hugged her knees closer to her chest. The thought that Stephen had been a witness to what she and Christian had shared caused her stomach to roil. She closed her eyes and bit her lower lip to keep from screaming. Her hands were clenched into tight, bloodless fists. Jenny swallowed hard, holding back her anger, pain, and humiliation.

The taut control Jenny placed on herself couldn't be maintained. It demanded an outlet and the outlet was Amalie. There was virtually no warning when Jenny attacked. Her feet struck out first, knocking Amalie on her back across the bed. The older woman's scream was cut short as Jenny pounced, caught her by the shoulder, and circled her neck with the chain. Amalie sputtered, gasping for air. Amalie raised her hands, reaching behind her to claw at Jenny's arms and face. Her manicured nails, sharp as talons, scored Jenny's forearm. Jenny cried out in pain, but didn't loosen her hold. Her knee pressed hard into Amalie's side, and Amalie was the one forced to give up her grip. The chain tightened around Amalie's throat, and Jenny's harsh breathing obliterated the sound of Amalie's pain.

It was Stephen Bennington's low, derisive chuckle that caught Jenny's attention. Simultaneously she felt John Todd's large hands on her forearms, drawing her inexorably away from Amalie. She struggled, flailing out with her hands and

396

feet, but from her first awareness that Stephen and John were in the room she had known the battle was lost.

John Todd pulled Jenny off the bed. His leg bumped the tub and water splashed the carpet and the hem of Jenny's shift. Todd recovered his balance almost immediately and pulled Jenny hard against him. Standing behind her, he crossed her own arms in front of her and pulled them toward her back in a one-man basket carry. Her weight shifted forward so that she was totally dependent on him for support. His superior height and strength made it absurdly easy for him to hold Jenny in just this manner for hours if he wished it.

Amalie scrambled to the far side of the bed, then off, retreating to the opposite end of the room and seeking safety behind the silk dressing screen. Her immaculate coiffure was pulled free of its anchoring pins, and resembled nothing so much as a bird's nest after a cat had found it. Her face was pale, and tiny lines whitened the corners of her mouth and eyes. She looked and felt every one of her fifty years. Her generous bosom heaved above the heart-shaped bodice of her gown. She held one hand to her throat and gently explored the mottled skin of her neck with her fingertips.

"She's mad!" Amalie rasped. She could still feel the iron chain around her neck. "There was no provocation for what she did! She tried to kill me!"

"Why are you so surprised?" Stephen asked dryly. He did not look at Amalie. His hard cobalt-blue eyes studied Jenny, and his handsomely chiseled features were cold now, predatory, and gave little of his thoughts away. "I've always maintained she's quite out of her head. You shouldn't have been alone with her. It's fortunate that Mr. Todd was in the next room."

"Yes, isn't it?" snapped Amalie. "I notice you've done nothing to help."

Stephen's laugh was without humor. "Be reasonable, Amalie. If Caroline killed you, my troubles would most likely be at an end. I'm advising caution in dealing with her. In the circumstances, that's all you can expect me to offer." He addressed Jenny. "Well, Caro, it seems that you've finally shown your colors—and in front of others. I suppose it was inevitable that your illness would surface again."

Jenny tried to tear herself away from John Todd's grasp. She strained, rearing her head like a filly being forced to accept the bit for the first time. Her thick, dark hair shielded part of her face and a strand of it was caught between her lips. She spit it out and made the gesture contemptuous, as if she were spitting at Stephen.

"There's nothing becoming about your rage, Caro. You don't look much different now than you did in the hospital. That's where you belong, and I think in some small, sane corner of your mind you know it as well." Stephen raised his eyes to John Todd. "You probably think that by holding her that way she'll eventually wear herself out. I can tell you it won't happen. I know all about my fiancée's treatment in the lunatic ward, and they found that restraining her, just as you are now, only agitates her further. Caroline requires a different sort of cure."

"You bastard!" Jenny cried hoarsely. "I knew this was your doing! You planned it! You didn't ask for the water because you want me clean! You want me dead!"

Stephen ignored her. With casual indifference to Jenny's presence, he adjusted the cuffs of his white shirt. "I hope the water is not too warm, Amalie. It's better cold."

"What has that to do with anything?" asked Amalie. She continued to eye Jenny warily even though John Todd's hold was inflexible.

"It's part of her treatment, of course. I've been assured by Dr. Morgan that when Dr. Glenn used it on her she responded very well. The plunge bath calmed her."

Jenny twisted hard. Her breasts ached because her own arms were crossed in front of them. When she tried to kick backward, she only succeeded in unbalancing herself so that her arms felt as if they were likely to pull away from her shoulders. "Bastard!" she said again. "I hate you! Do you hear me! I hate you!" Frustrated tears welled in Jenny's eyes. She blinked them back, glaring at Stephen. "Christian will find me. And when he does he'll find you. Think about that, Stephen. Think what he's going to do to you before you lay a finger on me."

A muscle jumped in Stephen's lean cheek. One corner of his mouth lifted slightly as he expressed his cynicism. His deliberate, steady stride narrowed the gap between them. When he stood directly in front of Jenny he raised his right hand. Jenny's chin was raised defiantly, her dark eyes dared him to touch her. He brought the flat of his hand hard against her cheek. Jenny's head swung sideways and the stinging pain made the tears in her eyes spill over. The imprint of Stephen's hand burned her skin. "I'm not afraid of Christian Marshall," Stephen said. "Perhaps you need to think about that."

John Todd retreated a few steps, taking Jenny with him. "That wasn't necessary, Bennington. There's no cause for slapping her. I think this has gone far enough."

Amalie, who could feel the bite of Jenny's chain as if it were still around her neck, disagreed. "If slapping is what it takes to calm the bitch down, then let him do it."

"Unless you're afraid of Marshall," Stephen added, studying Todd's grim features. "No? Good. Let Caroline go and take Amalie out of here. You can watch from the other room. If I need help, I'll call for you and I'll expect you to be here. Otherwise, let me handle my fiancée."

Todd, angry that Stephen had accused him of being afraid of Christian Marshall, pushed Jenny toward the bed. He didn't release her until he had forced her to crawl onto the mattress. Backing away quickly, he skirted the tub, took Amalie by the arm, and escorted her from the room.

"It seems we're alone now, Caro," Stephen said, sitting at the foot of the bed. "What's that name Marshall calls you? Jenny? I don't know if I can get used to it. You'll probably always be Caroline to me."

399

Jenny was turned partially away from Stephen. Her knees were drawn up protectively to her chest and she made furtive, impatient swipes at the tears which refused to dry up. Under her breath she called him a bastard again.

"I won't ask you to repeat that," he said pleasantly. "I can appreciate that you're overwrought. You shouldn't have attacked Amalie, though. That was a mistake on your part. What am I going to do with you, Caroline? You can't seem to resist showing others how perfectly mad you really are. I never wanted a lot of people to know about your illness. What will they think when I marry you?"

"Probably that you're after my money."

"Do you think so?" he asked rhetorically. "Perhaps it's true. But I pity you as well. There's no chance that any other man will have you to wed. Not when he'd have to worry that you'd murder him in his sleep."

"Aren't you afraid of that?" she snapped. "I still walk in my sleep."

"You don't frighten me, Caro. I know how to deal with you." Stephen stretched his legs, crossing them at the ankles. He ran his thumb and forefinger along the crease in his trousers. "I can have a minister brought here who will marry us," he said. "Minutes after I give Amalie her money you and I can be married. What do you think of that?"

"Go to hell," she said softly.

"I know you're not married to Marshall," he went on as if she hadn't spoken. "That was a quick invention on his part to keep me away from you."

"What makes you think that?" Jenny used the hem of her shift to erase the last traces of tears. Her face felt drawn and dry; her eyelids were puffy. Stephen held out a handkerchief to her. Jenny accepted it reluctantly and blew her nose.

"I saw the way you looked at him when he said you were married. It startled you. Lying was never your strong suit, Caro." He said the last as if it were a serious defect in her

400

character. "So . . . about our marriage . . . have I your agreement?"

"I'm not marrying you."

"Aren't you?" Stephen looked pointedly at the tub of rapidly cooling water. "I'd rather not go to the trouble of forcing your compliance, but I will if I have to. I know everything that was done to you in the hospital. Morgan described the techniques that Dr. Glenn was using to cure you of your madness. I'm certain the same technique can cure your reluctance to marry." He sighed softly, smiling ruefully. "But I'm no doctor, Caro. I don't know all the fine points of the treatment. There's always the possibility that I could injure you. I thought you should know that before we begin."

Jenny averted her head and remained mutinously silent.

"I had really hoped you wouldn't be so stubborn." He reached forward and made a grab for Jenny's ankle. She recoiled, trying to evade him, but he caught her calf. His hand slid over her leg and tightened around her ankle. When she kicked at him he grabbed the other ankle as well and dragged her toward him. "That's enough," he cautioned her tightly as she made a swing for him with her clenched fists. He ducked the blows easily, helped by the fact that the manacle restrained Jenny's reach with her left hand.

Stephen struggled with Jenny for several minutes before she exhausted herself. Although Jenny put up a formidable fight, Stephen never called for John Todd to assist him. He had something to prove to Jenny—namely, that he was in complete control of her well-being. He also discovered that he enjoyed her struggle. There was a certain sexual excitement in his thorough domination. She was forced to yield at every turn. Her husky breathlessness made him think of a lover. His voice was silky, threatening, when he told her what he was thinking.

"Get off me," she gritted. He was lying almost fully on top of her, and even if he hadn't told her what he wanted Jenny would have known. His arousal was hard against her thigh. Her thin

401

shift and his trousers were no barrier. When he laid the pad of his thumb against her lower lip and rubbed lightly, Jenny bit him.

Stephen swore and rolled off Jenny and the bed. Without giving her time to think, he picked her up and held her over the tub. The chain was stretched tautly and the manacle cut into the ball of Jenny's hand. "You leave me no choice, Caroline. No choice at all." He lowered her into the water.

In the other room, John Todd shuddered as Jenny's cries were silenced. "Jesus," he whispered, closing his eyes momentarily. "Shut the panel, Amalie. We don't have to watch. We'll be able to hear."

"No." Amalie placed her slender, beringed hand over the knob on the panel to keep Todd from shutting it. "I want to see what he does. How long do you suppose he can keep her under without drowning her?"

"Jesus," Todd said again. "You're enjoying this, aren't you?"

"She tried to kill me," Amalie reminded him. "I don't care what he does to her. I've seen the way you watch her, John. Don't think I haven't. You treat her like some damn princess. You should take a page from Stephen's book. He knows what to do with her. Look at his face. He's a sadistic bastard, but it wouldn't hurt you to be a little more like him."

"You want me to be sadistic?" Todd asked incredulously. "Listen to me, Amalie, if he kills her there won't be any money for you *and* you'll have a body to explain. Use some sense! Let me stop Stephen before he ruins everything!"

Amalie didn't say anything for a moment. She watched as Stephen lifted Jenny out of the water, dragging her to her feet by placing his hands under her arms. Jenny was so weak she needed Stephen's assistance to stand. Amalie could imagine how much Jenny despised herself for requiring her stepbrother's help. Jenny's limp and matted hair dripped water over her bare arms. Her shift clung wetly to her breasts, waist, and thighs. She pressed her manacled hand to her mouth as she

402

choked on the water she had swallowed. Her breath rattled.

"Oh, my God," Amalie said lowly. Her eyes had dropped to Jenny's waist again. She blinked widely. "I think she's pregnant."

"What?" Todd pushed Amalie slightly to the side so he could have a better view.

"She's pregnant. God, I should have suspected something like this! She's been ill most every morning. Why didn't I see it?"

John Todd didn't wait to find out what Amalie wanted him to do. He was running from the room even as Stephen was lowering Jenny back into the water. He pushed open the door and crossed to the tub in three long strides. "She's pregnant, Bennington," he growled, shoving Stephen out of the way. He yanked Jenny out of the tub. "You keep at this and she'll miscarry. Most likely die too. That's not why I brought her here. That was never part of the plan, not *my* plan anyway." He laid Jenny on the bed, turning her on her side, and covering her shivering body with a blanket.

"None of this was your plan, Mr. Todd," Amalie said. She stepped in the room from the hallway and shut the door behind her. In her right hand she held a derringer. It was leveled at her lover's chest. "I don't know how I could have been so mistaken about you," she said quietly, a frown creasing her brow. "We've known each other so long . . . shared so much . . . why didn't it occur to me that you might have a tender heart for this bitch? That's it, isn't it? You feel something for her, don't you?"

"Amalie," Todd cajoled, watching her carefully. He thought about reaching for his own derringer, then reconsidered. Amalie would kill him before his own gun cleared his concealed shoulder holster. "You're not making sense. I don't want her hurt because we can't afford it. I don't feel anything for her . . . not the way you think. I saved you, didn't I? I didn't let her choke you. Put the gun down, Amalie. Be reasonable."

Stephen backed away from Todd, making certain he was out

403

of Amalie's line of fire. "I don't know why you want to share anything with him," Stephen said softly, his eyes darting from one to the other. "Surely his usefulness is over. All that money could be yours, Amalie. You deserve it. You thought of everything; Todd here's only the muscle. That's all he's ever been."

Amalie stared at John Todd. Her expression was sad. "Stephen's right, you know. I can't depend on you if you've gone soft on me, and it seems that you have. I told you to let Stephen handle her as he saw fit. You interfered. Do you think I care if she's pregnant? It was an observation, not an excuse for you to become involved."

"Amalie," Todd said again. There was no pleading in his voice because he didn't believe for a moment that Amalie was seriously considering killing him. By the time he realized he should have pleaded, it was too late. John Todd died with a look of stunned amazement etched on his hard features.

The fist that Jenny had pressed against her mouth prevented her from screaming as Todd's body slumped to the floor. Stephen dragged his eyes away from the dead man and stared at Amalie, hardly believing what he had just witnessed. The falling out between partners had been swift and final. There was no questioning Amalie's seriousness. She had her derringer leveled at him.

"Don't even think of crossing me, Bennington," she said with icy calm. "I was a lot more sentimental about Mr. Todd than I am about you."

Stephen raised his hands, palms outward, and shrugged innocently. "I understand perfectly," he said. "What should I do with the body?"

"Take it to the fruit cellar. Use the back stairs."

"Do you think anyone heard the shot?"

"Above the music downstairs? Not likely. Someone would be here by now if they had."

Stephen lowered his hands as Amalie tucked her derringer into the sleeve of her gown. "Is she really pregnant?" he asked, jerking his thumb at Jenny.

"Yes. I only realized it moments before Mr. Todd came barging in here. I'd have told you if I'd known earlier. Her belly's thickening."

"I don't want the child."

"I realize that. It would be a complication."

He nodded. "What can you do about it?"

"Nothing . . . or everything. Are you familiar with Madame Restell?"

"By reputation."

"She advertises herself as a midwife, but I'm sure you realize she's an abortionist," said Amalie. "I send my girls to her when they get in trouble. Her little French female pills cost dearly, but she guarantees their efficacy."

"What do you want me to do?"

"Nothing tonight; it's too late. But tomorrow morning I want you to pay her a visit. Don't go to her brownstone on Fifth. She'd turn you away. Her offices are on Chambers and Greenwich Streets. Tell her I sent you and that I assured you she could help. Bring the pills back here. I'll see that your fiancée takes them." She ignored Jenny's low, keening cry. "Don't give it another thought, Stephen. You'll never have to be a father to Christian Marshall's baby."

Christian Marshall sat in the rocker in Jenny's suite. His head rested wearily against the ornately scrolled back of the rocker. His eyelids were heavy, shuttering the expression behind them. In his arms he held young Amy Turner. Her pale blonde hair was almost white against the dark fabric of Christian's jacket. She was fingering one of the buttons on his black satin vest.

Susan quietly motioned her daughter to come and sit on her lap, but Amy shook her head stubbornly. "Uncle Christian's sad, Mama," Amy whispered. "I'm staying here."

Susan and Scott, sitting opposite him on the chaise, glanced simultaneously at Christian to see if he heard their daughter's loud aside. He had. There was the slim suggestion of a smile playing at the corners of his mouth.

"She's fine where she is," Christian said. He looked down at Amy's blonde, curling hair and ruffled it with his fingertips. His smile faded so completely that it might never have been.

Susan's heart went out to Christian. She busied herself, raising a glass of red wine to her lips in the hopes of hiding the pity she felt. Trust Amy to see what she and Scott had missed. Yes, he was sad, deeply so, yet until Amy had pointed it out Susan had only seen anger.

Christian's anger lay just below the surface, held there by the sheer force of his self-control. It was the silent, imploding kind of anger, terrible and terrifying to look upon because one could not help but imagine that it would not remain silent. Christian's jaw ached from the tight way he held it, yet he could not relax. Inside his stomach roiled. There were faint shadows under his eyes from lack of sleep and tiny white lines engraved at the corners of his mouth. A glass of wine rested on the table beside him, but after one sip Christian had shown no interest in it. There was the need to keep a clear head, of course, but it was just as true that nothing he ate or drank since Jenny left seemed to have any texture, color, or taste. As a result his weight had dropped nearly ten pounds, and the hard lines of his face were as powerful as if they had been etched with acid.

Christian winced slightly as Amy moved on his lap and accidentally kicked his wounded leg. "It's all right," he said when Scott moved to take Amy from him. "She didn't mean to do it." He massaged his leg long after the pain had dissipated. The soothing, absent gesture was almost second nature to him. "Do you think Jenny and I will have a little girl?" he asked quietly, shifting his eyes to a point on the far wall. Copper threads in his dark hair were highlighted in the gaslight.

There was no way to answer his question. "Is that what you want?" asked Scott.

406

"A girl would be nice. My family runs to boys, though."

"Boys are nice too," said Susan for lack of anything better to say.

Christian's slight smile surfaced briefly. "I suspect I'll take whatever I get." He looked down at Amy, but spoke to his friends. "Why haven't we found her?" he asked softly, almost cautiously, afraid to admit failure out loud. "What the hell's happened to Jenny?"

Scott heard Susan's breath shudder through her. His wife was very close to tears. He reached for her hand and squeezed it reassuringly. "I wish I had the answers," he replied. "God, how I wish it."

"I keep thinking we're overlooking something," said Christian. "I was convinced early on that Stephen or William Bennington would eventually lead us to her."

Scott nodded. "We all felt the same way. None of us could have anticipated that William's routine at the bank would never vary. And Stephen . . . he's certainly made no unusual moves. If he's worried about losing any part of Jenny's inheritance, then he's drowning his sorrows in the arms and thighs of some—"

"Scott," Susan said reprovingly, pointing to their daughter. "Have a care what you say."

Scott ducked his head guiltily and mumbled an apology. "There's been no hint at the hospital of anything concerning Jenny," he went on. "If Stephen or William were involved, I think I'd have picked something up by now. They'd seek Morgan or Glenn out, wouldn't they?"

"That's what I thought," said Christian. "I just don't understand it. William's coming and going as if nothing's happened. One would think I never confronted him about Jenny's disappearance. Stephen appears to be unaffected by anything save Amalie's girls. And the hospital has given us no clues. We have exactly what we had in the beginning: an embroidered handkerchief still smelling faintly of chloroform and no idea to whom it belongs."

"We have a plan," Susan reminded him. "The day after tomorrow, with a bit of luck, we'll have evidence that Stephen and William are stealing from the bank."

Christian was silent for a long time. His arm stole around Amy's waist and she burrowed against his side, instinctively sensing that it was Christian who needed the cuddle. He wondered if he would ever hold his own child. The thought made it difficult for him to breathe for a moment. "I only care about the bank because Jenny did," he said at last. "I'd let William and Stephen walk away from it if it meant having her back." He raised his eyes to Susan and made no attempt to blink back the thin veil of tears. "I want her back, Susan. I just want Jenny with me again."

Chapter 16

Christian raised one hand to shade his eyes. After the near-endless winter New Yorkers had experienced, this particular Wednesday morning was unusually sunny, bright, and cloudless. Christian was not generally superstitious, but now, after so many turns of luck against him, he found himself thinking that the change in the weather and the onset of spring must be a good omen.

A light breeze whispered across the back of his neck. He was standing on the balcony outside Jenny's bedroom at the St. Mark. He stepped back from the balcony rail and turned slightly, squinting to get a better view of the activity in William Bennington's office. Sunlight bounced off the high, arched windows and made viewing difficult. Worried that he might be seen and identified as well, Christian hunched his shoulders and raised the collar of his jacket. It was probably an unnecessary precaution. From what he could see in The Trust, William and Stephen Bennington were too preoccupied with their own concerns to pay attention to anything beyond their windows.

Mrs. Brandywine opened the double balcony doors and poked her head out. "Mr. O'Shea says the guards are in place at the back of the bank. The last shipment should be here in minutes."

Christian nodded. "Thank you, Mrs. B. I'll be looking for it."

"Do you see Susan?" she asked.

"Hmm-mm. She's been pacing the block, Amy in tow, for the last half hour waiting for my signal. As soon as the payroll wagon arrives I'll give it."

"She has the hatbox?" asked Mrs. Brandywine.

"She has it," he said calmly, trying to soothe his housekeeper's frayed nerves. "Go back inside. We don't want to draw attention to ourselves." He turned away just as the payroll wagon moved into the alley behind the bank. Mrs. Brandywine disappeared into the bedroom, shutting the doors gently behind her. Christian checked his pocket watch. He would give them ten minutes, then signal Susan to proceed with the plan.

Amalie held a tiny white pill in the flat of her hand. She showed it to Jenny. "I've been patient up to now," she said. "I could have insisted you take this yesterday when Stephen brought the pills by, but I didn't. I've given you time to get used to the idea. You probably think I'm being unnecessarily cruel, yet I assure you that isn't my intention. I had to be certain that Stephen really intended to deliver the ransom I've asked. Early this morning he brought by a little over three quarters of a million in property deeds. Before noon he will have the rest. He's acted in good faith and I can do no less. I promised him I would get rid of the child. That's what has to happen. You really can't blame him for not wanting to be father to your child."

Jenny simply stared at the pill. Her eyes were vacant, her mind nearly so. Amalie's sentences seemed disjointed to her; nothing made sense. She hadn't slept since John Todd's murder. She'd been too afraid. She hadn't eaten anything, either, frightened that Amalie would put pills in her food, but she hadn't been so cautious about drinking. Jenny realized too

410

late that the tea she'd drunk had been laced with some drug, opium probably, and she was helpless before she had recognized the new danger.

"Have a bit of tea," Amalie encouraged, closing her hand over the pill. She poured from the silver-plated pot and handed Jenny a china cup and saucer. "Careful now. You wouldn't want to spill any and burn yourself. Here, let me help. I'll tip it ever so slightly for you." Amalie's smile was warm, encouraging. "Take it slowly. That's a girl. Doesn't taste so bitter now, does it? I'll wager you're even coming to like the taste. I should have done this from the beginning. It was Mr. Todd who talked me out of it. He thought you could be managed without any drugs. But then it turned out that Mr. Todd couldn't be managed. I blame you for that, you know." Amalie drew back, studying Jenny with flat, cold eyes that were at odds with her smile. "It was merely pity that he felt. Nothing else. It was me he cared for. He might have even loved me." Amalie's smile vanished, and the placement of her full lips became as hard as the green glass light in her eyes. "Before you I never doubted his loyalty. He never once interfered when I had to discipline a girl; never failed me when I asked him to throw out a gentleman caller. You changed all that. I don't thank you for it, Miss Van Dyke. No, I don't thank you for it."

Jenny blinked. Amalie's tight, bitterly accusing voice stung her and she recoiled, rubbing the gooseflesh on her bare arms. What was Amalie talking about? Why did the madam want to hurt her?

Amalie raised the china cup to Jenny's lips again. "Here, take a little more. Just a few sips. It helps, doesn't it? Gives the world a rosy glow. You won't mind so much; maybe you won't even remember." Amalie took away the cup, placed it on the table, and unclenched her fist. She waved her open hand in front of Jenny, showing the pill again. "You'll take this now, won't you? Here, Miss Caroline, just open your mouth. I'll put it right under your tongue."

The voice that commanded her was soft now, faintly pleading.

411

Jenny wanted to please, but she also sensed danger. It was difficult to keep her eyes open, yet the thought of going to sleep terrified her. She was frightened she wouldn't wake, and then how would Christian find her? The idea made complete sense to her, and that was cause for fear as well. With the small part of her mind that could still entertain rational thought, she knew she was losing her faculty for clear thinking. Jenny's lips parted. She moistened them with the tip of her tongue.

"That's right. A little wider and I'll put it in. Right in." Amalie raised her hand, holding the pill between her thumb and forefinger. "Just under your tongue. That's it, dearie. Just—ooowwww!" Amalie howled and jerked her hand away as Jenny's teeth clamped down hard on her fingers. "You little bitch!" She slapped Jenny across the cheek. Jenny's head snapped back and she spit out the pill. It disappeared into the wrinkled sheet.

Amalie groped for the pill, thought better of it, and put some distance between herself and Jenny. "It doesn't matter," she said under her breath. It was an effort to remain calm. "There's plenty more." Amalie stood and backed away from the bed, patting down her coiffure and straightening the neckline of her gown. "You don't really think you can stop me, do you?" she demanded.

But Jenny was looking at her blankly again and didn't answer.

Christian took the embroidered handkerchief from his pocket and raised it to his lips. He held it there for a moment, then let it drop. It caught the edge of the wrought iron rail, fluttered in the breeze, then fell to the balcony floor. It was fitting that the delicately stitched J was still visible when the handkerchief landed. Christian stepped on it and ground it with the heel of his shoe. The satisfaction was too fleeting.

He watched Susan Turner, below him and across the street, loosen the ribbon of her bonnet, then tie it again. It was her

412

acknowledgment of his signal. She bent down, spoke to her daughter briefly, then took Amy in hand again. They turned the corner and walked into the bank.

It seemed an eternity before Christian saw Susan again. For a while he feared that she hadn't been able to convince anyone of the necessity of seeing William Bennington personally. William certainly wouldn't have appreciated the interruption. He was sitting at his desk, a stack of ledgers before him, concentrating, Christian thought, on hiding the evidence of the loans he had made to himself. It was the simplest method of stealing from the bank. The false loans were written off as bad investments. William's trail was covered in black ink tracks among accounts payable and accounts receivable. He took the loan money directly, removing it from the bank in the manner Jenny had suggested—between the pages of the daily paper.

The breath Christian hardly realized he was holding was released softly when he saw Susan take a chair in front of William's desk. William had stood briefly upon her entry and now he sat down, sliding the ledgers to one side. Stephen, standing near the open safe, remained there. As near as Christian could tell, Stephen seemed unperturbed by the interruption. His pose remained casual.

In his mind Christian ticked off the instructions he had given to Susan. Hold the hatbox in your lap. Make certain the ribbon is over the pinhole. Don't dislodge the paper. Talk to William about a loan as if there was nothing else on your mind but getting money from him. Complain to him about the error in your account. Tell him how long you've been a customer and how The Trust is valued by the small investor. Be sincere, Susan. Don't let either of them see how much you despise them. Break it off in midsentence when you hear Amy crying for you from the lobby. Act ruffled, made anxious by your daughter's crying. Uncover the pinhole with your fidgeting fingers. Stand up. Place the hatbox on the table beside your chair. Leave the office hurriedly, murmuring your apologies. Pretend you don't hear them if they remind you of the hatbox.

413

Get out of the office quickly . . . take Amy . . . get out of the bank.

Christian permitted himself a small smile when he saw Susan and Amy emerge from the bank. Liam O'Shea was waiting on the corner to take Amy. The small girl wiped away her fake tears, smiled brightly for Liam, and took his hand. They crossed the street together toward the St. Mark while Susan went in the other direction and counted off the minutes.

The sun reflected brightly off the windows of William's office. Shielding his eyes didn't work anymore so Christian left the balcony. He had to trust that Stephen and William would be forced to move quickly. The guards at the back of the bank would be waiting for their orders. Gold and silver bullion needed to exchange hands, but William and Stephen would take their money in federal treasury notes. They could be invested elsewhere later.

Christian glanced at his pocket watch. Four more minutes before Susan had to return for the hatbox. Was it enough time for William and Stephen to incriminate themselves? Christian stepped into the sitting room. Mrs. Brandywine had moved away from the window where she had been watching, and was waiting by the door for Liam and Amy to return.

Events were proceeding smoothly, he thought, yet he could find no cause for rejoicing. It was still too early to be sure of success. And then there was Jenny. Victory would have a bitter taste if she wasn't present to share it.

"It was only a matter of time," Amalie said to Maggie. She pointed to Jenny, who was sleeping now, the shadows beneath her eyes proof of her exhaustion. "She couldn't fight the opium forever."

Maggie hesitated at the entrance to her own room. She hadn't been allowed in it for nearly a week. She hadn't wanted to know why and she still didn't. Maggie was happier not being involved in Amalie's schemes, and if she could have refused

Amalie and still found work in a good house, Maggie would have spit in the madam's eye. As it was, she found herself being pulled into the room and drawn closer to the bed.

"Why, it's her . . . that girl . . . the one who was here New Year's Eve!" she said breathlessly. "Do you mean to say that she's the reason I haven't been able to use my own room? Don't you think you're being ridiculous, Amalie? She's attractive, I suppose, but to go to such great lengths to have her as one of your girls? That's why she's here, isn't it?"

"Of course it's why," Amalie lied. "Marshall enjoyed her that night he was here. Why wouldn't someone else? She's just a thief from the Five Points, Maggie. No one's going to miss her."

Maggie's mind was working quickly. She began to connect pieces of information from things she had seen and heard recently. "Stephen Bennington wants her, doesn't he? That's why he's been here so often lately. He was watching that night when she was with Christian, and now he's decided that he wants her."

"You're so clever," said Amalie, preferring to let Maggie believe whatever she wanted. "Now, will you help me take her to the fruit cellar?"

"Take her to the . . ." Maggie stopped as Jenny turned in her sleep and the manacle was revealed. "Amalie! Why is she chained? Surely that's not—"

Amalie's voice was sharp. "I can find someone else. I thought—this being your room and all—that you'd be happy to get it back. Are you going to help me or not?" Amalie sat down on the edge of the bed, withdrew a skeleton key from between her breasts, and unlocked the manacle.

Maggie was uneasy. Her eyes darted around the room. Other than the chained balcony doors, she could see nothing had been changed. "Wouldn't it be easier to wait until Mr. Todd returns from Baltimore? Surely he doesn't plan to be gone much longer. He could move her easily."

"I want her moved now. I wouldn't have asked otherwise.

We'll take her by the back stairs. And, Maggie, this is between you and me. No one—*no one*—else is to know."

Maggie found swallowing difficult. She raised one slender hand to her throat as if that would ease the lump. Amalie's eyes were boring into her. She could not recall Amalie ever being so threatening. Whatever arrangement Amalie had made with Stephen Bennington regarding the girl, Amalie was taking her part very seriously. Maggie wondered about all the questions she had been told to ask Stephen about his stepsister. She glanced at the young woman on the bed again. No, she thought. She didn't want to know. "All right," she said. "I'll help you. We'll make a hammock of sorts with one of the sheets and carry her that way. I suppose we can manage that."

It took but twenty minutes to take Jenny from the room. She never stirred. The fruit cellar was dark, so dark that Maggie never saw the slightly raised mound that indicated the spot where John Todd was buried. Jenny found it later when she regained consciousness and crawled around her dark, airless prison on her hands and knees looking for a way out. She felt the freshly turned dirt with her hands, judged the length and breadth of the mound with her extended arms, and knew instantly what she had stumbled upon. She practically flung herself into one corner of the room then. Her arms were crossed protectively in front of her and her nails pressed deeply into her flesh. The pain was good, she thought. It meant she was still alive, that she wasn't dreaming. Christian would find her. He would find her!

Something furry ran over her bare foot. The dank, black walls of her prison closed in around her. The ground beneath her feet was damp. Jenny bit her lip hard. It didn't help. She couldn't stop herself. It started as a whimper and became the hoarse screams of her worst nightmares.

Liam O'Shea delivered Amy to the suite and waited by the window, watching for Susan. He stroked his mustache with his

416

fingertips. "You should have let me contact other policemen," he told Christian. "We could stop Stephen the moment he walks out of the bank and place him under arrest."

Christian was hunkered in front of Amy, telling her what a wonderful actress she was. With very little in the way of rehearsal, she had still managed to play her part to perfection, crying on cue to give her mother an excuse to leave William's office. He turned his head to one side and addressed Liam over his shoulder. "We won't know until we have Susan's photograph whether or not any money was taken. And if it was?" His brows lifted a notch. "We can't be certain it isn't ransom. That money could lead us to Jenny. I won't have anyone stand in the way of that."

O'Shea pointed out the window and drew Mrs. Brandywine's attention. "Here's Susan. She's carrying the hatbox." He checked his pocket watch while Mrs. B's eyes darted to the pendulum clock. "I make the exposure time to be eight minutes. Is it enough?"

"It will have to be," Christian said.

O'Shea's nervous pacing was finally interrupted by Susan's entry. "I've got it," she said breathlessly, holding up the hatbox. "I really hope it's going to tell us what we want to know. I think I just missed interrupting them when I barged in after my hatbox. Everything was neat and tidy then, but I'm almost sure that wasn't the case minutes before." Her excitement caused her words to trip over one another.

After prying Susan's fingers from their tight grip on the hatbox ribbon, Christian took the box into his own possession. "I'll develop the photograph," he said, gently removing Amy from his leg and pushing her toward her mother. "Keep an eye on the bank, Mrs. Brandywine. I assume Mr. Reilly and Joe Means are still in the lobby ready to go if either of the Benningtons leave."

"They're watching," Susan said. "I passed them in the lobby on my way up here."

"Good." He turned on his heel and disappeared into Jenny's

makeshift studio and darkroom.

Susan took off her coat and hung it up. "I'm glad that's over," she said, taking a seat and lifting Amy onto her lap. "I wish Christian had involved more policemen than yourself. I'm so afraid we're not going to corner the Benningtons. And Jenny . . ." She held her daughter closer.

"I said much the same thing before you came in. Mr. Marshall thinks that if Stephen has money it could be ransom. He doesn't want to jeopardize a chance to find Miss Holland."

"It can't be ransom," Susan objected. "We're all but certain that Stephen and William have not been contacted. William's been nowhere this past week. And Stephen's only been to Amalie's."

"And Madame Restell's," Liam said offhandedly, "but we're not going to find Miss Holland there now, are we?"

"What did you say?" she asked. The hand that was stroking Amy's hair fell still.

"I said we're not going to find Jenny at Madame Restell's."

"But Stephen was there?"

Liam nodded. "At her office. Yesterday morning it was."

"This is the first I've heard of it." Susan felt her stomach turn over as her thoughts began to race ahead. "Does Christian know?"

Liam shook his head. His brow furrowed at Susan's urgency.

"Why didn't you say something before now?" she asked.

"It didn't seem important." Liam looked at Mrs. Brandywine for some clue as to Susan's pale face. "It doesn't mean anything surely. Stephen's been a caller at Amalie's for a long time now. His visit to Restell's is a natural progression of things. Amalie doesn't like her girls carrying anything they shouldn't, if you take my meaning."

"I take your meaning," Susan said. "And it strikes me as unusual for Amalie to send any man to Restell's to take care of one of her girls. Wouldn't that be the girl's responsibility?"

Liam began to realize where Susan was heading. "Sure, and

418

you don't really think . . ."

"Jenny's carrying Christian's child."

It was Mrs. Brandywine's gasp that punctuated Susan's words. "Oh, no. You don't really think that . . ."

Liam nodded slowly, his eyes bleak. "Sure, and it makes sense when you think about it. How would one of Amalie's girls know who fathered her child? Stephen wouldn't be going to see Madame Restell for any common prostitute."

"Oh, my God," Mrs. B said softly. "But if that's true, then Jenny's most likely being kept at Amalie's. We have to tell Christian." She looked nervously at the closed door to the darkroom.

Liam glanced at the clock. "We can't go in there now. What if we're wrong? We'll ruin the photograph, won't we?"

Indecisiveness wasn't Susan's strong suit. She moved Amy off her lap and stood. "Mrs. B.? Will you watch Amy? I'm going to the hospital to get Scott. If our suspicions are correct, then Jenny is going to need a doctor. We may already be too late to save her baby." She wouldn't let herself think that they might be too late to save Jenny.

"Wait a minute," Liam objected. "Shouldn't you ask Mr. Marshall?"

"Just tell him. *Everything*. Tell him through the door if you have to. He won't thank you for waiting. I'll bring Scott here first. If you and Christian have left by then, I'm going to assume you've gone to Amalie's. Scott and I can find her house." Susan turned a deaf ear to other objections. She gave Amy a quick kiss goodbye and hurried out of the room. Less than a minute later Mrs. Brandywine spied Susan hailing a hack on Broadway.

In the darkroom images were beginning to form on the photographic paper. Christian was thorough and deliberate in processing the paper. There would be no second chance and therefore there was no margin for error. The focus of attention was solely on the task before him. His concentration was enormous. In the filtered yellow light of the darkroom the planes and angles of his face were tautly drawn.

He developed the image in a bath of ferrous sulfate, studied it, and began to feel more hopeful. When he believed the image was as clear and sharp as it was ever going to get, Christian quickly made it permanent by placing it in the fixing solution of potassium cyanide. This was later washed off in a bath of water. Christian hung the finished photograph on a line with a clip and waited for it to dry.

Ten minutes later he walked out of the darkroom with the photograph. There was no smile, but the light in his cool eyes was triumphant.

"Mrs. Brandywine. Liam. Look at it and be critical." He laid it down on the oval walnut table near the window. "What do you see?"

Amy sidled over to the table and stood on tiptoe to get a look also. "Jenny," she said. She pointed to the portrait behind William's desk. It had been photographed with remarkable clarity.

"Yes," Christian said softly. "That's Jenny."

"There's no doubt that it's William Bennington at the desk," Mrs. B. said. "Stephen's not quite as clear. He looks like a ghost."

"That's because he was moving back and forth between the desk and the safe," explained Christian. "As a result, his image appears in two places and in neither place is it as clear as his father's. William, on the other hand, was relatively stationary."

"Those are treasury notes on his desk," Liam said. "No question. But I don't know if it's enough for a conviction."

"Perhaps not," Christian said. "But it just might be sufficient for a confession." He glanced around the room. "Where's Susan? I want her to see this." Silence greeted him. He became aware of the tension in the room for the first time. "What's happened?" he demanded. "What aren't you telling me?"

420

Liam swallowed hard and recounted his conversation with Susan.

Christian's aquamarine eyes frosted over as he listened. He raked a hand through his hair. Recriminations and blaming would only take up valuable time. Jenny was at the forefront of his thoughts. And his child. Amalie and Stephen were trying to murder his child! He held up his hand, cutting Liam off as he saw Stephen Bennington entering the street from the alley behind The Trust. Stephen was crossing in front of his father's office and headed toward Broadway. Under his arm was a folded newspaper.

Christian spoke and acted quickly. "I'm going after him. Mr. Reilly should already be moving to follow. Liam, take this photograph, Joe, and whoever else you need—a judge, a lawyer, another policeman—I don't care who it is, but get William Bennington to dig a hole for himself. *He* knows what this photograph means." Christian shrugged into a coat and checked on the revolver he had pocketed. It was loaded. Out of habit he felt the other pocket for extra ammunition. "Work our advantage, O'Shea. Make him confess. Tell him the police are closing in on Stephen."

"But—"

"*Lie*, O'Shea. Do whatever it takes." Christian opened the door to the suite and partially stepped into the hallway. "Send Scott on to Amalie's, Mrs. B., and tell him to arm himself. I need a soldier first, a doctor second."

Christian's limp didn't impede his progress down the stairs or crossing the St. Mark lobby. He passed Joe Means and told him to go to the suite and follow the cop's directions. From Joe he learned that Mr. Reilly had left the hotel as soon as he saw Stephen on the street.

By the time Christian reached the thoroughfare there was no sign of the butler or Bennington. Trusting his instincts now, Christian hailed a cab and gave the driver Amalie Chatham's address. He sat back in the scarred leather seat. One hand absently massaged his wounded leg. The other was thrust into

421

his coat pocket and curled around the engraved ivory butt of his long-barreled Remington revolver.

William Bennington leaned forward in his chair. His elbows rested on the edge of the polished mahogany desk. His head rested heavily in his hands. He stared at the photograph that Liam O'Shea had placed in front of him. He wondered if he could destroy the picture before O'Shea stopped him. The little bastard traitor! O'Shea had been taking money from him and working for Marshall. William sighed. Anger seemed out of place at this juncture, a waste of energy. He was tired, very tired.

"What is it you want?" he asked, looking up. His eyes met Liam's first, then moved on. He felt the accusing gazes of Mr. Charles Vorhees, and Mr. Henryk Vandermeer, both directors of The Trust and old friends of Charles Van Dyke. Behind them, at the door which led to the bank lobby, stood two of Liam's friends and fellow policemen. They were expressionless, but their presence was threat enough. Standing beside the safe was a man William did not know, a small, wiry man who had the smell of horses about him. The man's gnarled hands were balled into white-knuckled fists.

"Your resignation will suffice for now," Mr. Vandermeer said. He was unaware that he was tapping his foot impatiently.

"It seems that I am to be convicted without a trial," William said. "Is that the way it's to be then?"

"You would prefer a trial?" asked Vorhees. His heavy jowls sagged over the stiff collar of his shirt. "Is that what you really want, Bennington, to bury The Trust? Because that's what will happen. In any event, I suspect the investors will lynch you before it comes to trial. O'Shea tells us Christian Marshall opened this investigation. That means *The Chronicle* and *that* means publicity."

William Bennington closed his eyes briefly. The tension in his neck was unbearable, and steady, pounding pressure was building behind his eyes. "It was Stephen," he said finally, lying because he had no choice. He was weary of the pressures that had been his lot of late. "It's been Stephen's idea from the very beginning. I did it for my son." Behind him he imagined that Caroline's painted smile had widened. She had won after all.

Christian met up with Reilly outside Amalie's. They stood on the sidewalk beyond the hedgerow. No one in the parlor house could see them. "Is Stephen already in there?" he asked.

Reilly nodded. "He came straight from the bank, no stops. He was still carrying the newspaper."

"There's a lot of money inside it."

"The photograph showed it then?"

"Yes."

"Are we going to confront him?"

"I am. It would be better if you waited here."

"But—"

"I'm almost certain Jenny's in there, Reilly. The embroidered handkerchief? That probably belonged to John Todd. He's Amalie's peacekeeper. Not a man to cross without a weapon."

"You have one?"

Christian showed Reilly the revolver. Instead of placing it in his pocket this time, he tucked the barrel in the waistband of his trousers. "Susan went after Scott, and he'll be coming here. There's a chance that Jenny's been given something that . . . she might have already lost the baby."

Reilly swore softly under his breath. "Are you certain you don't want me with you?"

"I'm sure. I know the layout of the house so I have an idea where to begin looking. It's still relatively early for most of the girls. Many of them will be abed. They're the least of my worries."

As Christian turned away to begin his route to the back of the house, Mr. Reilly touched his sleeve. "Good luck, sir."

Christian gave the older man a gritty smile. "I'm bringing Jenny out with me, Mr. Reilly. Count on it."

Amalie unfolded the newspaper on top of her desk. Stephen sat comfortably at one corner, his hip hitched on the edge. He watched Amalie for her reaction.

"Didn't your father wonder about the amount you took this time?" she asked. She didn't look at Stephen. Instead, she began gathering the notes, putting them into neat piles according to their denominations. Turning the pages of the newspaper quickly, she realized that Stephen had met her price exactly.

"He questioned me," he said, shrugging carelessly. "But he also left the matter of his stepdaughter up to me. Today is the first time he realized that I've known where she is."

"He was pleased?"

"I think so. He wanted to know the details, but I thought it would be better to keep that between us."

"Then he doesn't know I've had Caroline here?"

"No. He would have argued that you couldn't be trusted." Stephen smiled. That smile was noticeably absent in his cobalt-blue eyes. "I know differently, don't I?"

"Of course," she said blithely.

"Of course," Stephen repeated, studying her face closely. "Father agreed to make the appropriate entries in the ledgers. The three of us are the only ones who will ever know what's been done to The Trust. And only you and I know everything."

"You're feeling very smug, aren't you?" she said shrewdly. "Why do I suspect that perhaps you've skimmed a little cream for yourself?"

"Perhaps because it's true. You don't mind, do you?"

"Why should I? You've paid me what I asked. I had the deeds checked, you know. They were all good . . . everything quite legally registered to me now. Those properties will triple in value in a dozen years, maybe less. I'm a very wealthy woman, thanks to Caroline Van Dyke."

"Dear, dear Amalie," Stephen said without a grain of affection. "If I weren't betrothed to Caro I could be tempted, very tempted to plight thee my troth."

Amalie's derisive snort was hardly delicate. She had stopped counting her money and was watching Stephen warily. "I'm not flattered," she said, folding the newspaper into a tight roll.

"Fashioning a weapon?" he asked pointedly. "I assure you, it's not necessary. I have no intention of crossing swords with you, Miss Chatham. I saw how you treated John Todd, remember?"

"I was more concerned you would forget."

"May I see Caroline now?"

"Of course."

"How is she feeling? It occurred to me that losing the baby could push her right over the edge to complete madness."

"I was with her only a few hours ago. She was still carrying the child."

"What!" Stephen pushed away from the desk. "You promised me I wouldn't have to worry about Marshall's bastard!"

"Have a care with your voice," she cautioned. "You don't want the girls to hear you, do you? Anyway, I intend to keep my promise. It's only a matter of time before she miscarries."

"Then she's taken Restell's pills?"

"No, not yet. But she will. I've been giving her a mild dose of opium in her tea. Her resistance is fading. And I've put her in the fruit cellar to break her. That was a few hours ago . . ." She stopped, cocking her head to one side. "What was that?"

"What?" Stephen's head also turned. He waited, listening.

"I heard something." Amalie's ecru satin skirt whispered as she crossed the floor toward her living quarters. She paused at the entrance to her sitting room and listened again. "Nothing," she said finally. "I could have sworn . . ."

Stephen waved aside her concern. "Probably one of your girls taking the back stairs to the kitchen."

"No . . . no, it sounded as if it came from inside my suite."

"If you're that worried, I'll take a look. For God's sake, Amalie, do something about the money. It could be a little difficult to explain." Stephen moved fluidly across the room, unaware that Amalie watched him or that she found him attractive. The differences in their ages precluded any involvement or interest on Stephen's part, though Amalie was still a handsome woman. Primarily Stephen was concerned with how he was going to kill her. It seemed a bit of luck that she had moved Jenny to the cellar. Stephen enjoyed the irony that he would be responsible for reuniting Amalie with her lover.

Amalie was locking the top middle drawer of her desk when Stephen returned to the office. She made a point of dropping the key in her bodice and adjusting the neckline so the key rested comfortably between her breasts. "Anything?"

"No one's there. I didn't see or hear anyone in the back hallway. Maggie and a few other girls are in the kitchen. Will that be a problem?"

She shook her head. "The cellar is virtually soundproof. Besides, there's no way to it except the outside entrance. You won't have any trouble removing your fiancée as long as you bring your carriage around back."

"How did you get her down there?" A lock of Stephen's ash-blond hair had fallen across his forehead. He tossed his head back once to get rid of it.

Amalie's eyes went to the strong line of Stephen's throat. In some ways she regretted what she was going to have to do. But what choice did she have, really? She had to look out for herself. "Maggie helped me."

"What?" he practically snarled. "You fool!"

"Don't take that tone with me," she snapped back. "I knew what I was doing. Maggie didn't recognize her anyway. She remembers her from New Year's Eve. That's all. She thinks I've procured the girl just for you. As long as you don't say anything, Maggie won't bring it up. She's smart enough to

426

know when she shouldn't ask questions." Amalie raised one eyebrow, her expression haughty. "Satisfied?"

"I suppose I'll have to be. You give me little choice."

"If you're done grousing, do you want to see your fiancée? Good. Frankly, I'll be glad to be rid of her. Come this way. I need to get a lamp. We'll go through my suite and out the back and none of the girls will see us."

Stephen followed Amalie through her suite. They exited by the back door and went to the sloping double doors which led to the cellar. Amalie tugged on one of the handles and opened the door a notch.

"Didn't you lock it?" Stephen demanded.

"Does it look as if I did? Don't worry. She can't have gotten out of here. She was too weak. I can hardly lift it by myself. Help me, will you?"

Stephen bent and placed his hand over Amalie's. They heaved the door open together and descended quickly, Amalie first. She held the lamp in front of her while Stephen closed the door over his head.

"Back here," Amalie said, pointing to the room off to the left. "Where you buried John Todd." Amalie entered the moist, dirt chamber. Light scattered, revealing spiderwebs and baskets of rotting apples left from the previous summer. There was evidence that John Todd's grave had been disturbed, and Amalie could only imagine the terror that must have struck Jenny when she realized where she was.

Jenny raised her forearm to shield her eyes. The lamplight seemed unbearably bright. The bluish gray bruises from the manacle were clearly evident on her wrist. She cowered in the far corner, her knees drawn tightly to her chest.

"I thought you said you drugged her," Stephen said. "She's alert. Too alert. I can't move her like this." He took a few steps toward Jenny. Amalie's voice, cold and stiff, reminiscent of her emotionless state when she fired on John Todd, brought him up short. He turned slowly. Behind him he heard Jenny weeping softly.

The derringer that Amalie kept hidden under the gathered cuff of her right sleeve was now aimed at Stephen. "I'll save you the trouble of moving her at all," she said. "You had to have had some suspicion that it would end like this." Watching Stephen carefully, Amalie bent slowly at the knees and placed the lamp on the floor. "It just isn't possible to let you live, Stephen."

Stephen's face was impassive. "There really is no honor among thieves, is there, Amalie?" he asked dryly. "I had a similar plan for you."

"I thought you might."

"It's all very well that you want to get rid of me, but what are you going to do about Caroline?"

"I'm afraid I'll have to kill her as well."

"I see."

"I take it that doesn't surprise you either."

"Not really. But I wonder what Marshall would think about it."

"Marshall?" Amalie's brow creased. "What does he have to do with anything?"

Stephen's eyes left Amalie's face and looked beyond her right shoulder. "Tell her, Christian."

Amalie's tight smile held no warmth. Her lip curled cynically. "You didn't really think I'd fall for that trick, did you? I wasn't born this minute. You're as mad as your fiancée if you believe I could be distracted by—"

Stephen's careless shrug cut Amalie off. His focus stayed behind her. "Think what you will, Amalie. I'm quite certain he'll let you kill me, but he's not going to let you harm his precious Jenny. Isn't that so, Marshall?"

Amalie hesitated, listening. There was no sound behind her, no voice, no hint of breathing. She was angry with herself for allo___g Stephen to give her even a moment's pause. She ___ ___ r gun at him. "Don't reach for your pistol," she

428

"You're going to kill me anyway. Why shouldn't I try to defend myself?" He lowered his hands slowly, away from the weapon concealed by his vest. "I wonder how well you're going to fare when it's just you and Marshall left."

"Stop it!" Agitated, Amalie stamped her foot. "There's no one else in here!"

Stephen gave her an arch look. "I don't think you're as certain as you were earlier, Amalie."

She wasn't. Stephen was very convincing as his attention wandered from her to something just off to the right of her. As though it were a tangible thing, Amalie could feel Stephen's gaze brush the curve of her shoulder. What if he was telling the truth? "How would Christian Marshall get in here?" she demanded. "How would he even find us?"

"Well, Christian?" asked Stephen. "How did you find us?"

There was no answer and Amalie told herself she hadn't expected one. "It's no good, Stephen."

"He wants you to kill me," said Stephen. "Don't you understand? He's been waiting for us down here. We were so interested in Caroline that we never looked behind us once. He's been here all along. He wants you to kill me and then he thinks he'll overpower you. He won't let you touch Caroline. He has a revolver, Amalie." Stephen's eyes narrowed slightly. "I make it to be a Remington. Ivory handle. If I were in a position to collect on a bet, I'd wager it's the same gun he used during the war. The gun that got him a medal at Gettysburg."

Amalie's hand was shaking now. She raised her left hand to support her other wrist. "You're lying."

"Look over your shoulder and you'll see for yourself that I'm not."

"You'd like that, wouldn't you?" Amalie's finger tightened on the trigger. She was remembering the noise she had heard earlier when she and Stephen were talking in the office. There was tension in every line of her body. Again she asked herself, what if Stephen was telling the truth? Without warning she

429

swung around and fired blindly.

Jenny screamed as Christian dropped to his knees. With no thought for anything but his safety, Jenny scrambled across the floor. She narrowly missed being kicked by Stephen as he lunged at Amalie before her gun was turned on him again. Jenny rolled out of the way as Stephen knocked Amalie to the ground. The lamp fell on its side and the glass globe broke. Droplets of oil splattered on the ground and tiny yellow and orange flames rose up from the oil. They were licking at the hem of Amalie's gown just as Jenny reached Christian's side.

Even in the eerie light Jenny could see that Christian's face was nearly devoid of color. His voice was harsh, urgent. "Get out of here, Jenny."

"No, I'm not leaving you."

There was nothing Christian could do except curse himself for not getting Jenny out when he had the chance. But that was hindsight. He hadn't known the opportunity was there until it was gone. His grip on the revolver loosened and he sucked in his breath, trying to forget about the bullet that was lodged in his thigh. The pain was enormous and ignoring it was impossible. It felt like someone was branding exposed muscle with a white-hot iron.

Jenny took the Remington from Christian's hand. She'd never held one before and the weight of it surprised her. Stephen's breathy groans as he wrestled Amalie for her weapon were gradually drowned out by Amalie's own screams. The ruffled hem of her satin gown was a ring of fire now.

Rising slowly, Jenny braced herself against the wall. It was cold and damp at her back. She felt Christian's head and shoulder rest heavily against her leg. She thought he was unconscious, but then she heard him demand the gun. Jenny pretended he hadn't spoken, and raised the barrel of the revolver. Amalie's horrible screams sounded too familiar to Jenny, a reminder of hours spent in the treatment room when everyone ignored her own cries for help. Jenny's entire body was trembling and tears spiked the dark fan of her lashes. She couldn't listen to the screaming anymore. She couldn't! She wasn't this strong! Closing her eyes, she cocked the gun and slowly squeezed the trigger.

Within the confines of the cellar the report of the Remington was deafening. Jenny slumped to the floor beside Christian.

Chapter 17

May 1867

"It's a good likeness of her," Scott said as he examined the front page of *The Chronicle*. "Everyone in New York is going to be able to put a face to the name of Caroline Van Dyke."

"You've captured her beautifully," Susan agreed softly, looking from the paper in Scott's hands to Christian. "There's already a ground swell of support for her because of the stories in *The Chronicle*. This sketch . . . well, it's easy to imagine that Stephen and William are going to pay dearly for what they did. No one can look at this and not be moved."

A faint frown pulled the corners of Christian's mouth down. It had been six weeks since the confrontation in Amalie Chatham's cellar. Time had only had an opportunity to heal the most visible wounds. Christian glanced down at his left leg, which was raised on the ottoman. He touched his thigh. Beneath his trousers he could feel the spiral wrap of the gauze bandage.

"Is it bothering you?" Scott asked. He handed the newspaper to Susan and began to rise for the purpose of looking at Christian's leg.

Christian sat up a little straighter in his leather armchair. He warded off Scott's approach with an ebony walking cane, waving it back and forth in front of him. "Get away from me, you quack. I'm fine. And I'm not dropping my trousers in front of Susan so you can gloat over what you've done to me."

"More's the pity," Susan said under her breath, flashing Christian a flirtatious grin.

Scott gave his wife a dark look, then addressed Christian. "I was only going to refill my glass," he lied, lifting his crystal tumbler from the table beside the sofa. "Can I get you something?"

Christian raised his glass of whiskey to show Scott that it was still half filled. "Nothing for me." He lowered his cane as Scott went in the direction of the sideboard. "The leg's fine, really."

"No pain?"

"Hardly a twitch. I touch it out of habit, I suppose."

"You lived with that ball in your leg too long," Scott snorted. He filled his glass, turned away from the sideboard, and studied Christian over the rim of his glass. "I told Susan months ago that I'd eventually find a way to remove it. Of course I didn't expect it would take another bullet to give me the chance. Damn queer twist of fate that was."

"Amalie couldn't have aimed better if she had tried," Christian said softly, a trace of bitterness in his voice. It was still hard for him to admit that the madam's bullet had ultimately been of benefit. He wanted to go on hating her for what Jenny had suffered at her hands. His eyes darkened, losing their characteristic cool color as he thought of Amalie Chatham. His hand tightened around the brass knob of the cane so his knuckles were clearly outlined.

Susan knew the precise moment when Christian's attention was caught by the movement in the doorway. His features relaxed almost instantly. The line of his mouth softened and his brow smoothed. His eyes lost their hard, shuttered appearance. They became warm, tender, and boyishly eager. He released his punishing grip on the cane and leaned forward in his chair.

Amy charged into the study, welcomed by Christian's open

smile. Her parents laughed as she crawled onto Christian's lap and snuggled comfortably in the curve of the arm he put around her waist. Over the top of her pale hair Christian's eyes were rueful.

Jenny was still standing in the doorway, and her dark brown eyes were solemn, her smile gentle. She loved Christian all the more because the invitation in his eyes had been meant for her and he had hid his surprise from the child curled trustingly against him.

Scott raised his glass in salute to Jenny. "I'm glad you're finally back. Christian's been scowling since you took Amy up to see the nursery. It's just a guess," he added dryly, "but I don't think he likes having you out of his sight."

"What do you expect?" asked Susan. "That's the way newlyweds act. Don't you remember?"

Jenny was grateful that Susan had proposed a different reason for Christian's behavior. All of them accepted it and all of them knew it was a partial truth at best. Jenny remembered nothing of the time she'd spent in Amalie's cellar, but Christian was not so fortunate. In his sleep he still recalled every part of what had happened, and his most vivid memory was the moment when his Remington fired and he thought she had killed herself. It was at that point that he usually woke. He would reach for her then, sometimes just to hold her, sometimes to make love to her, always to reaffirm that he was awake, alive, and death was the dream.

Scott offered Jenny his seat beside Susan, but she chose the ottoman in front of Christian's chair. He moved his feet to one side and Jenny took the corner. Her slender arm rested casually across his legs.

Susan motioned to her daughter to come and sit with her. Amy slid off Christian's lap reluctantly and joined her mother. "I think she's going to be jealous of the baby," Susan told Christian. "She's somewhat proprietary where you're concerned."

"Amy still has me all to herself for four more months," he

435

said. "I think we can work out an equitable arrangement by the time the baby arrives."

Jenny nodded. "She approved of the nursery and she has promised to stay sometimes and help me with the baby. Isn't that right, Amy?"

Amy's smile dimpled her cheeks and she giggled. She put her hand on her mother's belly. "Do you have a baby in there?"

The natural color in Susan's cheeks deepened. "No. No, I don't." She glanced up at her husband, who was watching her over the rim of his tumbler. There was a wicked, suggestive look in his eyes. She averted her face quickly and pretended interest in smoothing her daughter's cap of curling hair.

Jenny placed her own hand on her rounded abdomen. "When we were upstairs I let Amy feel the baby kick."

Christian's feet dropped off the ottoman and he leaned forward enough so that he could put his hand near Jenny's, but he was disappointed when he didn't feel any movement.

"I'll let you know," Jenny promised.

Susan urged Amy off her lap and stood. "No, don't get up. Either of you. We don't have to stand on ceremony after all we've been through together. It was a lovely wedding. It was kind of you to ask us to be witnesses."

"The wedding supper was good," Scott noted, patting his flat stomach. He stopped when Susan poked him in the ribs with her elbow. "Well, it was," he insisted. Susan rolled her eyes while Jenny and Christian laughed softly. Somehow she managed to herd her husband and daughter into the hallway.

When the Turners were gone, Jenny made to rise from the ottoman. Christian stopped her. He pulled the upholstered footstool closer to his chair. "There," he said. "That's better. You were too far away."

Jenny turned partway around so she could see her husband's face. Husband. It almost seemed unreal. "I thought so too." Her head bent forward as Christian's fingers threaded through her hair and massaged the back of her neck. His touch sent a frisson of heat down her spine. "I think Scott and Susan knew

436

we wanted to be alone."

"We're newlyweds, remember?" he said, repeating Susan's excuse. "I make this marriage to be all of five hours old. Anyway, it's more likely that we gave them ideas. They won't be able to get Amy to bed fast enough tonight. I think there are definite plans afoot to enlarge the Turner family."

Jenny laughed lightly. "You think that, do you? You're probably right."

Christian didn't return her laughter. His expression was serious again. His eyes darted over her face, tracing the lines and curves. "I love you, Jenny Holland."

Jenny nuzzled Christian's palm as he cupped her cheek. She turned her head and kissed the heart of it. "It's nice to hear you still feel that way," she said.

"Still? After five hours? No, marriage was never likely to change the way I felt." His hand slipped away from her face and feathered in her thick hair again. "You were the one I was worried about. Any regrets, Mrs. Marshall?"

She smiled. It would take some time to get used to that name. The household staff was going to have trouble remembering to address her by it. Before the marriage she answered to Jenny, Miss Holland, Miss Van Dyke, and occasionally, when no one thought she was listening, she heard herself called the Princess. For Christian alone she was Jenny Holland. No one said her name the way he did. "No regrets, Mr. Marshall." None, she thought, except the fact that they had no family to share their joy. She kept her thoughts to herself. They were their own family now. "You'll notice I waited until Scott operated and rid you of that limp."

That made Christian chuckle. In truth it was he who had balked at marriage prior to the operation. He told Jenny she had no business being married to a cripple. Secretly, he was afraid of making her a widow. He knew from Scott that the surgery could take more than a limb, but Jenny's courage made him brave. "And you'll notice I waited until you got rid of that twenty-five million. No one was going to accuse me of marrying you for your money."

"You don't care that I came to you without a cent to my name?"

"You know I don't. The Van Dyke Foundation was a brilliant idea. It not only satisfied the terms of your father's will, but it's eventually going to help a great many people. Look at how much has been accomplished already. Morgan and Glenn have been removed from Jennings Memorial, and under the new head of the hospital Scott's been named chief of surgery. The treatment and practices on the lunatic ward are all subject to new policies. Doctors are committed to the patients' dignity and humanity. That was your doing, Jenny. You made people understand about that place."

Jenny shook her head. "No, that was *your* doing. I couldn't have described what it was like to live there. I had no words to make the public understand the kind of suffering that went on in Jennings. It was your photographs and sketches that allowed people to see. It was your newspaper that brought them to awareness."

Christian knew where she was heading, but he didn't want to discuss it now. "I haven't made a decision about selling *The Chronicle*. I do know I'm not going to decide anything until after Stephen and his father are sentenced. Short of bribing the judge, I'm not above using any means at my disposal to see that they get every year they deserve."

Jenny had to be satisfied with that. She knew Christian was leaning toward giving up all control of the paper, yet she believed that he would come to regret that decision. Lately, because of the interest he had in seeing the treatment of the insane exposed for the horror it was, Christian had been involved with *The Chronicle* as never before. It was the cause that inspired him, but it was the paper that gave him the forum. His sketches, most of them made from photographs, were powerful in their own right, but they would have been lost to the public if left to art galleries and private showings. *The Chronicle* breathed life into Christian's work. People couldn't ignore the stark drawings of Alice Vanderstell huddled on a thin mattress in her cell. Her eyes were glazed, her hair matted, and her fingers were stuffed in her mouth as if she would eat them whole. Christian's sketches showed that insanity was a great leveler, showing no favoritism for birthright, wealth, or breeding. If Alice Vanderstell could be given such ill-treatment, the public argued, then what horrors were suffered by the indigent?

Christian showed them that as well. With Scott's help he exposed the practices of the treatment room in editorials as graphic as they were scathing. The circulation of *The Chronicle* had increased ten percent, and more importantly to Christian, the reforms he called for were being acted upon. People rallied and legislators, always a beat behind their constituents' needs, were finally at the stage of proposing laws to bring the private hospitals in line with the public ones.

"All right," Jenny said. "We won't talk about selling the paper. But that doesn't mean I want to talk about Stephen Bennington." Jenny spied the latest edition of *The Chronicle* on the sofa vacated by Susan and Amy. She reached for it, unfolded it, and studied the front page. Her own face, courtesy of Christian's fine talent, stared back at her. Below her picture was the announcement of her marriage to Christian. "You didn't tell me about this," she said. "I suppose you showed it to Susan and Scott."

"Yes."

"What did they think?"

"That it's a good likeness."

"That's all?"

"They're inclined to believe that it keeps the public's sympathy with you, that it's going to seal Stephen's fate."

She looked at the picture again. "Are you sure that's all it is? This is more than a mere wedding announcement, and you'll never convince me otherwise. I can't help but notice that your picture isn't here." She sighed and her voice softened. "I don't want to be the subject of public pathos, Christian. I don't like that idea at all."

Christian slid the newspaper from Jenny's fingers and laid it on the floor. He tilted her chin toward him. "It's not pity," he assured her. "People want to know about the woman who stood up to both Benningtons, saved The Hancock Trust, and married the most handsome man in New York."

Jenny's smile was wry. "Don't think much of yourself, do you?"

"Not much." He grinned and his entire face was transformed. He didn't realize it, but in that moment Jenny was thinking he probably *was* the most handsome man in New York.

Christian stood, drawing Jenny to her feet as well.

"Christian!" Jenny felt herself being lifted. "What are you doing?"

"I'm carrying my bride of five hours to our bedroom," he said matter-of-factly. "I'll let you know when we get there what I'm going to do to her."

"But your leg," she protested. "Christian! Really . . . put me down." Her arms circled his neck when he threatened to drop her.

"That's better." His smile held a touch of arrogance.

"You're impossible."

"So I've been told."

Jenny nuzzled against Christian's shoulder. Her lips touched the warm pulse in his neck. "I love you, Christian Marshall."

At the foot of the stairs Christian paused. Mrs. Brandywine was on her way down the steps and she looked disapproving.

"What do you think you're doing?" she asked. "Where is your cane?"

"Be a dear, Mrs. B.," Christian said, "and don't fuss."

She snorted once and continued on her way. "It's not even eight o'clock," she mumbled under her breath. "And they're on their way to bed."

At the top of the stairs Christian stopped again. This time he was facing Wilton Reilly. "I'm taking my bride to bed," he said, anticipating the question.

Reilly didn't raise a brow. "Good for you, sir," he said dryly. "Have a care not to drop madam. There's the babe to think of." Having said his piece, the butler followed in Mrs. Brandywine's wake.

Christian's mouth gaped. He looked at Jenny to see if she was as surprised as he. She was trying hard to swallow her laughter. "It seems we each have our protectors," she said.

"Hmmmph." He started for the master bedroom.

"I think they're sweet. In fact," she said, lowering her voice confidentially, "I think they're sweet on each other."

"Then they should get married. I may even insist upon it. That would keep them too busy to worry about my leg and your pregnancy." He shifted Jenny's weight in his arms as he stood in front of their door. "Open it, please."

"Of course." She turned the handle and pushed it open. When they were inside the room Christian kicked the door shut with the heel of his shoe. "Now," Jenny said, standing on tiptoe, her mouth a mere fraction of an inch from his. "Tell me about those things you want to do to me."

"Come with me," he said softly. So softly. "I'll show you."

Dazed, a little giddy, definitely curious, Jenny allowed Christian to take her hand and lead her across the floor of the master bedroom. He stopped directly in front of the cheval glass, then turned Jenny so she faced it. Christian stood behind her. His hand rested on her bare skin just above the dropped shoulder neckline of her gown.

"Do you remember the first time we made love?" he asked huskily. "That was in front of the mirror too."

Jenny was speechless. When she closed her eyes for a moment she saw the powerful images he was evoking on the backs of her lids. "I remember," she said. "Everything."

Christian's fingers trailed along the neckline of Jenny's gown. Casually, as though it were unplanned, they dipped below the lacy edging. "I remember too," he said. "I can't forget."

Just when Jenny thought Christian was going to reach under

441

her gown and cup her breasts, he changed his tactics. His palms slid over her naked shoulders and down her arms. He circled her wrists with his thumb and forefinger. Jenny had no desire to break the flesh-and-blood bonds, and the look in her eyes told him so. He held the embrace a moment longer, then slowly drew his arms upward again. She felt his hands move across her shoulder blades. His fingers tugged on the buttons of her gown. After he had undone two, he eased her bodice down a little more.

Because of the baby, Jenny wasn't wearing a corset. Her silk chemise followed the lines of her gown, and just when Christian would have pushed the gown over the curves of her breasts, Jenny tried to turn in his arms to escape her reflection.

"No," he said gently. "Don't turn away. You're beautiful."

She smiled, shyly at first, then more widely. "You think so?"

"I know so." He stepped closer to her so she was cradled against his thighs. "Now, about this dress . . ."

He pushed the gown so that the bodice fell away to Jenny's waist.

It was just like the first time. She hadn't been able to look away then either. Now she watched Christian's hands cup the undersides of her heavy breasts. His thumbs passed across her nipples. Pregnancy had made them darker and more sensitive. Christian noticed the former while Jenny felt the latter. She bit her lower lip to keep from crying out her passion.

He undressed her. She turned, giving him her back in the mirror, and undressed him. It was Jenny who led the way to the bed.

"I like making love with you," she said.

"Mmmm." He was kissing the length of her throat. "It's a good thing. I don't intend you should like it with anyone else."

They shared a touch, traded a caress. Their mouths sipped, clung. They explored, whispered secrets, telling the other what they liked. The loving was still new to them, and a sense of discovery accompanied their actions. Curiosity made them bold. The pleasure they found was elemental and profound.

Christian's breath caught at the longing in Jenny's eyes. "God, how you make me want you!"

She regarded him steadily, a faint smile on her lips, but a flush stole across the delicate planes of her face.

His hands cupped her face, and when her mouth parted and her lower lip trembled, he bent his head until his mouth touched her. The kiss began as something tender and gently exploring. His tongue lightly stroked her lips before it moved against the barrier of her teeth. She opened her mouth and his tongue plunged in. He tasted her mouth, her lips, and could not seem to get enough of her heady sweetness. She reciprocated as he had taught her, and desire made her hungry for the warm taste of him. Her fingernails dug into his skin when he released her mouth and went on to explore the softness of her cheek and curve of her ear.

His hands and mouth became more demanding as his body hardened with desire and need. Jenny was breathless from the urgency of his caress. His mouth circled her nipples, and the already hard buds burgeoned beneath his tongue.

He whispered in raw, husky tones that he wanted her, had always wanted her. The pleasure of listening to him was enough for her for a time. He guided her hands to his waist, then lower, between his legs, and she felt the heat and strength of him.

Jenny watched Christian's face as he filled her, and she fell in love all over again with the man whose features showed such depths of passion and need. She saw strength in his vulnerability, in his openly expressed love, and knew he had trusted her with his very soul.

Much later Jenny turned on her side. Her head rested in the curve of Christian's shoulder; her tapered nails whispered across his chest. She could feel his heartbeat slowing, his breathing returning to normal. "You weren't this out of breath after you carried me up here," she said.

"Used different muscles," he said smugly. He caught her hand while it was still balled in a fist. "No need to take violent

443

exception. Ask Scott. He'll tell you the same thing."

"Because he's a doctor, I suppose."

"No, because he's a married man." He kissed her forehead. "And he knows all about this sort of thing."

"I see." Her hand relaxed, but Christian didn't release it. That was all right with Jenny. She didn't move for several minutes, content just to hold Christian and to be held by him. Gradually, almost against her will, her thoughts drifted.

"What are you thinking?" he asked.

She sighed. "I was thinking about Amalie."

Christian said nothing. He waited.

"It seems ironic that you risked your life to save her," she said, "and yet, as things turned out, she's the one person who's going to face the hangman."

"Even if I had been able to predict the future, it wouldn't have mattered. Stephen was doing nothing to help her. Her dress was going up in flames right in front of me. Until then I really thought I wanted to kill them both. It was one thing to set them up to kill each other, but to do the murdering myself . . . even when I thought you were dead . . . that you had committed . . ." His voice trailed off. He hated the memory. Jenny was so much stronger than he had given her credit for. "I realized I didn't want to be their executioner."

"Sometimes I wish I remembered what happened."

"And I give thanks every day that you don't. It was the shot you fired that scared Stephen and gave me a chance to help Amalie."

Jenny raised Christian's hand to her mouth. The tiny white scars on the back were the only evidence that he had beat out the flames with his bare hands. She kissed the faint ridges on his knuckles. She knew from Susan and Scott that Stephen had tried to make his escape while Christian was helping Amalie. It was Amalie who shot Stephen, stopping him with a bullet from her derringer that shattered his knee. By the time Susan, Scott, Mr. Reilly, and a half dozen of Amalie's girls, including Maggie, found the source of the shouting and shooting, there was nothing to do except tend to the wounded. Jenny had recovered consciousness in Maggie's bed, and the first thing she saw was her reflection in the mirror overhead. If Susan hadn't been at her side by then, Jenny knew she would have fainted again.

"I'm glad nothing happened to your hands—nothing permanent, anyway." Jenny brought Christian's hand to her breasts and held it against her heart. "Oh!" She moved his hand quickly, placing it over her belly. "There! Do you feel it? That's our baby, Christian. Isn't she strong?"

"She?"

"Susan thinks I'm going to have a girl."

"Scott says it's going to be a boy."

"Does it matter to you?"

"No. But if it's a girl, we'll name her Caroline. After you. Try to keep the name in the family."

Jenny laughed. She supposed she was never going to be Caroline again, not to Christian at least. "And if it's a boy?"

"We'll name him after you too," he said. "Holland."

"Holland Marshall." She tested the name out loud several times. "I like it."

Christian gave her a swift kiss full on the mouth. "Good. It's settled then." He kissed her again.

Perhaps the kissing would have gone on a little longer. Certainly that was the intention of both parties. It was the commotion in the hallway that brought them up short. Mrs. Brandywine was yelling at Mr. Reilly to be quiet. Mr. Reilly was shouting that she had lost her mind. There were other voices as well joining the fracas. Jenny and Christian exchanged startled glances.

"I didn't lock the door," he said.

"Neither did I," she said.

"I think they're coming here."

"I don't think a closed door is going to stop them."

Simultaneously they dove for their robes, which were lying at the foot of the bed. They had just finished tying the sashes

445

when the pounding on the door began.

"At least they're knocking," she pointed out.

"It doesn't matter," he returned calmly, straightening the covers on the bed. "I'm firing all of them."

Wilton Reilly breached the entrance first. "I told her that you would not want to be disturbed, sir," he said, shooting a sideways glance at Mrs. Brandywine. "I'm afraid I couldn't stop her."

"And there'd be hell to pay if you had," she retorted, crossing the threshold defiantly. Behind her stood four other members of the staff. Mary Margaret's cap was askew because she was nodding her head so energetically in support of the housekeeper.

"Isn't anyone going to tell me what this is about?"

"*He's* to blame, Mr. Marshall," said the butler. "He walked in here not five minutes ago, right past me he went, looking for you. Turned the place on its ear, he has. This sort of thing never went on in the Van Dyke home, I can speak to that."

Jenny laughed. "Don't be priggish, Reilly. As I recall we never had so much entertainment there either." She craned her neck, trying to get a look at the mysterious "he" that had so upset Reilly. "By all means, show him in."

The employees looked at one another, then as if their decision were made by a secret vote they parted. A young man stepped forward, filling the void.

"It's my fault, I'm afraid," he said.

Under the covers Jenny's hand found her husband's. She didn't need an introduction to the man who was approaching the foot of their bed. He spoke with Christian's voice. His eyes, pewter gray rather than aquamarine, held a similar coolness. His dark hair was threaded with copper.

"It was the story in the paper," he was saying. "The one that described how you caught the Benningtons with the pinhole camera. *The Savannah Press* picked it up . . . I read it. There was something about it . . . something familiar. It was the first time in two years that I remembered anything. In two days I

446

remembered everything. I came as soon as I could—" It shrugged helplessly, not really knowing what else to say suddenly aware of what he had intruded upon. Embarrassed, he grinned. "This is probably the most dangerous situation I ever put myself in."

Jenny's gaze strayed to her husband. Christian's face was beautiful in its stillness. His strong throat looked tight with the effort it took not to cry. Still, tears glistened at the rim of his eyes. Her heart swelled near to bursting with gladness for him. She squeezed his hand and waited.

Christian swallowed hard, unable to take his eyes off the man at the foot of the bed. It was because of Jenny that he was here, Christian thought. Without her there would have been no pinhole camera, no story, no sudden revelations. Jenny. His sweet Jenny Holland had already brought him so much joy. And now this. Christian returned the gentle pressure of Jenny's hand.

"Welcome home, Logan," he said.